JENNINE CAPÓ CRUCET is the author of *Make Your Home Among Strangers* and *How to Leave Hialeah,* winner of the Iowa Short Fiction Award, and named a Best Book of the Year by *The Miami Herald* and the Latinidad List. A PEN/O. Henry Prize winner and Bread Loaf Fellow, Crucet was raised in Miami and is currently an assistant professor of English and Ethnic Studies at the University of Nebraska-Lincoln.

ALSO BY JENNINE CAPÓ CRUCET

How to Leave Hialeah

Additional Praise for *Make Your Home Among Strangers*

"Jennine Capó Crucet's debut novel, about a whip-smart daughter of Cuban immigrants who leaves her Miami home against her parents' wishes to attend an elite college, will inevitably resonate among first-generation Americans . . . but the themes of the book are also universal enough to appeal to a wider audience. . . . Lizet will be recognizable to many children of immigrants who have a foot in two distinct cultures and, often, different social classes. Her flaws make her a believable character, and her flashes of insight . . . will compel many readers to nod their heads in familiarity."
—*The Guardian* (Best Latin American Book of Fall 2015)

"[*Make Your Home Among Strangers*] illuminates Lizet's conflicting emotions with honest prose, while an Elián González–inspired subplot underscores her struggle. Lizet's efforts to navigate a world of mostly white privilege are told with self-deprecating humor and an understanding of the awkward conversations many students must have in their first years in college."   —*Los Angeles Times*

"It's difficult to adequately capture the tension of first-generation college life in popular culture. The stress, the psychological and emotional conflict, and the strain placed on familial relationships and friendships are too often secreted away, in order to advance an inspiring narrative of achievement against all odds. Crucet is masterful at complicating that narrative of uplift, managing to make her fictional protagonist's struggles . . . haunting and compelling. *Make Your Home Among Strangers* is a deserving addition to a small, but necessary body of work committed to honest representations of academic striving among those who have been under-prepared and under-supported."
—Stacia L. Brown, *The Washington Post*

"Heartfelt . . . Being caught between two cultures is a usefully troubling condition for the writer intent on dramatizing the confusion, pain, and humor of having what Crucet calls "double vision," and Crucet, the award-winning author of a story collection delivers on all three. Sharp cultural observations and terrific dialogue keep the reader engaged." —Kathryn Ma, *The New York Times Book Review*

"A brilliantly crafted, sumptuous tale." —*Booklist* (starred review)

"A thrilling, deeply fulfilling journey of a young woman stepping into her own power. This debut novel from Crucet heralds the birth of a talented novelist to watch." —*Kirkus Reviews* (starred review)

"Superb . . . Crucet expertly summons the wrenching disconnect between immigrant parents and their offspring. . . . With this personal coming-of-age novel, Crucet offers us a piercing window into what it means to grow up." —*The Miami Herald*

"If you've ever felt out of your depth, you'll instantly connect with Lizet Ramirez, the protagonist of the new novel *Make Your Home Among Strangers*. . . . Her eye-opening year will encourage you to replace other people's expectations of you with your own." —*Redbook*

"Jennine Capó Crucet renders this coming-of-age story with dazzling élan, full of moments both bittersweet and messy, heartfelt and honest. This is the type of debut novel that leaves you wanting more—in a good way. I can't wait to see what Crucet does next." —*Buzzfeed*

"In her remarkable debut, Jennine Capó Crucet writes authentically about the experience of being Cuban-American on a macro scale, but also about the smaller heartaches of embarking on adulthood far from home." —*Bustle*

"In this dazzling debut novel, a young female protagonist is also caught between the impulse to define herself independently of her family's past and the pressure to never stray far from home and its bittersweet cultural values." —NBC Latino

"A classic coming-of-age tale . . . It's a playful and touching look at Miami and the lives that are lived in it, and it's definitely worth reading. Crucet just might be the literary voice that the Magic City has been waiting for." —*Miami New Times*

"An unusually comic and wise look at the dream of leaving home and that dream's ambivalent reality . . . As fun to read as it is essential. Crucet writes with insight and flair about resilience, loyalty, and the fight to find home again once you've left it." —*Ploughshares*

"This coming-of-age story achieves a wry and wistful tone. Debut novelist Crucet depicts with insight and subtlety the culture shock, confusion, guilt, and humiliations of the first-generation college student surrounded by privilege." —*Library Journal*

"Jennine Capó Crucet's sharply observed first novel captures the profound disorientation of leaving the world that reared you: once you have made your home among strangers, home itself often transforms into a strange place. Recounted with wry humor and heartbreaking honesty, Lizet's struggle is a poignant exploration of a young woman's evolving relationship to her culture, her family, and her own identity." —Celeste Ng, author of *Everything I Never Told You*

"*Make Your Home Among Strangers* is a vivid, exuberant novel begging to be devoured in one sitting. Hilarious and relentlessly honest, our narrator Lizet is the embodiment of the guilt, anger, and chronic homesickness, so often the side effects of being educated away from who you once were. Hers is an utterly American story, yet one hardly told, and Jennine Capó Crucet tells it with a combination of wisdom and urgency that is as rare as it is invigorating."
—Claire Vaye Watkins, author of *Gold Fame Citrus*

"*Make Your Home Among Strangers* is a gorgeous, sad, and poignantly hysterical exploration of what it means to be homesick for a place that doesn't exist. . . . Crucet is a distinct and important voice, and this novel is both a profound pleasure to read and a painful reminder of the real human costs of living in two places at once."
—Danielle Evans, author of *Before You Suffocate Your Own Fool Self*, winner of the 2011 PEN American Robert W. Bingham Prize

"Crucet's first novel is a masterpiece of contemporary fiction that dramatizes the intersection of race, class, geography, and education and shows the effects of being American on the human heart. Crucet manages the layers of self and emotion of her characters with wisdom and intelligence to create a commanding, urgent coming-of-age story. First-class work."
—David Treuer, author of *Rez Life: An Indian's Journey Through Reservation Life* and *Little*

"Crucet brilliantly brings to life the experience of a first-generation college student navigating an all-too-realistic elite school in an age where diversity initiatives do little to offset the air of privilege that permeates its halls, customs and—especially—its dormitories. Lizet is a heroine who is not only thoroughly believable but one we can't help but root for." —Adelle Waldman, author of *The Love Affairs of Nathaniel P.*

Make Your Home
Among Strangers

Make Your Home
Among Strangers

Jennine Capó Crucet

PICADOR · ST. MARTIN'S PRESS · NEW YORK

MAKE YOUR HOME AMONG STRANGERS. Copyright © 2015 by Jennine Capó Crucet. All rights
reserved. Printed in the United States of America. For information, address Picador,
175 Fifth Avenue, New York, N.Y. 10010.

picadorusa.com • picadorbookroom.tumblr.com
twitter.com/picadorusa • facebook.com/picadorusa

Picador® is a U.S. registered trademark and is used by St. Martin's Press under license
from Pan Books Limited.

For book club information, please visit facebook.com/picadorbookclub or
e-mail marketing@picadorusa.com.

The Library of Congress has cataloged the St. Martin's Press edition as follows:

Crucet, Jennine Capo.
    Make your home among strangers : a novel / Jennine Capo Crucet. — First edition.
    p. cm.
    ISBN 978-1-250-05966-6 (hardcover)
    ISBN 978-1-4668-6504-4 (e-book)
    1. Domestic fiction.   I. Title.
    PS3603.R83M35 2015
    813'.6—dc23   2015017167

Picador Paperback ISBN 978-1-250-09455-1

Our books may be purchased in bulk for promotional, educational, or business use. Please
contact your local bookseller or the Macmillan Corporate and Premium Sales Department at
1-800-221-7945, extension 5442, or by e-mail at MacmillanSpecialMarkets@macmillan.com.

First published by St. Martin's Press

First Picador Edition: July 2016

For Amara, Jose, and Angelica

and in loving memory of
Elizabeth Missel and Celaida Capó

Acknowledgments

Much thanks, love, and gratitude to the following:

My agent, the brilliant and thoughtful Adam Eaglin, not just for his belief in this book, but for the passion he put into making it stronger and finding it the right home, and for always knowing the right thing to say at the exact right time, even across several time zones. The whole crew at the Elyse Cheney Agency.

My editor, Hilary Rubin Teeman, a long-lost sister when it comes to unconventional first-name spellings and height. Alicia Adkins-Clancy, who answered e-mails from the altar; Dori Weintraub, dream publicist; the entire St. Martin's team, especially Laura Chasen and George Witte, for getting us down the home stretch.

The Institute for American Studies and the University of Leipzig, especially Florian Bast (eater of reindeer and undying Vikings fan), Anne Koenen, and Crister Garrett for opening up their homes and sharing their families with me during my time in Leipzig. Jennifer Porto and Andrew Curry for the late nights and the reminders of home.

The One Voice Scholars Program, the single most amazing organization for which I have ever worked. Sue, Mommi, Kelli/Kelly,

Irma, Ruth, Rosie, Sharmon, and especially Dan (Dan!) for their dedication to making college access a reality in this country. One Voice is the real deal: Please visit onevoice-la.org to learn about the vital work they do.

More of my One Voice Family: Amara, Angelica, Yaracet, Jenny, Jose, Steve, Pablo, and the rest of the One Voice 2010 class. Roxy and Arturo, my 2011 badasses. This book is for you guys and for those who'll come after you. Consider it a very long hug.

The Bread Loaf Writers' Conference, where so many of the best things that have ever happened to me got their start. Michael Collier, Jennifer Grotz, and Noreen Cargill for creating a supportive and inclusive home. The Waiters of 2008, 2009, and 2010—especially Tiphanie Yanique (waiter-mama and sister) and Aaron Balkan—and the 2012 Fellows (with extra love for Claire Vaye Watkins for her generosity).

The editors and magazines who supported this novel in its early stages: Roxane Gay and Catherine Chung at *Guernica*; Ken Chen at *CultureStrike*; my literary prima Laura Pegram at *Kweli*. Erin Belieu, Stuart Bernstein, Alexander Chee, Ru Freeman, John McElwee, Diane Roberts, Elizabeth Stuckey-French, and Alexi Zentner for valuable advice and timely guidance.

Peggy and Walt for the apartment on Alki, home to this novel's biggest revision. Peter Mountford, Urban Waite, Karen Leung-Waite, Brian McGuigan, Laura Scott, and the Richard Hugo House Family for making Seattle feel like home in every other way.

Holy hell, the Grind (especially summer 2012) and its cocreators, Ross White and Matthew Olzmann. Thank you for creating that beast. There is no book without the Grind.

My literary hermanas, Xhenet Aliu, Dara Barnat, Kara Candito, Reese Kwon, and Nina McConigley for their nonstop hustle and support; Charles Baxter and Helena Viramontes for being fantastic role models and mentors.

The M.E.A.N.H.O.E.s and the Skitsos of yesteryear, with a special thanks to Monica Hill, Ankur Pandya, and Chris Principe (and Renuka, honorary Skitso). Andrew "Best In Show" Missel, this book's very first reader, for his careful eye and his patience. Cindy Cruz, best friend forever and my favorite Gator, for letting me steal so much.

My little sister, Kathy, for getting back in the water. My parents, Rey and Maria, for always doing their best and for raising me to do the same. 4IFMLY forever. Everything is for you guys, always.

They had carved their names and address on me,
and I would come back.

—MAXINE HONG KINGSTON, *THE WOMAN WARRIOR*

I

CANALS ZIGZAG ACROSS THE CITY I used to call home. Those lines of murky water still run beside and under expressways, now choked by whorls of algae—mostly hydrilla, a well-known invasive, though that's likely the only algae I ever saw growing up in Miami. Even just ten years ago, before it took over, you could float tangle-free down those waterways from neighborhood to neighborhood, waving to strangers from your inner tube as they would wave back and wonder whether or not you needed rescuing.

While they were married, my parents used the canal across from the house they owned until just before I left for college in ways that make my current research group howl. Every Tuesday, at the weekly lab meetings I help our principal investigator run, each of us in the group is supposed to catalog the slow progress we're making toward understanding the demise of coral reef systems everywhere. But being one of the institute's lab managers means I've been working on this project longer than any of the postdocs or graduate students we hire, so *my* segment of the meeting has another goal: I try each week to make our PI laugh at least once by revealing, like a prize behind a curtain, some new and highly illegal thing my mom or dad tossed into that canal's water.

My dad: every single drop of motor oil ever drained from any of the dozen or so cars he's owned and sold over the years; a stack of loose CDs I once left on the couch and forgot, for days and days, to put away, each of them dotting the water's surface like a mirrored lily pad; an entire transmission. My mom: a dead hamster, cage and all, the failed project of my older sister Leidy, who was charged with keeping it alive over Christmas break when she was in fifth grade; any obvious junk mail, before I knew to grab the brochures from colleges out of her hands lest she send them sailing from her grip; dried-out watercolors, homemade tape recordings of her own voice, parched hunks of white clay—any and all signs of an attempt to discover some untapped talent she hoped she possessed wound up in the water. Too many things got dumped there. I know this was wrong—knew it then. Still, I say to my drop-jawed colleagues when they ask how we could've behaved so irresponsibly, what do you want me to tell you? I'm sorry, I say, but it's the truth.

Starting my segment of our meetings this way has let me turn Miami's canals into a funny family story. But I know which stories not to tell, which stories would make these particular listeners uncomfortable. Once, when my dad was thirteen, a friend from junior high dragged him and some other guys to a nearby canal to see a dead body he'd found there. My dad told me this story only once, the summer after Ariel Hernandez was sent back to Cuba after months of rallies and riots. I'd asked him if what people like my mom said was true: that Ariel had seen his mother's body floating in the Florida Straits, had watched sharks pick her apart before his rescue. This story was his only answer. So I asked him, What did you do, did you tell anyone? We just left it in the canal, he said. It got worse and worse, then one day it was gone, problem solved. My dad didn't say any more, even when I asked him why he'd kept the body a secret. He doesn't have any evidence to prove this actually happened, and there's no verifiable record I can look up to confirm it, but the fact that he's never mentioned it again— that he'll deny this story if I bring it up now—tells me it's true. My dad's canal isn't far from the one in front of our old house. The two waterways are probably connected, and though I don't know exactly how you'd navigate from one to the other, I'm sure it can be done.

Years after that summer, managing my first lab at the institute and working for a parasitologist studying the effects of sewage run-off on canal-dwelling snails, I slipped under another city's slick water: I lost my grip on the concrete shelf lining that particular canal and screamed as a reflex, which meant the contaminated water flooding my ears and nostrils had—via my open mouth—an additional (and an exceptionally gross) way to enter my system. My head submerged, the image of all these objects—the body, the CDs, the hamster cage, all of it somehow still intact and floating in Miami's water—surged over me. I found I couldn't kick my legs, fearing that I'd cut open my foot on a transmission that couldn't possibly be there: I was already on the West Coast by then, far from the canal my parents had abandoned to another family almost a decade earlier. The parasitologist hauled me out from the nastiness, made some unfortunate joke about Cubans and the coast guard, then spent the drive to the hospital apologizing for said joke, which he claimed was truly offensive in that *it wasn't even that funny.* Nurses plugged antibiotic-filled sacks into my arms, the hope being that intravenous administration would keep the various organisms that'd bombarded my body from calling it home for too long.

I called each parent from my sublet a couple days later once I'd been discharged.

—I don't know why you do that nasty work, my mom said, angry because I'd waited to call her. She preferred the rush of an emergency, the play-by-play of panic.

My father asked, after having me explain the basic facts of my treatment, Did you call your mother already? When I said yes, he

said, Good girl, Lizet—his voice the same as if I'd brought home
a decent report card or gotten rid of a Jehovah's Witness at the door
without bothering him for help. Good girl, Lizet. I was almost
twenty-eight.

Neither parent brought up the canal across the street from us
during that phone call—I didn't let either conversation go on very
long because I didn't want to hear that *other* story, another supposed
truth about our canal, one my family has always claimed but which
I don't know I believe.

It goes like this: When I was three years old and left under the
very temporary supervision of my then five-year-old sister while my
mother spoke with our backyard neighbor, I marched into the garage and rummaged through piles of old-clothes-turned-cleaning-
rags and half-empty bottles of detergents and oils, found the floaties
used to buoy me in the Atlantic Ocean, and blew them up on my
way across the street to the water. By my mother's account, I stood
on the sheer edge of the canal and blew these things up the way
my father always did—bending forward as I pushed air into them,
as if that motion helped—then licked them to slip them up my arms.
By my father's account, I went over there with the floaties already
on, my arms hovering out from my sides so that from behind, I
resembled a tiny body builder. (Sometimes they say I was barefoot,
but that can't be true. I would remember, I think, the asphalt
embroidering my heels, shredding the pads of my toes. I would
remember the sting of every step there.) By all accounts—even my
sister's, who you could argue was too young to have an account,
but that's not how stories work—I took several huge, shoulder-raising
breaths before launching myself into the canal's crowded water. In
some versions I pinch my nose; in some I know to breathe out
through it as I hit the water; and in others still the water rushes into
me through this and other openings, mandating that I be prescribed
antibiotics the minute my parents, who take embarrassingly long
to discover me floating across the street, explain to the triage nurse

in the hospital's emergency room from where it is I'd just been pulled. Versions of this story change from teller to teller, from time told to other time told. But every version ends with almost the same lines: She was fine! All that worrying, all that time and money and crying wasted—and for what? She was *fine*. It made us want to kill her.

2

A NOW-DEFUNCT AIRLINE IS MOSTLY responsible for giving me and Ariel Hernandez the same day as our Miami Homecoming: Thanksgiving 1999. He was a five-year-old Cuban boy rescued from a broken raft by fishermen earlier that day after watching everyone else on the raft, including his mother, die; I arrived that night, a day later than I'd planned because I underestimated, having never done it, just how chaotic flying on the busiest travel day of the year could be. And even though we each eventually set foot in the city our families called home, no one was expecting either of us to show up the way we did.

That first flight back home from college—which, I should confess, was only my second time ever on an airplane—started off badly enough that when I got to Pittsburgh and learned my connecting flight was overbooked, I should've asked the airline to just send me back to New York for Thanksgiving. Staying on campus for the holiday was the original plan anyway, the one designed by my dad months earlier, before he'd moved out, the plan my mother and sister thought I was following: I was not supposed to come home for Thanksgiving. It was not in the budget, or *el college lay-a-way*, or any of the other euphemisms my dad had used to describe how we would finance the astronomically expensive education I was mostly failing to receive. The four thousand dollars a year my family was initially expected to pay toward my tuition at Rawlings College seemed to my dad (and to me, back then) an insane amount of money, a figure almost as ludicrous as the forty-five thousand dollars Rawlings expected from each of its students every year. The aid package later approved after our appeal—the one with my parents' marital status revised to say "Formally Separated" and my dad's address changed to "Unknown"—brought the amount down to something me and my mom together could earn, a flight to upstate New York and another back in December being all our final budget said we could afford. But we hadn't taken into account something called federal work-study—a mysterious line in my aid package that I thought had something to do with working for the government or joining the army, and so I'd ignored it, hoping it would disappear. I got to campus for freshman orientation, marched into the aid office to pay my fall bill in person with a check my mom had written out three days before in tense, tired script, and learned from my aid officer that *work-study* was just a job on campus—an easy one, usually. Nothing to do with the government at all. I was one of the very first students to come in, which meant I had my pick of jobs, and so that fall, I'd spent the hours between classes working in the library, searching bags for mistakenly stolen books when the sensors hugging the doors went off. Which is how I'd managed to save enough for the Thanksgiving ticket and the shuttle ride to my mom and sister's new-to-me address.

I was surprising everyone, even myself: I was home for a holiday we didn't really celebrate. Eating turkey on a Thursday seemed mostly arbitrary to my Cuban-born-and-raised parents, and so to my sister and me growing up. Still, my entire school career up to that point celebrated America and its founding—the proof: a half-dozen handprint turkeys stuffed under my mother's mattress, now in a Little Havana apartment instead of our house—and I must've

been feeling sentimental for stories of pilgrims and Indians all getting along around a feast the night I scoured the Internet for a ticket
home. Also, the fact that everyone at Rawlings (in the dining hall,
around the mailboxes, before class while waiting for a professor to
arrive, even in the morning bathroom banter bouncing between
girls in separate shower stalls—all conversations in which I had no
place until I decided to fly home as a surprise) couldn't stop talking about family and food only made me want the same thing even
though I'd been fine without it my whole life. So as people talked
around their toothbrushes about the aunts and uncles they dreaded
seeing, I recast the holiday as equally important to some imaginary
version of the Ramirez clan and booked the trip, then mentioned
going home one October morning as I towel-dried my face. A girl
from my floor who'd barely ever noticed me finally introduced
herself—*I'm Tracy, by the way, but people call me Trace*—and told me,
as she spat toothpaste foam into the sink, how jealous she was that
home for me meant Miami Beach. I didn't mention that I lived miles
from the ocean, just like I didn't mention—to anyone—that I'd
drained my fall savings on this trip.

A day later than the Wednesday printed on my original ticket,
and a good hour after most of East Coast America would've
finished their turkey and potatoes and apple pie and all the other
All-American things all Americans eat on Thanksgiving, I shuffled
down the aisle of a plane, my bag catching on the armrests then
slamming back into me the whole way out. I stepped through the
squarish hole in the plane's side—I still couldn't believe this opening counted as a *door*—and the night's humidity swooped over me
like a wet sheet, plastering my already-greasy bangs to my forehead.
An old white man behind me huffed, Dear Christ, this place! Part
of me wanted to turn around and snap, *What do you mean,* this place,
you stupid viejo? You want to freaking say something about it? But the part
of me that had calmly worked with the gate agent in Pittsburgh to
find an available hotel room once it was clear they'd sold more tickets than seats on my connecting flight—the part that a week earlier

had borrowed my roommate Jillian's blazer for my academic hearing without mentioning the hearing itself—knew exactly what he meant. My bangs, which I'd blown out to give the rest of my hair some semblance of neatness, curled and tangled in that oppressive, familiar dankness. When I reached up to finger-comb them back into place, a motion that had been a reflex throughout high school, my nails got caught in the new knots.

The Miami International Airport terminal smelled strongly of mildew. The odor seemed to come up from the carpet, each of my steps releasing it into the air. That terminal was one of the last to be renovated, so the only TVs in it back then had one of three jobs: to display a pixilated list of ARRIVALS, or of DEPARTURES, or to relay the weather, updated every fifteen minutes. There was no recap of the Macy's Thanksgiving Day Parade, no local news about a food kitchen blaring overhead—the TVs weren't connected to the outside world that way. If they had been, my ignorance about Ariel Hernandez might've ended right then, before I'd even stepped through the airport's automatic glass doors and into the Miami night. It would've been at least a warning.

After explaining my overbooked flight and how my original shuttle reservation had been for Wednesday evening, and after an absurd amount of clicking on a keyboard and many *Mmm-hmm*s and almost no eye contact, the woman behind the shuttle service's counter managed to squeeze me onto a ride-share leaving in ten minutes.

—But you getting off last, she told me, the clicking suddenly stopping as she held up a finger to my face. Her acrylic nails—pink-and-whites that needed refilling—had slashes of diamonds glued across their long, curved tips. I could see her real nails growing up under them, like echoes.

—I got you, I said, happy to recognize something I hadn't seen in months.

I sat at the very back of the blue van after reluctantly handing over my bag to the driver: I didn't have any cash for a tip and almost told him so as we wrestled over it, each of us wanting to make sure we got the credit for putting it away.

The ticket in my hand said *Zone 8: Little Havana.* I read it twice before remembering that it wasn't a mistake. I'd lived in Hialeah my whole life except for the very last week before I left for Rawlings. I'd memorized the new address, but only because I'd entered and reentered it on all sorts of forms during orientation, correcting and updating it on anything I'd submitted before that fall. Even to someone from Hialeah, Little Havana was a joke back then, the part of Miami only the most recent of refugees called home, a place tour buses drove through, where old Cuban men played dominos for tourists and thought that made them celebrities. But none of these geographical distinctions mattered at Rawlings. There, when people asked, So where are you from? and I said, Hialeah, they answered: Wait, *where?* And so I gave them a new answer: Miami, I'm from Miami. Oh, they'd say, But where are you *from* from? I was *from* from Miami, but eventually I learned to say what they were trying to figure out: My parents are from Cuba. No, I've never been. Yes, I still have family there. No, we don't know Fidel Castro. Once I learned what I was supposed to say, it became a chant, like the address I'd memorized but didn't think of as home.

People packed in around me. An elderly white couple—the wrinkled man helping the wrinkled woman up the steps of the van, holding her by her bracelet-crammed wrist—creaked their way onto the seat bench in front of me, spreading out in the hopes of keeping anyone from sitting by them. It didn't work: a young-looking lady pushed in beside them. She wore smart gray pants and a matching blazer with patches on the elbows, and she looked like she could maybe be a professor somewhere except for the fact that she was clearly Latina; I'd yet to see a Latino professor on the Rawlings campus, though I knew from pictures in the school's guidebook that there were a few somewhere. But then I thought, Maybe she teaches at FIU or Miami Dade. Maybe she's new there. Her hair was pulled back tight, slicked smooth with gel. To the old couple she said, Good evening, and they nodded back at her. The old woman scooted closer to her husband, the orange cloud of her hair touching his shoulder. She turned her face—the side of it dotted with brownish spots, a few whiskers sprouting from a fold under her chin—and inspected the young woman the way I'd just done before turning away.

—Coral Gables, the old woman said. She leaned forward, put her hand on the driver's chair. Our stop is Coral Gables, near the – Gerald, just tell him how to get there.

—The man knows, Sharon. It'll be fine.

He grunted this with a sturdiness that would've shut me up. *It'll be fine.* I rested my forehead against the window—surprised, after so many cold weeks in New York, by the warm glass. Outside, the sun dipped behind buildings and palm trees, only the red welt of it still visible. I hadn't decided yet if I should use this trip home to confess my issues at school to my mom; I'd bought my ticket weeks before things started to look so bad. I was straight-up failing my chemistry course, but by Thanksgiving this problem was only a footnote to a list of other issues, the most serious being that I had accidentally plagiarized part of a paper in my freshman writing class and would soon be meeting again with the Academic Integrity Committee about what this meant in terms of my status as a student at Rawlings. I'd testified at my hearing a week earlier: I'd *attempted* to correctly cite something, but I didn't even know the extent to which that needed to be done to count as correct. The committee said it was taking into consideration the fact that I'd gone to Hialeah Lakes High. Several times during my hearing, they'd referred to it as "an underserved high school," which I figured out was a nice way of saying a school so shitty that the people at Rawlings had read an article about it in *The New Yorker*. They'd expected me to know about this article—*You mean to tell us you aren't familiar with the national attention your former school is receiving?*—as well as that magazine when the only one I ever read back then was *Vanidades*, which my mom sometimes mailed me after reading them herself during her shifts directing calls at the City of Miami Building Department. I'd swallowed and told the committee no, I was not aware. The committee was also, in general, worried about my ability to succeed at Rawlings given that I was considering a biology major. The truth was, I didn't really know if I should major in biology, but I planned to major in biology anyway because I'd read it was one of the largest, most popular majors at Rawlings, and therefore (I reasoned) couldn't possibly be that hard. The truth was, I had enough to worry about that Thanksgiving before my flight got canceled, before I'd ever heard the name Ariel Hernandez. And just like the fact of me even being in the city in a van headed her way, my mother knew about none of it.

3

IN PITTSBURGH, THE AIRLINE HAD sent me to a hotel that was only a short "courtesy" ride away from the airport, and like the hotels we now passed—scummy buildings on the fringes of Miami International, on the fringes of the definition of *hotel*—the rooms could be rented either for the night or by the hour. There was a time when hotels like this terrified me, but I'd spent enough hours in them with my boyfriend Omar during my senior year of high school that I was no longer shocked to see a prostitute hanging out by a vending machine or waiting in a car and sniffing her own armpits, thinking nobody's looking. Still, I'd never spent the *night* in a place like that, and I was alone, and the room—which just as recently as that summer had seemed so fun and illicit and beautiful in this murky, hope-filled way—just felt gross, the sheets and towels, to the touch, all one step shy of dry.

We rolled through the city, our route apparently not needing the expressway. Around us, the noise of rumbling sound systems and way-too-much bass faded in and out depending on the stoplights. We eventually pulled up to a sprawling ranch house in a nice part of the Gables I'd never seen, and the old people left the van without saying goodbye to anyone, and I was relieved, now that I was back in Miami, that there was no need to be polite. Even this far inland, I could smell the salt in the air every time the door slid open. I hadn't been this close to the ocean in months, and out of nowhere, the air made my mouth water. My eyes welled with tears—more water rushing to meet the ocean that I didn't even know I'd missed.

My imaginary profesora and I were apparently the driver's last two stops. She'd scooted in from the edge of her row after the old people left and was now directly in front of me. The mass of her hair was corralled into this thick bun, shiny and hard from the gel keeping it under control. The dark center of the thing, like an entrance to a tunnel, seemed to stare right at me. I had the urge to stick my finger in it, see how far it would go, but then she let out this big sigh and her shoulders drooped forward and shook. She brought her hands to her face, sucked in a wet breath through her fingers. The driver's eyes swerved to the rearview mirror, and he lifted his eyebrows at whatever he saw there. He looked away to the road, but then his eyes met mine in the mirror and he shifted in his seat, cleared his throat when he looked away again like she was my problem. So I grabbed onto her bench and scooted forward, saying with mostly air so she wouldn't really hear me, Uh, hey.

She leaned back on the bench—I moved my hand out of the way just in time—and, still through her fingers, said, *God.* Then she wiped her cheeks with her whole palm, pushing with the same fierceness that Leidy's son, my baby nephew Dante, used when smashing his own hands into his face as he cried. She bent down and snatched something from off the floor—her huge purse. It hit her lap with a sound like steps creaking, the leather stretching as she rooted around in it. She pulled out a compact and flipped it open. In the mirror she used to inspect her face, I could only see a tiny circle of her at a time: her weak, ruddy chin; her bare, wide lips, the almost-straight teeth they revealed then hid; her flared nostrils as she used her pinkie nail to swipe something from the right one.

Then, a flash of her full, dark eyebrow—and below it, her right eye, still ringed in perfect black eyeliner, the lashes still well-shellacked with mascara. None of it smudged by tears at all. I sat back against my bench, confused as to whether or not what she'd just been doing, not five seconds before, was crying. She tugged at the corner of her eye, lifting it, and I'd been staring for exactly too long when I realized what she watched in her mirror was me.

She snapped the compact shut, slid her purse off her lap and onto the bench, and turned to face me. She smiled—a square, forced grin that even showed the crooked bottom teeth I'd missed before—then dropped her head back to her purse. She said, Sorry, I'm being weird.

Her voice didn't sound like I thought it would, and I was surprised I'd expected something specific. It was deeper and quieter than I thought it should be, and there was no Miami accent in it, no sharpness to her *I*. And what she said made her sound like my roommate Jillian, who was constantly describing the things she did as *weird* or *random*, even when they were neither weird nor random. Her face still turned to her purse, she asked, Are you headed to Hialeah, too?

—Yeah, I lied.

—Wait though, she said. Where did you go to high school?

She hopped in her seat and twisted her whole body my way, her hand now on the seatback between us. In seeing her get so excited about such a stupid, irrelevant question, I wanted to take away all the distinction I'd given her by thinking of her as a professor. But I didn't know yet that this question—when you're from Miami and talking to someone else from Miami after you've both left it—was the shortcut to finding out which version of the city had raised me. Out the window, the sun disappeared along with the clean, empty streets of Coral Gables, and that neighborhood started to melt away into the run-down strip malls—with their bakeries and liquor stores and Navarro Pharmacies and neon-signed cash-only restaurants—that looked more familiar.

When I didn't answer right away, she said, I went to Hialeah Gardens.

She said the school's name like a punch line, pointed to her chest with four of her fingers, her thumb back at me, as if saying, *Can you believe that?* But I didn't get the joke: Gardens was our big rival in football, a sport we tended to dominate, but they killed us almost every year in soccer. A handful of kids from both teams at both schools went to college on athletic scholarships each year; that was how most of the few students headed to college at all from either school managed to make it there.

—Oh cool, I said. I went to Hialeah Lakes.

—*Wow*, she said, nodding. Yikes, she said. That's *rough*.

She lowered her head and nodded harder, waiting for me to nod along with her. A rectangle of light came in through the van's window and scrolled over her face, turning her skin greenish, and I thought maybe she was lying about going to Gardens, or that maybe I was wrong and she wasn't some kind of Latina like me.

—Were you crying just now? I said, crossing my arms over my chest. Because it looked like you were crying.

The woman let her hand drop from the seatback, and I added, I'm just saying.

—I'm, she said, I was being weird is all. She laughed a little and said, I just flew in from Michigan. I'm in my last year of a postdoc there.

Then she rolled her eyes, as if the definition of *postdoc* were written in the air above us. I lifted my chin and squinted, but she didn't say more, and I tried not to think about how much I still didn't know, even after almost a whole semester away at a real school. The rectangle of light slinked over the seat and found my arms, passing over them and turning them the same green.

—I'm in college, I said. I'm a freshman. I came home for the break but my flight got screwed up yesterday.

She showed me all her teeth again, but her lips slipped over them in a more natural way. She asked where I went to school, but

I flapped my hand in front of my face, like the question smelled foul. I didn't expect her to know the school. My boyfriend Omar had never even heard of it before I'd applied, and my own sister had trouble remembering the name, though she blamed *me* for that, since I'd applied to Rawlings without my family knowing about it and—as a necessary result of that—without their permission.

—It's this school in the middle of nowhere called Rawlings.

—Rawlings *College*? she said more loudly than anything she'd said so far. *That's* where you go? As in, one of the top liberal arts schools in the country? *That* Rawlings?

I couldn't believe she'd heard of it. I couldn't believe she knew to say *liberal arts*. My surprise at this almost matched hers. She shook off her open mouth and said, Hold up, so you must be a super-genius.

—Not really, I said. But yeah, it's – it's like a *really* good school.

We both nodded, and I felt ready to brag a little, to tell her how a few weeks earlier the school had thrown an all-day party for everyone on campus—even us new students—under this huge tent on the quad to celebrate this one professor winning the Nobel Prize in economics. The school had sprung for hundreds of these goofy caps with part of the prize-winning theorem (which meant nothing to most of us, as several of the speakers that day joked) printed on the front and the words '99 NOBEL BASH on the back. After eating my weight in free fancy cheese, I got up the courage to ask the now-super-famous professor to sign my cap's bill, and that request made him chuckle. (I feel like a movie star! I didn't even bring a suitable pen! he said.) Then, after we located a suitable pen, his hand shook as he signed and he accidentally smudged the signature. To the smudge he said, Oh drat!, which apparently meant he felt badly enough about it to find me *another* free cap, and he signed that one, too. I wanted to say how later, I caught him *offering* to sign other people's caps, and I couldn't believe *I'd* given a Nobel Prize winner an idea. Maybe I'd even tell her—since she was from home, since she'd gone to Gardens—that eating all that cheese had backed me up like nothing I'd ever felt, and so I didn't shit for two days, but neither did my roommate (she'd dragged me to the celebration in the first place but had disappeared by an ice-cream bar I didn't find until I was already too packed with cheese), and how just as my roommate confessed her no-shitting to me, she ripped this huge fart—the first of hers I ever heard despite us living in the same rectangle for almost two months—and I laughed so hard I fell out of my desk chair and onto the floor with a fart of my own.

But this woman, before I could think of how to best tell the story, put her hand over my hand and set her face in this serious way, her eyeliner thick under her bottom lashes, and said, It's *not* a really good school. It's a *fantastic* school. Congratulations.

I shrugged, said thanks, and tried to slide my hand out from under hers, but she grabbed it and said, No, really. Getting in there is a huge freaking deal. You should be proud as hell. And from a school like *Lakes*? Holy shit, girl.

Outside, the houses whizzing by had bars over their windows, which meant we were closing in on my old neighborhood, but those bars—it's like I'd never noticed them before. I shrugged again and looked down at the floor; it was covered in clear candy wrappers. I imagined someone here before me, on this same route, eating a thousand mints, readying her breath for whomever she'd come to Miami to see.

The woman lifted my hand off the seat and said, You know that, right? That you should be proud?

Her mouth was shut, the muscles on the sides of her jaw flaring in and out. I finally pulled my hand away, balled it into a fist. I said, Yeah, I know.

She said, Good, and slid her palms along the sides of her head to check the gelled-back precision of her hair. I shifted my feet and the wrappers crunched beneath them. Water stains climbed the canvas of my sneakers, where winter slush had soaked in and dried and soaked in again. They were ruined, and that officially made them my winter shoes.

—How are you doing in your classes so far? she asked.

I looked up from the floor and caught the driver staring at us in his mirror. He yelled, Hialeah! And since I knew that wasn't really my neighborhood anymore, and since this woman's question proved she didn't want my Nobel Bash story, I figured I'd try out how it felt to stop the game of me being this credit to where I was from, this beginning of a success story, and instead, finally admit the truth to someone who maybe would understand.

—I'm doing bad, I said.

Her thick eyebrows slid together and they somehow looked *more* perfect like that. She leaned her face forward, closing her eyes and crinkling the skin around them in a pained way that I thought said, *Go on, tell me, I'm listening.*

I said, I'm doing *really* bad, actually. I don't know why it's so hard. Everyone else seems to just *know* stuff and I – I *don't*. It's like I'm the only one. I don't even know how I got in sometimes, that's how hard it is, how much I'm messing up. So yeah. It's going really, really bad for me.

—Oh god, the woman said. It's – what's your name?

—Lizet, I told her.

—Lizet, she said. It's bad-*lee*.

—What?

—You're doing *badly*. Not bad. Bad-*lee*.

I sat there with my mouth open, possibly making a dumb sound with the air seeping out from it. I could taste it then: my bad breath, the breath of someone who'd kept her mouth shut all day.

I blamed the new sting in my eyes on this breath and said, Right, okay.

Out the van's window, we passed my old high school, which hadn't changed since the summer: the eight-foot-tall, barbed-wire-topped fence surrounding the city block on which it stood, the windowless two-story facade with the words HIALEAH LAKES painted on it in all capital letters, the whole building the same gray as the concrete surrounding it. It was the gray of the winter I'd just left, and I had to touch the window again to make sure it wasn't freezing. When my hand felt the warm glass, I let it rest there, my fingers a barricade sparing me from the next block we sped past, then the next block, with the mini-mall that housed the My Dreams II Banquet Hall, where, if we could've afforded the formal party, my Quinces would've probably happened. I tried to remember who I'd been friends with at fourteen, before Omar came along and replaced them: which girls or boys I would've asked to make up the fourteen couples of my quinceañera court. I chanted their names, first and last, in my head and over the word *badly* as each couple added themselves to the list; I invented last names where I no longer remembered them, all to distract myself from the salty water brimming at the edges of my vision.

—Oh no, the woman finally whispered. No, don't – I didn't mean it like –

—¿Señora? the driver said.

The van stopped.

—Shit, she said. This is me.

She dug around in her purse and said, Here, take this. I want you to e-mail me.

She held out a little card—a business card. I took it from her, making sure my thumb covered her name. The seal for the Michigan school took up the whole left side, the side my thumb couldn't cover.

—I know you don't know me, she said. But I'm – I'm a resource. We're two girls from Hialeah who left for, you know, better things, right? More opportunities? And I want to help you any way I can. We have to stick together, right?

That same square smile, wrecking her face. The driver unbuckled his seatbelt. He turned on the blinkers—the tinny, rhythmic tick of them flashing on and off behind me—and got out of the van. I nodded.

—Awesome, she said. Cool. OK, well.

She scooted her purse along the bench, pushing it ahead of her like a boulder. As she slid open the door, the humidity outside flooded the van again, and it hit me from behind too, as the driver opened the back doors to get her suitcase. I felt my bangs curl, but her hair stayed perfect, the gel doing its job. She hopped down, hauled her purse to her hip, then straightened out her pants and blazer, tugging at the wrinkles as she stood just outside the van. She leaned a little away from the purse, struggling to keep it balanced on her shoulder and looking crooked as a result. The wheels of her suitcase dragged against the asphalt outside. The grating sound they made moved away from me, ended when the driver placed the bag by her side.

—Gracias, she said to the driver, who'd already left her there and was on his way back to the van. She watched me for a little too long, her eyes zipping around my face like she was trying to memorize me sitting on that vinyl bench before sliding the door between us closed. She inhaled then, so hard that her shoulders rose, the purse slipping.

—Please e-mail me, she said. Do it, OK?

She shifted the purse to her other shoulder, said, Good luck with everything.

I got the feeling she really meant it, like she was saying this to some old version of herself, but when she shut the door—not hard enough; she had to open it again and then slam it—I took the card in my other hand and ripped it in half, then ripped it in half again, then again and again, until the feathery edges of the paper wouldn't let me pull them apart any more. I let this bland confetti, dampened by the sweat on my palms, slip piece by piece down to the van's floor, where they nestled in with the mint wrappers left by someone before me, someone who'd done a better job of planning for this last leg of their trip. I wished for a piece of gum, for something to bring the saliva back to my mouth. I knew I had nothing, but I tugged my backpack closer to me and looked anyway, hoping some other version of myself had thought ahead.

The driver—after shouting, ¡La Pequeña Habana! over his

shoulder to me, his final passenger—left me alone in the back. I eventually found a stub of an eyeliner pencil at the bottom of my bag's front pocket, and I used my reflection in the now-dark window to line my eyes as best I could, the blocks of my old neighborhood blurring by. I also found an unwrapped cough drop, and after smudging the lint off with my thumb and blowing on it a few times, I decided to pretend I knew how it got there in the first place and tossed it in my mouth. It was so old that it didn't taste like anything, and little traces of the paper wrapper once protecting it somehow materialized and scratched around in my mouth like bits of sand. I swirled this almost-something for a long while, tricked myself into believing the cough drop hadn't yet totally disappeared.

4

I DIDN'T RECOGNIZE MY MOM'S new building in the dark, couldn't remember right away which window on the second floor was hers: I'd lived there only three days before leaving for Rawlings. The complex was a brighter peach than my memory had made it over to be, an orangey hue that too closely matched the Spanish tiles curving their way across the flat roof. A reggaetón remix blasted from the open windows on the building's first floor, the noise giving me permission to ignore the male neighbors leaning against the chain-link fence that separated a block's worth of sidewalk-hugging grass into lawns. On my last day there, Mami, Leidy, Omar, and I had each pulled a stuffed suitcase down the stairs; now I replayed each turn we'd taken in reverse, decided on a window, and tugged my bag up the too-tall front steps of the building's entrance.

My knock on the apartment door was answered only by the suddenly-gone sound of the television as someone on the other side muted the volume, pretending no one was home. I heard Dante's baby-quack, then a sharp *Shh*. I'd planned to yell *Surprise!* from outside the door just as it opened, but instead, after knocking two more times, I had to say, You know I can hear you guys. It's me.

Then, a few seconds later, Me as in Lizet?

I heard the chain slide back, then hands moving down to the other locks. My sister opened the door, Dante on the floor behind her.

—What the fuck are *you* doing here? she said.

Her emphasis should've been on the word *fuck*, or maybe on *here*, but not on *you*. She'd been expecting someone else? But seeing how much she looked exactly like herself—her smooth cheeks with only the left one dimpled, her almost-black eyes and their long lashes, her dark and falsely blond-streaked hair pulled up in the same loose, messy bun she always wore around the house to avoid denting her blowout—made me so happy that I didn't think to ask what she meant.

—Leidy! I screamed. Oh my god, Dante! He's so big!

—Lizet? my mom said from somewhere behind the door, which Leidy still hadn't opened all the way. I pushed it slowly with my whole hand just in time to see my mother rushing at me from the couch, already crying.

—Pero niña, she said, her hands in the air like someone getting called on stage for *The Price Is Right*, que tú haces aquí? You're supposed to be at school!

I didn't even recognize the squeal of my voice when I said, Mom!

She coiled her arms around my neck, latched her hand to the back of my head and pulled, buried my face in her shoulder. Her own neck was damp—wet from sweat or tears—and the salt from either or both met my lips.

—You're not supposed to be here, she said, then said again.

She swayed our hug side to side. Her fingers fanned open to cradle my head, and one of her rings got tangled in my hair, tugging my scalp. Instead of *ouch*, I said, I know, I know.

Behind her, the TV glowed with the still-silent news, which wasn't normally on at that hour. On the screen was the dirty, tanned face of a little boy not looking at the camera: my first glimpse of Ariel Hernandez. A young woman was dragging a wet towel up and down and across his cheeks. Without me knowing, without me even being aware of the race, he'd beaten me to Miami by a few hours. I looked away from the TV and over Mami's shoulder back to Leidy, whose hand still rested on the doorframe, her mouth a half smile.

—But – here I am, I said. Surprise, happy Thanksgiving.

—Get inside, come come, Mom said, ending our hug by pulling my arms, her rings taking with them several strands of my hair. You must be starving, que quieres?

She hurried toward the kitchen and began listing what was in there—did I want a snack like crackers with cream cheese and guayaba, or should she microwave the leftover rice and chicken, or some plátanos, or she could also slice up the rest of an avocado that was going to go bad any minute now so *someone* should eat it. The stream of options trailed away as Leidy swooped down and grabbed Dante, who let out a sharp, brief scream, then went silent. He raised his hand and smacked Leidy flat on the mouth. She seized his arm and pinned it to his side with one hand, and he turned and gawked at me, his mouth open but grinning, as Leidy, left with nothing else to do, dragged my bag in from the hallway.

After searching for soap to wash my face in a bathroom that felt more foreign than the massive one in the dorm, I eventually emerged from that white-tiled closet and sat next to my mom on the couch. A plate of cold chicken and rice waited for me on the glass coffee table as the news about Ariel played in front of us. I told my mom detail after detail of my trip, all the planning that went into it, every word of my story bouncing back to me off the side of her face.

—It's a Thanksgiving miracle, Mami said, echoing the news anchors.

But she was talking to the TV. She turned to me only during commercials, staring at me while I ate, her mouth wrinkled with a sort of regret.

—I was looking forward to getting you at the airport your first time home! she said during a local commercial for Mashikos Menswear. And during the next commercial—this one ringing with the familiar jingle for Santa's Enchanted Forest—she said, I was gonna bring you flowers, that first time! You stole that from me!

I pushed my food around my plate.

The jingle played on, and over it she said, How could you keep this from me all these weeks? All this time you've been lying.

—I wasn't lying, I just didn't tell you –

She shushed me as the news came back on. The coverage seemed to reset her reaction to me: she forgot she was shocked I was there each time the screen flashed back to the live shot of the house belonging to the relatives who'd claimed Ariel—a house not two blocks from our building. Leidy tried to ask me if I'd seen the news truck when the shuttle dropped me off—I hadn't—but Mom silenced us with a palm in the air before I could answer. So during the next commercial, I invented a story about my night in Pittsburgh that involved a sad Steelers fan and a prostitute in the room next to mine, hoping it would keep my mom's attention.

—I couldn't sleep thanks to the crazy sex noises and all the crying, I said.

But she cut off my mocking of the groans I'd supposedly heard.

—You think it's funny? A place like that, you could've gotten raped. You know that, right?

I half scoffed a *Mom, please* but she was glaring at me. I pulled my legs up and hugged my knees to my chest, and she turned back to the screen, the corner of the nail on her middle finger rooting around her bottom teeth for leftovers. Around that finger, she said, It's like you don't think about things, like about anyone but yourself. Like you forget how bad the world is.

Leidy gave a collaborative grunt, and I thought about confessing my lie to undo the very unintentional direction my story had taken the conversation. I hadn't really heard anything while trying to fall asleep the night before in Pittsburgh—just sirens outside, cars rushing down the street below, nothing I wasn't used to from home—but I didn't know how to tell them, without it sounding like bragging, that once I figured out how to turn off the disco ball overhead and got used to the weird staleness of the sheets, I fell asleep watching myself breathe in the mirror on the ceiling, my too-long hair fanned around my head like a dark cloud, amazed at where my own planning had landed me.

Leidy paced around the living room with Dante in her arms, bouncing him in an effort to make him fall asleep but shouting questions at the TV at the same time: But this Ariel kid, why is he famous? So okay, he just got here but so *what*, take a number, bro. I mean, what makes *him* so special?

—His mother died, my mother said, then kept saying: a new chant, this one to the TV, to the bare walls of her apartment.

She grabbed the remote and scanned up a few channels, but every one of them ran the same footage on a loop, my mom engaging with it through a one-sided call-and-response that reminded me of the very few times we'd gone to Mass. They'd show the shot of the inner tube, and she'd whisper, His mother died. The snippet from an interview with the fisherman who'd first spotted him: His *mother* died. The beachside reporter (why was he even *on* the beach when they'd brought Ariel in hours earlier?), foam-topped microphone in hand: His. Mother. *DIED.*

When the Spanish-language news showed, for the eighth time, Ariel's hand being waved for him by his uncle's grip as they left the hospital that afternoon, I asked my mom if she was trying to tell me something. She said to the TV, Tell you what? and so I stood up and walked away—she yelled to my back, Well I'm glad you're home even though you lied to me!—and went to what I thought of as my sister's room. It was technically *our* room, but I hadn't slept there enough nights to really feel that, and I didn't have a real bed; we had left it in our house, knowing it wouldn't fit in the new room. I'd be sleeping on the pull-out sofa that separated Dante's crib from my sister's mattress.

I pushed a pile of blue and white baby clothes and blankets to one side of the sofa and lugged my suitcase up onto the other, unzipping it just as Leidy came in behind me.

—We could've cleaned if we knew you were gonna be here.

—No, I know, don't even worry about it, I said. Did you guys do Thanksgiving dinner?

She lowered Dante into the crib and handed him a stuffed bunny, the long ear of which he shoved in his mouth. I opened the top drawer of the dresser and tried to make space for my stuff.

—Sort of. It's Dante's first Thanksgiving so yeah, we made like a chicken and some mashed potatoes or whatever, and Mom said grace.

She sat down on the floor next to the pile of baby stuff and pulled a shirt loose from it, then folded the shirt into a tiny square.

—But this stupid kid on the news! Mami couldn't stop watching it, and so I was like *hello?* So in the end dinner sucked.

I should've asked for details about the day then, for more about Ariel Hernandez, or about Dante's dad—if he'd called or been over—or about our own dad (same questions), but I thought I already knew the answers. As recent as the end of our parents' marriage was, Leidy and I were not at all shocked that they were no longer together. They got married a couple months after Mami found out she was pregnant with Leidy, and they each blamed the other for having to drop out of high school so close to finishing. They should've left each other dozens of times before that summer, maybe right after my dad refused to buy Mami a plane ticket to Cuba to see the dying mother she hated for disowning her from afar after getting pregnant before marriage; or later, when I started middle school and Mami became a Jehovah's Witness for a few intense months and bullied my dad to convert or else she'd take us away and go live with my tía Zoila. Because my parents married as teenagers, their relationship sort of froze there, stuck at that age where every fight is The End and probably should be. We were known on our Hialeah block as the family whose arguments spilled into the front lawn. Leidy and I knew to listen for the words *Are you fuck-ing crazy, Lourdes?*—which meant: time to go outside, get in the grass on our hands and knees, and look for Mom's wedding ring. They fought constantly, more so in the couple years leading up to that fall and mostly about Leidy's pregnancy and her boyfriend's refusal to marry her—the exact inverse of the choice my dad had made when he got my mom pregnant. It should've been a family disaster except that it coincided with me announcing that I'd applied to out-of-state schools months earlier without their knowledge and would be leaving at the end of the summer. Which is why my father decided to leave, too: he no longer saw the point, he said, of being around women clearly set on behaving as if he hadn't stuck around in the first place.

The air conditioner kicked on, sending a buzz through the window trapping it in place. It jarred me to hear an AC in the winter, and the whole room, with me in it, seemed like a huge freaking mistake. I felt stupid for even wanting the attention I thought I'd get by coming back. The processed air hit me and I shivered. If I was going to be invisible and miserable and cold, I could've stayed at school, saved myself the money. I kept unpacking my suitcase.

—Why did you not tell me you were coming? Leidy said.

I shrugged. I said, I wanted it to be a surprise.

—So nobody – like nobody *here* – knows you were doing this? Not even Omar?

—No one, I said.

She sucked her teeth and stood up, a tiny tower of folded baby clothes in her hands. And you're supposed to be the smart one? she said.

Her face suddenly next to mine at the dresser, I said, What the fuck is your problem?

—Mom's right, something could've happened to you and who would've even known?

—Oh come *on*.

—I'm just saying you should've told me. I can keep a secret, okay?

I mean, at least I would've kept her away from the TV so she could enjoy how you showed up here. Now she's like all *distracted.*

I crammed my underwear into my half of the dresser drawer, then went back to my suitcase for more clothes.

—Look, maybe you know how to buy a plane ticket on a computer to go wherever, but that doesn't make you somebody that can just be all like whatever about it. That's not what being independent means.

—Okay Leidy, I get it.

—I'm not trying to say anything, okay? I just get why Mami's pissed, because honestly, you had *me* you could've told, and for like a whole twenty-four hours no one knew where you were, and just because we didn't know that we didn't know doesn't mean it's all fine now, okay?

—Fine. *God,* I said.

I slammed the drawer shut. She opened it back up slowly and tucked the baby's things next to mine.

—That's it, all right? I'm not gonna say anything else about it. I just feel like somebody should say it, and it's not gonna be Mami right now.

She stood by the dresser and raised a hand to her mouth, chipped away at her nail polish with her teeth.

I sat down on the sofa bed, my arms folded across my body. Beyond us, in the living room we could see if we poked our heads out from the bedroom door, the TV screamed with an interview of some government person saying Ariel's arrival could turn into a political issue, and our mother screamed back, *Political* issue? Is this guy serious? His *mother* is *dead!*

—Fine, you know what? I'm sorry I'm here.

—It's not like that, Leidy said. Don't be sorry. I'm happy you're home.

I thought then that she'd sit next to me, but she stayed standing up, pulling another soft thing from the pile shrinking next to me, this time holding a onesie against her chest as she folded it in half, then in half again.

—I don't gotta work tomorrow, she said.

—Awesome, I said, meaning it.

She stopped mid-fold and almost laughed.

—*Awesome!* she parroted back, her voice high and in her nose. She threw what she was folding into the drawer, pushed it shut, then slung her hands under Dante's arms. She raised him to her face and cooed to him, *Awe*-some, *awe*-some! What other stupid words you picking up at that school?

5

MAMI WOKE UP BEFORE THE SUNRISE on my first morning
back—a habit left over from marriage: she always made our dad
his café before he headed to a jobsite—and learned from Radio
Mambí that the very first rally to support Ariel's Miami family not
only was happening that morning but would be held just two blocks
away, in front of the house owned by Ariel's U.S. relatives. She kissed
me on the forehead while I was still asleep, told me she was going
and that she'd left café con leche for me in the microwave. All you
gotta do is press start, she said, and from the bedroom door, she
either said or I half-dreamed, *I'll be back by lunch.* So I spent Friday
morning on the living room floor, playing silly singsong games with
Dante, who I was surprised to realize I'd missed. He was eight
months old by then and could do several new things that made
him more appealing to me: crawl, talk a little, sleep through the
night. More than my mom's new apartment, or our old house belonging to someone else now, or the things from my old room
stuffed into half a new one, it was Dante's unexpected heft when I
lifted him out of his crib that made me understand how much
could change in three months.

Thanks to the holiday, Leidy was off from the salon, where she mostly worked the phone and booked appointments, swept hair off the salon floor, and sometimes did makeup. She spent her day off just sitting on the couch, flipping between back-to-back episodes of *Jerry Springer* and the news coverage about Ariel, avoiding what seemed like the chore of playing with her son or taking him to go see his father. I wasn't sure if Leidy and Rolando were talking to each other and, though I never admitted this to Leidy, I didn't blame him for wanting to stay away from her, considering what she'd done: When Roly didn't propose to her during the last slow dance at prom, or in front of Cinderella's Castle at Grad Nite, or while receiving his diploma in front of a couple thousand people at graduation, Leidy decided to force the issue and stopped taking the pill the week after school finished in June. On a mid-July morning the summer before my senior year, while our parents were at work, she screamed my name from the bathroom, and seconds later, she blasted into my room holding a stick she'd peed on three minutes before. I figured from her joy that the test was negative, but then she showed me the plus sign as she laughed and cried at the same time. She smashed me in a hug and said, Roly is gonna *freak out*! I started crying too and saying *Oh no oh no*—the same reaction I had while waiting those three minutes for my own results from my scares with Omar. What was happening inside Leidy, I realized, was my own worst-case scenario, but Leidy shook my shoulders, the stick still in her fist and now against my skin, and said, Aren't you gonna congratulate me?

—You're *happy* about this?

—Of course! Lizet, I graduated from school. So did Roly. This makes sense, this is what's next for us.

Leidy looked down at the test again, and I wanted one for my-self: some test that would measure whether or not I was really headed for the same future. When she left for Roly's house, I went to the library and found those lists made year after year by important people, the lists of the very top schools in the country. These schools, I saw, were next to impossible to get into, but like the plus sign on Leidy's test, I wanted whatever result my actions brought—positive or negative—to indicate something irrefutable about me.

Leidy correctly predicted Roly's freak-out, but she didn't predict him leaving her once she confessed, a few weeks later, that she'd stopped taking her birth control and had purposely not informed him of that decision. Our dad wanted to step in, maybe talk to Roly's parents, but Leidy said she didn't need his help: she was certain Roly would see his son growing inside her and forgive her, would go back on his decision to throw away the four years they'd been together—basically since *freshman year*! she told anyone who'd listen—and do the right thing, even if it was true that she'd lied to trap him. We all kept waiting for it, buoyed by her certainty, by the example of our own dad's choices, our own family's origins. I made a mistake of my own, thinking that the biggest difference between a college and a university was that a college (which I thought must be more like Miami Dade Community *College* than Florida International *University*) was easier to get into. So I sent off applications to that year's top three colleges without anyone's knowledge or help or blessing just to see if I could get in: just to know if I was meant for something other than what Leidy and my mom had done for themselves.

A couple days after mailing them, I told Omar I'd applied on a whim to only one out-of-state school: getting rejected from one wouldn't sound as bad as three come April.

—I thought you didn't want to leave Florida, he said.

His hand reached around and hugged the back of his own neck, and I knew for him *Florida* was another word for *Omar*.

—Leidy's pregnant, I said.

He made the requisite *Whoa*s and *Holy Shit*s, but those eventually led to *I'm not totally surprised* and, finally, *At least you'll make a cute maid of honor.*

I thought of how three phone calls and a few faxed pages of the tax return copies my dad had already given me (for verifying my reduced school lunch application) was all it took to get the fee waivers for those three applications, and for the first time, I wanted not just to get into one of those colleges but to go—like immediately. I wanted to be gone already. It was a relief to think maybe I'd given myself a chance, and with that came a new feeling: guilt.

Omar elbowed me in the ribs and said, What? You know it's true. He's gotta marry her, probably should've proposed to her already.

But he never did, and even when Leidy went into labor, he refused to show up, instead dropping by the hospital hours after (with a couple friends but no gift) to see Dante—just Dante—on his birthday: March 25, six days before the arrival of my Rawlings acceptance. I'd spent the intervening months driving Leidy to her doctor's appointments, going with her to Babies R Us and La Canastilla Cubana, planning her a baby shower that Roly's mom refused to attend but for which Blanca—Omar's mom—made three kinds of flan; all this while barely missing class and staying on top of the clubs I'd joined as a freshman, back when I had time to waste. I didn't know the rule about thick or thin envelopes—I wouldn't get the two rejections for another week—so when I read *Congratulations* on the Rawlings letter, I thought the sleep deprivation from having Dante in the house was making me see things. But I read it again, right there with the driveway's hot concrete burning my bare feet, and I started to organize my arguments as to why I should be allowed to go. I folded the letter back into the envelope and ran on my tiptoes to the house, already knowing none of my reasons would work: unlike with Dante, my parents hadn't been warned this was coming. And unlike Leidy, I couldn't even try for a little while to pretend this was an accident.

The next morning, on the anniversary of Dante's first full week around and with no more visits from Roly to hint that meeting his son had changed his mind about Leidy, I faked my mom's signature on the deposit waiver the school had mailed along with my letter and returned with it the card saying I accepted my spot in the class of 2003. I eventually mustered the ovaries to show them the folder full of papers Rawlings had sent me with my financial aid package, using the official-looking forms to confuse them into thinking it was too late to fight me about it. Leidy didn't really care; she'd miss the help but was relieved there'd be one less person around to see how completely wrong she'd been about her own plan and Roly. But my betrayal—that is the word my parents used over and over again for what I'd done—gave them permission to finally abandon their marriage, and my dad took my impending fall exit to mean he could do the same, but even sooner.

6

THE STREET IN FRONT OF OUR BUILDING buzzed all morning, the sidewalks overflowing with crowds that trampled each yard's overgrown grass. From our apartment window, the rally below looked more like spectators camped out for a choice spot along a parade route than an actual rally. Some people had salsa or talk radio playing out of boom boxes. Some sat on coolers and handed out water and cans of soda whenever a new person they seemed to know walked up. Wisps of conversations reached our window from the street: such-and-such reporter had said something about Ariel going back by the end of the weekend, so clearly she was a communist. The people down there, on the street, all nodded their heads and said, Claro que sí. I leaned forward more, Leidy, Dante, and the TV behind me, my cheek touching the window screen, and looked up and over the blocks of houses and palm trees spreading far out like stripes parallel to the horizon. It was gorgeous outside—bright white sky, not so hot you could kill someone, not so humid, almost a breeze—the beginning of winter in Miami. I couldn't believe I had to go back to the gloomy half-lit days of upstate New York, to snow turned to dirt-slush pushed into every corner for miles, to inescapable cold everywhere you turned. Before ever seeing snow, I thought that even if I couldn't bear the cold that came with it, its novelty would carry me through at least four years, no problem. I'd actually been eager for it to come after the surprise of fall colors wore off, after maybe half the leaves on campus ended up pressed between the pages of my textbooks. Once those were gone, everything looked stark enough that I asked Jillian one night, while she studied on her bed and I sat at my desk highlighting pretty much every sentence in my chemistry textbook, when the snow would show up and cover it all.

She pulled her headphones off and said, My brother told me that one year, they had snow here on *Halloween*. Three, four feet overnight. He said all the girls in slutty costumes couldn't stand to put coats on over them, and like a dozen stupid bitches ended up in the hospital due to exposure.

—Wait, you have a brother? I said, and she gasped and smacked her book with both her hands, then pointed with a *He-llo?* to a photo of her and a guy much taller than her, their arms wrapped around each other's waists, her in a bikini top and shorts and him in a tuxedo. I'd assumed he was a boyfriend she only talked to when I wasn't around, the way I did with Omar. I asked if he'd gone to Rawlings too, and she told me no, he went to another college—one I'd never heard of but that was just a few hours away by bus, and so he'd come to Rawlings to visit a high school friend a few years earlier. He was already a senior, she said.

—I can't believe you've never even *seen* snow in real life, she said.

I looked out our window and tried to imagine a snow-friendly sexy Halloween costume. Sexy astronaut? Sexy female polar bear?

—I can't believe you didn't know I had a brother, she said a few seconds later. That's weird, I thought you knew that..

A door slammed in the hallway and a male voice laughed.

I eventually said to my reflection in the window, It's not *that* weird. You don't know I have a baby nephew, do you? His name is – my sister named him Dante.

I'd imagined this moment already—the moment where I'd explain Dante's name to my roommate—back when Jillian was just an idea, just a name printed in a letter from the school. I'd planned to tell the theoretical Jillian that Leidy named Dante after the famous writer, a name she came across when she looked over my shoulder at something I happened to be reading (not for school, just for fun, I'd say). This was nowhere near the truth: Leidy said the name Dante was *super original* and that's the only reason she gave anyone for picking it. At the sonogram appointment where we learned the baby's sex—I'd skipped sixth period to drive her—the tech had swirled a finger over the screen and said to us, There's the penis, and Leidy was relieved: she thought Roly would be more likely to forgive her if she gave him a son instead of a daughter. I was relieved, too, since by then I'd learned about history's Dante, and I could tell people, when they asked, that she took the name from that.

But I hadn't anticipated utter silence as my roommate's response when I planned this conversation in my head, hadn't visualized the bags under my own eyes staring back at me in the dark window. I couldn't bear to turn around and see Jillian's open mouth, or maybe she was laughing so hard that she couldn't make a sound. I waited for the rustle of her turning a page, but there was nothing. Down the corridor from us, a rollicking song with a female singer started playing from someone's stereo, but the stereo's owner closed their door seconds after the first notes hit the hallway. From the kitchen came a peppery smell—someone cooking instant soup.

—You smell that? I tried. When Jillian didn't answer, I decided to go back to snow and said, You know, there's places in America where people can trick-or-treat without worrying about freezing to death.

She didn't laugh, so I turned around to face her judgment only to see her nodding along to a song: at some point—I couldn't tell when—she'd put her headphones back on.

The morning that snow finally came—a week into November—
Jillian woke me by slapping two damp mittens on my back. I jumped,
and before I could ask why her hat and coat were flecked with water
(Had she showered while dressed? Got caught in a sprinkler?), she
screamed: Liz! It snowed! All last night and this morning!

I rubbed my eyes and slurred, Class is canceled?

She barked just one *Ha!* and pulled my comforter all the way
off me.

—Wake up, *wake up*, she said. Let's go, before you have to get
ready for class.

She ran from our room and left the door open, pounded her
hands on the doors down from us and yelled, You guys! It's
Lizet's first snow! Let's do this! Tracy, get your camera. Is Caroline still – Shit, Caroline, finish drying your hair and come outside!

As her voice disappeared into the cave of the hall bathroom, I
looked out the window. I'd seen snow on TV, had played in some
soapy, manmade snow at the mall when I was little, but to see that
now-familiar square of campus totally transformed: what was, as
I'd fallen asleep, a brown swath of dead grass and trees suddenly
cleaned up and covered. I couldn't believe it was the same Outside. I would've bought that I'd been moved in the night to a different planet; I couldn't believe the planet I'd lived on for eighteen
years was capable of looking like this—and I couldn't believe people lived in it, vacationed specifically to glide over it. More than
anything, I needed to touch it—immediately—to know it like everyone else did as quickly as I could. I flung myself from the bed,
slid my feet into my shower flip-flops, ran past Jillian and her *Hey,
wait!* in the bathroom doorway, and charged down the stairwell at
the end of the hall to the nearest exit—the dorm's loading dock—
throwing my whole weight against the metal double doors.

Those first fifteen seconds: down the loading dock steps, flip-
flops slipping on ice, stepping on the snow—two feet high and still
falling—and expecting to walk on top of it. Hearing a soft crunch,

then one leg then the other crashing down, the snow reaching just past my knees, hugging my feet and calves. And I was stuck. And I laughed so hard I fell on my butt into more snow, soft but not soft enough, the white stuff packing into my armpits because I'd extended my arms to brace for the fall. Those first fifteen seconds, I got it: I got how people could love snow. But then, creeping in like the very real tingle I started to feel in my feet, was the fact that snow was frozen water—that snow was *wet* and not fluffy like cotton or like the mall's soap-bubble snow. I'd locked myself out of the dorm by accident, and as I held a clump of snow in my hand for the first time and squeezed it hard, my skin turned red. It burned. My toes burned, too—I scrunched them to make sure I could still feel them, thinking of those stupid girls on Halloween—and I looked up to find Jillian next to Tracy, both waving from the other side of the door's glass square. Then Tracy lifted her camera to her face.

Jillian pushed her way out and yelled, Oh my god, you are *crazy*! You're practically naked! She pulled off her coat and twirled it over my shoulders.

Tracy took another shot from inside, this time of Jillian with her arm around me and giving a thumbs-up.

—Make sure you get her flip-flops, she yelled.

More people came down, from our floor and other floors. I ran back up to get socks and real shoes, threw a pair of baggy jeans over my soaked pajama pants, and returned to a full-on snowball fight. Later, amid Jillian and Tracy and other people I'd seen all fall trekking in and out of the bathroom in nothing but towels but whose last names I didn't know, we collectively decided to skip class without saying this directly. One girl, a brunette named Caroline in a lilac vest and sweatpants, made hot chocolate for everyone using milk and not powder but actual chocolate, and we all sat in the hallway outside our rooms drinking it. I had the idea to call Leidy and my mom and tell them what it was like, my first time in the snow, but I didn't want to be the only one to get up and leave, the first to say *Thank you but* and give back the mug. So I wrapped my fingers around it even tighter, let them get warmer.

A day later, during Jillian's twice-weekly night class, I told my mom and Leidy about the snow over the phone. I almost blew the surprise of the Thanksgiving trip when I said I was thinking of getting a cooler so I could bring some down so they could see for themselves, saying *at Christmas* just in time to cover it up. Mami asked if I had any pictures of me in the snow and I said yes, someone took some and that I'd track them down. But I still hadn't done that, thinking if Tracy wanted me to have them, she'd come to me.

Now that I was back home, I felt bad for not bringing any evidence along—no props to show my sister to make talking to her easier. I sipped the coffee Mami left for me and asked Leidy about Dante's daycare, about her hours at the salon, about nothing that mattered as much as what I wanted to ask her: if she'd seen or spoken to our dad. I didn't know how to bring him up. I hadn't heard from him since the night before I left for New York, when he'd stood outside my mom's building, hands in his pockets, and asked if I needed anything. I'd only shrugged and said no. After a few other vague yes-or-no questions (You know where you're going? You know how to get there? You sure?), we hugged for a second too short and he left in his work van for his new place. He didn't even have a phone there yet. He probably had one by now, but I didn't have the number. I wondered if Leidy did and just had not given it to me any of the times I'd called home. I'd tried his work number when I made it to campus, to let him know I'd survived my first plane ride, but I got an answering machine. I called it again after moving in, meeting my roommate, and setting up my side of our room—things I'd imagined both my parents helping me do, though I don't know how we would've afforded their tickets or if they would've left Leidy alone with a five-month-old Dante—but that time, it just rang and rang. After that, tired of wasting phone card minutes on answering machines, I left it up to him to call.

I wanted to ask Leidy if he'd been ignoring her the same way he was ignoring me, but we hadn't so much as uttered *Papi* since the night before I left for New York: we still blamed him for our move. Our home was only in his name—something neither of us knew before that June when, a couple weeks after he moved out, some woman from the bank came on his behalf and told my mom he wanted to put the house up for sale. My mom was too confused and proud to fight it, and by the end of July, the house belonged to some new family—another set of Cubans. For three weeks we stayed with my tía Zoila, with Roly not even hinting that Leidy and Dante could stay with him and his parents, and the three of us plus Omar moved everything from Zoila's to Little Havana just before I left for school. And because the second move of my life came so close to the first, I just *missed* the house; I didn't really get to say goodbye to it, didn't even know how to do that, since it was the only place I remembered ever living.

Leidy bounced Dante in her lap as she watched the TV. She rubbed his back and said, I freaking *hate* this neighborhood. It's so freaking reffy, everyone got here like five minutes ago from some island.

Dante shoved his fist in his mouth, muffling his own noise. I let the blinds clink back into place and turned around, settled onto the couch next to them.

—So how's school going finally? Leidy said.

—It's okay, I said. I swallowed and rubbed at the sore spot on my neck, feeling for the old home of the strands twisted up in Mami's ring the night before. I said, It's way harder than I thought it would be.

—Ms. Smarty Pants can't hack it, huh?

She flipped back to the news, where people in front of a chain-link fence a block away gave speeches. She tried to raise the volume, smacking the remote a few times to get it to register, and I was grateful for her distraction, since it meant she missed my recoiling at what she'd said. In my mind, I called her a stupid bitch, then pushed my anger into pity—of course she'd say that, she had no idea what college classes were like. She'd probably never know. I imagined myself paying her utility bill someday, or her calling me to help Dante with his biology homework. It wasn't fair, but it helped me answer her.

—I can hack it. It's just that Hialeah Lakes was a joke compared to the work I gotta do now.

She returned to the talk show, where a woman's hands were lost in another woman's hair. I let Dante wrap his hand around my finger and said in a voice that sounded a bit too high, So have you talked to Roly?

She nodded to the TV.

—He came by here to see Dante last week. He brought him that.

She gestured to a toy on the floor, the one with colored panels that I'd spent the morning showing him, singing along with the songs it played.

—It's stupid, she said. He's too little for it still.

—But that's nice of him, right? I tried.

Leidy put her hand to her mouth and gnawed on her middle finger, her face twisting to look too much like our mom's. She pulled her hand away and spit a sliver of nail from the tip of her tongue. It flew sideways and landed on my foot, and I wiped it off on the carpet, pretending to lift my leg to tuck it under me. She moved on to her ring finger and said, Roly really is so freaking dumb. He really could have everything, like a whole family, but no. Not *him*. He needs to freaking grow up, is what he needs.

She said all of this to the TV, as if Jerry were asking her to tell America why she was so angry. I imagined us on this trashy show, sitting in those perfect-for-throwing chairs in front of the angry-for-no-reason crowd, me trying—when Leidy's words inevitably fail her—to explain her make-Roly-marry-me plan to Jerry as he roams the stage, batting the microphone against his own forehead, blurting out to the audience to stoke their rage, *Oh yes, the joys of fatherhood!*

—And what about – You heard anything from Papi? I finally, finally asked.

She turned Dante on her lap to face her, kissed his dark hair. He twisted his head to look at me, and she grabbed underneath his chin and squashed his cheeks, making his lips pucker but also pulling his face back to hers.

—I think Mom's given up on him, she said.

—That's not what I asked.

—I know that. I can hear, she said.

A commercial came on so she went back to the news. There, a woman was crying and nodding and wiping her face while a man stood next to her, yelling about something so much that his neck burned red.

When Leidy didn't say anything else, I waited a few more seconds and whined, Are you gonna answer me? I hated the way my voice sounded: too high, too pleading, the same voice I'd had to breathe through to steady my answers at my academic integrity hearing. A big laugh rolled up from the street below and filled the living room, and while Leidy turned to it like a reflex, I had to close my eyes and blink away the thought of the next time I'd be in that long wood-paneled room, waiting for a different sort of answer.

—Papi has called a couple times, she said out the window. But Mom just hangs up the second she hears it's him.

I jumped up to get away from her, half-tripping my way to the small kitchen, to the sink, saying *Oh for real?* with a calm so false I coughed afterward to cover it up. I started scrubbing the inside of my café con leche mug as if trying to dig a hole in it.

—It's not like I talk to him or anything, she said. Don't be like that.

—I'm not being like anything, Leidy.

I poured more soap onto the dishrag, scrubbed it against itself to make lather, then crammed the whole rag into the mug and scrubbed harder.

—Well whatever, *you* knew you were leaving and *you* got your own place, but *I'm* the one who was all stressed about being basically homeless when what I wanted was to just like *deal* with my own freaking kid and my own freaking *life*. Mom's still super mad about the house too. Dad selling it made things harder for like *no reason.*

I looked over my shoulder but kept the water running. Behind me, Leidy—still looking outside, Dante back on the floor and on his belly—mumbled, Freaking asshole.

I wanted to ask who was the asshole, our dad or me, but instead I faced the sink and said, I don't have my own place. I *have* a roommate.

I scanned the kitchen counter for other dishes and decided to rewash everything already in the drying rack to calm down. The skin on my hands was chapped and cracking thanks to my reluctance to wear the one pair of mittens I had; along with her coat, Jillian had tugged mittens over my hands after Tracy took the pictures I'd never seen. She pulled them out from the coat's pocket and said, as she put them on me, Mittens are better because then your fingers keep each other company. I tried to give them back to her later that night, but she said to keep them. I have like thirty pairs, she said, and the crazy color suits you better anyway. I never left the dorm wearing them, though: The distinct green (WILD PEA, the tag inside one of them read) and brand name printed inside the wrists gave them away as Formerly Jillian's to anyone paying attention. I left them in my desk drawer at school but had wished for them when I got stuck in Pittsburgh. The cold there had peeled back the skin on my knuckles, and now the hot water and soap made them look even worse, made my skin itchy and angry. But I kept rinsing and scrubbing until everything was back on the drying rack, just like I'd found it. I shut off the water and, behind me, the program went to commercial. I dried my hands with a paper towel and returned to the couch, trusting that I'd taken enough deep breaths, my eyes on the carpet the whole way there. I sidestepped Dante at my sister's feet before sitting down.

I knew I wanted to go by our old house and see it. Maybe the family there now was nice and I could explain everything and they would let me really say bye to my old room. Before he moved out, my dad kept saying to me, You betrayed us, this is a betrayal. He said it so much that the word stopped meaning anything— *betray betray betray betray betray betray*—until the woman from the bank sat us down in our own living room and explained what was about to happen. No one said *betrayal*, but as I filled out my financial aid appeal form—alone in my room, the door closed, half my things in boxes marked *Send to Rawlings* and the other half in boxes marked *Lizet's stuff*—I knew exactly how much hurt could fit into a word.

The backs of my hands burned red, the skin flaking in rows like fish scales.

—You want to drive by the house? I asked Leidy.

—You don't want to do that.

She switched an earring out from the first to the second hole in her earlobe, then said, They fucking paved over every fucking piece of grass. They have like eighteen SUVs parked there now. Probably they're running a garage or some car-alarm installation thing. It's freaking the *worst*.

—So you been there then?

—Relax, she said. I went by there maybe once.

She adjusted her other earring and said, But it was like – *too* much.

The news came back with some of the same footage from the day before of Ariel being carried from place to place, in some new relative's arms in every shot.

—Why are they always carrying him? I said. Can't that kid fucking *walk*?

—I should change Dante's name to Ariel, Leidy said.

We laughed a little, and in it she said, Maybe then Roly would want to be around.

—Don't say that, I said.

The people in the street—on TV and behind us, outside—started pushing each other, wrestling for a spot in front of Ariel's new home.

—Should we be worried about Mom? I said.

I faced Leidy, wanting to look serious and grown-up, but she stayed focused on the TV.

—She misses you I think, she said. I know she's like happy for you now, for your new life or whatever, but it's hard. A lot's different for her, what's she supposed to do?

On the floor, Dante flailed his arms, looking to climb up to my lap, but I couldn't move, couldn't bend forward to haul him to me.

—I didn't – I wasn't asking that. I meant now, outside with the –

—No, I know, she said. I'm just telling you Mom's probably not really happy.

She leaned down and grabbed Dante, squeezing him around his basketball of a belly. She said, Obviously it's my fault too. She doesn't talk about it when you call. She doesn't want you to worry. She doesn't want to mess up your *awesome* life.

—Things *aren't* awesome, I said, but Dante blasted over my words with a high scream, and instead of trying to explain, I reached down and grabbed the toy Roly had brought him. I held it in my lap and waited for Leidy to say *What did you say* as Dante punished it with smacks.

Leidy switched fast between the commercial on the Springer channel and the commercial on the news channel, flipping to see which came back to its program first. The news won, showing the weather, focusing on the swirl of snow hovering over New England before zooming down to Florida. I was twenty-four hours away from the plane ride back to New York: I'd booked the return for Saturday afternoon because it was two hundred dollars cheaper than leaving Sunday morning. Dante kept slapping the toy, and I felt the sun through the window pressing on the back of my neck. Then a new feeling: the skin stinging a little, maybe starting to burn. I hadn't been sunburned in years. None of us ever really burned; on days we'd go to the beach, we never wore sunscreen—we were dark enough that we didn't think we needed to. I touched my neck, felt how hot my skin had become in those few minutes on the couch, and couldn't believe how cold I would be again so soon. That heat made me feel brave, as if the sun were pushing me, gently on the back, to say what I knew would make Leidy turn off the television.

—So I'm having some – issues. Serious issues, I said. Up at school.

I moved the toy off my lap and Dante froze.

—Holy. Fucking. Shit, Leidy said. She slid Dante over to me and stood up. She pointed the remote at the TV. Look who *that* is!

I stared at the screen and blinked hard. But when I opened my eyes again, the camera was still on the same person—our mother.

—That's our freaking mom, Leidy shrieked. She snatched up Dante and bounced him toward the TV, saying, Es Abuela. ¡Abuela! ¡Abuela!

She grabbed his arm, made him point.

Our mother's mouth moved, a microphone in front of her face. Leidy dropped Dante's arm and turned up the volume, the green bar on the bottom of the screen creeping right.

—But he *is* home. That's the end of it. His mother made the ultimate sacrifice to get him here. That *must* be honored. That *must* be the end of it, Mami said.

Her eyes suddenly filled and she swiped at the bottoms of them with her middle fingers, like she was flipping off the cameraman.

—Ah-Bee! Dante screamed. He clapped wildly.

—Mom's fucking famous! Leidy said. She spun around to face me. Let's go down there. We can get on TV! Where are my earrings?

I couldn't find the words to say, *You're wearing them.* She tossed the remote on the couch and ran off to our room, whispering in baby talk, We gotta get your shoes!

Our mom kept talking. Her voice was too deep—it sounded like a stranger's. I lowered the volume, lowered it all the way to nothing. The camera zoomed in on her now-silent face—the new, heavy lines framing her mouth—then zoomed out to show her arms flailing down the street. *I live right on this block*, she was probably saying. Never mind that she didn't want to be here, that she was from Hialeah, not Little Havana. There was a pause in her talking, then a nod, then her mouth moved again as she held up a peace sign. Peace for what? And then I realized it was not *peace*, it was *two*. I have two daughters, she was telling the world. *This is personal; we live right on this block; I have two little girls.*

I stood up from the couch and shot at the TV with the remote, afraid of what she'd do next. My mother's wet face disappeared.

—Leidy! I yelled into the next room. Forget his shoes, we need to hurry.

Only when the ghost of my mother's image—her metallic outline—faded away into the now-dead screen did I let go of the remote, its thud against the carpet the last sound I heard as I ran out the front door.

7

LEIDY DIDN'T SEEM TO HEAR my almost-confession about Rawlings, never asked, *What were you saying?* Not even when she caught up with me on the sprint to Ariel's house, me wearing a broken pair of my mom's flip-flops that she left by the mailboxes downstairs, her in a red tube top and cutoffs and strappy sandals, earrings still in, her nameplate now dangling from her neck—*camera ready*, she called the look. Dante spent the run trying to rip the nameplate free from the gold chain.

The cameras had moved on to someone else by the time we got there, though Leidy did manage to stand—as seductively as is possible when one is holding an eight-month-old—behind the man they were then interviewing. My mom was on the sidewalk, watching the new interview, and when I asked her what the hell was going on, she shushed me hard and crossed her arms over her chest, then rose up on her toes to see better.

That night, as we sat to eat dinner in the area we called the dining room but which was really just a table and three chairs set off by a square of linoleum a few feet from the couch, my mom was too frantic—too happy—talking about being interviewed, about the people she'd met, and I didn't want to spoil that for her with news of my Rawlings hearing, not after what Leidy had told me that morning. Mami was in such good spirits that she'd cooked bistec palomilla—my favorite, with tons of extra onions, the meat pounded so thin that before she'd fried it you could see light through the sinewy slab—and I knew from the meal that she'd forgiven me for my stupid plan to come home without telling her. I lowered my face over my plate and let the steam and the smell of almost-burnt onions fill my whole head and displace the foreign college-world terms—*plagiarism, academic integrity, student code of conduct*—as well as the word those would boil down to were I to try and explain things to them: *cheating*. For most of dinner, I was grateful for the distraction of the Ariel conversation. My mom smiled at how slowly I chewed, not knowing that I was just trying to keep my mouth busy.

—What everybody's saying is that he made it here, right? Mami said. So that's it, he can stay, that's the law. If you're Cuban and you make it to dry land, when you ask for asylum, you get it. Done. Everybody knows that.

She worked a chunk of the thin steak between her molars. I didn't want to say that what she thought of as *the law* was probably very much open for debate; he hadn't made it to the U.S. unassisted— he'd been picked up at sea and brought in—so the wet foot/dry foot element, which already seemed like a tricky way to distinguish which Cubans got sent back and which got to stay and eventually apply for political asylum, was more complicated than my mom wanted to admit. Plus, Ariel Hernandez wasn't just a minor; he was a little kid. How could my mom—who was friends with so many people who'd been brought by their parents from Cuba—think that some- one so young would get to decide in which country he'd grow up? I cut another sliver of meat, speared a perfect loop of onion for the same bite, chewed and chewed.

—You know the coast guard? She pointed her fork at me, then Leidy, then said, They almost didn't believe the fisherman that called them. They thought Ariel was a doll when they saw him, he was sitting so still on the raft. They almost left him there.

She told us that pretty much everyone she met—her *vecinos*, she called them now, neighbors she hadn't talked to until that day—was somehow related to Ariel's relatives here or to Ariel himself. She would not be surprised, she said, if we were somehow related to him, too.

I asked what I thought was a simple, obvious question: What about his dad?

My mom stopped chewing, swallowed, and said like a speech, Well it's the father's family that's taken him in. They knew Ariel was coming – it was the father that told them. And what does he care? He let them leave. He has a whole new family in Cuba. New wife, new baby, everything. He gave them his blessing.

She had her fork in her fist as she said this. She stabbed the next piece of meat on her plate and shoved it in her mouth.

—Where'd you hear that? I asked.

—From everyone!

I closed my eyes, the word *citation* suddenly coming to me, and said, Right, okay.

Then, after more chewing, But who exactly?

—What is your *problem*? Leidy yelled. What do *you* care who said it? Of course it's true. We're on the freaking front lines here.

—I'm just asking about sources, Leidy. Not every ref standing on the street knows –

—So you don't believe me now? Mami said.

She threw her fork onto her plate. The clang of it sounded like the start of so many other fights, but my question really came from an honest desire for accuracy. She picked up her napkin and started wiping imaginary crumbs off the edge of the table and into her hand, mumbling something about disrespect, and I wanted to tell her how my writing seminar professor had—as we sat in the high-ceiling box of her office three days after I'd handed in my first research paper—shown me a highlighted block of sentences in my work, then pulled out another sheet, a photocopy from a book I remembered using at the library, the same sentences surrounded by a red square. She placed them side by side and asked me what was going on. I said I didn't know, because that was the truth: I did not know what the problem was. I said, I copied that from the book I cited in the bibliography—the last page of my paper? Had she missed it? No, she hadn't missed it. What's wrong then? I said, but she slid the pages away from me, tucked them into a folder she'd already labeled *Ramirez, L. (plagiarism issue)*, and suggested we hold off on the rest of this conversation until we each spoke with the Dean of Students. I was so bewildered that I'd stupidly said *Thank you* and then bolted, my chair making a hideous noise against the wood floor. My mom wouldn't understand any of this as an explanation for my sudden sensitivity to how one cited their information; she'd backtrack and ask me, *Wait, why's a teacher talking to you outside of school?* She raised the hand catching the crumbs over my napkin and dumped them on it, her fingers opening and closing to shake them loose.

—I believe you, Mami, I said. I didn't mean anything bad by it. I was just asking if you heard that on the news or something, is all I meant.

My mom leaned back in her chair, calm now, but Leidy snorted and said, We *are* the freaking news, Lizet. She tore a slice of steak into tiny gum-able threads and pushed them one by one into Dante's mouth with the tip of her finger.

Like the TV still running in the background but on mute during dinner, my mom eventually circled back to the facts and events she'd started with, and I piled more rice on my plate, ready to pack my mouth with food if she asked, *Now tell me the truth, Lizet, how are things really going up there?* I would need the chewing time to figure out what to say that wouldn't be considered lying. When she noticed the hill of rice, she stood at her chair and leaned over the table, picked up the serving plate in the center and slid the last hunk of steak from it, tipping it so that all the juice and onions smothered

everything. There was no way I could finish it, and I said, Mom!
I'm fine! I just wanted rice!

—You haven't told me, she said, how's the food up there?

She scraped the serving plate clean with her fork and then sat
back down. The food at Rawlings was decent, though everyone else
talked like it was amazing, singing the praises of what we were told
was the largest salad bar in the Northeast. There were other supposed wonders: sandwiches that everyone called speedies, made on
demand by a chef and not a work-study student; something called
the Mongolian Grill that I hadn't tried because the color and con-
sistency of the sauce choices made me think of house paint. I ate a
lot of peanut butter and jelly, a lot of soft-serve ice cream, a lot of
pasta with grilled onions on top.

—Actually the food is great, I said. My school has the largest
salad bar in the Northeast. It's like a thing they brag about.

—*Wow*, Leidy said. That's ah-*maze*-ing.

—You eat salad now? Mami said.

—What's your hardest class? Leidy said. She pushed the last few
grains of rice around on her plate, picked one up and crammed it
into Dante's mouth.

I thought about her question for longer than I had to, watching
globs of oil on my plate separate themselves from the rest of the
steak's juices. I picked up my fork and tried again.

—English, I said. My writing class. But for a reason I should
probably explain.

—You're taking English? my mom said. Why? You already *speak*
English. *Great* English. If anything you should be taking Spanish.

I dragged my fork through the separated oil, tried to get its circles to break and slip back where they belonged.

—They make you take it, I said. It's a requirement, Mami. But
the reason –

—Why do they make you take something you already know?

—It's not just me that has to take it, *Mom*. It's everyone.

—They make *everyone* take English, Leidy said. For real?

—I call that a waste of time, Mom said. Making you take classes for stuff you know almost your whole life already.

With my fork I lifted the edge of the steak; the rice underneath was now stained the same gray as the meat. I lowered it and cut off the corner, gave up and tucked it in my mouth.

—It's not English like *speaking* English, I said. It's writing and research and stuff.

—Do they teach you to talk with your mouth full? Leidy said.

My mom waved her paper towel napkin at Leidy and shushed a *Stop*.

—Whatever, Leidy, I said. Because you've got *great* manners. Because you're *so* classy.

My sister stood from the table and grabbed the empty plates, stacked them on top of each other. Dante reached up for her with two oil-slicked hands.

—Excuse *me* for asking you a simple question, she said.

I chewed and ignored the clash of plates and cutlery in the sink behind me. I cut the steak into tiny pieces and then mixed them in with the rice, focusing very hard on only this and ready to say, if asked, that I was just making it Tupperware ready. I heard my mom push her seat back from the table, but she didn't get up.

—So, Mami said. Are you gonna see Omar? While you're here?

Leidy turned off the water and waited, a plate in her hands, for my answer.

I'd planned on surprising him, too—I hadn't told Omar I'd be home for Thanksgiving—but I hadn't spoken to him since we talked on the phone a week earlier, the night before my plagiarism hearing. We were, I guess, officially still a couple, but I'd made up my mind after that last phone conversation to end things the next time I saw him in person. I didn't want to face him yet, but I didn't want to set off any alarms for my mom either. She loved him; he called her Mom; she'd known his mother Blanca for years, ever since Omar and Leidy got placed in the same seventh-grade homeroom in middle school.

—I wanted this to be more of a family trip, I said.

My food had stopped steaming and didn't smell like much of anything anymore.

—He *is* family almost, Mami said. He'll be hurt if he finds out you were here.

—You really should call him, Leidy said like a warning. He's *gonna* find out you were here. You know Mami will say something to Blanca.

—No I won't! I can keep a secret. Plus it's only Thanksgiving, Mami said to her. Blanca won't even think to ask if Lizet came back for some random days. It's no big deal, not like Christmas.

I couldn't help thinking of the nights in the dorm where I didn't go in with my hallmates on pizza—I'm just not hungry, no big deal, I'd lie—because after paying so much for the flight, I was just plain broke.

—But it is. It's a big deal, I said. I wanted to surprise you guys.

—No, of course, Mami said. You did, really. I'm just saying, you know what I mean about Thanksgiving.

She patted my hand and said, Of course you coming is a big deal. But really mama, think about calling Omar. It's a waste of a trip if you don't see him.

The cold food in front of me—*that* was a waste; the time Leidy spent waiting for Roly to come around—another waste; but until my mom said that about Omar and my trip, I hadn't considered the money I spent to come home as belonging in the same category.

Leidy came back to the table, the drying towel smushed up in her hands. She smoothed it out, then folded it into a square—the skin of her hands strong and tan, almost glowing, nothing like mine, with its winter-induced alien damage. She picked up our napkins and said, What time you need to be at the airport tomorrow?

I scratched at the back of my hand. Noon, I lied.

My flight actually left at two, but almost as a family rule, we always ran late, and since I was the only one who'd seen my

itinerary and my true time of departure, I gave us plenty of pad-
ding for our tendency to run on Cuban Time.

—Perfect, Mami said, smiling. I need to be down the street by
one for an Ariel meeting. You think I'll make it back in time?

I almost said no, almost gave her the real time. *My bad*, I could've
said, *I had it mixed up in my head*. But if I kept it from her, then that
was me letting her go to that meeting—granting her that—rather
than her picking the meeting over me. Somehow that made me feel
better about the money I'd wasted to be there.

I said, You should be more than fine.

She squeezed my hand, then let it go and reached for my
plate. With her fingers she picked the meat from my rice mess,
placing each bite in her mouth as she looked out the living room
window. Her shoulders lifted with a heavy breath, but her jaw
kept grinding.

—This is such an exciting time, Mami said, mouth full, toward
the night.

—I know, I said, pretending she meant it for me.

8

OMAR AND I HAD BEEN a couple since the summer before my junior year. He graduated a year ahead of me, was taking one or two classes a semester at Miami Dade while working part-time at Pep Boys, which is where he spent most of his paycheck in an effort to make his Acura Integra *the* most-tricked-out-est Integra in all of Hialeah. Though he never talked much about a future that was more than a year or two away, he had, the night after my own high school graduation, wondered out loud about getting engaged, and I'd made us both laugh by saying, You'd be smart to put this on lockdown. But I left for Rawlings without that promise, not wanting to be the one to bring it up again and thinking—because he'd admitted to being proud of me for going—that we were headed that way no matter what. I'd drifted away from that kind of certainty since leaving, and I talked with him less and less about school in the two weeks since he'd made me admit, when I started to sob on the phone the night after the meeting with my writing seminar professor, what was *really* freaking me out (another set of *Holy Shit*s and *Damn*s—he barely said anything else, and I started to suspect he didn't understand how seriously a place like Rawlings took honor-code violations). But my decision to break up with him came after our most recent phone call, when I explained why I was so nervous about the hearing: that it could result in me being kicked out of school. He'd stayed quiet on the line and then finally said, That ain't the worse thing, right?

I only managed to say, The *worst* thing, Omar. And yes. It would be.

You're so dramatic, he said back. Then crackly sounds like he was breathing right into the phone. You don't even *like* it there, he said.

During my first weeks away, not wanting to admit to my mom or sister what a huge mistake going so far and to such a hard school felt like sometimes, he was the only person I'd confessed my home-sickness to—and he had my sad list of Reasons Why I Shouldn't Be There memorized by that point. But instead of telling me the usual (You *are* smart enough, Lizet; no, it's *better* being away from your sister and the baby right now, she needs to figure her shit out; you *won't* freeze to death, stop exaggerating), he presented the list back to me as evidence, used it against me. I sat on my end, silent, letting him pelt me with everything I'd cried about since August, each of my unspoken retorts sounding childish as they scrolled through my head (I don't *hate* Jillian; I'm not the *stupidest* person in *all* my classes; not *every single person* on this campus is rich). As that new, defensive list formed inside of me, I decided I needed to start thinking of Omar as *my high school boyfriend*, leftovers from *the old me*. I loved Omar, but his reaction told me that he thought of my going away for school as an experiment that could fail, or an ad-venture that I might, at any time, give up. *You can always just come home*, he kept saying, but after that conversation, I heard it as a threat.

The night before my very first trip on an airplane, in the hours before I left for New York late that summer—after the too-short hug and too-short talk with my dad in front of my mom's building, after I promised my mom that everything needing to be packed was packed, so yes, I felt fine going out for a little while—me and Omar were *together* together for one of the last times I let myself remember. We were parked in a new spot, one we'd never tried out before, and we were kicking ourselves for thinking of it so late, after a year of wasting gas while we argued the pros and cons of every other spot on our list of places one could park and fuck. Omar had made the trek from Hialeah to Little Havana to get me—had come into the apartment wearing baggy jeans and this gray V-neck shirt that stretched tight across his chest and shoulders, and then moved some heavy boxes around for my mom without so much as sweating, Leidy gawking at him, then at me for being *such an idiot* to leave such a perfect guy, one who *obviously* dismissed the fact that I wasn't on *the same level of hotness* as him—and from there we went north, up through Miami Lakes, to a golf course we'd passed a million times, with its big islands of grass and spats of sand and palm trees and some other trees that didn't belong in Miami.

It was my idea—we were both trying to save money, so neither of us offered to cover the cost of a couple hours at a hotel by the airport—and I wasn't sure it was a good one until we made the familiar climb into the Integra's backseat: I looked down at Omar's jeans to tear off his belt and realized we were shrouded in such darkness I couldn't see the buckle. We couldn't believe it was as easy as just driving over a curb and onto the grass, out to the darkest place—the very middle of the course, behind the trunks of banyan trees whose branches spilled back to the ground to make more trunks. We couldn't believe that we could just turn off the headlights and become invisible. We couldn't believe there were no cops around. Cops were everywhere we went—our school's parking lot, the back road by the abandoned overpass, behind the Sedano's Market some gangbanger guys Omar sort of knew had tried to burn down. Here were most Saturday nights that year: Omar would come, and I'd be just about to, I thought, and we'd hear the *thud thud thud* of a flashlight against the rear window and see, behind me, a beam of light searching for my bare ass. It got so predictable that I joked that Omar was telling the cops where we'd be and then flashing them some signal when he was done and it was time to bust us—why else were they not giving us tickets for public indecency like they said they would with every *next time*? Omar didn't laugh at my joke though. Omar didn't think of me as particularly funny.

That last night, he made his sad faces and looked into my eyes more than usual and handed me all his excuses (*But I trimmed the hair around my dick and everything*; *I showered with that soap you like instead of the soap at the gym; I brought baby wipes, the ones with the aloe stuff you say makes your skin soft*), which is why I gave in to his pleas not to use a condom. That, and I'd been on the pill since Leidy learned she was pregnant, just over a year by then—something I couldn't tell Omar because he'd think it meant I planned on sleeping with other guys now that I was about to be *one of those college girls*. Before that night, we'd only had no-condom sex when I was on my period and when he remembered the towels—had them waiting in the Integra's trunk—to put down on the backseat.

He'd pulled out, and I'd cleaned up, and then we sat there, sticky and holding hands, his thumb not stroking the back of my wrist in a soft way, but instead each finger gripping around to my palm, owning it. Every minute or so, he'd squeeze it and hold the squeeze, sending some secret code through our hands, his pulses reminding me of just a few minutes before, when I'd felt that same kind of throb up in me—that sudden fullness meaning I needed, quick, to slide off and get out of the way. I thought I could sense Omar's thoughts, and in between those squeezes—the weird smell of bleach and musk surrounding us, a balled-up baby wipe in each of our free hands—I was sure that we'd stay together. That we wouldn't break up the way our school's guidance counselor, a sad woman I'd only talked to twice who never weighed in on *anything*, warned me we inevitably would if I left. That his plan to maybe get married, maybe the summer after my junior year of college, could actually happen. Yet at that same instant, Omar's hand squeezing mine, I saw some foggy future me—flanked by smart women with tame hair—already looking back at Lizet in the car, there in the backseat, with her hair matted at the base of her neck, her chest slick with saliva and sweat, saying to that animal girl: No, no, no. I don't know how, but I believed both versions: I believed we would find a way to be together, and I believed there was no way I could let that happen.

I turned to Omar and shoved my face into his neck. I bit him around his ear, tugged with my teeth on his fake diamond earring. He squeezed my hand again.

—Me and you need to have a serious conversation, he said.

I dropped the baby wipe on the car floor and splayed the fingers of that hand and mashed his mouth with my palm, laughing to myself and poking my fingertips into his eyes. I pushed his whole face away from me and swung my leg into his lap. He let go of my hand and grabbed my thigh, pulled it then slapped it, then grabbed it again.

—See? he said. Now why you gotta go and do something like that? Fuck it, El, you're making this tough.

Puffy little bags hung beneath his eyes, each shiny with sweat. He was trying to tell me, through the slats of my fingers, that this was hard for him, that he wanted to not miss me, to not want me to stay. He pulled my hand off his face and bit my palm, my wrist. I flipped him off, then tried to pick his nose with my middle finger.

—Maybe I don't need to be worried, he said. You're too weird for anybody but me to want.

—That's true, I said.

I was convinced he was right, but I could've only felt that way in Miami, in that car.

He pinned my wrist behind my back and pulled me toward him. He breathed out hard through his nose—something he did a lot and a sign he was mad at himself for liking me so much. He imagined himself a tough guy; he thought of us as a couple that shouldn't

be but *had* to be, that some outside force made him want my perceived weirdness despite his better judgment (and I was weird, in
that neighborhood, in our school of five thousand people with only
a slim percentage of us going off to college full-time). He had to
think this, because otherwise he had to admit I was always on my
way to being too good for him. He kissed my forehead, and it
felt less like a goodbye and more like the start of something much
more dangerous for each of us: the beginning of who we were going to be.

He put his chin on the top of my head. He said, You really don't
think your parents are gonna work to save their marriage?

His stubble scratched my scalp as he said this. It was such a
formal, unnatural way for him to phrase the question that I knew
he'd practiced it in his head, had maybe heard some TV doctor
say it. He must've felt a change in my body, a tensing, because just
then he slid his hands under my ass and hoisted me up onto his
lap all the way, pulled my hips toward his and held me there, my
stomach against his half-hard dick, so that I couldn't squirm away
or look at his face. I loved and hated his physical strength—the
way he could just move me in and out of his way. I wanted it for
myself.

I pushed what probably sounded like a snarky laugh through
my nose, but mostly, I was just tired of thinking about my parents.
Before my dad forced our frantic move by selling the house, I'd
imagined both parents at the airport, a send-off that was officially
and formally impossible. Now I couldn't even picture my dad
waving goodbye to me at the gate. Omar didn't know the details
behind what I'd called the *choice* to sell the house; the three of us—
me, Leidy, our mom—all agreed it was too ugly a thing to admit,
even to Omar.

—I really don't want to talk about it, I said.

Out the rear windshield, white and red lights blurred on the expressway, unsteady beams of color. When I was a little girl trapped
in the backseat on our way home from visiting one of many aunts

in other parts of Miami, I'd relax my focus on the road ahead and let the red on our side of the median blur into a torrent of blood, the white on the other side—coming toward me—a smear of lightning. I always wished we were going the other way, not realizing that nothing about my view would change with that flip.

—You know, you're not the first person ever whose family hates each other, he said.

—Shut up, they've always hated each other, that's not it.

But I didn't move away from him. I just kept staring out the back windshield.

That first semester of college, as I grew more and more impatient during phone conversations with Omar, I started to tell anyone who asked that Omar was a monster. He was an animal—more like an animal than a human. It seemed like what other people wanted to hear. To them, Omar looked the part, with his earrings and the close-cut hair and goatee, the wide shoulders, the dark brows, him leaning on his Integra and throwing a sideways peace sign in almost every photo of him I owned. The girls on my floor would ask, Is that a *gang sign?* and instead of saying, No, you're an idiot, I said, Maybe, who knows with Omar? Other girls would feel bad for me and claim they understood: the girl who'd made everyone hot chocolate, Caroline, even went so far as to mention she'd read *The House on Mango Street* in AP English. She said she knew about *the kinds of relationships that plagued my community*, had nodded in a solemn way when I told her yes, Omar could be rough. Part of me was angry that they were half right: my parents *did* have a version of that relationship, but it wasn't at all accurate for me and Omar. Still, I was happy to have something to add to those late nights in the dorm's common room when I was otherwise quiet, to be included in conversations even if I didn't totally understand the part I was playing. When everyone around you thinks they already know what your life is like, it's easier to play in to that idea—it was easier for me to make Omar sound like a psycho papi chulo who wanted to control me. At the very least, it made trying to make friends simpler than it would've been had I tried to be a more accurate version of myself.

The truth is, I had to abandon some part of myself to leave Omar in Miami. I had to adopt some twisted interpretation of everything that came before college to make my leaving him the right thing—I had to believe the story I made up for other people. A few weeks into the fall, I stayed up late one night listening to Jillian and half a dozen other girls like Tracy and Caroline talk in our room. I'd been invited by default, since I'd already climbed into bed before the first set of roommates from down the hall came in with an over-sized bowl of popcorn. But then these people I knew only from our brief, shower-caddy-toting bathroom hellos sprawled across the foot of my bed like we were really friends. And even though the next morning wouldn't bring anything more or less friendly when we skimmed shoulders at the bank of sinks, I listened hard to their stories, to what they said about the boyfriends they'd broken up with just before coming to Rawlings. How their mothers all had stories like theirs, how their mothers had all met their fathers in college after having wasted tears on some high school boy that *so wasn't right* for them: I understood that the worst "best" thing that ever happened to my mother was falling for my dad. For your heart to screw over your brain—that's the worst best thing that could happen to anyone.

Omar tugged my hair and said, Everything's gonna be fine, El.

—I know, I said.

—I'll come out next semester for sure, once I can save a little, he said.

—I know.

—And we've got three weeks at Christmas, he said.

—Right.

He held both my shoulders in his rough hands. Do you want to go? he said.

I didn't think he meant the golf course. I thought he meant to New York, so I said, Yeah, of course. I think I'm ready.

He blinked twice like he'd just placed contact lenses in his eyes. Then he slid his hands down to my hips and tossed me onto the seat next to him. I bounced there and he reached for his boxers on the floor.

—What? I said, pulling my knees up to my chest.

—You're ready, huh? He jerked his shorts up his hairy legs, found his jeans and belt, his shirt. You think you're the guy? Like, *I got mine, so peace, I'm out.* Then fuck you, bro.

I held up my hands to him, palms out, and said, Okay, *what?*

He pulled his shirt over his head.

—Wow, you really need to calm yourself down, I said, reaching for my bra between us on the seat. I snapped it on and adjusted the cups.

Omar hated being told to calm down. In fact, saying *calm yourself down* was the best way to get him to not calm down at all. He grabbed the front seats and hurled himself at the steering wheel, his T-shirt hanging bunched around his neck, his arms still free.

—No, I got it. You're fucking ready. Let's go then, he said.

He pushed his arms through the sleeves, grabbed at the keys and turned them, revved the engine. I tugged on my underwear, seeing that, though I'd picked them out because I thought they matched, the bottoms were actually navy blue, the bra black.

—Omar, for *real?* I yelled. Then, like a mom, I said, *Oh*-mar, *please.* Then, Oh! Seriously! Come *on* already!

He put the car in drive.

—You know what? I said. You're right. Let's fucking go.

He turned in his seat and screamed, You're the one who says she's ready!

I realized then the confusion, and I almost lowered my voice, but I didn't know yet how effective that could be. I yelled, To *New York*, asshole! I'm ready to go to New York, not go from *here*! But whatever, do whatever you want!

I struggled to find my pants, then twisted them around until I found the leg holes. I shook them out and wiggled them on while

Omar cursed up front. I found my blouse and tried undoing the buttons—Omar had just pulled it over my head to get it off, hadn't bothered the buttons with his bulky fingers—but it was inside out. Omar kept changing gears on the car, which kept lunging forward, then backward, not really going anywhere. I flipped the blouse and opened it, then wrapped the fabric around me, making sure the holes lined up with the buttons by starting from the bottom.

—Hey genius, he finally said.

I didn't answer, just looked out the window as my fingers climbed up, fastening me into my shirt. He pressed his head against the steering wheel, then lifted it and smacked his forehead with both his hands four or five times.

—We're fucking stuck, he said.

My hands froze. What do you mean we're stuck?

—I mean the car. He put his hand on the latch to open the door, but before he pulled it, he asked, You dressed?

I murmured yes, and he opened the door, and dim light from the dome overhead suddenly yellowed everything.

I scrambled up to the front seat in time to hear Omar say, Oh *fuck*.

All he'd done was stand up, so I said, What?

He stepped forward and I heard what sounded like a wet fart, and then he said, Are you fucking *serious*?

I tried to look past his legs in the doorway at the ground, but my eyes were still used to the dark. I couldn't see anything but him.

How could I not have thought about the possibility of mud? About the Miami rain that soaked the grass every day in the summer? We'd driven onto the *rough*—a word I didn't yet know meant the long grass, grass meant to be long, to slow things up for a golf ball. We'd glided onto it in the dark and rocked the car with our bodies enough to dig us in deep.

I will always—always—give Omar credit for trying everything

he could to get us out of that mud without anyone's help. His sneakers were ruined that night, along with the shirt he was wearing and the jeans. The towels from the backseat, already wet with sweat, were also ruined once he used them to clean the mud off his face, arms, body.

I got to keep clean, mostly. Everything I was told to do—press the gas, then try neutral, then turn the wheel all the way left, then all the way right, now straight, *straight!*—involved me staying in the car, not getting slapped with mud. I stepped out only once, right after I'd pressed the gas down all the way like he'd said to do while he rocked the car from behind. I heard Omar scream and I thought maybe I'd been in reverse and had killed him—*Oh my god*, I thought, *I ran him over!*—so I threw the car in park even though it wasn't going anywhere and jumped out, felt my flip-flops sink and the mud seep between and over my toes. It wasn't even cold; the mud was as warm as the air around us. I'd sunken in so fast and deep that when I lifted my leg, my shoe made a sucking sound but wouldn't budge: if I'd tried to step forward, I would've fallen face-first. So I turned at the hip, holding on to the Integra's roof for balance, and saw Omar, who, covered head to toe in so much mud, really looked like a monster.

Only when it hit one A.M.—after an hour and a half of trying—did I venture to say, Omar, it's late. My flight was at seven forty-five the next morning. Omar called his friend Chino, who found the number for a tow truck and gave it to us. Chino offered to come out himself, but thankfully Omar said *Don't worry about it* and hung up before he could ask any questions.

The tow truck didn't even take ten minutes to find us. The swirling yellow and red lights mounted on top of the truck reminded me how even this last time, we'd never really gone that far from anything.

—What were you guys doing out here? the tow truck guy said.

Neither of us answered because we figured he already knew. He couldn't be older than thirty or thirty-five. He laughed, and then, on the way back from the bed of his truck, chains in hand, he said, Which of you two had the smart idea to park in this shitfest?

We left that question unanswered, too.

The tow truck's lights were what attracted the police. Omar finally got the ticket we'd been promised so many times before. When I told him I'd help pay off both—the ticket and the cost of the tow—he said forget it.

—A going-away present, he said.

I wanted to laugh, but Omar wasn't even hinting at a smile. So I kept the laugh to myself. I never thought of him as particularly funny either.

In the airport on Saturday with two hours to go until my Thanksgiving return flight really left, I sat near my gate across from a bank of pay phones and thought about calling Omar. I wondered if I could get him to come out to the airport. It was a longer trek from Hialeah, but the way he drove, he could make it in twenty minutes if he caught all green lights. I wondered if he'd waste time being mad over the phone and use that as an excuse not to spend the gas, or if he'd just rush over, wanting to see me so bad that he didn't care I'd been home and not told him. I wondered if I'd have to beg him—if I *would* beg him—to come see me. We'd have a couple hours to talk before my plane would start boarding. I'd maybe get to hear someone say they were going to miss me.

I decided to make it a test. He picked up on the third ring.

—What do you mean, you're *here*? he said. You're like, outside?

—No, I'm at the airport.

—No fucking way, he said. So, *shit*! You need me to come get you?

—Not exactly.

It turned out not to matter: he was stuck at work, asked everyone around to cover for him and not one person said they'd do it.

I didn't know if this meant he'd failed the test or not. I could turn it whichever way I needed.

Eventually, after a pointless conversation about his pizza-for-dinner Thanksgiving and the Ariel news and the custom rims he'd saved for and just bought and which friends were doing what that night, he asked me why I hadn't told him anything about the trip.

A voice over the airport's PA system answered in my place, announcing a gate change for a flight that wasn't mine.

—I would've paid for you to stay an extra night, he said after the voice finished.

—I couldn't let you do that.

—Why not?

—Because we weren't talking, I said. Because of that last fight about my hearing.

He was silent for a second, then said, I didn't know we were fighting like *that*.

I almost said, You don't know *anything*, but could already hear him shooting back, *See what I mean about dramatic?* And he'd be right.

—Plus, you're probably broke after those rims, I said.

—*God* El, he said. You are so fucking stupid.

I was ready, then, for the conversation to be over. I said, I know.

He told someone on his end to give him five more fucking minutes, then said into the phone, Are you gonna pull some shit like this at Christmas?

I mumbled no, but then reminded him that he already knew my travel plans for that day. It was the return flight for my original ticket.

—We'll see if I remember, he said, but he laughed.

—We'll see if I care, I said.

—How you gonna be like that when you're the one who comes home and doesn't even tell me?

There was still so much time left until we'd start to board, but I said, Omar, they're calling now, I gotta go. I'll see you in a few weeks, okay?

He sighed into the phone, then said, Fine, Lizet. I gotta go too. But will you at least call me tonight? So I know you got there alive?

—I thought you were going out with Chino and them, I said.

I wanted to hear that he'd stay home tonight and talk to me, that he'd carve out a chunk of time from his boys and give it to me so we could figure things out, and if he did that, he'd pass some other little test, and I'd stay his girlfriend.

—I'll have my phone with me, he said. I'll pick up.

I said okay even though I wasn't sure if I meant it. We both knew that I wouldn't call him—I'd let *him* call me that night, give him one more hurdle, and if he never did, that would settle the other tests he'd only half passed.

I was about to just hang up on him when he asked, So you hear yet?

—Omar, I told you I've *been* here but I'm leaving.

—No, I mean the thing at school. The investigation thing. What happened?

—Oh *that*.

I considered lying to him, saying everything was fine, that I'd already heard and I was clear to stay. But he'd know that wasn't true, would sense it in the way I'd force those words out, as false as the thug image of Omar I'd given people up at Rawlings. The difference between him and the Rawlings audience was that he knew me better, or more precisely, he knew the version of me that couldn't lie to him, not yet.

—There's another stupid meeting, where they'll tell me the decision. I'll probably find out when that is like the minute I get back, I said.

The weight of that truth made me clutch the phone to my face and slide down in the plastic seat.

—Well good luck with that, he said.

He cleared his throat, the sound crackling in my ear, then said, Seriously, good luck. I actually mean it.

And then he hung up on *me*.

9

FROM THE ROWS OF SHUT DOORS and the absence of wet boots outside of them, I figured I was the only person back on my floor. I was in our room just long enough to leave my bags in the middle of the carpet separating Jillian's side from mine—she'd be back Sunday, and I planned to spend my night alone spreading myself over the whole room just because I could—before turning around and heading immediately back into the cold, to a building everyone called the Commons, where our mailboxes lived.

It had snowed all day, but some miraculous group of people apparently still worked that weekend, plowing the sidewalks and paths for those of us unlucky enough to be on campus. Everything felt louder for the unnatural silence—no cars searching for spots in the parking lot, no one smoking or talking on their dorm's front steps. My sneakers against the clean pavement made soft, dry taps; the only real sound around me was my jacket's plasticky swish.

The Commons could feel deserted in the mornings whenever I made it to breakfast, but that Saturday night, the place felt post-apocalyptic empty. Inside, the snack shop that served fried things—normally open until two A.M.—was closed, a metal grate I'd never

seen before pulled down over the entrance. In the TV lounge across
from it, a screen glowed a beam through the dark over the body of
just one person, a guy with his head thrown back against the recliner holding him, a baseball cap over his face.

At the bank of mailboxes, I reached into my coat pocket and
pulled out a fistful of plastic and metal, more key chains than keys.
I fumbled for the tiniest one while eyeing the crush of papers waiting inside, visible through the slit of a window lodged in my mailbox's face. Through that slit I spotted the bright red envelope the
school used to mail out the bursar bills. I had these sent to myself
at my campus address because at first, when they went to my mom's
apartment, her and Leidy lost their minds over numbers so big, not
realizing that most of the figures in one column were canceled out
by the figures in another. I'd switched the delivery address and dealt
with it myself after a second month's round of panicked calls from
home. In the box, too, were flyers for concerts I wouldn't go to, ads
for events in the Commons about which I didn't give a shit—pool
tournaments, marathon game nights, free popcorn and screenings
of French films—paperwork for a housing lottery I might or might
not be around to experience, and in the smash of all of it, in that
little bin, there was, as I'd predicted for Omar, a sealed letter from
the Office of the Dean of Students.

I dumped the flyers in the recycling bin and shoved the bill and
the lottery info and the letter into the mesh pocket inside my jacket.
As empty as the Commons was, I wanted to open the letter in my
room to guarantee I'd be alone, in case the reality of the set date
made me cry.

I didn't even stop to take off my shoes. I stood on Jillian's rug—
I'd clean up any mud later—and unzipped my jacket, then the mesh
pocket, let the other envelopes drop to the floor, and opened the
Dean of Students letter. The paper was thin and beautiful, the
school's seal glowing through the middle of the page like a sun. It
felt too elegant to be a piece of mail I'd been dreading. At the end
of my hearing, an older white woman waiting outside of the con-

ference room had touched the back of my arm as I'd left—I'd almost darted right past her—and walked me through another set
of doors and around her desk in the lobby, telling me that she'd
send a notice via campus mail with information about the next
meeting once a decision was reached. I'd nodded but said nothing,
staring only at the bright lipstick clinging to her mouth; she wore
no other makeup, and the effect was both cartoonish and sad. As
she opened one half of the wooden double doors I had come in
through over an hour earlier, her mouth added that we'd likely meet
in the same place. I saw now that she was right: I was to report to
the same office in the same building on Monday at three thirty P.M.
There was a phone number listed to call if that time was a problem, but also a sentence (one of only four on the whole sheet) stating that my supervisor at the library had already been notified of
the conflict and had agreed to excuse me from the first half of my
Monday shift.

I read those four sentences over and over again, bringing the
letter closer to my face as I slid off my shoes, then as I sat on Jillian's bed. I took the meeting being scheduled in the afternoon—
after a full day of classes—as a bad sign, thinking it meant that
the committee wanted to give me one last day to enjoy being a Rawlings student: one last morning bathroom rush among dozens of
the country's brightest students; one last hundred-year-old lecture
room with heavy, carved desks; one last glasses-clad professor in a
real tweed jacket at the chalkboard; one last walk across the snow-
covered quad. *Let her have at least that*, I imagined the lone woman
on the committee telling the four men. Let's at least give her that.
It didn't feel like enough, and I thought about calling the number
and saying that I wouldn't be there, that I was still in Miami and
involved in a local protest about a boy who'd come from Cuba, that
as eager as I was to hear their decision, it would have to wait—or
maybe not even matter, because maybe I'd have to stay in Miami
and be *proactive*, have to *advocate* for something; I could use the
committee's own vocabulary against them. Sorry I can't make it

(I imagined myself saying after some beep), but don't feel bad about kicking me out because really, there's a lot going on down here, and really, I need to be home right now anyway.

I placed the letter on my desk and picked up the phone, but there was no dial tone. I gawked at the receiver—even the *phones* were gone for break?—then almost dropped it when I heard a voice: Omar telling someone to shut the hell up.

—Whoa, it didn't even *ring*, he said after my confused *Hello?* You just sitting there waiting for me, huh?

—No, I said.

Behind him, I heard Chino's voice and another guy—a voice I didn't recognize—both laughing. I shoved the letter into my desk's top drawer, heard it tear as it crinkled against Jillian's gifted mittens. I pushed the drawer shut.

—I was about to call somebody, I said.

—Who?

—Don't worry about it.

I grabbed my sneaker off the rug and launched it hard at the closet door.

—Oh it's like *that?* he said. I thought you were gonna call me when you got there.

—I just walked in the door, Omar. Seriously? Can I get a fucking minute?

—Are you serious right now? *I* fucking call *you* and you talk to me like this?

I heard Chino say, Oh *shit*, and then a car door slam, then the voice that wasn't Chino's yelling, Bro, just hang up on that bitch already, we gotta go.

—Who the fuck is *that?* I said.

—Don't worry about it.

I took the phone in both my hands and crashed it into the cradle, then lifted it and slammed it again. I picked up my other sneaker and hurled it in the general direction of the first one's landing spot, then hauled my suitcase onto Jillian's bed so I could pace in my socks around her rug while waiting for Omar to call back.

The longer the phone went without ringing, the more the things in my bag made it into my drawers, smashed back into place, until after a while, I reached in and found nothing. So I filled the suitcase with the dirty clothes I'd left in a pile under my bed and zipped it shut, then shoved it where the pile had been. On Jillian's desk, which sat at the foot of her bed, lived the white egg of her Mac desktop, angled so that she could see the monitor from bed like a TV. I pulled back her butter-colored quilt, slipped one of her DVDs into her sleeping computer's drive—a movie I'd never seen called *Life of Brian* by Monty Python, a comedy group I'd mistakenly called "The Monty Python" when Jillian first asked me if I liked them and I tried to play it off like I knew who they were— and got in her bed, tugging the quilt up around me. I'd never so much as sat on her bed before that night, but now I reached over from it to the dresser and grabbed the box of cereal I'd left perched there. I tucked the box under the quilt with me.

The movie played—the screen's glow the only light in the room— and I had a hard time understanding the actors because of the British accents and the cereal's crunch filling my ears between the jokes I didn't know to laugh at. So I watched the movie two more times, looking for clues to the jokes, for the setups—the warnings I'd missed. I even turned on the subtitles the third time through. I laughed when it seemed like I should, until the act of laughing itself triggered the real thing.

During orientation week, I'd missed a different sort of warning the day I met the handful of other incoming Latino students (we comprised three percent of that year's class) as well as the black students (another four percent) at an assembly. We each showed up to the lecture hall with the same letter dangling from our hands, an invitation from the college's Office of Diversity Affairs promising fun at yet another ice cream social. I'd already had so much ice cream that week that I wondered if Rawlings made some deal with a local dairy farm—I'd seen enough cows during the ride in from the airport to think this possible. The letter stated, in bold type, that this meeting was mandatory (which sort of detracted from the *fun* aspect), and it also stated that this would be our chance to familiarize ourselves with the various campus resources available to students of color. It was the very first time I saw that phrase—*students of color*—but I was still brown enough from life in Miami to understand it meant me.

I sat near the aisle in the last row of the lecture hall and watched the room fill in that direction: from last row to first. A small group— maybe seven people—came in together like they already knew each other, rowdy and talking loud as if headed to a pep rally. I later learned they were from the West Coast and part of a program called TROOP—an acronym for something—which meant they were all bound by that program to enroll at the same college as a unit, the program's premise being that having each other on campus would make things easier, would keep each of them alive. But most of us came in alone, or in pairs if we were lucky enough to have bumped into someone else who'd gotten this rare letter in their orientation welcome packet.

Eventually a girl sat two seats away from me, close enough that we had to talk. I said hey first and told her I liked her earrings— gold dangling things with feather-shaped pieces hanging from quarter-sized hoops—and the twang in her voice when she said *Well hi there* back made me wonder what she was doing at that meeting. She said her name was Dana and that she was from Texas; her father was from Argentina, and she visited relatives there every year, sometimes for a whole month. She'd spent most of the summer there, had just returned from relaxing on the family's ranch before coming to Rawlings.

—Hence this tan, she said with an eye roll.

She held out her arms, turned and inspected them, then lifted her legs and wiggled her Christmas-red toenails, her feet in gold sandals. She said her mother was American, which was why she didn't really speak Spanish. She was rooming in a program house called the Multicultural Learning Unit, a new building I'd thought about applying to live in until I read about the extra fees associated with program houses—I wasn't sure if financial aid would go toward covering those. I nodded at everything she told me, relieved like nothing I'd ever felt that she wasn't asking about my family, my summer, my tan.

—Don't worry, she said. I think this meeting is more for the black students. It's hard to be black on a campus like this.

She looked at her nails, long and polished and completely natural—not the acrylics I thought I'd spied when she first sat next to me. She watched the group who had come in together settle down in the very front row.

—I *love* black guys, she told me. My ex-boyfriend was black.

—That's cool, I said.

—He gave me this, she said.

She tugged a thin chain out of her blouse. A gold medallion hung at the end of it, the letter *D* raised on its surface, little diamonds dotting the letter's backbone. It was the kind of jewelry I imagined rich husbands who worked too many hours giving their wives on some anniversary.

—We're still friends, she said. I still love him a lot. He's at Middlebury.

—Oh, I managed.

I pretended to pick something off my knee to avoid giving away that I didn't know if Middlebury was a school or a city or something else entirely.

—Yeah, I didn't get in there, but whatever, it's time I live my own life, she said. Plus I'm a legacy here, but still, this is probably where I would've picked anyway.

Each word she spoke had the unintentional side effect of

convincing me that she was some sort of alien, or maybe a poorly designed alien robot. I'd never encountered anyone like this in my life, and that meant I knew better than to ask how someone could *be* a *legacy here*. She asked me if I spoke Spanish (Yes) and what kind (Cuban, I guess?). She said this would be of little help to her, as the instructor for her Intro to Spanish course was from Bilbao, Spain, and so probably spoke *real* Spanish.

Because Dana had glossy brown hair and exquisitely applied makeup and elegant yet somehow still flashy jewelry, it wasn't long before a guy came and sat between us in the seat closer to her. His name was Ruben and he was, he said, from Miami. I almost pissed myself with happiness until I said, Where in Miami, and he said, A part called Kendall? And I said, That's not Miami, and he said, How do *you* know?

I told him I was from Hialeah, had just graduated from Hialeah Lakes High.

—Really? he said.

And when I nodded, he said *Oh* and pointed to himself, shrugged and added, Private school, then turned his back to me and encouraged Dana to talk about herself as much as possible. They hit it off so easily and had so much in common that I began worrying that *I* was at the wrong meeting, but just then someone sat on my other side and said hello, introduced herself with a last name and everything.

—I'm Jaquelin Medina, this new person on my left said.

—Lizet, I told her. Ramirez.

I held out my hand for her to shake, something that still felt awkward and unnatural; I was used to kissing people on the cheek to greet them. From the way she leaned forward and then corrected herself before putting her palm against mine, I knew she was battling the same tendency.

Within a few seconds, she was crying—just quiet, smooth tears falling down and off her jawline, following each other down the streak the first had made. I didn't know what else to say but, Are you okay?

She didn't turn to look at me.

—I gotta go home, she whispered. This is a mistake.

Ruben and Dana laughed about something, and when I glanced over at them, Ruben had her hand in his, was turning a huge gold ring on her middle finger.

—We've been here like a week, I said to Jaquelin. The meeting hasn't even started yet. Look, where you from?

—California, she said. Los Angeles.

—I'm from Miami, I said.

—I miss my mom, she said. I miss my sisters. My stuff still isn't here yet.

—Neither is mine! I lied with a fake laugh.

She sniffled and wiped the drops from her jaw, dragging the water onto her neck. She turned her face to me and said, So your parents didn't come to help you move in?

I folded the letter still in my hands into a very small square. On move-in day, I'd watched from my bed as Jillian's parents hauled suitcase after suitcase up to our room; the clothes I'd wrapped around the other things I'd packed had filled only three of my four dresser drawers. Later, her parents lugged up maybe a hundred bags from Target, each one containing a plastic contraption intended to house more of Jillian's stuff. No, *Mom*, she'd barked at one point, that's the *sweater* box. Her mother, who was trying to force the empty flat container into the closet, instead hurled it in her daughter's general direction with a resigned *Fine!* and Jillian tossed the box onto her bed, packed it with sweaters, snapped on its plastic top, and slid it under her bed, which they'd already lofted to fit a mini-fridge. They were all so stressed and unhappy that it hardly seemed like a *good* thing to have your family there, except that later, as I sat on my side of the room, I thought about how, when Jillian called her parents, they'd be able to picture where their daughter sat, would know where the phone was. I unfolded the letter in my lap, then refolded it, going against every just-made crease.

—We couldn't afford it, I told Jaquelin. The flights up here, I mean.

Jaquelin nodded. She said, My mom doesn't have papers.

I didn't know why she volunteered this until I registered that it meant her mother couldn't get on an airplane. One of my dad's brothers had a friend who owned a speedboat, and twice a year, the two of them raced out into the Florida Straits and intercepted rafts that they'd arranged to meet and brought them closer to the coast—just close enough that they could relaunch their raft and make it to shore "unassisted" and eventually seek political asylum thanks to the Cuban Adjustment Act. My uncle's friend charged these people ten thousand dollars each and gave some of that money to my uncle for helping with the runs; my uncle had quit doing this a couple years earlier, after getting his own girlfriend and daughter over from Cuba. I wondered if Jaquelin's mother knew about this law, this system: she could start the process now, leave but come back via raft as a Cuban, so that in four years she could easily board a plane and fly out to see her daughter graduate from one of the best colleges in America. I wondered if this was really an option, if her mother could take advantage of the holes in the system the way my family and so many others had.

Jaquelin began crying again, sniffling into the heel of her hand to stay quiet.

—I'm sorry, she said. It's just – it's hard, right? Wasn't move-in day the worst?

—It was, I said, praying that someone would get behind the podium soon.

The mandatory meeting was run by several people, most of them minorities, all of them having the term *retention specialist* in their job title. Before anyone passed out any ice cream, I learned that students of color struggle more in college than our white counterparts. I learned that, when combined with being from a low-income

family—the case for some of us in that room, one specialist said—
your chances of graduating college fall to somewhere around twenty
percent. They told us to look around and imagine most of the
people in that auditorium disappearing, and I did that, not really
realizing that when Dana and Ruben looked at me, they were
imagining me gone.

We learned that the high schools some of us went to, because
they were in low-income areas, probably did not prepare us for the
rigorous coursework we would soon encounter. We were told to
use the writing center, the various tutoring centers. We were told we
had to do our homework, told we had to go to class. Dana whispered to Ruben, Is this a fucking joke? I don't need to hear this!
And I sort of felt the same way, but she was the one to get up and
storm out of the auditorium, Ruben ducking out a minute after her.
No one stopped either of them. I ended up leaving once the ice
cream came out, ashamed that some important people at Rawlings
felt we needed this meeting, needed to hear things that, the moment
after they were said, seemed painfully obvious. I didn't even stay to
sit with Jaquelin, who'd written down every word—*get plenty of sleep,
take advantage of your professor's office hours*—and who I left alone with
her bowl of ice cream. I hadn't seen her again, not since that day.
Not in any of my classes, not even in the dining hall. I hadn't even
bothered to look for her at the airport or on the campus shuttle—I
knew without her saying so that her work-study money was being
sent home, that she had to stick to her budget in a way I didn't.

As a bunch of British dudes pretending to be Romans whistled from
crosses on Jillian's computer screen, I was the one silently crying,
the one days away from disappearing. I calmed myself down by
thinking something horrible: at least my mom could get on a plane.
At least *Beloved Family Member Getting Deported* wasn't on my list of
worries. Jaquelin was proof that someone at Rawlings had it harder
than me, and if only twenty percent of us were going to make it,

then at the very least I had a better chance than her, didn't I? My home life *had* to be more stable than Jaquelin's, right? Maybe I belonged just a little more than this one other person, and ugly as it was, that felt like something—like an actual advantage.

The last of the credits scrolled away. I kept Jillian's quilt around my shoulders like a cape, dragged it with me over to the phone. I dialed the apartment after punching in the numbers on my phone card, and after a couple rings, Leidy answered.

—I was just calling to tell Mami I made it back okay. Let me talk to her.

—She's not back yet.

—Back from where?

—The meeting.

It was just after ten at night. I pulled the quilt tighter around me, gathered the material in a fist at my chest.

—The meeting that started at one? *That* meeting?

—No Lizet, the meeting for future Miss Americas. *Of course* that meeting. What other meeting *would it be*?

Her voice sounded tired and so far away. I went over to the heater and dialed it to its highest setting. After we hung up, I put my hands on the warming metal, wondering how long I could hold them there before they burned.

10

I TRIPLE-CHECKED JILLIAN'S SHEETS FOR cereal crumbs the next morning, eventually managing to arrange her quilt back on her bed with the same disheveled elegance she achieved whenever she made it. The DVD was once again in its case and nestled on her shelf between *The Big Lebowski* and *The Sound of Music*—two other movies everyone at Rawlings but me had seen. Jillian didn't even look at her bed before dropping her duffel bag on the rug and launching herself onto it, snuggling her face into her pillows before turning to me at my desk and saying, Liz! It's *so* hot in here!

It took a second to remember she was talking to me—I was Liz again, no more El—but I reached over and turned the heater's dial to low. Going by Liz was easier than correcting people when they said, *Sorry, Lisette?* or *Like short for Elizabeth?* after I told them my name. I liked Liz fine, and it seemed more and more weird to me that no one had ever called me by that nickname before, but just a few days home had made it strange to me again. Even though Omar and other Miami friends had called me El since kindergarten, asking new people to call me El seemed annoying of me, like I was trying too hard, like how it hit my ear when any Rebecca wanted to be

called Becca instead of just Becky or a Victoria, Tori instead of just
Vicky. So I'd embraced Liz, had even covered up, with a lopsided
heart filled in with blue pen, the *E* and *T* on the nametag our RA
had taped to our door.

I hadn't noticed the room was too hot, and said so.

—How have you not died of heatstroke? she said, not really wanting an answer.

Jillian was Jillian, never Jill. She'd said it just like that the day
we met—*Never Jill*—and I liked her for it. She flipped over on the
mattress and said, How was your break?

I meant to say great but instead I said, It was okay.

—Oh my god, that's right! she said, bolting up from her pillows.
That baby from Cuba. Was any of that happening near you? My
parents were all, Isn't your roommate Cuban? And I was like, she
sure as fuck is.

I turned around at my desk, confused the news had made it that
far north.

—He's not a baby, I said. He's like five or six.

—Whatever, were you near anything?

—Sort of, I said to my hands, to my lap. My mom lives around
there. But how was *your* break?

—It went well. She reached to her nightstand drawer for a hand
mirror. Same old same old, she said. *Amazing* food. My brother is
a jackass. The bus back was a nightmare.

In the mirror, she inspected her eyelid for something, picked at
whatever she saw, then said to her reflection, So did you see any of
it? It's such a crazy story, right?

—How'd you even hear about it?

She lowered the mirror and looked at me in a way that felt dramatic but that I'd come to learn was only her way of teasing me.

—Are you kidding? she said. It's *everywhere*.

I leaned back in my chair until it hit the desk's pencil drawer,
where the notice from the dean's office still hid along with her
mittens.

—Why is the news in Jersey about some Cuban kid in Miami? I said.

Jillian tossed the mirror onto her quilt and hopped off her bed, swinging her slick black hair over her shoulder and saying a deadpan *You are so funny, Liz* as she opened the mini-fridge under her bed. She pulled out a bottled water and stared at me as she took a long drink; she had eyes I can honestly say I'd never seen before in real life, blue flecked with gray, crisp, the kind of color I'd seen only on models in magazines. Her eyebrows were perfect though I'd never seen her pluck them. She had very, very smooth skin, which she'd started wrecking a couple times a week by going to tanning salons with some girls she knew from intramural softball. She was one of the most beautiful people I'd ever seen, but she made no sense to me back then: she was athletic but kind of prissy, super smart and always talking about being a feminist but still spending hours a day applying five different shades of eye shadow to various zones above and below her eyes before heading out to class or softball practice. I'd pegged her, on our first day as roommates, as Greek or Italian—way more interesting than Cuban because there was so much more ocean separating this country from either of those (you couldn't build a raft out of random crap and make it across the Atlantic)—but when I'd asked her where her people were from, she said, Cherry Hill, and then, when it was clear I didn't know what that was supposed to mean, she added, In Jersey—the good part. She climbed back on her bed with her water after putting the mirror away in her nightstand.

—You have to tell me what it's like down there. Is it like World War Three or what?

On my desk sat my bio textbook, opened to the chapter I was supposed to have read already. I said to it, You know, I didn't even really notice anything?

—Why are you *lying*? she blurted. They had people losing their minds on television. It looked totally nutso.

—That's just TV, I said.

—And now that kid is basically stuck living with strangers until he goes back home. Jesus, what a nightmare. What could possibly possess a woman to force a little boy to make that kind of a trip?

I sat on my hands to keep them under control. I'd encountered this a couple times so far at Rawlings—people hanging up Che posters in their rooms, not realizing that most Cubans know him as a murderer; people talking about the *excellent healthcare system* in Cuba and just not believing me when I explained how my mom sent a monthly package that included antibiotics, Advil, soap, Band-Aids, and tampons to my aunts still over there—but I hadn't heard any of this from Jillian. Her worst offense (which I wasn't even sure *counted* as an offense) was that, without fail, she introduced me to anyone she knew—the softball girls, the friends she'd brought along from high school—this way: *This is my roommate, Liz. She's Cuban.* Her doing this bothered me but I didn't know why exactly, so I kept telling myself: It's not like it isn't *true*, what would I even *want* her to say?

I said, I don't think you understand how bad things are in Cuba.

I almost said, *His mother died trying to get him here*, but I didn't want to risk sounding like a hysterical TV Cuban, so I pulled my book from my desk and held it in my lap to give my hands something to hold on to and added instead, She wanted a better life for him. It's really, really bad there.

—But you've never actually been there yourself, she said. Right?

Another question I got a lot at Rawlings, usually after Jillian's *She's Cuban* introduction. I never got asked this in Miami, and I'd never asked it of anyone after learning where their parents or grandparents had been born (*You're Irish? Have you ever been to Ireland?*). I knew saying no to Jillian's question would, for some reason, wreck the credibility of anything else I said, which is maybe what she was trying to do, so I said the truth: I have a lot of family still there, on both my mom's side and my dad's side.

—And you talk to them? I've never heard you talking to anyone in Cuba.

—It's not like calling someone in another *state*. You can't just
call people.

—That's ridiculous.

—Not everyone has phones, I said as she hoisted her duffel by
its long strap onto the bed and started pulling out clothes I'd never
seen.

—And I'll tell you what else is ridiculous, she said. All the Cubans down there saying he's going to stay. No offense, but that's
just insane.

I couldn't talk—I dropped the textbook on my lap and held on
to the arms of my desk chair to keep from jumping up. I'd been on
the other side of this conversation with my mom and Leidy just a
couple days before, but I suddenly couldn't remember any of it, what
I'd said or why I'd said it—only the part where I'd asked for sources
and made my mom angry. When everything in Jillian's bag was
newly sprawled on her bed and I still hadn't said anything, she announced with a sigh, I'm just saying it seems totally clear he shouldn't
stay.

I slammed my book shut and slid my chair back into my desk
to block the drawer where I'd hidden the hearing notice. Jillian
didn't know anything about my academic integrity hearing, had
no idea that the blazer she'd loaned me before Thanksgiving break
was not for a presentation in my writing seminar. I said, No, I don't
think it's *that* totally clear.

—Of course you don't, she said. You're too connected to the
whole thing.

I tossed the book on the desk behind me and said—too loud and
leaning too far forward—What the fuck does *that* mean, *connected*?
I'm not fucking *related* to the kid.

—Don't get ghetto, Liz, she said. I'm just saying that, no offense,
but as a Cuban person, you can't really expect people to believe
that you'll be completely rational about this.

She held the water bottle loosely now, between only a couple fingers. I tried to match her ease by leaning back in my chair.

—I was born in this country, I said, not knowing what point I was trying to make.

I righted my chair and tried again. I said, Look, I would argue that I – I can speak *more* intelligently about this than you because I know more about it than you ever could.

—Wow, she said, her water bottle heading back to her mouth. Let's just leave that there before you get any more racist.

I didn't think I'd said anything racist, and I'd let her *ghetto* comment slide because I couldn't in that second articulate *why* it bothered me. Jillian had read more books and had taken more AP classes than me; I guessed she knew how to cite things properly in a research paper; she'd even been to other continents already: if she thought I was being ghetto, then there was a chance, in my head, that she was right. She screwed the cap back on her bottle and turned away from me, to the clothes on her bed.

—I am not being racist, I said to her back. I can know things you don't know because of where I grew up. That's not me being racist.

She kept ripping tags from the clothes, mumbling *Shit* and checking the corner of her thumbnail after one gave her trouble. She didn't look at me as she dropped the tags in the recycling bin, then grabbed a fist's worth of hangers from her closet.

—Well, whatever, she said to a long-sleeved blouse as she tugged it onto a hanger. I'm sorry, but I'm just saying people of color can be racist, too.

I covered my face with my hands, finally feeling the heat of the room on my neck, in the sting of my armpits. I dragged my hands down and let them slap my lap.

—Fine. That kid lives in a house two blocks from my mom's apartment, I finally admitted.

She dropped the hangers on her bed—her new clothes suddenly way less interesting—and came over to my desk. She looked down at my textbook, capped one of my almost-dried-out highlighters, and said, Well, I hope for your mom's sake that people can manage to stay calm.

So she hadn't assumed that my mom was part of the perceived hysteria, and I was grateful for that. I took the highlighter from Jillian's hand—her nails still wet-looking with a burgundy polish, her cuticles nonexistent—and dropped it into my desk drawer.

I said, I hope so too.

I shoved my hand in the drawer, pushed the mittens and the letter back even more, and asked Jillian if she minded, but could I borrow that blazer again.

II

———

THE OLDER WOMAN WHOSE LIPSTICK had marked off her mouth greeted me Monday afternoon with another levitated smile— the fillings in her molars glinted at me from the very corners of it. As I sat in the lobby, Jillian's blazer scratching the back of my neck, I tried not to watch her typing at her desk, a pair of glasses perched on the tip of her nose. Then, as if God himself had tapped her on the shoulder and told only her that it was time, she stopped typing and tugged off the glasses, stood and said, They're ready for you.

Before she opened the second set of wooden doors that led into the conference room, she told me, Don't be worried, sweetheart. The last thing I felt before stepping through the doorway was the cold replacing her warm hand, which had, without me registering it, rubbed a circle on my back to push me forward.

It was the sort of room you only really needed when staging the ceremonial signing of a new constitution—ornately carved wood panels reaching halfway up the walls, paintings of someone else's wigged ancestors groaning against their frames—old and regal in a way that stunned me even this second time inside, though as

I entered I didn't repeat my original mistake of staring at the ceiling, something that afterward I worried made me look like I didn't care that the committee was already there, seated around the massive table taking up most of the room. This time, I mostly ignored the elaborate masks huddled up in each corner, looking at them only just long enough to see that I'd been wrong—the masks, I saw now, were actually shields.

Each member of the committee sat in the exact same spot as the first time, which gave me the very freaky feeling that they'd never moved, that they'd skipped their own Thanksgivings to instead stay right there and talk about my case. I laced my fingers and put the ball of my joined fists on the table. The wood was lacquered with something thick and yellowish that reminded me of the cheap bottles of clear nail polish into which Mami and Leidy dropped chopped-up chunks of garlic, the resulting phlegmy goop supposedly making your nails grow twice as fast. I knew, because I'd looked it up after my hearing, that the table was very old; it had been built for this room (and *in* this room, its builders foreseeing that it wouldn't fit through the doors), commissioned by the college's first president for this—the college's first conference room.

—How are you, Lizet. Did you have a nice break.

I nodded double-time though I didn't know if I should, as the phrases didn't sound like actual questions. Still, I wanted them to see I was listening. I made sure to look each of them right in the eyes: four white men and one white woman, each with the word *Dean* in their title. The men spanned maybe thirty years, their hair creeping along various stages of gray except for the bald one, who was, ironically, the youngest-looking of them all, the tufts ringing and dolloping his head still black. He was officially my faculty advisor, though I'd only met him once before, during orientation week. The woman—seated closest to me, to my right—looked around forty, a faint streak of gray-blond darting up and over her otherwise dark head. Nothing sat on the table now; the last time, they'd each had a thick folder in front of them containing copies of all

the same documents. I leaned forward in my seat, using as little
of the chair as I could, feeling the strain of this choice in my
thighs.

The oldest man, seated directly across from me at the head of
the table, said, I'm sure you're anxious to know the findings of the
committee.

He twisted his nose in a lazy attempt to work his glasses back
up his face. He went on, As I'm sure you're fully aware by now, we
take our duties very seriously, and we have given your case in particular very careful attention.

—Lizet, the woman said, almost interrupting him. This case is
unusual for a variety of reasons. On paper it seemed pretty clear-
cut, but the facts that surfaced during the hearing itself brought
with them new considerations.

I kept slowly nodding during all of this, throughout each sentence.

—So please don't be alarmed by what we're about to say, she
said.

Like telling Omar to calm himself down, this too had the opposite effect.

—What Dean Geller is saying is that we have indeed found the
claim of egregious plagiarism justified, the oldest man rushed forward, leaning up in his chair with his words. However, he said,
while the penalty of that charge is normally quite severe, it's absolutely clear to us, based on your testimony and on your initial response to the charge when your professor confronted you, that
this penalty should be mitigated, and that's our recommendation.

When no one spoke, I said, Okay.

Under the table, I shifted my weight to my right leg, ready to
run out the door. I wasn't sure what they were telling me. I was
waiting for the word *expelled*.

The woman—Dean Geller—spoke again.

—Lizet, this means you aren't being asked to leave Rawlings.

As soon as she said this, my spine touched the back of the chair for the first time since sitting down. The tension in my body shifted to this new spot.

—I'm not?

—No, she said. She looked around at the others, as if daring them to jump in. We're recommending that you be placed on a kind of probation. We think that makes the most sense based on the answers you gave at your hearing.

I kept nodding. At the hearing, they'd all asked me questions, saying *Go on* when my answers were short—for some reason, I thought they'd want short answers: Yes miss, No sir. Go on, they kept saying. Go on, it's OK, we're asking for a reason.

The balding man pushed closer to the table, his hands coming alive as he started to speak, so much so that I remembered—I didn't during the hearing, where he'd been fairly reserved—that his great-grandmother was Cuban; he'd said so after scanning my file as I sat across from him during orientation, the one time we'd met before all this and where we'd discussed my fall schedule. I'd almost asked if that was why he'd been assigned to me, but I didn't have to: the answer was yes—he told me so himself. This accident of heritage had trumped the fact that I'd applied to Rawlings as a biology major and he was a classics professor.

—In particular, he said, we were deeply concerned by what we learned about your high school. No counselor we spoke to there was able to provide us with a copy of a code of academic integrity. One went so far as to say that none existed.

The oldest man made a kind of snort—his version of a laugh. They'd called Hialeah Lakes: I tried to tamp down the shame I felt at someone there possibly knowing about this with the fact that there were almost a dozen counselors—most lasting a year or two before transferring somewhere better—and so maybe whoever they'd spoken to was new and hadn't thought to connect the call to me. I had some sense that I could trust a place like Rawlings to respect my privacy while conducting their investigation—that they took their own rules as seriously as they took their honor code—but did they realize that even if they never uttered my name, just saying *Rawlings* to anyone at Hialeah Lakes led to no one but me? I looked up from my hands and caught Dean Geller glaring at the old man. I squeezed my palms together tighter when she turned back to me, to keep from showing any sign that I'd noticed.

—So our decision to place you on probation is based on things like that, she said, which taken all together means that we think your old school didn't foster something that we're calling a culture of success. And that isn't your fault, but I wanted – we wanted to give you a chance to ask what this means, or anything else you want to ask. We want you to feel empowered by this information, not afraid of it.

I hadn't said anything yet, but I was confused that they were talking about home instead of what I'd done. I stuttered a little, saying, I'm not sure –

The old man leaned sideways in his chair as if his back hurt and half barked, What she's trying to say is we believe you sincerely didn't know better. You haven't been given, at any point in your academic career prior to coming here, the *tools* to know better. So yes, you are guilty, but you are also blameless, and so that requires a more nuanced penalty.

I didn't remember saying at my hearing that I *didn't know better.* I didn't remember saying anything about tools at all. They'd asked me questions about my high school, about my teachers there, information I thought they already had on a sheet in front of them provided by the admissions office. They'd asked irrelevant questions about my parents and why they didn't go to college, why they hadn't finished high school (They were with child, I'd said, wincing inside at how my attempt at formality—*knocked up* and even *pregnant* had seemed too casual in my head—came out sounding overly biblical). They'd even asked about any siblings I might have, what they were doing with their lives (You mean my sister? I'd said). We'd gotten off track from my offense so fast that I'd thought I was doomed, and now it was happening again.

Dean Geller leaned my way, and this movement silenced the old man. She stuck her arm out across the table, although from where she sat there was no way she could reach me.

—Lizet, we feel strongly that, having admitted you, it is our responsibility to help you succeed. And we see no better place for you to do that –

—Remaining at Rawlings, the old man interrupted again, is the fastest way we can see you overcoming these deficiencies.

The balding man and Dean Geller shifted in their chairs, and Dean Geller fixed her eyes on the old man until he met her glare. She seemed embarrassed for me, but I felt humiliated enough on my own, though I didn't really understand why. When whatever passed between them was over, Dean Geller leaned to her left and produced some papers from somewhere beside her near the floor, then placed them on the table. She slid them my way, said they stated the terms of my probation.

I fanned them out: four sheets of that same beautiful onionskin paper, three of them covered with lines and lines of what looked like a list of instructions. The last page had just a couple sentences near the middle, and then five signatures stacked near the bottom left. Another signature—belonging to the school's president—was next to these, alone in the middle. On the right was a blank line, my full name typed in all caps beneath it.

—It's a kind of contract, she said.

They each went around the table and said something about this probation, about how my offense had actually provided an opportunity for them to address other serious concerns about my performance so far at Rawlings. *Your performance*, they kept saying, and so I pictured Leidy in her camera-ready outfit working her way into the frame, my mom's face on the TV before I'd turned it off and run down the street, and I nodded at the things they told me: some conditions about my fall grades, how they would factor into what happened next; something about possibly being placed in remedial classes in the spring; an *unfortunate and unforeseen complication* those remedial classes would pose on my credit hours that would impact a grant in my financial aid package, causing it to be replaced by an unsubsidized loan (this portion sounding so complicated and terrifying that I must've looked physically sick, because the woman interrupted the person covering it and asked me if I was all right, if perhaps I had a question). When I asked what the difference between a subsidized and an unsubsidized loan was, they all looked at each other, something seemingly reassuring them as they met each other's faces. Dean Geller answered and then said she'd have my financial aid officer contact me soon. The old man ended discussion on this point by saying there were plenty of deserving students in line for this money, and if anything, the committee felt that this complication would motivate me to reach out to the academic resources available on campus over the next three weeks.

—The letter makes all this very clear, Dean Geller eventually said. We'd like you to read over it. Your signature indicates you understand the committee's decision and that you accept the terms of your probation.

—Okay, I said. I sign it here then?

—On the line above your name, she said.

That seemed obvious; I'd meant *here* as in, *in that room*, right at that moment. Instead of clearing this up, I asked for a pen, slid the top three pages to the side, and on the fourth signed my name. When I looked up, the same grim faces watched each other, again sharing some secret. Then I realized my mistake: they'd expected me to read it through first. I'd signed something without reading it, made a commitment without knowing what was expected of me—something else Rawlings would have to teach me not to do.

I slid the pen away, and the man who'd attempted to explain the financial aid problem asked me, Do you have any questions?

I had so many, but most were not about the hearing's results.

I wanted to ask: Where was everybody *before* that day? Why did it take this plagiarism hearing to get someone to notice that I was in major trouble in a whole other subject? If things were as bad as this letter indicated, why hadn't I seen my advisor since orientation? When he'd asked me what classes I planned on taking and I told him—bio, chem, calc, using those shortened versions in the hopes of sounding ready for it—why did he only say, Sounds hard for a first semester. You sure? Of course I was sure: I took six classes senior year of high school, all of them honors or AP, and I'd been an extracurricular junkie, so it made perfect sense to me that I could downgrade from six to four core classes—classes that *didn't even meet every day!*—and be fine. The Office of Diversity's mandatory meeting had warned us against that exact sentiment (it was, I think, number three on the list of "The Five Biggest Mistakes You Can Make Right Away," a handout I left on the floor of that auditorium). Yes, I was sure, and he signed some paper—without really reading it!— saying I was good to go. Why had I found the handout insulting? Why did I feel like I'd tricked Rawlings into letting me in at all? How could I make that feeling go away?

—Can I – Is the meeting over? I said.

—This meeting? Yes, I believe so, Dean Geller said. She turned to the old man, deferring to him voluntarily for the first time all afternoon. Dean Tompkins?

—We've concluded the proceedings, yes. You are free to go, Lizet. We wish you the best of luck, young lady.

I pushed back from the table and couldn't help but think of my sister, the sound of her name the last word in the room. *Like they even know anything*, she would tell me now. *Don't listen to those people, what do they know about anything?* She'd managed to get herself on TV just as she'd planned, hadn't she? Couldn't that count as a culture of success? I gathered the four sheets in my hands, tapping them against the table into a stack as I stood.

—Oh, no Lizet, sorry for not making that clear, the old man— Dean Tompkins—said as he raised his hand to his glasses. The signed copy is for the college's records. Please leave that here. The secretary will have a copy for you as you leave.

—As I leave? I said.

—Linda, Dean Geller snapped at him. The assistant's name is Linda.

—Linda, yes. She's just outside, he said. She'll escort you out.

I left the papers there and dragged myself from the room, still half convinced that whatever I'd just signed actually gave my spot in the class of 2003 to the next person in line for it; hadn't one of them said something to that effect? Linda—I was glad to know her name—was there again, though this time I didn't rush by her. She clicked the door shut behind me, her hand back between my shoulder blades and pushing me forward, right up to her desk. An envelope with my name on it sat just on the desk's edge.

I asked her if it was a copy of what I'd just signed, and she said yes.

—Did you see it, like I mean, read it? Because I don't know – do they mean I can stay for just my freshman year, or for longer? For all four years?

She looked back at the door as if it should've already answered my question. The chunk of color sitting on her mouth had faded to the faint stain of fruit punch, and it showed off the saddest smile. She reached for the envelope and handed it to me.

—Oh, sweetheart, she said. Her hand went to her chest, genuinely sorry for something. You poor dear, she said. You're staying for good, sweetheart. You came through it OK and you can stay as long as it's worth it for you.

—Really? You read this whole thing and that's what it means?

She made to speak but just opened her mouth, then closed it. She must've thought I was an idiot, to have just sat through that whole meeting but still need to ask her this. She put her hands on my shoulders and almost whispered, I'm the one who types these up, and I promise you, you came through this fine. It's complicated, but you'll figure it out on your own time. You're a very smart person. They wouldn't let you stay if that weren't true. OK?

I made the mistake of hugging her—standing on my toes to throw my arms around her neck as I crumpled my copy of the letter against her back. She didn't seem to mind the hug. She even did her best to hug me back.

I read over the letter several times during the rest of my shift at the library's entrance desk, distracted only by the scuffs of people's boots as they whooshed in or out of the building. Again, Linda was right: it made more sense once I was out of that room, away from that table that predated Miami's founding. I could concentrate better in the library—a fact about myself I should've recognized earlier in the semester. The letter detailed a series of *if this, then that* scenarios: If I failed chemistry—likely, since I'd failed the midterm after freezing up and not finishing most of it—my spring probation would involve a limit on the classes I could take and I'd be forced into a noncredit remedial course that didn't count toward my eventual graduation. If I earned lower than a C-minus in any of my courses in addition to failing chemistry, there'd be more remedial courses—which meant I'd dip below the necessary credit hours to officially count as full-time and, as a result, a six-thousand-dollar grant in my aid package given to high-achieving minority first-generation college students (a crammed line in my bursar bill that read "Rawlings Minority Student Success Initiative: Fulfilling the Family Dream Scholarship") would be revoked and replaced with an unsubsidized loan come the following year. Considering I already had five thousand a year in all kinds of loans, this was very bad news, and it also made me understand Linda's comment about Rawlings being worth it. If I somehow passed all four of my classes with a C-minus or better, I'd be allowed to continue working toward a biology major and wouldn't have to take anything with the word *remedial* in the course title. Most importantly, my financial aid wouldn't change. But this seemed the least likely outcome: along with the failing chem grade, I had a D in biology and a C-minus in calculus. On their own, these two classes weren't super hard, but taking them both the same term as chemistry made each worse. And because I'd failed the paper that I plagiarized (something the letter made clear but that I hadn't left the meeting understanding), and because it counted for thirty percent of my grade, I was hovering at a D in my writing seminar. I had an A in my required PE—swimming, which was easy since I'd grown up doing it—but the grades in our PE courses didn't count toward our final GPA. Had I understood that earlier, I would've taken the course pass/fail instead of for a grade: I could've missed a few classes, then, to study for the others without hurting my chances of passing.

Someone's bag beeped as they went through the security scanner, and I jumped high enough at my tall desk that he laughed into his hand at me.

—Sorry about that, he whispered.

He couldn't have looked less like Omar—ear-length red hair parted down the middle in a style well on its way out, a smattering of freckles across his nose, greenish eyes, eyebrows so pale they might as well not exist—but my brain understood he could count as attractive to a certain kind of person and so classified him as a new kind of male specimen, albeit one that would burst into flames if left unprotected on a South Florida beach. I put my letter down; my hands shook as I reached for his bag, which was covered with so many buttons and patches that I couldn't discern its original color.

—I guess you never get used to that sound, huh?

—No, you do, I said. You get used to it if you work at it.

I checked his bag—his portable CD player the sensor's culprit—and cleared it though the scanner, then slid it back to him with a cheesy smile and a thumbs-up.

He thanked me. I'm Ethan, by the way, he said, and I said, Okay.

I went back to my letter.

He drummed his fingers on my desk, then said, Right. OK. See ya around.

He pushed through the glass doors a few feet from my desk. Through the library's huge front window, I watched him walk toward the quad, wishing I'd said, *Yeah for sure, see you around* back to him, making a kind of promise to myself that way: that I'd be around to do such a thing. I told myself I'd wave at him—a big, obvious one that used both arms—if he turned around, but he didn't.

The commotion with Ethan was the night's only distraction at work. For the most part, as I planned out the next three and a half weeks, people passed me in silence. For the most part, it's like I wasn't even there.

12

THE THIRD ITEM DOWN ON the page of "Relevant Campus Resources" I'd printed off the Diversity Affairs Web site—listed after the mental health clinic and the financial aid office—was the Learning Strategies Center, which was divided into various "learning labs" based on whichever subject was slowly killing you. Like the salon where Leidy worked, each of these places gladly welcomed walk-ins, so my first visit to the chemistry learning lab between classes on Tuesday was spontaneous.

It was housed, along with a couple other offices, in a three-story brick building on the corner of the quad. I'd passed it dozens of times but never entered, thinking it was someone's house: it looked more like an old mansion than an office building. But it actually *was* an old mansion, the former home of Rawlings presidents of yesteryear, before the civil rights era convinced college officials that having the president's house right on campus maybe made student protests a little too easy for us. Inside, tucked up against a wall in what was clearly once a living room, sat a modern cubicle, its reddish panels the same color as the carpeting. The stairs—each step extra wide and pleated with the same carpet—ran right alongside this front desk. After easing shut the front door so that it didn't make a sound as it closed and saying hello, I asked the student sitting there, So how does this work?

He said, Oh! Ummm, then chuckled. He pushed a chunk of straight black hair from his eyes and off his forehead, but it flopped back to the same spot the minute he pulled his hand away. He showed me a brochure and explained that upperclassman majors in various subjects were standing by to help me work through any and all assigned problem sets and to further explain concepts that I didn't pick up in class or on my own. He ran a finger down the list of subjects covered, then down the different locations on campus.

—It's other students that do it? That help you?

He said yes but assured me that the process to become a peer tutor was, like everything else at Rawlings, fairly grueling. He was, in fact, a tutor for several physics courses but couldn't go near chemistry.

—For instance, he said, I'm pretty sure the center coordinator for chemistry has banned me from even saying the word *chemistry* more than twice in one day.

—You better watch out then, I said.

He blinked at me, so I said, You said *chemistry* three times just talking right now.

—Oh! he said, then laughed hard through his nose in spurts.

I swung my backpack around to my chest and opened the zipper, looking for my wallet and thinking of the money I'd thrown away on my surprise flight home.

—They charge by the hour or what? I said.

—Oh, no no no, he said, waving his hands. This is totally free. Or rather, to be more accurate, it's part of what our tuition covers.

My hand was already around my wallet. I let my fingers relax and felt its weight slump back in my bag.

—How many do I get? I mean, appointments.

—As many as you need? I don't think there's a limit.

He slid papers around on his cubicle desk, checked a list tacked to the wall. He said, No one's ever asked me that.

Before I left that day, I booked twice-weekly slots for chemistry all the way up to the final exam, and I made initial biology and calculus appointments for the next day. I took the brochure for the writing center, which was apparently housed in the basement of the student union, right next to where I worked, and during that afternoon's library shift, while checking my e-mail during my break and seeing the string of appointment confirmations in my inbox, I created an online account and booked even more appointments in every subject, grabbing multiple time slots on the weekends and each day of study week. It's free, I told myself, imagining them as mall-bestowed perfume samples hoarded in the hopes of never having to buy a whole bottle.

On my way to the writing center—where I'd made standing appointments on Tuesday and Thursday mornings and Saturday afternoons, and where I would eventually bring draft after draft of my final paper and its bibliography, driving my tutor close to insane with my paranoia about plagiarism—I had to pass several large-screen TVs mounted on a wall that also had clocks set to different time zones. Without fail, over those last weeks before winter break, one of those TVs had something about the impending Y2K doom (we got e-mails "preparing us" for this from the Office of Technology, but we didn't seem to have to actually *do* anything to prepare) and another invariably blasted the latest development in "The Battle for the Boy," which was what some stations were calling the Ariel Hernandez situation. Ariel's father had emerged from wherever he'd been the first few weeks Ariel was in the United States and was now demanding that his son be sent back. On my way to my first Thursday writing center session, I walked by those TVs just in time to see a line of demonstrators stretching from Ariel's house to beyond my mom's apartment building, which glowed orange on the screen. The shot zoomed in and I stopped and stood on my toes to get closer to the screen, scanning the line for Leidy or my mom, but the camera angle was from above, from a helicopter, and the tops of everyone's heads both looked and didn't look familiar. A row of words popped up, white letters in a black bar: AND AS YOU CAN SEE, SUSAN, THINGS ARE UNDER CONTROL NOW BUT AUTHORITIES ARE STILL STANDING BY IN CASE THE SITUATION ESCALATES AGAIN. The black bar rolled away and another scrolled up to replace it: *SUSAN:* BUT DAN, ARE YOU SEEING ANY FLAMES OR SMOKE NOW FROM THE SKY SEVEN NEWSCOPTER? EARLIER YOU SAID—

Before the next box could roll up, I found the volume button on the underside of the screen, and even though a small placard asked that we not change any of the settings, I reached up and tapped it just a little louder so that the closed-captioning the mute setting triggered disappeared. I didn't care if anyone saw me, but I had a joke ready—*We have enough reading to do, am I right?*—if anyone said something. No one did.

I stood back from the row of TVs and decided the marching looked almost peaceful now that there was no mention of fire scrolling across the screen, especially when compared to the nearby Y2K-related report showing the pandemonium of the Wall Street floor, where the hysteria of men in suits flapping paper around was matched only by the scroll rate of the words flying on and off the screen.

Halfway down the steps, the TVs safely behind me, I turned on the landing and slammed into the overstuffed backpack of Jaquelin Medina, who I hadn't seen since the mandatory Diversity Affairs welcome meeting. Despite this, she gave me a tremendous hug, but I was too stunned to return it in time—my arms stayed pinned to my body as her hands pressed into my back.

—I was just thinking about you, she said.

Something moved across my face that made her say, No! Not like that, I mean I was just worrying because, you know, I heard about how bad things are getting.

I thought she meant my grades and my probation, so in too mean a voice I said, How'd you hear about that?

She pointed slowly behind me, up the steps. The . . . media? Plus we've been talking about it a lot in my government class.

I shook my head once and said, Sorry, I'm just – it's hard. I know it's everywhere, I'm just busy, I'm just – trying to ignore it.

—Is your family doing okay? They're staying away from all the like –

She finished her sentence by waving both hands in front of her chest and giving an exaggerated frown, like she'd just been asked to dissect a cat and had to say no. I didn't know what to tell her: part of my study plan for finals was to not call home as much as usual, since I didn't think I could handle being much more than a Rawlings student for a little while. For three days in a row, I'd stayed in the library after my shifts until it closed at two A.M., and the four or five messages from Omar that Jillian wrote down on her yellow Post-it notes over those days had gone straight from my fist to our garbage can. The one message from Leidy I planned to return when I knew she'd be at work so I could keep it short and talk to the answering machine instead of her.

—I think so, I said.

Someone came down the steps behind me, and I searched his face as he looked at me and Jaquelin in the stairwell, but I couldn't see his eyes behind his sunglasses. Had he stopped to watch the Ariel coverage and now gotten the bonus of catching probably the only two Latinos he'd see on campus all day discussing the exact national issue he expected us to be talking about?

Jaquelin put her hand on my shoulder and pressed her lips together. Do you want to get dinner? I have a swipe on my meal card for a guest.

—I already ate, I lied. And I have my own meal plan, I said, this time meaning to sound rough. Were you just coming out of there?

I pointed to the glass doors of the writing center.

She looked back at the entrance, smiled at the place.

—Yeah, she said. I come every Thursday for a couple hours and work with a tutor on my papers. Have you been? It's so good, it's helped me so much.

—No, I haven't been, but I'm thinking of going now since – because of finals.

—You should! she said. My tutor's an English major and she's so good with structure and helping me even just talk through paper topics sometimes. I can't believe you haven't been yet. I had to start going the second week, after that meeting where – where we met? – and they told us to go, but I was like, whatever, you know? Then right away we had this response paper due in my history class? And I got a B-minus and I was like, *uh-oh,* I better hustle if I want to stay here. That feels like a million years ago, right?

I blinked a couple times, said yeah.

—Okay, so no dinner, but maybe – what are you doing Saturday? My roommate invited me to this party but I don't really want to go alone.

I wanted to say something sharp to keep up the ruse that I was smarter than her—*You aren't alone if you're going with your roommate*—but then I got what she meant: her roommate was white. She didn't feel like going to a party where she might be the only *person of color.*

—We can just meet there, she said. We don't gotta like, get ready together or anything. I just think it would be cool if, since us two are from real cities, right? We can show them what's up. It's a dance party supposedly.

The two or three Rawlings parties I'd gone to in early fall blurred together as one long night where I stood against a wall holding a red plastic cup filled mostly with foam as progressively drunker frat boys walked over to me and asked me what my problem was. Despite whatever Omar thought, I wasn't interested in cheating on him and hooking up with white boys wearing frayed visors with RAWLINGS SAILING stitched across the front, and this version of night-life was so vastly pathetic compared to the places in Miami Omar could get us into that I preferred staying back at the dorm and waiting for Jillian to come home drunk, her careful makeup all smudged, and tell me and half the hall about *some jerk who was totally hot though*. But Jaquelin saying this was a dance party—god, I missed dancing, missed moving around in a crowd of hundreds while music pulverized me from every direction. Before Omar and I got serious, I used to be close with some girls at Hialeah Lakes, and we lived for the weekends, for putting on the worst animal print we could find and using our older sisters' IDs to get into eighteen-and-over clubs, for dancing in a tight circle all night long. We'd claim we were sleeping over at each other's houses, but we'd come home the next morning straight from the clubs, changing in the back-seats of whatever car we'd been allowed to borrow for the night. Once we all found ourselves with boyfriends, those nights slowed down, then stopped, replaced by us hanging out in couples, then just each couple on its own until we either got engaged or broke up. I'd never thought of Rawlings as a place where I could maybe find a version of that fun again. Those first few parties—their hosts blasting music sluggish with guitar and devoid of booty-moving bass—had each ended with me walking back to the dorms a few feet behind the first random group of girls to leave, my arms hugging my shoulders against the cold night.

—Is there gonna be a DJ? I asked.

Jaquelin smiled.

—I could lie and say yes, but really? I have no idea. I just know my roommate said there'd be dancing, because she knows otherwise I'm not interested.

I said I'd come and she gave me the details. We arranged to meet just inside the entrance of the off-campus building—another huge, old mansion, this one converted into event space and high-end student housing—playing host to the party.

—That's funny, there's a club called Mansion in Miami, I told her. It'll probably be just like that, right?

—That's hilarious, she said. But you know what? I don't really care if it's lame, I'm wearing my club clothes because why the hell not? I haven't worn them once out here. I'll probably take them back home and leave them there at break. But maybe they deserve a last chance here at Rawlings.

Behind us a clomp of footsteps charged down the stairs, and them coming after her *last chance here at Rawlings* made me wish they'd run me over, grind me into the concrete and make me part of the campus in a way I could live up to and that didn't cost anything. As they passed, Jaquelin scooted closer to me, said Hi! and waved at this group of students—all talking to each other—even though not one of them acknowledged that she stood there.

—I'll wear mine too, I said. You don't want to be the only one.

The night of the party, Jillian caught me sitting on the bathroom floor in front of the full-length mirror, flat-ironing my hair.

—Oh, she said from the doorway. I thought I smelled something burning in here.

She came and stood by me, inspecting the reflection of her outfit. Her black leather boots and the zippers running up their outside seams went to her knees, and under them she wore reddish tights that accented the red gumball-like beads of the necklace wrapped twice around her throat. Her low-cut top was gray and looked like a bodice made out of felt, and it matched perfectly with the fedora tipped forward on her head: she must've bought them as a set. The whole outfit looked too grown up, too coordinated to be any fun. Her makeup case—like a plastic toolbox—hung from her hand as she talked to the mirror.

—From the hallway it smells like there's a fire in here, she said. I was really about to get the RA.

—It's just me, I said.

She moved to the counter and set her case down, placed her fedora next to it. A stream of smoke came up from my flat iron as a twisted strip went in on one side and came out stick-straight and only a little crispy from the other. Straightening my hair made it twice as long: it reached past my waist.

—It can't be good for your hair to have the iron set that hot.

—That's the only way to make it straight, I said. I always do it this hot.

I was wearing a pair of hip-hugger jeans that looked stitched up the sides, but the openings weren't real; I wouldn't end up like those girls on Halloween Jillian's brother had warned her about. I'd never worn jeans to a real club in Miami, only to the places we went as a joke, the places tucked into mini-malls in Broward County that promised free drinks to all females until midnight.

—Am I to take this hair frying as a sign you're actually going out tonight? Or are you staying in to finally call your boyfriend? He's really tired of leaving messages, I'll tell you that.

She pushed her hair back with a hairband, the first move in crafting the layers of makeup that constituted Party Face Jillian.

—I haven't straightened my hair since graduation, I said. I wanted to try it up here. It'll probably last a while in this cold.

I fed another section through the iron, clamped it as close to my scalp as I could stand.

—But yeah, I'm going out tonight, I said. To some party near west campus? Someone told me there'd be dancing, so I figured I'd see if it's true.

—The party at Newman House? Down on Buffalo Street? We're going to that, a bunch of us from the hall. You should go with us. Tracy might drive.

—Tracy might *what*? a voice yelled from the hallway. A second later, Tracy's over-blushed face hovered in the bathroom's entrance. Is someone barbecuing in here?

I put the flat iron down by my leg to hide it, waved away smoke with one hand while finger-combing the freshly straightened piece with the other.

—Sorry, that's me, I said.

—Trace, will you drive everyone down to Newman House? Then we'll only have to walk back. It's *so* cold out.

—I'm not driving, she said. I'm already drinking.

She wrinkled her nose at the air, then said, But we can take my Jeep and you can drive if you want.

Jillian daubed a foundation-soaked sponge across her forehead and pouted like a baby. She said, I already did shots with Caroline and them in her room.

—When did you do shots? I said. How long have I been in here?

—*She* can drive, Tracy said, thrusting her chin at me. If she's going.

Jillian said, Who? Then, Oh, *Liz*!

—Or not. Whatever, Tracy said. I don't really care.

Her head disappeared from the doorway, and Jillian said to the mirror, You feel like driving her car to the party? It's one way to guarantee you won't have to walk. I don't know how many people'll end up wanting a ride, if there'll be room.

I picked up the flat iron and grabbed a chunk of hair from the base of my neck, singeing by accident some skin there. If I drove, I'd be warm, but then I imagined what I knew would happen: no parking for blocks around, the girls in the car I didn't know—and Jillian, too, with any more booze in her—all insisting on getting dropped off at the house's gate, leaving me to find a spot big enough for a Jeep on my own; Jaquelin witnessing my devolution into Rawlings chauffeur as she freezes outside; me panicking that, after I tap an Audi behind me, some old dent on Tracy's Jeep is maybe my fault; freezing anyway on a still-long walk from the parking spot to the party, Jaquelin so disgusted by me that she takes off before I make it back.

—I shouldn't drive either, I said. I think I'm – I'm pretty buzzed too, actually.

—Really! No wonder you're OK doing that to your hair, she laughed. No biggie, we'll figure something out.

She swept some colorless powder all over her face. I slid the iron down the last section of hair and headed back to our room. I changed into my strapless bra and pulled on a black tube top, threw on every bracelet I owned, and shoved my biggest set of hoop earrings through my earlobes. Jaquelin would recognize it as a lazy clubbing outfit, but it was more like Miami clothes than anything I'd worn in months. I parted my now-straight hair down the middle, rubbed a little pink lotion on my hands and smoothed it over the ends and the pieces that stuck straight up from the crown. I pulled Omar's silver chain out from where it sat pooled at the bottom of the cup that held my pens and highlighters and draped it around my neck.

After a little while in my room, some fierce makeup on my own face now, I went into the hallway to find Jillian and the other girls. I bumped into the RA in the bathroom.

—Someone was smoking something in here, she said.

—No, it was – people were straightening their hair. With a flat iron. It was on a really high setting.

—You look amazing, she said to me. Jesus, I didn't even recognize you for a second. Your hair is so long.

She reached out her hand to touch it. I let her. It feathered out of her hand and fell back stiff at my side.

—Jillian and them left a couple minutes ago, she said. Were you looking for someone?

—They left? I said. Like all together?

—You can probably still catch them. They said they were taking the campus shuttle.

I thought Jillian would come back to our room, at least to put her makeup away, but the case wasn't on the counter—she must've left it somewhere else. I pulled my hair into a cord and wrapped it around my fist, out of anyone's grip.

—No, it's fine. I wasn't really going with them anyway.

I'm meeting up with a real friend, I almost said, but that would only make my RA ask me questions and act interested in me, since that was essentially her job.

I went back to our room, taking a long body-warming swig from the bottle of vodka Jillian kept on the freezer shelf of her mini-fridge, and when I put it back, I didn't bother to make it look like I hadn't touched it. Let her say something to me about it, I said to the fridge door, then to my reflection as I checked my makeup again. But I knew I was stalling, waiting until I was sure the next campus shuttle had come and gone.

13

APPARENTLY JAQUELIN DIDN'T FUNCTION ON the half-Mexican, half-Honduran equivalent of Cuban Time: I was almost an hour late—so pretty much on time by our standards—but she wasn't standing just inside the foyer like we'd planned, and as someone took my coat and someone else put a paper wristband on my outstretched arm, I searched for anyone I recognized. The only thing that kept me from panicking about being there alone was the music—hip-hop playing so loud that I'd heard it from a block away, meaning actual speakers and not some shitty computer ones buzzing a song beyond recognition. Meaning, at the very least, a PA system—maybe even an actual DJ. Huddles of females tittered just inside the door, screaming nonsense over the music into each other's ears, radiating a kind of fear I'd never seen on them: no one in their pack was willing to take the lead and go in. But the music gave me the courage to walk down the gauntlet of males holding up the entrance's walls while they sipped like mad from their beers. I safety-hoisted my tube top—made sure things were as secure as they got in a shirt like that—and strutted down the long foyer past all of them, flipping my hair over my shoulders and showing off my collarbone, refusing to make eye contact with even a single person, my face set to look as bored and unimpressed as possible. *This is how you enter a club, motherfuckers*, I thought, and I knew they could hear me thinking it, because they all turned and watched me.

A few steps before the archway leading to the dance floor, I heard a guy's voice yell, Hey you!—a little different from the *Hey girl, come here*, or the *Hey baby, lemme talk to you* one normally heard while traversing the male-lined entryway of a Miami club, but it would do. I kept my eyes on the dark room in front of me, where the music came from, picturing those girls in the herds behind me totally incapable of taking even one step forward, until I heard, Hey OK! Hey OK! OK OK OK!

I tilted my head so I could see (without obviously looking) who was having some kind of OK-breakdown against the wall—but he *wasn't* against the wall: he was lunging forward, reaching toward me, beer in one hand, the other hand and its different color wristband going for my arm as he yelled, OK! OK, hey!

When his fingers glanced the top of my arm, I swung out of his way and said, Who are *you*, trying to touch me? I scowled at his hand in the air between us, but even in the dim, red light, I could make out the freckles dotting his knuckles.

—It's Ethan, remember! From the library? And you're OK! You're OK, get it?

I did. It was lame enough to remind me where I really was.

—You straightened your hair, he said. It looks rad.

I dipped my head forward to bring my hair in front of me, then pushed it back again like it was *so annoying* to have to deal repeatedly with something so substantial. Then I pretended to yawn.

—I have a boyfriend, I said.

He didn't even blink. Good for you, he said.

He glanced around, trying to nod with the beat but missing it by a little each time. Now that I stood next to him (instead of towering above from my library desk), I saw he was thin and a good eight inches taller than me. He kept leaning down, as if trying to see the room from my height, and the terrible plaid shirt he wore over some faded T-shirt kept falling open in my direction, as if lined inside with stolen watches he wanted me to check out.

—This party is way loud, he yelled into my ear.

The red light bulbs illuminating the entrance made his already-red hair look orange. Disorganized red scruff glinted from his chin.

—I know, he said, I'm a freak, right? This light. It's like I'm glowing.

He'd caught me staring, so I said, Sorry.

—Nah, it's cool, he said.

One team of girls from the front door grew a little brave, tiptoed their way behind me. I didn't want to move—I wanted to break them up like a school of fish around a shark—but Ethan touched the top of my half-exposed back and scooted me closer to the wall. It was a little quieter there, without the beam of sound from the dance floor's entrance directly hitting us.

—So I can keep calling you OK, he said. But if you have an actual name, you can tell me what that is at any point.

—Okay, I said.

And I couldn't help it; I laughed. So did he, his throat flashing as he sent the boom of it toward the ceiling.

A pair of hands clamped down on my shoulders from behind me.

—Liiiiiiz, Jillian slurred when I turned around. Where *were* you? We were *looking* for you!

Her necklace was now wrapped around her wrist. Her hat was gone, her face glazed with so much sweat I would've guessed she'd just been jogging.

—You guys left me at the dorm, I said.

—Wha? No we *did-it*. Tracy said she could-it *find* you when you left the *bathroom*.

Ethan yelled over the music, Who's your friend? and I said, She's not my friend, she's my roommate.

—She's pretty wrecked, he said.

—No, she's just a little sloppy, I said. Right, Jillian?

—Li-*zet*! she said, a hand still on each of my shoulders. I. *Love.* Dancing!

—Who knew! I said. Hey, maybe go get some air?

She closed her eyes and nodded, then jolted them open and squealed, I want to see you dance later!

I kept my mouth shut but smiled.

She grabbed me in a bear hug—said, You are one fucking *hawt mamacita!*—then freed me and ran away, yipping as she sprinted outside.

I shrugged at Ethan and said, She sucks sometimes.

—I can see that, he said. He took a sip from his cup, leaned down even more, then said, Li-*zet*.

—Are you drunk, too? I said.

He tipped the cup down. This is water, he said. I don't drink shitty beer.

—There's non-shitty beer?

—*What?* he laughed. Where are you *from*?

—Miami, I said. I braced myself for the follow-up *But where are you* from *from?* by watching people's shoes turn slush into water on the floor, but it never came.

—Well that explains you not knowing there's good beer in the world.

I asked him where he was from, and he said Seattle.

—Which explains *my* excellent dancing outfit, he said. He pulled open the plaid shirt even more. The T-shirt underneath said YIELD.

I grinned. I didn't say anything about your clothes, I said.

—You didn't need to. He sipped more water, then sniffed his armpit. Damn, I *really* have to do laundry.

I recoiled with extra theatrics but then turned to stand by his side against the wall. I said, I can smell you from here, and he laughed and said, Right on.

—*Yield?* I said. I prefer *Stop*.

—Oh, right, so you're too *sophisticated* for Pearl Jam, like every-one else now?

—What does Pearl Jam have to do with anything?

He scratched the red hair sprouting on his chin, then pointed to the word on his shirt. He said, You know this is a Pearl Jam al-bum, right?

I didn't. I couldn't even name a Pearl Jam song, though of course I'd heard of the band. I looked at his shoes—big, black boots—then up at his face, to his eyes, which sort of startled me with how light they were. A blast of cold came down the foyer as the song playing melted into another—one I loved. I knew exactly how many sec-onds I had until it got to the hook.

—But it's also – I work on campus as a street sign, he said.

I bent forward and laughed. The next school of girls flitted their way into the vast room where the music lived. Inside that room, just past its entrance, was some of the worst dancing I'd ever seen up to that point in my life. Even though the song playing had a heavy bass beat, had been all over the radio for months, even though the music video for it showcased a wide array of booty-dancing op-tions for the viewer to imitate, either no one in there had seen that video, or something got lost between their brains and their bodies. Some people were just sort of jumping in place, not even moving their arms, while others thrashed from side to side—all to slightly different rhythms, as if they had on headphones and were listen-ing to other songs. The girls who'd just walked in shoved out their butts, squatting as if doing some slutty aerobics. One girl started pumping her shoulders and high-stepping like a bird searching for a mate. I looked back at Ethan and expected to see him laughing at them, but he wasn't—not at all. He was tapping his foot. I slung my thumbs into my belt loops and tugged my jeans down my hips a little more.

—You gonna go dance or what? I said.

He smiled into his cup. I don't dance.

—You *don't* dance? Then why are you here?

—I came with some of my residents – I'm an RA in Donald Hall. Before you got here I was actually about to go.

—Uh-huh, I said.

He held up his arm, turned his wrist, showing off his wristband.

—Really, he laughed, I was *really* leaving. Probably head up to the bars and see who's around. It's twenty-one-and-over, though, so, sorry.

He pointed at my wristband and I snorted. The new song had been on for at least a minute by then. If I moved now, I'd catch the chorus.

He said, You're a freshman, right?

I looked away from him, back at what passed for dancing.

—Dude, he said, don't be ashamed. Enjoy it.

There was no way I looked only eighteen and he had to know it. He raised his cup to his mouth in an awkward move meant to hide his eyes as they moved over my waist, then my chest. I leaned back on the wall, pinning my hair against it with my shoulders.

He said after the long sip, I'm graduating this spring, and every time I think about it, I feel like I'm going to hurl. Time flies, Lizet.

I said, Would you say it *yields* for no one?

He cringed and said, OK, that was a good one, that was clever. But, on *that* note.

He pointed down to the ground. He said, The underage beer is in the basement, but you didn't hear that from Ethan the RA.

—You're really leaving.

He handed me his empty cup, gave me a crooked salute, then shot each of his thumbs toward the house's front door. He took one step away, then swung back to me and said, Do you like ice skating?

I scrunched my face, shook my head no. Never been, I said.

—*What!* He shoved his hands in his outdated hair and pulled it. You're *kidding me.*

—Remember when I said I was from Miami?

—So what? That means you're too cool for ice skating? I mean, it's *ice skating*!

—You don't *dance*.

He hopped in place and said, OK, tomorrow? One thirty in front of Donald Hall, I'm in charge of – it's a program for my residents. Not that many people signed up. You should come.

He stopped hopping and held up both his hands and said as he rolled his eyes, Don't worry, I know you have a boyfriend.

He backed away with his hands still up, like I was suddenly dangerous.

—I don't have skates or whatever, I said.

—Don't need 'em. Provided free of charge courtesy of Rawlings College.

He raised his arms to the ceiling as if Rawlings was God in the sky.

—Maybe I'll be there, I said.

—Stop being a poser and just show up tomorrow, he yelled from a few feet away.

—I'm not being a –

He made a buzzer sound, then yelled, Poser! Look at you posing! before ducking into the new crowd at the door.

The other people in the foyer all looked at me as he left, and I wondered if I *was* too cool for ice skating. I wondered what he'd meant by that—if I'd come off as snotty as I'd walked in rather than just confident and in control, finally in my element. Maybe it was simpler than that: maybe RAs got bonuses for recruiting another dorm's residents to their programs—double points for minorities! Why go through the show of inviting me otherwise, if I seemed *too cool* for it?

Jillian tumbled down the foyer toward me, way too excited about something.

—And who was *that*? she said.

Her hands slipped back to my shoulders. She pressed them

against the wall, but I pulled her hands away and freed my hair by swinging it forward.

—Some guy I met at work. He's an RA.

She lurched at me and said, He *totally* wants you.

—And he's *totally* not my type. He's – it's like someone set fire to a palm tree.

—No! He's *cute*! she said. Wait! Is *he* why you've been avoiding Omar?

She wagged her finger in my face and I smacked it away.

—Don't you fucking do that, I said.

She cradled her hand and said to it, Whoa Nelly, calm down, Miss Thang.

—I don't even know that guy. And why do you – you smell like shit.

She stood up straight and grinned—said, I. Vomited. And now? More dancing!—then she darted back into the music before I could say anything.

A minute later I surveyed the perimeter of the massive room— the ceiling high and crisscrossed with wooden beams, the windows twelve feet tall and swathed in poured-looking curtains. Hundreds of people pulsed on the dance floor, and a DJ and his equipment stood far off on a platform in front of it. I finally found Jaquelin near that platform, right up against a speaker. She hugged me— her arms damp and cold from her sweat—then yelled, Look! and pointed to the DJ, a muscular guy wearing a red bandana over his hair, a pair of mirrored sunglasses shielding his eyes. It's a miracle! Jaquelin yelled, and we immediately started dancing together, immediately fell in sync. When we'd lift our hands in the air, the girls around us did it too, a few seconds later. When we went from a slow grind to shaking our asses as fast as we could, the girls around us tried to match us. Eventually the DJ threw on a song with a beat enough like a merengue, so then we danced as a couple, deploying every turn and spin we knew, and a circle started to grow around

us. I was happier than I'd been in weeks, just moving like that, but
Jaquelin kept pulling people into the circle with us, trying to show
them a turn we'd just done. I heard her yell, Like this! to one girl,
then she put her hands on the girl's hips and pushed them from
side to side. Even though the girl was half a beat off, Jaquelin said,
You got it! You're doing it! She came back to dance with me for
another thirty seconds before spinning out and pulling another
shitty dancer back in with her. When enough of them were around
us that the circle had collapsed, she told me she was going to the
bathroom, not to move from that spot. I closed my eyes and con-
centrated on the chill of some guy's sweat-soaked shirt as he edged
behind me, pressing against me to dance, and I felt closer to home
in that moment than when I'd been back there for Thanksgiving.

The DJ, a guy they'd brought from the closest big city, had been
watching over the top of his sunglasses as me and Jaquelin danced,
and now that it was just me grinding on some faceless stranger, he
leaned down from his kingdom and yelled an invite up to the platform in my direction. I didn't need to answer: he grabbed my whole
forearm and yanked me the three feet up to his side. A silver ring
circled each finger he'd wrapped around my elbow. He wore a white
tank top—a *wife-beater*, is what Omar would've called it—and what
I'd first thought was a Mexican flag tattooed on his shoulder was
actually an Italian one. He slid a headphone back from his ear, put
his arm around my shoulder, and pulled the side of my head to his
mouth.

—I'm not supposed to let people up here, he said. But you're
not people.

He asked me what I was doing at *a party like this*, and when I
said I was a Rawlings student, he said, No fucking way! When I
said, But I'm from Miami, he kissed the top of my head.

He set up the next song—another intense favorite, this one by
a morbidly obese Puerto Rican rapper who, at 698 pounds, would
be dead of a heart attack in less than two months—and as I danced
with him, I slid his sunglasses off his face. From so close I saw he

was older than I'd thought. I hid my own eyes behind the mirrored lenses. The heads in the crowd, hundreds of them, bobbed and swayed and jerked, their bodies packed together. Jaquelin was edging closer to the speaker again, standing in a new circle, the only nonwhite girl in it, her back to me. I spotted Jillian near one side, up next to one of those colossal windows, doing what looked like a very drunk impression of someone who couldn't dance. The farther out she stuck her ass, the more obvious it was that she didn't have one, and I laughed, hard.

Behind me, the DJ put his thick hand on my waist. I shifted so we stood side by side, bodies churning in front of us. He leaned over and said, Baby, tell me what you want me to play for you. I pulled my hair off my back—it was hotter up there, a few feet closer to the ceiling—and tied it into a loose knot on top of my head.

—What songs you got, I said out to the crowd, with the word *ass* in them?

He lowered the hand to my hip, and I pretended not to notice. I slipped the headphones from around his neck, avoiding the film of sweat clinging to him, and put them over my own ears.

14

I LEFT JILLIAN (IN HER CLOTHES from the night before, minus the boots) sleeping facedown on her still-made bed, getting dressed and leaving without waking her. After a few hours in the library rereading the early chapters in my chem textbook and outlining them the way my tutor had suggested, I hauled myself and my stuff to Donald Hall. It was one of the more modern dorms, with a wide entrance and a sort of concrete porch, which is where a group of ten or so people—Ethan not among them—stood waiting, a few with skates hanging from their shoulders. As I walked up to the circle, I glanced through the building's glass doors and realized I'd never been inside any dorm but mine.

Ethan materialized from a stairwell door and met me with a huge wave, saying, You made it! as he came outside. He introduced me to the other residents all up for ice skating that afternoon, most of them freshmen like me. Everyone looked exhausted, pale: Ethan even said, I'm thinking this is a much-needed break, you guys. Just one week left before study week starts. We can do this!

We slouched across campus to the rink where the hockey team played and practiced. I'd seen it from the outside during an orientation week tour, but it was up near the athletic fields—a part of campus I never needed to visit. Ethan asked me how the party had wrapped up, and all I said was, Good. He mentioned that a few of the people walking with us now had been there, had I seen them? He herded us together into a little group of three and then abandoned us for another subset of residents. We proceeded to have an awkward conversation about the DJ and whether or not he was *sketchy*. They declared me the ultimate authority on this issue, since they recognized me as the girl who'd gotten closest to him.

—I guess he was pretty sketchy, I said, trying out the word.

It was sweeter-sounding, more innocuous, than *skeezy* or *grimy*—words that would've felt more natural coming from my mouth but that didn't really describe him. *Sketchy* was it. *Sketchy* was perfect. I wondered if people used that word in Seattle.

We kept walking, the piles of old snow lining the sidewalks and paths reaching almost to my thighs, the sky clear and so the cold extra brutal. I still couldn't understand why the sun, when out like that, couldn't do its job and warm us even a little bit. I kept my hands in my coat pockets, though I'd brought Jillian's mittens with me in my backpack for skating; there was only so much cold I could take for so long without them.

Ethan would occasionally jog up to the front of the group and point out some *awesome* or *rad* thing about Rawlings, grinning like a fool at a plaque that commemorated the graduation of the first woman admitted to the college—We were the first of our sister schools to go co-ed, he pointed out—or the building that housed a brain collection.

—We have a *brain collection*? someone said from the back of the group, and I was glad I wasn't the only one who didn't know about it.

Ethan told us that, among other brains, there was the brain of a local serial killer (supposedly bigger than Einstein's brain, he said) and the brain of an orca. He told us that orca brains had a part of the corpus callosum that was far more developed than that of humans, and that this likely meant they were not only smarter than

us, but capable of more complex emotions than anything we as a
species could ever feel.

—Holy shit, someone said.

After a second of walking in silent awe of this new fact, I asked
Ethan what his major was. Whatever he said—marine biology, neu-
roscience—I would make myself study it: I wanted to know things
like the things he was telling us, even if facts like that made the
field trips my elementary school had taken to see Lolita the Killer
Whale at the Miami Seaquarium so morally wrong that I'd spend
my life trying to make up for it.

—History, he said.

I stopped walking without meaning to, and the person behind
me slammed into my back, said, Oh sorry, even though it was my
fault.

I didn't ask Ethan if he'd learned that fact at Rawlings or somewhere else, but I promised myself I'd see the brains by the end of
next spring. I'd see everything, cram four years of exploring into a
semester if I had to. Maybe I'd ask Ethan for a list of recommen-
dations, assuming I could do it without letting on that one year at
Rawlings might be all I could afford. He pointed out a building
that had a twin in New York City: it was made out of a metal that,
when exposed to atmospheric pollutants, would turn a brilliant,
aquatic blue. But our version, on this crisp hill, was a dump-in-the-
toilet brown.

—Too clean here, he said, walking backwards so that he faced us.
But seriously, guys, check out the one in the city if you're ever there.

He turned around with a little hop, an honest-to-goodness skip,
and seeing him do that made me hope that after graduation, Ethan
could find a job as some sort of RA for the world.

The skates surprised me the most: their bulk, the very unnatural
feeling of walking in them, the way I was sure I'd snap both my
ankles within seconds of putting them on. Then there was the fact

that I had to step onto ice—*onto ice*. *Step* onto it. I didn't know how to do that, so with my skates on, I sat in the stands surrounding the rink, watching people do it for a little while, how they transitioned from regular ground to a surface so slick. Some people launched into big graceful laps, but I ignored them, scrutinizing instead the ones pulling themselves along the edge of the rink, hand over hand. I spent the afternoon in that latter category, so afraid to let go that even at the urging of the group and Ethan, I never tried it. My knuckles would hurt the next day; my arms and shoulders would ache. But despite never leaving the edge of the rink, I fell flat on my ass three times when my legs flipped out from under me.

The third time, Ethan glided over to where I sat on the ice. I was leaning back on my hands, Jillian's mittens protecting them, but when he bent forward and sped over, his own hands tucked behind him, I pulled mine to my lap, imagining his skates sharp enough to slice off all my fingers.

—You OK? he said. That one looked bad.

I was sure my tailbone was now embedded into some other bone right above it. I tried very hard not to cry from the pain of it.

—It was, I said. You know what? I think I'm done for now.

—Fair enough.

He reached down a hand—no gloves for him—and I took it, my other hand latching on to the rink's wall.

—This might not be for me, I said, letting go of him the instant I was up.

He let me inch back by myself, circling the rink a couple times as I did it, then joined me on the bench once I was safely off the ice and over the threat of tears.

—So, not for you, huh? he said, his hands clasped together between his legs.

—I don't think so, I said.

We both looked at the skates wobbling on the ends of my legs.

—Did you at least have fun today? Even a little?

I told him yes, a little, and he grinned.

—Good! He clapped once and said, My work here is done.

—So this is work?

He shrugged and said, Sorta. Planning stuff like this, coming up with programs? It's part of my job. But it's fun, too, sometimes.

He raised his hands and curled two fingers on each into air quotes. You know, he said, *building community*.

He sat there as I untied the skates and struggled to pull them off. I tried to make that very awkward motion look smooth, because he was watching the whole time; I tugged at them—one foot, then the other—and searched my tiny, non-orca brain for anything to say.

He tapped his pointer finger on my knee and said, You interested in being an RA?

—Do people in Seattle say *sketchy*? I blurted out.

He reeled away from me on the bench.

—Are you saying I'm being sketchy? Because I'm not. I'm sure it happens all the time but I swear I'm not hitting on you. I don't hit on freshmen – why would I hit on a freshman? And I don't hit on freshmen with *boyfriends*. I'm not *that* lame.

I felt my face heat up despite the proximity of all that ice—though *his* face flushed so red it looked painful. I ducked down to hide my cheeks and tie my sneakers back on my feet, my legs feeling a thousand times lighter without the skates.

—Uh, no, bro, I said (mostly to my ankles). I'm really just asking that. I never heard *sketchy* before coming here and I didn't know – whatever. But yeah, thanks for clearing up that other thing!

He shoved his hands in his hair and said, Oh, dude, no, I – you're obviously cool, I didn't mean –

—No, it's fine.

I finished the last double tie on my laces and said, I really don't care.

—I'd never heard *sketchy* either! Not before Rawlings. But *everyone* says it here.

—Good to know, thanks.

—Like *everyone*, he said out to the ice, his face still searing.

A girl out on the rink leapt into the air, spun, and landed perfectly, a spray of ice erupting from the spot her skate touched. We both watched her for longer than the move deserved.

—So the deadline is coming up – to be an RA, to apply, I mean. It's a tough gig to get but it's a sweet deal if you land it.

I thought about saying that sophomore year was a little up in the air for me right now, but I knew he'd ask why—that he'd ask because, if nothing else, he was someone whose job was to listen. Of course he'd ask why. I was only a couple weeks away from escaping campus without any other student knowing about the hearing. Out on the ice, the girl went for a second leap.

—Like for starters? he said to my silence. It's free room and board. If I'm being honest, that's a big reason to do it.

He looked at my sneakers for too long, then said, And if I'm being *really* honest, it's probably the only way I could afford this place.

I sat up very straight then, feeling so exposed—what about me made him think I couldn't afford Rawlings?—that I crossed my arms over my chest and rubbed my shoulders through my sweater. Not one conversation about money existed for me outside the financial aid office; I sometimes thought I was the only person getting aid even though I'd seen other people walking in and out of there. I worried I was hallucinating those people—that's how little anyone at Rawlings seemed to think about how much anything cost.

—That's amazing, I said. But yeah, no. I'm not sure that's for me either.

He looked down at the floor, and I caught him staring at the label on Jillian's mittens, which in my hurry to take off the skates I'd tossed on top of my backpack without even realizing it.

—Oh. Got it, he said. No worries, just thought I'd mention it in case you were curious, but I get it's not something you, like, *need*. Don't take it that way, OK?

He was already standing, already halfway to the rink's entrance by the time I looked up.

He stepped onto the ice. OK, OK? You get me?

I said, No, hey, thanks for thinking I could do it.

He shot me a corny thumbs-up. Time yields for no one, he said.

He cringed at his words and I laughed too loud so he wouldn't regret saying them.

As he glided a couple feet backward, he said, Can I say something completely unrelated to all that?

—Please, I said, and he said, Don't get mad.

Skating to the spot right in front of where I sat, he leaned over the edge as if about to tell me a secret. With a deep bend he picked up the mittens from his side and ran his thumb over the supple green leather, then handed them to me as he looked from side to side, making sure no one but me would hear what he was about to say. He even looked up at the lights as if they cared.

—And it really is an honest-to-god observation, I'm *not* hitting on you, but, OK. I've never seen anyone, like, *ever*? Just *bounce* like that. When they fall.

He pushed off from the edge and put his hands up like the night before, skating backwards for a second as he said, Sorry, I don't mean to be disrespectful, it's just – it's *true*.

He skated away fast, ice flying off the backs of his skates.

My hands, still clutching the mittens, went straight to my back pockets, a reflex to protect the ass I'd bounced on out there. If I should've been offended, I failed that test: I flung my head forward and bent over, letting my hair fall over my shoulders, then covered my mouth and eyes with my hands, crushing Jillian's mittens against my face. I only indulged the urge to hide my laughter for a moment; I made myself look up because I didn't want Ethan to make another wrong assumption, to mistake my shaking shoulders and the noise muffled by my hands as crying.

He turned and put his hands on his head and sort of shrugged, and I waved him away with those stupid gloves, thinking hard about how and when I would make it clear to him that they weren't mine.

As classes ended and study week began, any social activities that did not involve studying came to a halt. Rawlings students prided themselves on the campus's stress-inducing finals culture, one of the most intense in the country. I saw Ethan a few times coming in and out of the library, his wave and hello and occasional joke tinged with the strain I noticed on everyone's faces. The tutors at the center were less patient, the dorm's hallways quieter. Every table in the dining hall featured both a plate of food and a book, everyone choosing to eat alone. Leidy had stopped leaving messages halfway through study week, or maybe Jillian had stopped writing them down: neither of us spent much time in our room, as she'd started studying with her softball friends somewhere off campus. She didn't come back one night, then the next, and when I saw her leaving the library one afternoon and I asked her where she'd been, she just said, as if I was the biggest moron around, Studying.

Even though I worked hard to avoid what other students jokingly called "the outside world"—the news, anyone back home who loved you—I did suffer from one moment of weakness: a Sunday, the afternoon before finals officially began. I had my chemistry exam the next afternoon (my first one), and I didn't need the Office of Diversity Affairs to tell me sleep was more important than another last-minute session at the learning lab. I'd slept maybe eight hours total over the previous three days. (The number of hours you slept became a kind of shorthand when you ran into someone on campus—the lower the number, the more impressive, the harder you were working.) The lack of sleep, coupled with the nausea that accompanied too much coffee and not enough food, along with the fact that I was about to get my period (and therefore prone to crying into my chem textbook whenever I remembered

that the exam would last three whole hours) pushed me into believing that there was no way I could face the week ahead of me
without hearing my dad's voice. I thought his distance from the
things going on in my life would remind me that I'd survive, and if
I could make him talk to me after so many failed attempts, then
maybe I could do other difficult things. Unlike Omar, my dad
wouldn't ask to be filled in on my hearing's outcome; he didn't
even know about it. And unlike my mother or Leidy, my dad
would talk about his own job and ask me questions because he
probably couldn't care less about what was going on with Ariel; he
was not, as he liked to say, political. He'd been a U.S. citizen for
ten years but had never voted in an election. He only became nat-
uralized because he literally lost his green card—could not find
the original document, only a copy—and, because he worked in
construction (roofing, electrical work, hired by whoever needed
something pulled or wired or covered in tar paper), he didn't want
to keep getting confused with the workers who had fake documents.

I found the calling card I'd used the few times I'd tried to reach
him stuffed far back in my desk drawer, his work number—a cell
phone assigned to him by his boss—scrawled in red marker on the
front of it, the phrase *(emergency only!!!)* underneath.

He picked up by saying, This is Ricky, and I was so thrown off
by that—and by the fact that he answered at all—that I just said,
Papi? without realizing until later how pathetic it must've sounded.

—Lizet! he practically screamed into the phone. Hey! Wow!

It was late afternoon, and he was on his way to a jobsite, a middle school expansion that should've been done by the time classes
started but got delayed when some investigation exposed the contract as being full of kickbacks for the brother-in-law of the school
board's superintendent. Work could only happen when kids weren't
there; they paid him overtime because of the shift in hours. He
blurted out these details as I got used to the sound of him talking,
of his voice suddenly in my ear, that easy.

—I haven't heard from you in so long, he said, as if it were my fault.

He told me he'd finally managed to talk to my sister a couple days earlier, that she'd bragged about how I'd been home for Thanksgiving. He didn't sound hurt that I hadn't tried to see him while in town, but him bringing it up in the first place meant this was definitely the case—and that Leidy had told him hoping to produce that exact effect.

—Yeah, I said. It wasn't the best idea. Ariel Hernandez showed up and kind of stole my thunder.

—What about thunder?

—I just shouldn't have gone, I said. It wasn't worth the money.

Cars honked on his end of the line. I imagined him sitting in his work van, his cooler sweating on the floor in the space between the seats. I wondered where he was picturing me, if he had any idea how beautiful the snow outside my window looked with the sunset gleaming off it.

—Is it cold there? he asked.

—Yeah, it's snowed a lot.

—I saw that on the Weather Channel, that it's been snowing there.

I said yeah.

We didn't talk for long. He didn't ask about my mother or Leidy or Dante, not that I expected him to do that. I waited for him to give me the number to wherever he lived now so I wouldn't have to call him on the work cell phone he'd said was only for emergencies, but he never gave me that. He didn't ask when I'd be home next (granted, the date on my return ticket hadn't changed, but still). He just kept saying, So you're doing okay? So you're really doing fine? So you're really okay? And I kept wishing he'd believe me when I answered yes and ask something else.

—I went ice skating a couple weeks ago, I told him before hanging up.

—No shit, he said. I bet you fell a lot.

—Not *a lot*, I said. But yeah, I did, like three times. No big deal. It was still fun.

—Falling is fun? He laughed in a tired way and said, Okay, if you say so.

The sound of the van's engine disappeared on the line, and when I said, Hello?—thinking we'd been disconnected—he said, No, I'm here. I just got to where I'm going.

He said, I guess good luck on your tests. I said thanks.

As he hung up he said, See you later, and those words loomed like a forecast behind each chemistry-related fact I reviewed that night. Hours later, at exactly midnight, every student on campus stuck their heads out of whatever window they were closest to and screamed. It was a Rawlings tradition: a campus-wide shriek the midnight before the first scheduled exam. But I didn't know about it that year, and so when I heard those screams, I thought for sure I was going crazy: that all the various voices in my head—my dad's, those of my professors, even an imagined one for Ariel that I'd silenced—were hell-bent on pushing out the facts and formulas I'd lived in for the last three weeks. And I was even more convinced the screams were in my head a minute later when I decided that, after I made it through finals and got back home, I would figure out where my dad lived, go there, and make him answer for selling the house, for not caring if he ever talked to me while I was away. And the second I made that resolution, the very instant that goal was certain to me, the screaming—it stopped.

15

THE FIRST THING MY MOM SAID when she saw me—what she screamed right into my ear as she hugged me in the airport terminal—was, You are so skinny!

It sounded more like a compliment than anything she was worried about. I lost eleven pounds that fall, seven of them in the weeks between Thanksgiving and my last exam. Unlike most students, who'd put on weight all fall like pigs before a Noche Buena slaughter, I had a healthier diet at Rawlings than I did at home, having finally made use of that famous salad bar to get through finals.

—I could say the same about you, I told her.

She looked several pounds thinner, her makeup weirdly askew, her body draped in a faux-silk gold blouse and matching leggings I'd never seen. When she broke our hug, she looked down at the airport carpet and tucked her short, coarse hair behind her ears. Her roots needed a serious touch-up, the gray and brown pushing up in a solid band around her head. The blond streaks she'd always maintained looked detached from her scalp. She pried my fingers from my carry-on bag and started wheeling it away from me.

—I've been so busy since you left, I barely have time to eat, she said. But look at you, you look so smart!

I didn't ask what looking smart meant. I scanned the crowd of waiting people around us for Leidy, to give her a hug and take Dante off her hands, but my mom was alone. She was already walking a few steps ahead of me and then, as if realizing she'd left something behind, she stopped and said, It's so good to have you home!

—Where's Leidy?

—Work, Lizet. She's at work.

She looked at the inside of her wrist, her watch's face having rotated there.

—Though she's probably on her way to get Dante from daycare by now.

—Oh, I said. Of course, right.

She started moving again, my suitcase in tow. I jogged to her side, and she fished something out from between her breasts and handed it to me—the ticket from the parking garage, stamped almost an hour before—and told me if we hurried, we could save the extra five dollars. I was secretly relieved that her rush was due to something unrelated to me: I'd barely talked to Mami without Leidy as my go-between since the last trip, and I worried the whole flight home that she was still angry about Thanksgiving, about how I'd planned that trip on my own—that it had made her draw some conclusion about me, that I was turning into someone she either didn't like or didn't trust.

As we swerved around the parking garage looking for the way out, my mom's left leg shook and jumped under the steering wheel. We made it to the bottom level of the garage and paid—a breathy *Yes!* from Mami when we came in under the hour—and then she asked a slew of questions: about the trip, the planes, who I'd sat next to on each and what they were like, whether or not I'd had a chance to sleep, how many degrees it was when I left—each question interrupting the answer to the one before it.

What Mami didn't ask about was school. She spent the bulk of the car ride in conversation with the drivers of other cars, cursing them or begging them or ridiculing them, then saying to me, I'm right, right? She asked me if I was too hot or too cold, or hungry or tired, and I kept answering, No, I'm fine. I was exhausted and very near tears, actually. I was shocked to find that it did not feel good to be home, to have seen her standing there in the airport. The entire three hours of the last flight, though I'd been nervous about seeing her, I mostly felt very happy to be getting away from Rawlings and that first semester. But spotting her before she saw me in the terminal—in that fake gold outfit, her face oily, her hands fidgeting with the rings on her fingers—had made my stomach turn, and I just wanted to be alone somewhere to catch my breath, to have a minute to sync up my idea of home with reality. I'd seen my mother in that moment as *not* my mother; I saw her as a tacky-looking woman, as the Cuban lady the girls on my floor would've seen, alone in an airport. And I did not like that I suddenly had this ability to see her that way, isolated from our shared history. I didn't know if she'd changed or if she'd always looked that way but now I could just see through my feelings somehow. I felt instantly cold, and then I panicked: if she looked that way to me, what did I look like to her, with my uncombed hair and my newly pale skin and the greenish, studying-induced bags under my eyes, with my horrid plane breath? By the time I'd spotted the sign for the restrooms, it was too late: she'd snagged me, thrown her arms around my neck, had said I looked *smart*.

As much as I was ashamed of my hearing results, by what that long letter stated the committee had decided—that I was the product of a poor environment—I willingly took it: I wanted to be at Rawlings, and I was grateful that they'd taken my background into consideration. I wanted to rise—I used exactly that word in the thank-you e-mail I wrote to the committee after printing out the resource list—to *rise above* what I'd come from. I'd felt sick as I typed it, felt like a traitor after I hit send, but now, at the clash of my mom's bangles as she turned the steering wheel to cut off a car in retaliation for *them* cutting *her* off moments before—all the while lowering her window, her arm extending out, then her middle finger at the end of that arm, waving a *fuck you* as she yelled the same phrase in Spanish at the driver—I knew I'd meant it.

I eventually stopped paying attention to the street signs and turns and let myself feel lost in what still felt like my new neighborhood. Leidy was right: Little Havana *did* feel reffy, in a different way than Hialeah did—more like theme-park reffy, the reffiness as main attraction, on display. At a red light, we stopped a few cars back from a tour bus. A voice from its loudspeaker floated to us: And next up, on the left, you'll see the eternal flame monument dedicated to those who died in the Bay of Pigs Invasion. The light turned green, we kept going, and then, as if they were getting paid to do it, some old Cuban guys were actually there by that flame, in sparkling white guayaberas, saluting at it and everything, and people from places like California and Spain snapped pictures of them, and the Cuban guys smiled for these pictures.

We eventually turned onto the street of my mother's apartment building, something I registered only because she slowed down. What I saw there was another kind of spectacle: signs down the whole block, saying WELCOME and YOU ARE HOME. I blinked and breathed through the rush in my chest, then remembered who the signs were really for.

There were Cuban flags and American flags, signs with writing in too many fonts declaring: ¡ARIEL NO SE VA! Blown up and hanging on almost every fence was a picture of Ariel—looking chubbier than he had a month earlier—hanging onto the neck of some girl maybe a year or two older than me. Above the photo, in bold print, were the words, NO DESTRUYAN ESTA FELICIDAD.

—Who's that? I said.

When I pointed, I touched the glass of the window, something my dad spent years training me and Leidy never to do. I smashed my fingertip against the glass and left a greasy print. Mami's leg was still shaking.

—Esa muchacha, she said, is Ariel's cousin but is like a mother to him now. Her name is Caridaylis. Cari. They are never apart.

Mami now had both hands firmly on the steering wheel. She sat up too close to it. I imagined, in an accident, how it would ram her chest into her spine just before her head hit the windshield.

—She's like an angel, Mami said. She is like a saint.

—I don't remember her from the news.

—She's only nineteen. Think about taking that on, being a mom to him when he's gone through so much. I bet you can't even imagine it.

The girl had coppery hair and dark eyebrows. In the picture, she's smiling widely and looking behind her, at Ariel. She has a too-thick gold chain around her neck, and I imagined it as on loan from a boyfriend, having belonged to him first. She looked less like a mom and more like a big sister to the boy hanging on her back, but I kept this to myself.

I shrugged. Leidy's twenty and she's a mom, I said.

—Your sister's different. She went looking for trouble.

She didn't say anything else, but it seemed important for me to try: Yeah, but Dante's still a baby, I mumbled. And I'm sure that girl Cari has help.

If my mom heard me, she pretended not to.

As we pulled into the complex's parking lot, Leidy swung through the building's door, keeping it open with her hip. Dante sat perched on the other. She grabbed his chunky arm and made him wave to us, staying put on the tiled entrance because she was barefoot. She looked tired in a way that suddenly made me incredibly sad—her hair greasy after a day of washing dozens of other heads. As she and Dante waved, the baby looked at the car, at my mother and me opening and shutting its doors.

Mami tugged my suitcase out from the trunk before I could get to it—I was waving back to Dante and yelling, Hey, Big Guy!— and slammed the trunk closed before I could make it back there to help. She rolled the suitcase up to the front entrance and left it there, then squeezed through the doorway past Leidy after an automatic hello kiss that caught more air than cheek. Dante reached for his grandmother's hair but missed.

Leidy bounced him on her hip and he started grunting *Bah! Bah! Bah!* She looked down and traced the grout surrounding a square of tile with her big toe as I came up from the parking lot. When I reached her, she hugged me hard with her free arm and kissed me on the cheek—real and sloppy—and that's when I admitted something big had been off about Mami's welcome.

We followed my mom's voice as it ricocheted off the concrete stairwell. She was talking, talking, talking, talking: This person moved out, this apartment has a parakeet even though it's no pets allowed, did you see they painted this wall to cover up some graffiti? I lugged my bag up the stairs and wished she would keep her voice down. She seemed excited to have people close by to spy on and talk about. The wheels of my suitcase slammed again and again against the steps, the echo like an audience clapping.

The apartment was clean, the carpet in the living room section of the main room vacuumed so recently that I could still see the lines from it and Leidy's latest footsteps. It smelled like laundry, like a spray-can version of fresh sheets. In every electrical outlet, there was some kind of deodorizing thing plugged in, and immediately I imagined Dante ingesting the chemical goop heated inside each of them. There were some papers stacked neatly on the dining table, flyers with slogans and a poor-quality photo of Ariel on them. There was only one poster, which took up the bottom half of the window facing the street and which said, ARIEL ***IS*** HOME— that middle word underlined several times and written in a different color than the other two. I was happy the sign wasn't in Spanish; it meant my mother wasn't blending into the neighborhood as easily as she thought she was.

Mami stood next to the television and opened her arms wide, her bracelets sliding toward her elbows. She yelled, Welcome back! and then gestured to the coffee table at a plant, a mix of jagged-edged leaves and tiny flowers clustered together like a colorful brain. A stick topped with a small Mylar balloon, the words CONGRATS, GRAD! on it, was shoved in its dirt. And on the couch behind the coffee table was a large, clear balloon dotted with white stars and topped with coils of red bow—and inside the balloon, a blond teddy bear with a similar red bow around its neck, holding a fabric heart. The bear sat on a pile of shredded green plastic ribbon meant to look like grass, the same stuff that padded our Easter baskets when we were little girls. I stepped forward to read the writing on the heart. I LOVE YOU, it said, and I feigned delight.

—You guys, I squealed. I hugged Leidy again and Dante let out a half-burp. When I turned to hug my mom, she'd disappeared.

—Where'd she go? I said.

I stroked Dante's arm with one finger, then placed his open hand on his mother's shoulder. We heard Mami's bedroom door shut.

—She's being *weird*, Leidy said. I think you're weirding her out.

I pulled my sweatshirt off over my head. Dante started to cry, but Leidy stared past him at me, looking almost sorry for me. I left my bag by the door and stepped over to the bear on the couch. I yelled, Mami?

Through her bedroom door, I heard a muffled, ¡Ya voy!

I sat down and put the balloon on my lap. The bear inside shifted and fell against the balloon's back side, reclining.

—I'm not *weirding her out*. I barely said anything to her on the drive here.

I rolled the balloon to try to right the bear inside: it flopped over too far, landed facedown in the shredded plastic. So I rolled it the other way.

—Well whatever it is, she'll get over it. Just ask her about Ariel or Caridaylis. *That'll* make her talk.

It was late afternoon, the time of day when I usually fell asleep at my desk, my face in a book, an unofficial nap. I was so exhausted. I felt like I might cry. Instead I said, I saw her picture outside. Is she his new spokesperson?

Leidy laughed then said, Not really. I think Mami's still auditioning for that part.

She plopped down beside me and Dante's hand immediately went to the balloon, which he rubbed and which made a fart-like noise. He yanked his hand away and examined it for traces of the sound. I should've asked Leidy what she meant, but instead, I just swirled the bear and mumbled, Yeah.

—Don't worry, she said in a fake-cheerful voice. She'll get over it. She *has* to. You're here for like three freaking weeks!

Mami still hadn't come out of her room. Part of me was proud of myself for having such good intuition—I *knew* something was wrong—until I realized that my mom's reaction meant she, like me, must not have liked what she saw coming toward her at the airport.

—And plus? Leidy said. You got enough days here this visit to maybe go sit in the sun for a while. You look worse than last time, she said. You look so freaking *white*.

Dante went for the balloon a second time, pulling his hand away and inspecting it when once again the rubbery noise came out from under it. He kept at this until Leidy finally stopped him.

16

MY DAD CALLED THE APARTMENT only once: the night I got in from Rawlings, to make sure my flight had landed and that I'd been on it. But since he sensed my mom standing nearby—*She's right next to you, isn't she?*—he didn't ask anything else or arrange to see me, said only that he'd call back. Three days later, by the morning before Noche Buena and the rowdy family party that came with it, I still hadn't heard from him, and because I wanted to remind him of what he'd be missing—he had less family in the United States than my mother did, had celebrated Noche Buena with her side since he was seventeen—and because my campus-wide-scream-induced decision to finally confront him about the house still hung over me, I decided to set off to my tío Fito's apartment, starting my search with the brother who took him in right after he left my mom. I came to this plan after asking myself, *What is the most Latina thing I could do right now?* I'd thought about my choices in these terms since my first night back, when during dinner I described the new coral paint job on the house across the street as *sufficiently tropical* and Leidy laughed back that I should *quit talking like a white girl.* I decided the most Latina thing I could do was this: drive to my dad's brother's apartment, demand whoever was there to tell me where my dad lived now, then drive to *that* place and yell as many fuck-as-adjective expressions at Papi as I could generate while standing in the street in my flip-flops. It would be a lot like the fights between him and my mom, and therefore definitely *not* white.

I got to Fito's Hialeah apartment half dreading that my dad's van would be in the visitor's spot, but it wasn't, which meant I would get a practice run at yelling at someone in addition to the lame sassing of the rearview mirror I'd done at red lights on the drive there. Two of Fito's sons, cousins a little older than me, stood talking and smoking in front of the apartment's sliding glass doors, which led out to a railing-surrounded patch of concrete just off the complex's parking lot. I locked the car and walked up to the railing into the open arms of my cousins, who were, as they put it, *chilliando* (not a word, but I kept that to myself, since identifying something as *not a word* was a Leidy-certified white-girl thing to do). We hugged and they held their cigarettes way out from our kiss-on-the-cheek greeting. I stood still for a second, the railing against my hip bone as my hand worked the gate's latch, and waited for them to say welcome home or something, but the blank faces watching me from behind swirls of cigarette smoke just said, So wassup, prima?

—I just got back from New York, I said, knowing they'd think I meant the city.

—You went on vacation? the older one said.

I only knew him as Weasel—most of us just called him Wease— and wasn't positive on his or his younger brother's actual names even though we all counted each other as cousins: they always called me and any other girl cousin prima—primita if we were little. The younger one we all just called Little Fito, after his dad.

—No, college, bro. I was away at *college*. I just got back from like four months away.

—No shit, Little Fito said. All the way in New York? That's fucking crazy.

—Woooooow, Weasel said, obviously less impressed. He put his cigarette back in his mouth and held it there, turning his head to the parking lot.

—I thought we didn't see you because of your dad! Little Fito said. Or, I mean, you know, your mom?

He looked at his cigarette like it could answer the delicate etiquette question of how to reference my parents' separation.

—My dad never mentioned I was away at college? I said.

The tip of Weasel's cigarette flared orange.

—No! Little Fito said. I mean, yeah, he did, but we figured you were *around*, like at Miami Dade or FIU.

I was a breath away from telling him about Rawlings before thinking of Leidy. The fourth or fifth time she accused me of acting white was the afternoon of my second day home, when I told her how, when I'd gone to pick up Dante from daycare, the girl ranked ninth in my graduating high school class was there, working as a teacher's helper and five months pregnant with her boyfriend-turned-fiancé's kid. Without really thinking about it, I told Leidy that seeing that girl there was depressing. I think my exact words were, *It just really bummed me out.* She'd said, What the fuck is *bum you out?* Jesus, you sound *so freaking white.* I'd said, What does that even mean, stop saying that, and she'd said, Then shut the fuck up already, before storming from the living room, claiming Dante needed his diaper changed. I'd hurt her feelings without realizing it, which, based on my time at Rawlings, felt to me more *white* than anything else I'd done since being back—that, and what seemed like my atypical reaction to the daily Ariel Hernandez protests, which I felt were pretty intense but which most of Little Havana treated as a totally acceptable response. My inability to get as upset as my mom about Ariel's possible deportation made me for the first time worry that Rawlings could change me in a way that was bad.

I decided to explain Rawlings to these cousins by saying how I'd first thought about it, which wasn't accurate, but it would get me past them into their apartment.

—The school I'm at is more like UM than FIU in that it's freaking expensive, but it's sorta different, like the football team is shitty, and I got this stupid scholarship that covers a lot of it, so, yeah, that's why I'm there.

Little Fito nodded and smiled, said, A scholarship, damn.

Weasel pulled the cigarette out of his mouth, tossed it over my head into the parking lot, grabbed the sliding glass door's handle, and said, You want a beer?

Inside sat Tío Fito—Fito the Elder—eyes glassy and with a can of Becks (la llave, we called it, because of the little drawing of a key on the logo) snuggled between his legs. He was watching a Marlins game, which confused the hell out of me until Little Fito explained it was a tape of the 1997 World Series.

—Two years later and he still don't believe we won it, Little Fito said.

Weasel laughed and went to the fridge to get cans for everyone. I almost joked that I was just happy they were watching anything other than the news like my mom, but then I thought better of saying her name, or Ariel's.

Tío Fito stood up after placing his can on the tile floor and staggered over to me for a hug. He was shirtless and, aside from the preponderance of gray chest hair, the broken little veins sprawling over his cheeks, and the deep lines on his forehead that spelled out the eleven years he had on his younger brother, looked pretty much like a beer-drenched version of my dad, down to the goatee and the heavy eyelashes. He was the only one of my tíos to come from Cuba on the Mariel Boatlift, and his English wasn't as good as it would've been had he arrived earlier and as a young teenager, like my father.

—Meri Cree ma! he slurred.

His hug was loose and floppy. The warmth of his bare chest and back felt weird—almost damp—against the insides of my arms.

—Merry Christmas, Tío. Where's Papi?

He shuffled out from our hug and dropped onto the couch. He breathed in sharply, then pressed his hand to his belly and burped.

I laughed, then said toward Little Fito, He's drunk already? Isn't it maybe too early for that?

From the kitchen, Weasel said, Shut the fuck up.

—Eh? Tío said. ¿Tu papá? No here.

He shook his head and flapped an arm around to indicate the living room and kitchen of the apartment.

Weasel yelled in my direction, You forget how to speak Spanish in New York?

—Relax, Wease, Little Fito said behind me.

—No, Tío, I mean where does he *live*?

—You don't know where your dad *lives*? Weasel yelled into the fridge.

—Okay, *that's* just messed up, Little Fito said.

I whirled around to him and yelled, He never *told* me.

Beers in his hands, Weasel yelled from the kitchen doorway, You ever *ask*?

I hissed at them, *Of course*, and believed it for all of two seconds. Because, as I turned back to Tío Fito, whose face, in the glow of the TV screen, looked brighter and younger than it should, I scanned the last four months—the short phone conversation at the end of study week, the messages I'd left him, the brief goodbye on my mom's building's steps—for the moment where I actually said the words, *Papi, can I have your address?* Or even, *This is my phone number here at school*. I couldn't find it—it wasn't there—and I started to worry that Papi had a good reason to be mad at *me*.

—He's still in Hialeah, Tío said in Spanish.

He kept his eyes on the screen while picking up his can and said, In the apartments by your old house, what are they called? The Villas, him and that Dominican guy from his job, they're roommates.

The idea of my dad having a roommate almost made me laugh: all this time, the stories we could've told each other, maybe helped each other out. Then I thought about Jillian, now back in Cherry Hill, gearing up to celebrate not Noche Buena but just regular storybook Christmas Eve, sledding and drinking boozy eggnog and reading Dickens around a fire and hunting geese or whatever real white people did on Christmas. If my dad's roommate was the Dominican guy I'd seen a few times who hung drywall, who'd lived in the U.S. maybe a couple years and who Papi met at a jobsite a few months before I left, then our experiences of having roommates probably didn't have much in common.

—Apartamento dos, Tío said.

—No, Papi, el doce, Weasel said to him. He stepped across the tiny living room and tipped a can in my direction. He means unit twelve. He's bad with numbers.

—Why do – wait, *you* know where my dad lives?

—You mean *my uncle*? Weasel said. He pulled the can away. Yeah I fucking know. You want to say something about it? You want to bitch about it like your mom?

Little Fito stepped between us and yelled, Chill bro! It's like Christmas and shit!

He put his hand on Weasel's chest.

—¡Oye! Tío Fito yelled. He shushed us and pointed at the TV.

The most Latina thing I could've done then, I think, was smack Weasel and tell him there was more coming if he wanted to talk shit about my mom. But the slashes of his eyes, the aggressively cocked head, the fist choking the can of beer, the muscles around his jaw—all of it said, *Get out*. And I felt suddenly cold and scared of him. Had he always been so quick to get mad like that? Did me noticing it for the first time right then mean that I'd already been gone too long, that I was already used to nice, mostly quiet people like Jillian, who showed they were mad by folding their laundry extra sharply and clearing their throats while they did it?

—Number twelve, I said to Little Fito. In the Villas?

—Yeah, he said, letting his hand drop. He took the beer his

brother had offered me. I stepped back toward the sliding glass door. Tell your dad we say wassup, he said, opening the door for me.

—Or don't, Weasel said.

He stared me down hard, then disappeared down the apartment's hallway, his words—in an annoying, high-pitched girl voice and in an accent I knew Leidy would have a word for—trailing behind him: *Oh he's drunk? It's maybe too early for that!*

Out by the railing, Little Fito said, Wease is a dick. Forget him.

He kissed me on the cheek and opened the gate for me—the bitter beer on his breath wafting across my face. I wanted to ask him what I was missing, but to need him to tell me was worse than not knowing. Asking questions would only show him that his brother was right to hate on me.

—Merry Christmas, he said, the gate still open. Hope things get better with Tío.

I said, Me too. I clicked the gate shut and hurried to my mom's car, only getting it when I turned the key in the ignition, the car baking me inside even in December: he didn't mean Tío Fito. He meant *his* tío. My dad. He meant that what came next could be worse than just a drunk uncle. That the person guilty of so much silence could be me. By the time I pulled out of the spot and passed their apartment, no one waited outside, new cigarettes in hand, to wave goodbye. The glass door was shut, and through it, the glow from the TV, the green of the baseball diamond on its screen, washed over my uncle, making him look like a memory of someone—a ghost I barely recognized—as I drove away.

The trip to my dad's apartment through my old neighborhood made me feel a little like those tourists on the buses that went through Little Havana—*Look, there's that high school I went to that those deans told me they'd read about!*—but I couldn't help that I felt hungry looking at everything, proud of myself for remembering what was on the next corner before actually seeing it. A stack of banged-up grocery carts humped each other in a metal orgy in the far corner of the new Sedano's parking lot. On the next street down, a heavy woman wearing not enough of a bikini under a neon mesh cover-up screamed at a shirtless man holding a rooster to his chest. I laughed at how everything looked like something I was and wasn't surprised to see. I fought off the urge to pass by my old house even though I could on my way to the Villas; I didn't want the sight of it to muddy my original intentions any more than the fight with Weasel already had. I didn't want my sadness about no longer living there bleeding into my anger. I didn't want Papi getting a boost from a loss he'd caused.

The Villas were a city block of squat town houses alternatingly painted yellow or peach. A nine-foot-high concrete wall surrounded the whole development, but it wasn't a gated community; you could move in and out of it freely, without someone writing down your license plate number for no real reason other than to say they wrote it down. The wall was more for keeping the run-down Villas hidden from the busy avenue running alongside them. The speed limit was forty-five on that street, and the base of the concrete on that side showcased a collage of plastic bags, paper food wrappers, cans, bottles, napkins smudged every color. Tall weeds poked out from the garbage, looking themselves like a kind of trash. The walls were tagged in only a couple places, but each wall was a quilt of different paint shades from where tag after tag had been covered week after week, a patchwork of primer and gray. I turned the air conditioner to high, pointed the vents at my suddenly-drenched and stinging armpits, and pulled into the neighborhood.

I slowed down to twenty miles per hour—the speed limit inside the walls—and what seemed like the same two town houses scrolled by on each side of the street. The Villas had a reputation for being trashy: leases were month to month, driveways were places to party and fight, and no one enforced rules about the number of saints

you could prop up in the small squares of lawn. There were no sidewalks. There were no speed bumps. I'd never been inside the neighborhood, though I'd apparently spent the first months of my life
there: my parents had moved to the Villas while saving for the house,
which they managed to find and buy before I turned two. Number twelve came up quickly enough, in the section of the Villas
where the town houses didn't have their own parking spots. I couldn't
tell if any of the white work vans in the wide lot ringed by the
units was my dad's. I parked in one of the spots marked VISITOR,
directed a final blast of cold air down each of my T-shirt sleeves,
then turned off the car.

I sat there until the heat coming through the windshield started
to rise again, until my cheeks pulsed with the sun beating down
on me through the glass. Maybe I was trying to darken myself up
before he saw me—maybe I was worried he wouldn't recognize me.
Maybe I was stealing some fire from the sun, something to fuel a
rage I was certain I should unleash but that my time away had
morphed into something more subdued—what Leidy would call
more *white*. I shook my hands out and thought of Weasel's flaring
cigarette, then got out of the car.

My dad's rental looked less lived-in than the others. The lawn
was uniformly dry, with nothing on it to give away the religious
leanings of its inhabitants. I walked up the concrete strip connecting the asphalt to the front door, stuck my fist between the bars
guarding it, and knocked.

A man coughed from inside. I almost turned and bolted for my
car—the fingers of my left hand all of a sudden went numb. But
within a couple seconds a male voice I definitely didn't recognize
yelled, ¡Ya voy!

The drywall man swung open the door, a gold cross dangling
from his neck and resting on his dark chest. His shirt was draped
over his shoulders, unbuttoned. ¡Ay dios mío! he said when he saw
me. I started to introduce myself but his fist went for the lock on

his side of the bars, and he opened those, too, swinging them out so that I had to step away from the door to avoid getting hit. He smiled and said, ¡Es la hija!

He hugged me like I belonged to him, said, Come in!

Over his shoulder, I could see the rectangular living room with a small kitchen on the left, the sparse, mismatched furniture—a trunk acting as a coffee table, a beige faux-leather love seat I remembered from our house, a black vinyl recliner I'd never seen before—all arranged around a huge projection television that was on but with the sound muted.

He let go of me and said in Spanish, You're Ricky's youngest one. Lizet, right?

—Uh, yeah, I stuttered. And you're . . .

He pointed his broad hands at his own chest. Hunks of gold the size of class rings sat like extra knuckles on each of his middle fingers. He said, Rafael!

I smiled, then raised my palms between us as if offering an invisible tray of food, my shoulders inching toward my ears.

—¡Pasa, pasa! he said, waving me in and closing the bars behind me.

The room smelled like my own armpits and bleach and cigarettes. I wondered if my dad had started smoking, then noticed the pack in Rafael's front shirt pocket, hovering near his purplish nipple. He wore white jeans, which made him look darker, and the hair that trailed down his stomach disappeared higher up. He leapt over to the love seat and held out his hand, told me to sit.

He said in English now, I hear so much of you! From Ricky!

He dropped into the vinyl recliner, grinning and grabbing his knees, his feet tapping against the tile.

—What? I said. *Really?*

—Ha ha! Rafael almost yelled. You home from the college – is cold there.

He rubbed his thumb against his other fingers and said, ¡Cuesta mucho dinero, eh!

A wall-mounted air conditioner kicked on, filling the room with a low buzz. I scooted to the edge of the cushion and spotted, down the hallway, the shut bedroom doors.

—Is my dad here? I said.

—No no no. He is work – trabajando todavía.

I felt the heat rush from my face as the noisy AC pushed new cold onto me. I took a big breath of its moldy, wet air, pointed down the hall and said, Just tell me if he's here, okay?

He looked at the doors—said, Oh! See, I show you—then darted the few feet to them, opened each to display the made beds they hid. On his little jog back—Rafael crackled with energy—he laughed and said, You are the smart one, I understand now, ha ha! He sat again and reached across the trunk posing as a table, wrapped his hand under my chin, turned my face from side to side. I'd never spoken to this man before in my life. I should've been a little more polite, but as he held my face in his hands, I felt paralyzed by how he seemed to think he knew me well enough to inspect my face like an artifact he'd spent years tracking down, so I blurted through squashed lips, Wait, how do you know that? About my college being expensive?

—Tu papá, Rafael said. He tell me.

He let go and leapt from his chair, a finger in the air, and rushed away to the kitchen, yelling over his shoulder, Wait! I show you!

He dug around in a drawer and then scrambled back with a stiff magazine in his hand, something dark blue that, when he landed back in the seat, he held out to me across the trunk. I recognized it right away: the Rawlings viewbook—the familiar, well-worn glossy pages I'd stashed under my mattress like my own dorky porn.

—This is you, no? he said, thumbing through it. The diverse pallet of co-ed faces in various poses of concentration and fulfillment flipped by.

—That's where I go, yeah.

—He show me. He so proud of you! Rafael said with a smile that hid his teeth.

I wanted him to say it again, so I could really believe it. He slid the viewbook onto the trunk, and my eyes watered: I looked up at the ceiling to make the stinging of it stop. A brown stain, like a ring, clung to the corner back by the front door, where water had seeped in and ruined the already-shitty popcorn ceiling. My dad would've noticed something like that, would've probably gone up to fix it himself rather than wait for a landlord, then argued with the landlord later, after he'd taken the cost of repairs out of his portion of the rent, his labor rate exactly what it should be. I tried to convince myself that the presence of that stain meant something, maybe that my dad didn't spend very much time here, in that living room.

—Que te pasa, mamita, Rafael said. You okay?

I pointed at the viewbook and said, I didn't know he had this.

I tugged it onto my lap, asked its cover: Why does he have this?

Rafael started to say something, but I shook my head and said, Listen, does my dad talk about my mom or my sister?

His hands went for the cigarette pack in his shirt pocket. He slipped it out and opened it but then shut it again right away.

—Maybe we call him? Rafael said. I call him.

He lunged to his left for the phone.

—No! No, don't.

—You come for him, no me!

—Right, but – I think maybe I need to go.

—No, por favor, he said, his hand reaching out for me again, his eyes flicking around the room as if watching a fly. ¿Quieres café? I make you café!

He darted to the kitchen. Down in my lap, the viewbook's pages showed off places I now knew well—the library, the stunning student union—even the hockey rink, a picture I'd never dwelled on for too long but that now meant something to me. All of them did. I went there: my dad kept it because I went there. He'd shown it to this man he'd known for only a few months but had never told his brother or my cousins that I left the state to go there. Rafael banged around the kitchen, searching the cabinets for a cafetera. I couldn't imagine either man making their own Cuban coffee, not when so many places in Hialeah brewed it all day long and for so cheap, not when my mom had made it for my dad every single morning for as long as I could remember. I pushed the viewbook away; I didn't need to look at it any more.

—Look, I shouted as I stood up and moved to the door. I was trying hard to hold off on crying until the car ride home. I said, Can you just *not* tell my dad I was here? Please?

He rushed into the room, a fork in his hand—another thing I didn't understand.

—Mamita, he said, you know I can no be doing that.

I didn't want to respond, feeling the crack in my voice before I could hear it, but I said, I'll come back tomorrow.

He shook his head, scratched the back of his neck with the fork. He knew I was lying.

—Mañana es Noche Buena, he said.

His shoulders drooped as he looked toward the bedroom doors, still open to the plain, empty beds, and it was clear he knew a lot more about my life than I knew about his, and that he felt sorry for me, for my father. I didn't recognize either bedspread, couldn't tell which room belonged to which man.

—Tell him, just, that I called. That I'll come by tomorrow, I said.

Rafael lunged forward to the trunk. He went to tear a corner from the viewbook, then thought better of it and tugged a page from a magazine instead. He pulled a chewed-on pen from his back pocket and scribbled something on it, then handed the page to me.

—The telephone number here, he said. I think you no have it.

He took several steps to reach me by the door, then pressed the paper into my hand. I shut my fist around it and nodded, my other hand pushing against the bars. I ran down the burning concrete walkway, the heat somehow rising through my sandals, the car feeling like home base in a game I'd never played before.

17

MY MOTHER SAT ACROSS FROM me and Leidy at the table as we picked at some bagged salad—a light late dinner in preparation for the next day and the onslaught of food that came with Noche Buena. They asked me what I'd done all day while they were each at work, but I only mentioned the branch library, where I'd stopped to check my e-mail and calm down after running from Rafael. I stayed there—dodging homeless people and a librarian with a plastic name badge slumping from her shirt's breast pocket that read *Hello, I am LIBRARIAN*—until it was time to get Dante at day-care, my mom having made me "volunteer" for that job (along with picking up Leidy at the salon an hour later) so she could go straight from work to Ariel's house, where she too was "volunteering," though neither Leidy nor I knew what that really entailed.

—They have so much planned for this Noche Buena, Mami told us, a wad of lettuce in her cheek. They've had a lechón picked out since right after Thanksgiving. I heard Cari say that to the news-people.

My mom talked about Ariel's pseudo-mom, Caridaylis, like she knew her, which she sort of did. They'd met a few times, and my mother watched live as Cari gave interviews, Mami's face occasionally showing up in the background of the newscasts she'd force Leidy to later watch with her. Leidy bitched about this to me the night before, whispering about it in our room while Dante slept in his crib. She thinks they're friends, Leidy had scoffed, and when I asked, Well *are* they, she'd rolled her body away from me to face the wall and said, Why do I try to tell you anything?

Dante smashed his hand into a hill of white rice, leftovers from the Chinese takeout Leidy had ordered during her lunch break at work.

—You guys realize it's the last Noche Buena of the century? I said.

My mom slapped her hands on the table. Dante jumped once in his baby seat, then swatted his hand, scattering most of the rice on the linoleum square demarcating the space under the table as *kitchen* rather than *living room*.

—That's right, Mami said. She shoved a chunk of dressing-saturated lettuce in her mouth and said, I hadn't even thought of that.

—Ugh, don't say it that way, Leidy said. That makes it sound scary.

When I'd logged on to change my mailing address back to the apartment—a new e-mail from the registrar's office warned that final grades would be mailed out after Christmas but before the new year—there'd been yet another warning on the Rawlings Web site preparing us for possible doom.

—It *is* kind of scary, I said. Isn't it?

My mom laughed.

—That's the kind of thing people worry about when they don't have *real* problems, she said. Then she put her fork down, looked right at me, frowned and said, Speaking of problems.

She then asked if this would be my first Noche Buena as Omar's ex-girlfriend. He'd gone to our party the year before, his very presence a welcome distraction from Leidy's pregnant body and the silver band she'd bought herself to wear not on her left but on her right ring finger (You can't outright lie about it, my mom had said exactly a year ago). All night, Leidy told people before they'd even asked, Roly wanted to be here but couldn't get off from work. Papi had warned her: The fewer details you give, the better.

—I haven't really talked to Omar, I said.

Leidy bobbed between the table and floor, piling now-dirty rice onto a paper towel.

—He called here today. Like three times, she said.

—What? When?

—Why didn't you say something sooner? Mami yelled as if Omar were *her* boyfriend.

—Jesus, relax, Leidy said. He called around six? Then when you were in the shower, around seven. But he didn't say it was him. I was like, *Hello?*, then he hanged up on me.

That didn't sound at all like Omar, who always made a point of being charming with my mom and sister.

—Did you talk shit about me to him? Leidy said.

—What? No, why would I talk about you to Omar?

—¡Pero *Lizet*! Mami said. Go call him back! Right now! What is *wrong* with you?

—Mom, it's not a big deal.

—Of course it's a big deal! He loves you, he hasn't seen you in *how* long, he's calling here and you –

She sputtered like she'd run out of words, then found one more: Please?

—Fine! God! I said.

I pushed my plate away and stood, then said to my mom's smile, I'll be right back.

I grabbed the cordless, dashed over Dante's toys and around our overstuffed furniture, and locked myself in the bedroom. I sat on Leidy's bed just after I pulled the torn page Rafael had given me—folded into a tiny square—from the very bottom of my front pocket. I smoothed it out and rested the page on my knee, then dialed.

He picked up on the first ring. He even said, playing it off as one word, Hellolizet?

I had to keep my voice down, but I still couldn't help but say, Dad!

He paused and said, Yeah?

—Hey! Hi, sorry, hey.

I tucked my hair behind my ear, passing the phone between hands, the sound of a television show whirring on the other end. I said, Have you – did you call here before?

—What? he said. Then he coughed for a good five seconds.

—Never mind. Just that, Leidy told me someone was calling here before.

—But a few hours ago, he said. Right?

This was the closest he came to admitting the calls had been him. Right, I said.

—No, right. So, he said, you happy to be back?

There was an enthusiasm—a cheeriness even—that suddenly came to his voice. I heard a door shut on his end, the TV sound gone. He said, It was cold there when you left?

—Yeah, it was. Really cold.

I looked at my suitcase, still sort of packed, my clothes flopping out of it and over the edges like guts.

—So, he said. It went okay?

—What did?

—School! The semester! Did it go fine or what?

It was the first time anyone had asked me this in the three days I'd been home. I'd thought that Leidy and my mom were pretending they didn't care so as to hurt my feelings or to put me back in my place, but the conversation with my cousins at Fito's apartment showed me otherwise: it wasn't that they didn't want to hear; it's that they didn't even know to *ask*. That their idea of me had no room for what I was doing with my life made me want to fold in half—I told myself the pain was from eating nothing but salad for dinner.

—I think so, I said.

—Because I wouldn't know, because you never call me from up there.

—But you never gave me –

—Listen, he said. Do you have time tomorrow before your mother takes you to that stupid fucking party happening at her cousin's house?

I said yes, and in the other room, Dante began to whine.

Papi coughed some more, then said, Listen, I hate the phone. You know I hate the fucking phone, okay? You know the Latin American Grill we used to eat at?

The *we* meant the four of us. I said of course.

—The one by the *old* Publix, not the one by the new Publix.

—Dad, I said. I know which fucking Latin American Grill it is.

—Oye, he said. Watch it.

When I didn't say anything, he said, I thought people in college didn't talk like that. That's *vulgar*, no? Isn't that what you'd call it?

I was deciding whether or not to say, You're right, it *is* vulgar, when he said, Oh come on! Don't get so sensitive! I only say it because there's like fifty-five Latin American Grills all over fucking Hialeah.

I laughed then, and beneath it, someone shushed someone else on the other side of the closed door. Slips of shadow suddenly disappeared from the slice of light at the floor.

—No, you're right, there's a bunch of them, I told him.

—Come tomorrow. I don't have work but I need breakfast anyways.

This was his way of inviting me—of saying he wanted to see me. The difference between me and my mom and Leidy was that I could sometimes see between his words, behind what he said; I could sometimes hear the sad echo of what he wanted to say. It wasn't a skill I learned or that I could summon when I really needed it—sometimes I just had it, I suddenly just *understood* him. Whenever this happened, it was like getting a gulp of air after holding my breath at the bottom of a pool. I hadn't felt it since the day before he moved out of the old house, when he brought his leftover boxes to my room and shoved them against the wall, saying only, I don't need these. But he'd already written *Lizet Ramirez* on them in clear, thick letters using black marker, above a drawn-in blank square in which I'd write a Rawlings address he didn't know. I didn't say anything then—I didn't want him to know I understood his gesture, and him putting our house up for sale a month later would erase all the guilt I'd felt for staying quiet that day. But him keeping the viewbook, him showing it to Rafael, even if it was just to brag: I wanted to acknowledge that. I wanted to say something. So I forced out the words.

—Papi, I went by your apartment today.

—I know, he said. I was at work.

I pretended to cough like he had, tried again.

—I know, I said. I mean, I met your roommate. I talked with him.

—Who, Rafael?

—Yeah, who else? I said. He's nice.

—He's fine. He told me you came by. What's the big deal?

He shifted the phone to the other side of his face—the scratch of him losing his patience—and just as suddenly, it was gone: I was no better than Leidy or my mom at reading him. But he'd been right; I ended up needing every single box he'd given me.

So I said, I'll be there. Just tell me what time.

The next morning, just before leaving the apartment, I kissed Mami goodbye on the forehead as she was waking up, her car keys already in my hand. I whispered a reminder of the lie I'd told her the night before: that me and Omar were getting breakfast and talking things out, but I'd be back early, with more than enough time to properly shellac myself in hair gel and makeup for Noche Buena.

Before she pulled the comforter back over her face, she said, Be sweet to him, Lizet. He loves you so much. He knows you, you love each other.

—I don't know, Mami. I think it's over.

—Don't ever forget that, she said into her pillow. Be careful.

Leidy was already up, warming milk for Dante. I'd let both her and my mom believe it was Omar and not my dad on the phone.

—You want some more advice? she said as I walked past the kitchen. She gave me some the previous night, gems like, *Don't be the first one to say sorry unless he brings a present* and *Don't wear a black shirt because you'll look more pale.*

—Not really, I said.

—So you're gonna break up with him then?

She turned away from the microwave, where Dante's bottle spun in a slow circle on a glass tray, and faced me.

—I don't know, I said. I forced a grin. Let's see if he brings a present.

The microwave beeped as she said, *There* you go! and nodded at me. She snatched the bottle and repeatedly throttled it up and down, her bicep flexing with each shake. With her other hand on her hip, she said, You do you, girl, you *gotta* do you, as I shut the apartment door.

18

I GOT TO THE RESTAURANT by seven thirty, half an hour before
my dad said to meet him, but it was a mistake to come so early: it
meant I'd be at a table by myself for thirty minutes, different overweight waitresses asking me, You *sure* someone's coming? ¿Estás se-
gura? I was groggy enough to be confused at their questions for a
second, thinking, *Of course no one's coming! I made the Omar thing up!* I
flipped over the laminated menu and thought of Jillian, of how
whenever she was up against a due date, she'd spend all night alone
at the one diner in town—a dingy place open twenty-four hours
that was called, for no reason connected to anything Latino that I
could discern, Manolo's—claiming she'd return only once she *finished this goddamn paper.* I imagined her sitting in a booth, her notes
and books strewn over a sticky table as other overweight waitresses
(white versions of the ones here at Latin American) poured her cup
after cup of coffee but otherwise left her alone to work. She always
went by herself; I never offered to come along and she never asked
for my company. I sat up straighter, imagining Jillian's black hair
cascading down my own back. I called a waitress over and asked,
in Spanish but not inflecting it as a question, for a café con leche.

The minute the café—in its small Styrofoam cup—and the mug filled with steamed milk arrived, I felt more at ease. The task of pouring the froth-topped espresso into the milk, of stirring in several heaping spoonfuls of sugar, of making the whole thing the right shade of creamy brown before tasting it and then adding more café—these small maneuvers consumed my attention. To anyone watching, I was a woman preparing her morning coffee, not a girl made jittery by the clang of silverware and chairs and plates around her, not one surveying the surrounding patrons in an effort to decide if she looked like she belonged there. I was doing something I'd done hundreds of times before, but I was suddenly aware of my *performance* of making café con leche, of trying to pass for what I thought I already was. I shook loose my shoulders, then watched the milk's spin die down. I poked the spoon's tip into it and lifted off the skin that formed on the surface, flicked it onto my waiting napkin. I was *camera ready*, a total pro.

My father's van pulled into a spot in the parking lot just as that first sip scorched my top lip, the roof of my mouth, my tongue. My eyes watered immediately and I tried not to cough too loudly, but the damage was done: a different waitress altogether hustled to my table and slid me a glass of water. I hadn't asked for it, and no one around me seemed to have one.

My dad was ten minutes early and no doubt banking on my own tendency to be late, so he was surprised to see me there already, table obtained, café procured and prepared, glass of water pushed to his side, a still-wrapped straw waiting beside it. I waved as he swung through the restaurant's door, a bell jingling overhead, even though he'd seen me from the parking lot; I wanted him to understand that I didn't expect him to recognize me—this young woman with better posture than he remembered who could sit alone at a restaurant and order her coffee and take care of her business.

He looked mostly the same. He wore his work clothes—a white V-neck T-shirt, stonewash jeans splattered with ancient paint—but also his gold chain and wristwatch, which meant he'd dressed up to meet me. I stopped breathing for an instant at the sight of his chin and upper lip: he'd shaved the goatee he'd sported almost every day of my life so far. The only other time I'd seen his face bare (one of my earliest memories), I clung to my mom's shirt, crying, *That's not Papi!* over and over again, cords of spit and tears soaking my mom's blouse until sections of it turned sheer. Despite years of work in the sun, he only had a few wrinkles around his eyes and only a smattering of gray hair at the temples. He looked much younger than a man with two grown daughters should look.

—I got you a water, I said when he was still a few feet away.

I pointed at it, focusing on the cup's bumpy plastic so I wouldn't have to watch him as I decided whether or not to risk looking stupid and stand to greet him. For all my earlier anger, and then my confusion at what Rafael did and didn't tell me, I had no idea how to feel now, how I should act toward my father at this moment— had no clue what I expected either of us to do. On the way to his apartment the day before, I'd hissed some challenge into the rearview mirror at every red light: So what, you're too *busy* to give us your home number? Or: You didn't have the balls to tell Mom to her *face* you were selling the house so you send some *bitch* from the *bank*—real fucking brave of you, huh? But watching Rafael's broad hands flip through the pages of the viewbook I'd hidden from everyone, out of which I'd torn an application I mailed off in secret—it mattered now, that Papi had kept it, had even moved it to his new home. When Papi's feet stopped just by my chair, I couldn't help but look up.

He stood at the edge of the table, his shirt stretched a little tight over his belly, faint yellow stains nestled near his armpits, his arms spread out wide to hug me.

—Come on, he said. And as I got up, deciding not to think and just reaching to him, my chair scratching the floor, he whispered as he squeezed me harder than he ever had, You look like *shit*.

I stayed tucked under his arm, smelling the mix of sweat and deodorant.

He clapped me on the back, squeezed me again, and then just as abruptly dropped me. As he pulled away his eyes were locked on the table, and I wondered how shitty I really looked; it seemed hard for him to face me. He scooted his chair in and pointed to my seat, as if he'd been the one here early holding this spot for us.

—Sit already! he said. When I did, he said, So what's going on? You a doctor yet?

—Ha ha, I said. Not yet.

Like any good first-generation college student, I planned to follow up my biology degree with a stint at med school, followed by whatever came after med school, followed by me opening my very own clinic back home, where I'd see everyone for free and give kids shots without making them cry. It was a good plan, one I believed in even after I heard it come from the mouth of almost every other student at the Diversity Affairs orientation meeting.

My dad's leg hopped under the table, making the water in his glass shimmy.

—Listen, he said. I know you're busy up there doing your studies and whatnot. But me too, with work. It's crazy how much I'm working these days. I mean, really crazy.

He ran his hands through his hair three times and said, I'm at five or six different jobsites in one week sometimes, so, you know, I'm not around, like . . .

He looked up at the lights sprouting from the bottom of a fan overhead. He shrugged. I thought of Weasel a day earlier, saying into his father's refrigerator, *You don't know where he lives?* as his brother tried to make excuses for both of us.

—I know, I said. People get busy. I'm the same. It's okay.

I smiled and he nodded and said, Good.

He picked up his menu like something was finally settled for him, and with that action, he was, somehow and suddenly, the easier parent for me to understand. A waitress with a head covered in tight curls came over and took our full order: a second café con leche, two orders of buttered Cuban toast, two plates of scrambled eggs with thin slices of fried ham chopped up and mixed in.

—¿Revuelto? she asked after I said the number of the special I wanted. She raised a painted-on eyebrow at me, like I didn't know what the word meant. It's the only way I'd ever ordered it. Sí, claro, I said.

She hustled away and within seconds, the waitress who'd brought over my café con leche swept by with a matching set of beverage-assembling supplies for my father. He mumbled a gracias to her back.

—So you get straight A's or what?

He poured the café into the milk, then streamed a line of sugar into it right from the dispenser, skipping the act of measuring it out into his spoon. In my hesitation, he looked up from the glittery trail tumbling into his cup and said, Oh no, did you *get a B* in something? He put the sugar down and laughed.

It wasn't hard to do as well as I had at my high school. Our teachers ranged from the passionate (our saviors: those who'd started off as Teach For America recruits and stuck around long past their obligatory two years) to the supernaturally lazy (those who depended on movies to kill time: for instance, our Honors World History teacher, who over the course of one nine-week grading period, between classes devoted to "silent reading" from textbooks we couldn't take home, showed us *The Ten Commandments*, *Cleopatra*, the entire Roots miniseries starring—as the teacher put it—"the guy from *Reading Rainbow*," *Schindler's List*, *Good Morning, Vietnam* starring "the guy who was the genie in *Aladdin*," and, for some reason, *The Fifth Element* followed immediately by *Stargate*, which was the one he'd "*meant* to show us" when he accidentally brought in *The Fifth Element*. But if you passed an AP exam with a score of three or higher (a rare occurrence at our school but something I'd done, to my own shock, for the first time in tenth grade), or if a guardian managed to show up for parent-teacher night, those were ways you could end up on the list of "good kids" I imagined the teachers circulating.

I don't know when it happened, but my teachers knew me as a good student even before I'd decided to be one. It probably had to do with Leidy being a so-so presence in their classrooms, the teacher logic being that, when you have two sisters so close in age, they can't both be disappointments.

—I don't know my *official* grades yet. They get mailed out soon, I said, as if waiting for them wasn't an ordeal. But it's way harder to do good there, I said. Way, way harder.

He finished a sip of coffee and said, Oh yeah?

I didn't let much spill out. To give him the entirety of what I'd been through academically would require me to back up way too much, to admit how far I now was from his idea of me when it came to school. To tell him everything, to let so many feelings just plop onto the table, would make him so uncomfortable that I wouldn't be surprised if he left his coffee behind and walked out to his van. He'd done much worse before.

—It's really intense, I finally said. The professors – our teachers? They're like obsessed people about their subjects. They are *crazy*.

—Sounds like people here with the Ariel Hernandez bullshit, he said. Sounds like your mother.

He sipped his coffee, twisted his napkin with his free hand. I waited for a laugh, for some indication he was joking. He put the cup down and said instead, Are you in any clubs like before you went over there?

His changing the subject almost worked, as the question got me thinking about how the high school version of me had been a member or officer of almost every club our school had to offer—even, for one very misguided summer, the JV cheerleading team (I liked the exercise and the stunts but hated the idea of actually *cheering* for something; I quit after the first game of the regular season). I'd forgotten how that version of me spent most lunch periods not eating at Taco Bell with Omar, but in front of a classroom counting raised hands voting on where to go for our senior trip or on the various theme days for spirit week. *That* Lizet stayed after school every day but Friday, making banners to hang in the building's central plaza, bossing other girls around and complaining later to Omar about how nobody cared about anything, coming home with marker-smudged hands and glitter speckling my knees. I'd almost forgotten that girl. And as I tried to answer my dad, I realized I had no idea what clubs, outside of sports like Jillian's intramural softball, existed at Rawlings. There were so many flyers on the bulletin boards around campus that to me they blurred into one huge flyer advertising colored paper.

—No, I said. That's how hard it is there, that I don't even do any clubs.

He was about to ask me something else when I said, But wait, what do you mean about Mom and Ariel Hernandez?

He drank more coffee as an answer. A new waitress stopped to toss two plastic baskets filled with parchment-wrapped slabs of squashed Cuban bread on our table, her arms piled with maybe six more baskets headed for other customers. As he tried ignoring my question by ripping a hunk of tostada from his basket and shoving it into his mouth, I said, Have you – I didn't know you'd talked to her.

—I haven't, he said, chewing.

He wrapped his hands around his mug, laced his fingers together around it, each finger coming to rest in the nest of black hair on the backs of his hands. A couple of his fingernails were splitting from his habit of biting them down so severely, and lodged in the swirls of the calluses on his fingertips were smudges of what I figured was tar: when we'd hugged, I'd smelled Irish Spring soap, so the black stains filling those creases couldn't be dirt—dirt would've washed off. He swallowed the bite of tostada and said, Do you get any news up there? At your school? Like on TV?

I barely ever stopped to watch the TV in the dorm's lounge on my way in from classes—I didn't have time—but I said, Yeah.

—But do you get Univision or Telemundo up there?

His leg started to rattle under the table again.

—I don't know. Maybe? I haven't really checked.

He slid the mug close to his body. He looked at another one of the ceiling fans and said, I've seen her on some of those reports, the stuff they tape right at Ariel's house.

He shook his head at the fan and then looked back at me, right at my face.

—I've seen her on there a bunch of times, he said.

—So what? I said, though I couldn't match his stare. So she's making the best of our new neighborhood. How is that *her* fault?

I sipped my own coffee as he had, giving him space to defend himself. But he didn't hear it—the blame. He pushed flakes of bread around on the table with his pointer finger.

—That's one way to put it, he said to his plate. Forget I said anything, fine.

Him even bringing it up meant he was very, very worried about whatever he'd seen, and that made *me* worried, but I couldn't help that my instinct was to defend her: he was the reason she even lived in Little Havana now, whether I could make myself say that or not.

—Just tell her, he said. Look, just tell her to relax, okay? She needs to relax.

He ripped off another piece of bread and plunged it into his coffee. I did the same. I let the piece dissolve in my mouth, swallowed the sweet mush.

—Listen, he said, pointing a shard of bread at me, I know it's hard for her to hear what people are saying and what he's going through. *I* can barely listen to it, okay? And I was *fourteen* when I came here, so I remember more than her. She was only twelve, thirteen.

He leaned back and lifted his hands as if being held up at gunpoint, one fist still gripping the bread.

—But listen, the way she talks about it? She has to admit she's not, whatever, that he's not her kid. That's not her life. Besides, she's *got* two kids, and she's got Dante now too, so that's plenty.

—Me and Leidy aren't really –

—You know what I mean, he barked. He shoved more bread in his mouth and said, crumbs flying out with his words, And you know how she gets. So tell her to relax about it.

I choked my fork in my hand to keep from saying *No duh* the way Jillian would. Another waitress came by and slid two identical plates of scrambled eggs on the table, the pink flecks of ham scattered atop each heap like wet confetti. We both looked down and sat up straight, away from our plates, neither of us seemingly very hungry at all.

—I don't have to tell her anything, I said.

—¿Todo bien? the waitress asked, and we said yes without looking at each other.

He unwrapped his silverware, tossing the little paper band off to his side. Digging into the eggs, mixing them even though they were already very much mixed, he said, You know what? Do whatever you want.

—She's just volunteering, I said. But I couldn't even convince myself: my mom would say exactly that in her own defense. I pushed my eggs around my plate.

—Volunteering. Sure she is. If that's what she calls what she's doing.

He waved one hand like a blade across his throat and shut his mouth, started over.

—Like I said, do whatever you want. It's not my problem.

I shrugged and said, Fine, not mine either then.

He didn't speak again until his eggs were gone, though that was only maybe a few minutes. About halfway through them, with me still on my fifth or sixth bite, I faked a mean laugh and said, Hungry much? But the only response was the clank of his fork on the plate.

When nothing but specks of egg were left, he grabbed his napkin and pulled it to his face. He wiped around his mouth in a wide arc, and from that move, I knew he'd shaved recently; he was still used to a goatee, to a big food-catching swath of hair clinging to his face. The empty feeling was still new to him.

—So the party's at Zoila's house again?

I had a freak flash of panic—he was planning on coming and making a scene. My dad had missed Noche Buena only a couple times before: one time because of a fight with Mami, after which he went instead to Fito's apartment and hung out there; and one time because his grandmother was dying and he wanted to spend it with her, since she'd pretty much raised him. I imagined him making his last stand in Zoila's driveway, but then he leaned back in his chair and let out a puff of air—a muted burp.

—Yeah, I said.

As he rubbed his belly through his shirt, I searched for what to say next: What are *you* doing for Noche Buena? Are you sad you aren't coming with us? Where did you even go before you came to Mom's family's party? Do you feel bad now that you aren't invited? As bad as we felt when you decided to make us homeless?

—I have something, he said.

He sat up in his seat. A present, I thought, and something shot through my hands, the pinkie and ring fingers going numb. I hadn't gotten him anything—hadn't expected anything from him. I hadn't gotten gifts for anyone, not even Dante. I'd planned to explain that I was going to shop the day after Christmas—*I was so busy up at school!*—but I'd forgotten to give this explanation to anyone.

—Papi, you didn't need –

—It's nothing, he said.

He lifted himself from the seat a bit and reached his hand behind him. In his fist, when the hand returned, was his wallet. He flipped it open.

—No, really Dad.

He shushed me. From the gap where money went, he tugged out three bill-sized crumpled envelopes. Two were blank, but scribbled on the third was the word *Dante*.

—It's not a lot, so listen, just take it. There's one for Leidy and one for the kid. You give it to them for me, okay?

He held the envelopes out across the table, the three of them fanned out and trembling a little. Please, he said. It's fine, just take it.

The one marked Dante was on top. The name was written in all caps, with the *D* written over and over again, like the pen had stopped working. Almost every Christmas before this, he'd sneak off in the days leading up to the holiday and buy Leidy and me something that he hadn't discussed with my mom: when I was nine, it was a Nintendo; the year before Leidy got pregnant, he bought both of us a really nice Seiko watch. The next year, with Leidy three months away from having Dante and Roly still staying away, it was nothing. Later, I understood that his not getting us something on his own was a sign he was planning on leaving, even before I made it easier for him by confessing what I'd done. And later, his choice to forgo gifts would be vindicated when I showed him the acceptance packet to a school he didn't know I'd applied to, that he didn't even know existed. But now, with these envelopes, a new possibility opened up: he'd been too disappointed in Leidy, by her and Roly's choices—too angry at how little control he had over anything— to pick something out.

He placed the envelopes, still in their fan, down on the tabletop. The corner of one poked a small puddle left by the glass of water. Darkness rushed into the paper, the envelope's corner absorbing the water faster than he could slide them away and mutter, Shit.

—Papi, I said. You should do it.

He was putting his wallet back in his pocket. Do what?

—Give them to Leidy and Dante yourself.

—Oh *please*, he said. He searched the dining room for any waitress willing to make eye contact with him. I'm not interested in the drama, Lizet.

My knuckles were white, wrapped around the handle of my mug.

Maybe I was going to throw it across the table. Maybe I was ready to be explicit—to bring up the woman from the bank, the drama of *that* act. Maybe I just wanted more coffee and was waiting for any of those waitresses to see me.

—Are you kidding me? I said. Yes you are.

His eyes darted from a waitress to me, then moved away again just as fast. He mumbled *whatever* and I let go of the mug.

—All I'm saying is you should come see them. You should give them this yourself.

He looked down at the dregs of his café, the bottom of his mug home to clumps of bread and undissolved sugar, same as in my cup.

—I can't, he said. He stopped his search and said, You know I can't.

I shrugged. Do whatever you want, I said.

He didn't answer, just placed four fingers on the envelopes and pushed them even closer to my side of the table.

—Listen, you're not gonna steal this, right?

I blocked them from coming any closer. You know what, Dad?

—I'm joking! he said. Jesus! I'm asking because maybe you need money for stuff up there at that school.

I did. I always did. But I said, I don't.

He tapped the envelopes and said, Just tell me if you do, okay?

His fingers left them then and touched my wrist. My hand clenched the mug's handle and then just as suddenly released it, and his hand encircled my wrist completely. He squeezed it too hard, not a comfort but a warning—a parent seizing an arm to wrench a child from an intersection, from the path of oncoming danger. Then he let go, and as he pulled his hand away, I felt the traces of his grip on my wrist, like small rounds of sandpaper taking something with them, leaving only the idea of softness behind.

—Okay, I said. I will.

—Good, he said. Because you can. You can tell me. But you know that, because you're the smart one.

I didn't really mean it then but I felt I had to say it: Papi, Leidy is smart, too.

A waitress dropped a small plastic tray with our bill between us. My dad took the same four fingers from before and pulled it to him. He lifted the slip, examined the numbers.

—Sure she is, he said, glaring at the receipt.

The envelopes were in my back pocket. In the restaurant's parking lot, where we said a goodbye that felt more like a see-you-later, my dad warned me against putting the money in so unsafe a place, but I wasn't worried about losing it: I was worried about how I would explain the money at all when I'd supposedly spent the last hour eating toast and eggs with Omar. I turned the wrong way out of the lot automatically, heading home out of habit, and I figured maybe that was a sign—maybe seeing the old house would give me the answer. *The house will tell me what to do,* I thought: I'd learned about magical realism in my writing seminar, when the TA had made weirdly consistent eye contact with me during the two class meetings where he was in charge and where we discussed it. He held his palm out to me at the end of every point he made and kept saying, *Right?*—his assumption being, I guess, that I knew what he was talking about because pronouncing my last name required the rolling of an *R*. At one point he referred to magical realism as my *literary tradition* and asked me to explain that concept to my classmates. He held *both* his hands out to me then, like I was supposed to drop my genetically allotted portion of magical realism into them, pass it between us like an imaginary ball at a rave.

I tried my best. I said, I don't know if we have any traditions like that, sir. My parents don't really . . . read.

He gave a short laugh like I'd just offended him, and, after blinking hard, grinned through closed lips. And I knew from that tightrope smile, from the slow way he talked me through what he presumed I meant to say, that he thought I was an idiot.

And so now, as I navigated the city's asphalt grid toward my old house, I fantasized that it would happen: that a parrot or an iguana would drop out of a tree and trudge over to me, talk in Spanish about my destiny and tell me what to do. Or maybe some palm fronds from the trees lining the street would reach down and cradle me, then ferry me to an old spirit woman who'd call me by some ancient name and inscribe the answers to my problems on the back of a tiger/dragon/shark. Better yet, maybe she would become my temporary mom, since Ariel was borrowing mine. I had high hopes for my old house as *metaphor*, my old house as *fantastical plot element to be taken literally*, my old house as *lens via which I could examine the narrative of our familial strife*. I was ready for what I'd been taught about myself, about what it meant to be *like me*, to kick in.

But when I got there, the squat palm trees that had lived in a clump in our front yard had been cut down. I looked down the avenue, thinking I must be at the wrong place, but of course I wasn't: Leidy had tried to warn me about this at Thanksgiving. The bars on the windows and door weren't white anymore but had been painted black, which somehow made them *less* noticeable. The fence around the house—that was gone, replaced by a stronger-looking low wall that seemed not so much a gate but more a bunch of cinder blocks stacked in a row along the sidewalk. There wasn't a carport anymore either, and the mango tree that had always dropped its fruit on that carport had been ripped out, a concrete slab covering the patch of grass in which it had grown. The sun bounced off these new cement surfaces, making the house look like it was burning. The stucco exterior was still painted bright green, but with the sun pounding on it like that—with no grass to absorb the glare—it seemed more like the irritating yellow of a glow stick swirling in a club's darkness. There wasn't a parrot or a fucking iguana for miles.

I pulled off the street, the nose of the car inching past the cement wall. It felt like an accident, is the only way I can think to say it, like a bad copy of my house, or like a voice I was supposed to recognize but couldn't place. I was of course alone in the car, but I said, *Oh my god, look what they did! What should we do?* to the empty passenger seat. My hands trembled on the steering wheel; out of nowhere I felt like I had to pee. I wanted to pretend I wasn't alone. I tried one more time: *Help me know what to do.*

The yard stood solid and still. No part of that concrete was going to speak to me. If I indulged this sorry excuse for magic and kept talking to imaginary people about imaginary choices, I worried I'd never go back to my mom's apartment, or to the freezing dorm room a thousand miles away, or to anywhere I didn't belong. I couldn't let my imagination give me other options; it was too painful to admit they weren't real. I shifted my eyes to the dashboard, refusing to look into the house's windows or at the front door, and watched my hand as it forced the car into reverse.

Once I'd parked in the lot behind my mom's building, I rested my head on the steering wheel before turning off the car. I'd wanted to see the house and be calmed by it, feel somehow like it was still mine, not realizing that the mere act of observing it in that way, like a particle under a microscope, meant it had changed. I shifted in my seat just like my dad had at the restaurant, lifting a hip to pull the envelopes out of my back pocket. They weren't there. They weren't there! I almost yelped with happiness—the spirit of my old house had taken them, relieved me of their burden; the TA was right and *this is more than a metaphor!*—until my hand slid toward the other pocket, almost as an afterthought, undoing the magic.

19

LEIDY NOTICED THE ENVELOPES IMMEDIATELY, said, What are those? as she tried to tug them from my grip seconds after I found her in our room, changing Dante on the bed.

—No *wait*! I said, pulling them away and holding them behind my back. I have to tell you something.

Her smile twisted off her face, and she went back to her wad of dirty baby wipes.

—Those you and Omar's divorce papers?

She snorted as she crossed Dante's legs at the ankles and lifted them with one hand, folded the dirty wipe in half with the other. She shoved the wipe, the crap smudge a shadow under its still-unused side, under his butt and pulled it toward her. More crap smeared its surface as she brought the wipe out from between an otherwise clean-looking pair of butt cheeks.

—I didn't see Omar. I went to see Dad.

She dropped Dante's legs, but they still stood up on their own for a second before curling back toward him. His face, along with his mother's, was now set on me.

—Papi? she said, like that wasn't who I meant. *What?*

—Don't tell Mom, I said.

She dashed behind me, dirty wipe in hand, and closed our bedroom door.

—Are you kidding me? *I'm* not telling her shit. I freaking value my life.

I flicked my thumb toward the door and said, She's still *here?*

I'd made enough noise coming up the vault of the building's stairwell, then through the apartment's door, then tossing the clump of my mom's keys into the ceramic plate on top of the TV to draw people into the living room if they were home. Leidy had yelled, In here, and through my mom's open bedroom door, the mountain of sheets topping her unmade bed didn't look tall enough to be her.

—No, she's down at Ariel's house. Leidy scrunched her eyes shut and shook her head at this. But still, she said.

She sat back next to a naked-from-the-waist-down Dante. He reached for his toes and made faint grunting noises as he opened and closed his fists, missing his feet with each flail. Leidy's mouth was open a little, the tip of her tongue perched just behind her bottom teeth, the hand not holding the wipe now gripping her opposite shoulder.

I said, Are you mad?

She blurted out, No! Then said, I mean, I don't know. Just tell me what happened. Where's he living now?

I almost let out a gust of *Oh-thank-god.* She didn't know where he lived—she hadn't known all these weeks and been keeping it from me. I felt like a turd for ever thinking otherwise, for assuming that, like me, Leidy could be a terrible person.

—We met at Latin American.

—The one by the old house?

—Yeah, I said.

—So he doesn't want us to know where he's staying. Freaking asshole.

—Have you ever *asked* him? I said, accidentally sounding a lot like Weasel, so I said, Sorry, I didn't mean for it to come out that way.

She tossed the wipe in a plastic bag hanging from a knob on her nightstand and then waved that hand at me, saying, No, it's fine. She grabbed Dante's legs and spun him ninety degrees on the bed, then pulled the clean diaper by her pillow to him, unfolding it and sliding it under his legs. You're right, she said, shrugging. It's not like I ever asked him. Did you?

If all I did was answer this specific question, it wouldn't be a lie. She was not asking if I'd been to his apartment, how I'd found that apartment. This kind of logic—this tendency to reason away a question so that I kept certain facts only for myself, making me feel special over her, as if I didn't have enough to make me feel that way: that's what made me a terrible person. No, I said.

—So we both suck. What else is new?

She pulled the sticky tabs of Dante's diaper so tight around his belly that I thought it *must* be uncomfortable for him, he *had* to feel too cinched in, but he smiled at her and flapped his arms. I held the envelopes out in front of me.

—He gave me these, I said. Christmas presents.

I added to this explanation what I knew to be true, what I'd understood as hovering between Papi's words from the way he'd talked about all those different jobsites.

—He said he didn't have time to get actual presents. He'd planned on it, but just ran out of time. His hours are crazy. He's working on schools again. He's really sorry.

She held out her hand.

—Sure he is, she said.

I gave her one of the blank ones and the one marked *Dante*.

—This other one's for him, I said.

She held the two of them in front of her face. She sucked in air—sharp—through her nose, held it in as if a doctor were about to give her a shot.

She said, This one says Dante on it.

—I know, I said.

—He got something for Dante, she said.

She turned the envelope over, still unable to open it, still somehow not believing it: our dad acting in this small way like an abuelo; our father doing something that in her book counted as sweet. She fingered the seal, tugging at the taped-down corner, then shook her head and shuffled the envelopes so that the other was on top. She turned the unnamed one over in her hands, too, ran her fingers over its wrinkles, its beat-up looking seal. Then she stopped and pulled her face away from it. She handed it back to me.

—This one says your name on it.

—No it doesn't, I said.

But as she passed the envelope back to me, I saw it—faint and small and in pencil, trapped under a slice of clear tape, in the blocky caps he always used—the letters scribbled on the back along the angle of the tattered seal: *LIZET.*

I turned the one I still held over and saw the word *LEIDY* scribbled in the same faint handwriting, also in pencil. He'd written these out at a different time than the one he'd done for Dante. Dante had been an afterthought.

—If he gave you more money than me I'm gonna be pissed, she said.

She snatched her envelope from my hand and tore it open. For a quick second, it was almost the sound of wrapping paper being shredded by small hands, but it was over too soon.

I opened my envelope slowly, peeling the tape from a corner instead of ripping through it, to keep my name intact. A fifty-dollar bill, crisp from the bank, sat in there. And on the inside triangle of the seal's flap, more words, more of my father's block letters.

—Fifty bucks, Leidy said, the money between her fingers, another perfect bill. You?

—Same, I said.

She tossed the envelope on the bed and I leaned toward it. I stuck a finger inside to see if there was any writing. There wasn't.

—What, you don't believe me? she said.

She'd already folded the money.

—No, I said. It's just . . . it's weird. What about Dante's?

She ripped open his envelope and pulled out another fifty.

—Great, she said. What's a baby supposed to do with fifty bucks? Eat it?

She smirked at me and held that face, actually waiting for me to answer.

I closed my eyes and then opened them, and she shoved the bills—both now folded over and over like an accordion—in my face.

—Leidy, are you for real?

—Whatever, she said. It's the thought that counts, right?

She dropped the bills on the bed but then grabbed them back not even a second after tossing them away. I reached for Dante's envelope, picked it up along with hers. No writing in his either.

—Let me throw these away, I said.

She started undoing the crinkles she'd only just made, unfolding the bills and smoothing them against her thigh.

—For real though? she said. What the fuck does he want me to do with this fifty bucks? If he wanted to buy Dante a toy, then buy him a toy. Or if he means it for Pampers? Buy him some Pampers.

She covered her eyes with the hand not holding the money against her lap, and I opened the door and backed out of the room, all three envelopes in my fist.

I hid behind the wall that marked off the kitchen from the living room, tossing the two other envelopes onto the counter and holding the one meant for me with both hands up against my chest to steady it—my hands made the paper shake. I pushed the flap open with my pointer fingers and pressed my chin to my chest to read, the whole note seemingly underlined by the money still inside.

Lizet: I forgot about your sister's "accident" (ha ha) and had to take half your $ for him at the last minute—I know I had to give him

<u>*something*</u>. *But YOU were supposed to get more—I know you need $
up there. $50 for your nephew = $100 for your sister = That's not fair.
Call me so I can give you the $50 I owe you before you go. <u>YOU</u> deserve
it.—DAD*

I read it again, half listening for Leidy's footsteps in the hallway. He'd meant to give me twice as much as he'd given Leidy, and
even though he'd done the right thing by giving the money to Dante
instead, he equated that with rewarding Leidy and punishing me
even though we'd both disappointed him, the only difference being that *my* choices had no way of evoking for him the very origins
of our family. They hadn't added a whole new person for him to
feel wary of loving.

And the note meant more than what it said: I really thought their
anger at me applying behind their backs would dissipate once they
saw me preparing to go, once the reality of their youngest daughter leaving home set in. I kept waiting for either of them to say they
were proud of me. My teachers had said it, but in an automatic way
and always using the plural: *We're so proud of you*. That phrase, in
the overanimated voice of an assistant principal, had boomed over
the PA system during fifth period AP English one day in April
after the main office got word that I'd been admitted to Rawlings:
Teachers and students, he'd said, pardon the interruption, but we're
proud to announce that we've *just* learned senior Lizet Ramirez has
become the *first* student in Hialeah Lakes history to be accepted to
Rawlings University. We're so proud of you, Lizet, and we hope other
students follow your example and start *taking school seriously*. As if
all you had to do to get into Rawlings was take school seriously.
As if calling it Rawlings *University* over *College* was somehow a
needed upgrade. The administration was so overwhelmed by what
I'd done that they couldn't help gushing via loudspeaker to almost
five thousand completely uninterested people: I thought that pride
had to infect my parents eventually. But when my dad said goodbye to me months later in front of my mom's building, he hadn't

said it. When my mom, who'd insisted no one could come with her to the airport to see me off, pressed her thumb to my cheek to smear away something that wasn't even there, she hadn't said it. In phone calls, at the end of recorded messages, no one said it. And now, right there in my hands, I had written proof—I could see it between the small print, the words in their crammed blocks building to what I'd been waiting for one of them to say: I'm proud of you.

I pulled the money out, then folded the envelope into a tiny square and shoved it in my pocket, and, to make facing Leidy again even possible, I told myself I would not see my dad again, especially since he'd think it was just to get more cash. And what was the point, when I'd already proven at breakfast that I lacked the guts to confront him about the house? I took leaping steps down the hall to try to cover the fact that I'd been gone for a few beats more than I should've, only to find Leidy not wondering what took me so long, but with her back to me as she stood by the dresser. She was holding the bills with both hands by their corners, rubbing them against each other and then pausing to watch them, as if waiting for a message. She rested her wrists on the edge of the already-open top drawer; she must've pulled it open slowly so I wouldn't hear from the kitchen. She took one hand off the money and pressed it to the stack of her underwear in the drawer, pushed them to the side; she pressed the same hand to the stack of bras and swept them over, too. She laid the two almost-crisp-again bills, one at a time, at the very back of the drawer, then slid the bras and the underwear back into place, everything right where it belonged.

Fifty dollars once seemed to me like a lot of money, and it still did as I stood there in the doorway, watching my sister slowly close that drawer before she turned and saw me and pretended to be messing with the stack of diapers piled on the dresser. But I knew that in a couple weeks I'd be gone again and it wouldn't be enough: there was no way his present to us could cover all the things we needed. And because Papi hadn't written anything to Leidy, because she only had those two pieces of paper now tucked behind and under the thinnest things she owned, he'd given her even less than he'd given me.

She squared the stack of diapers and placed the box of wipes next to it, then said in the most bored voice she could find, So did Papi say what he was doing for Noche Buena?

—He didn't, I said. But I don't care so I didn't ask.

I slipped my shoes from my feet and lined them up outside our bedroom door against the wall. Down the hallway and through Mami's half-closed door, clothes—shed like snakeskins—dotted the floor in complete-looking outfits, pairs of shoes in their centers, each outfit apparently created in its entirety but then declared wrong for whatever she'd be doing.

—We should start getting ready soon, I said to Leidy's back. I looked down at the scuffed fronts of my flats and said to them, Why is Mom even over there today?

When Leidy didn't answer, I said, You want to shower first? I can watch Dante.

She spun around and said, You know, I almost wish it *was* Omar you'd seen?

She snatched the used grocery bag holding the dirty wipes from the knob on her nightstand.

—God no, that would be worse, I said. And for sure *he* wouldn't give us money.

We laughed, but too hard; we were both pretending. She knotted the bag's handles to seal in the smell, then rehung it on the knob.

—I'm surprised he doesn't run away, I said.

—Huh?

I came all the way into the room and pointed at Dante, who was still on the bed and gazing at his mom, his belly button peeking out over his new diaper. I sat down by him and traced my finger around the tiny hole. He didn't so much laugh as he did scream, a piercing noise like a parrot's shriek filling the whole apartment. It disappeared so suddenly when I flinched away that Leidy and I cracked up in the emptiness ringing after it.

—Yeah, that's a thing he does sometimes, she giggled. Watch this.

She sat on the bed and leaned over, pulled his shirt higher and blew hard—really hard—on his stomach, the farting sounds quickly drowned out by the same scream-laugh.

—You are so freaky sometimes, she singsonged to him as she sat up and smushed his face between her hands, the pads of her fingers on his cheeks.

I laughed more and said, Why does he *do* that?

—I have no idea, she said. It's just what he does.

Together, up until Mami came home glowing with the news of everything going into Ariel's first Noche Buena in Miami, we hovered over Dante and tickled the bottoms of his feet, the skin behind his knees, the palms of his hands before he could shut them to keep out our fingers. He did it almost every time, in response to almost every spot we tried—the parrot shriek taking over his throat as he tried to roll away from us. We did it for too long, covering up our private thoughts with Dante's noise, our normal-sounding laughter rushing in every time to fill the silence that took over the instant we pulled our hands from him.

20

WE DIDN'T SEE MY MOM'S whole family often—mostly just at Noche Buena, weddings and births, funerals—but we acted like we did. That half of my family was big and messy, sprawled around the city and good at pretending we cared very much about lives we knew little about. As we drove over to Tía Zoila's house, after watching my mom fling on the same gold shirt and pants she'd worn to pick me up at the airport (ignoring Leidy's pleas that she wear something less reffy-looking), I realized I wasn't sure if everyone in my mom's family knew about my parents splitting up for good—or, if they knew about it, whether anyone would mention it to one of us. And thanks to my cousins on my dad's side, I was almost certain no one really understood that I was away at college, that I was getting a college degree and not just my AA or some certificate. Still, we ignored most facts and thought of ourselves as close, as sufficiently up in everyone else's business, and we always were on Noche Buena.

As my mom walked ahead of us into Zoila's house with a Tupperware full of tostones she'd fried at our apartment (the cooking making our clothes reek of oil and food hours before we even got anywhere near the pig roasting in our tía's backyard), we heard Zoila scream, Look at that fucking skank! Baby, look who's here!

She came running from outside, spotting us through the glass door as she prepared a vat of sangria with her second husband, Tony. She was already drunk from tasting it to get the flavor right; her recipe for sangria included, among other things, an entire bottle of Bacardi 151. Even with all the fruit, the first sip always tasted like straight-up poison.

—Who you calling a skank, you puta? my mom laughed back. She handed me the Tupperware and then let her cousin body-slam her into a hug.

Zoila and my mom liked to say they were more like sisters than cousins. This wasn't true—even when you considered the fact that my mom had lived with Zoila and Zoila's mother when she came from Cuba up until getting pregnant and married—but they really, really believed it. Yelling obscenities at each other was something they thought sisters did.

—You are so fucking skinny, you slutty chicken, Zoila said into my mom's hair. And look at this one! she said to Dante, scooping him out of Leidy's grip. ¡Mi gordito!

She rolled the *R* for way longer than she needed to. She started to pretend-bite his arms. Dante, who should've been used to noise, sat on her hip, stunned.

—This one I'm gonna eat instead of lechón, Zoila said.

She fake-chewed the fat she fake-bit from Dante's arms. Then she greeted me and Leidy, calling us various combinations of the words slut, whore, bitch, skank, and chicken—that last word being her new one this year. The cursing was also connected to Tony; he was, at twenty-eight, twelve years younger than her, and she used moisturizer and profanity the same way since meeting him, hoping to seem younger than she was.

Tony came inside, his fingers stained red. The more he tested the sangria, the more acceptable it seemed to him to stir it with his hand instead of a long spoon after each adjustment.

—Hey Lizet, Leidy, he said, kissing each of us on the cheek as he said our names.

He'd grown a stubby ponytail since his wedding to Zoila, but he still had the same creepy facial hair—a thin, too-many-cornered beard outlining his jaw—that every other guy in Miami between the ages of twenty and thirty had in 1999. Tony looked at Leidy's chest and said, Being a mom is making you more beautiful than ever, sweetie!

He tacked on the *sweetie* to sound like the uncle we were supposed to think he was now, but it didn't work: he was only eight years older than Leidy, and cute enough that we'd wondered aloud to each other, while chewing mustard-slathered Vienna sausages at their wedding reception a couple years earlier, what the hell he saw in Zoila. Leidy's theory was that she let him put it in her butt. I hear guys *love* that, she'd said, her mouth full. After trying to think of any other reason—maybe he needed citizenship, maybe she was dying and secretly rich, maybe he thought she was fun and beautiful and was going to age well—I'd tossed back another sausage and agreed with her.

Zoila held my mom out at arm's length, zipping her scrunched, liner-shellacked eyes around my mom's face, clearly wanting to ask about something—probably about my dad. She would say, *Where is that motherfucker? Where is that cocksucker tonight?* But she was not so drunk to bring this up right away. It was coming, though; whatever was making the gossip-fueled questions hover over her mouth now would find its way out before the food hit the table. She kept looking over our shoulders, as if waiting for one more from our gang to come through the door. I wanted to tell her the way I'd told Leidy: *I'm* the one who's seen him. It would likely be a more welcome topic of conversation than what classes I'd taken or what snow felt like. Zoila handed Dante back to Leidy, effectively obscuring Tony's view of my sister's chest, and he wandered away to wash the sangria stains from his hands.

When we got to the backyard, about half the family was there and already in various states of inebriation, and my heart filled with a sort-of-happiness at the fact that the scene looked like it did every year.

—¡Llegaron las niñas! someone yelled, and everyone turned to us, *the girls.* Some people held up their drinks in recognition of our arrival but stayed put, knowing we'd eventually take a lap around the yard to greet everyone. My mom, although still a Ramirez in name, was the only one from her branch of the Rodriguez clan— her brother, our real uncle, went every year to his wife's sort-of-religious family's Noche Buena party, which was alcohol-free and therefore tamer than ours. He'd managed to convince his wife to come to our family's party only once: it ended badly, with one of the other uncles siphoning all the gas out of their car and using it to start a fire in the driveway "to help Santa find the party." They hadn't been back since.

One of my cousins, Neyda, who was my age but in her senior year of high school, came over, kissed us each on the cheek, and then, without even making small talk, asked Leidy if she could hold Dante. Except she didn't know his name: she asked if she could hold him just before asking what she should call him.

—I love babies, Neyda said in a voice that made her sound like one. Maybe when I finish school, me and my best friend, we're thinking of opening like a daycare?

—Cool, I said. My smile felt too wide.

—Just don't put him on the ground or anything. He's not crawling super good yet, Leidy said as she handed him off. Neyda's eyes popped at him, and he swung his hand at her face, as if trying to smack her.

Leidy turned her head from us and said, Where's that sangria?

I followed Leidy across the uneven cement patio, through the haze of smoke surrounding the aboveground pit where the pig roasted, and stood next to her at the folding table propping up the family booze. She slid two plastic cups off the stack by the punch bowl and served each of us too much; she was careful to leave the ice in the bowl lest it take up any precious room in our cups. Poison or no poison, I suddenly felt like celebrating the first normal feeling I'd had since being home: Noche Buena, me looking like nothing more than the echo of my bored sister, both of us ready to watch the yearly show play out, neither of us important enough to be at its center. Her son was a nameless baby floating around the party, our dad a worry we left back in our room. She jutted her chin out at me and said, Cheers, but didn't push her cup toward mine. As she sipped and scanned the backyard, she held the cup in both hands, looking like the girls at Rawlings parties, like how I must've looked against a wall with my own plastic cup. I took a big gulp of sangria, and Leidy said, *Okay* then! She seemed to be standing up straighter now that she didn't have Dante in her arms, and her long earrings—the only part of her outfit she hadn't swapped out for something else while we got ready—brushed her shoulders, tangling and untangling themselves in the chunks of her hair. She dropped one hand from the cup and let it dangle at her side and said, What?

—Nothing, I said, my eye twitching at the drink's aftertaste.

—Zoila is freaking crazy, right? She looks *old*!

We both took another sip, trying to hide how tough it was to swallow.

—Tony was looking at your tits, I said.

She almost spit out the sip she'd just taken and said, I know, right? He's so gross.

—Nice ponytail, I said into my cup.

—Shut *up*, she laughed. She slugged my shoulder.

A few seconds later, she said, Oh my god, look over there. She gestured with her cup to Zoila, who'd followed us outside and was now hoisting up her shirt. She pressed her breasts together, each of them encased in a black lace-striped cup; her nipples peeked at us from behind the stripes like neighbors through slats of a fence. Our mom and the other older cousins watched as Zoila shoved her breasts up under her neck and shouted, Once I have the surgery, they'll be like this but bigger.

Leidy and I looked back at each other, shock melting into stifled laughs. It felt like Zoila's wedding again—before Dante, before her plan to get Roly to commit had backfired so fantastically, before I'd even heard of Rawlings College—the two of us on the same team. If there'd been a way to hold on to that—to stop Neyda from hustling across the cement to us, Dante's spit all over her halter top—I would've used it then.

—Okay, so your kid? I think he shit or something.

—Maybe it's your upper lip, I said into my cup again, but Leidy didn't seem to hear me that time. She handed me her drink and reached out for Dante. She stuck her finger down the back of his diaper and just said, Nope.

Neyda clapped her hands like she was dusting them off and said to me, So is Omar coming later?

Omar had impressed my family last year by being handsome and just showing up, but I was still surprised Neyda remembered his name. Then, right away, I wasn't: I remembered what I looked like to them this time a year ago; I was graduating high school soon, Omar had a decent job, and the family probably circled the word around the yard that they expected him to propose or get me pregnant by the time summer rolled around. Come on, mira la otra, they'd probably snickered, throwing an eyebrow at Leidy's belly. It was worth their time to remember the name of someone at whose wedding reception they planned on having too much to drink.

—We broke up, I told Neyda. I shrugged and sipped, wondering if it was true.

—Oh no! she squealed. That's so sad, oh my god! Who dumped who?

—She dumped *him*, Leidy said, the *him* having the same ugly sound around it as it did when I'd given her the envelopes earlier, when the *him* was our dad. She kicked him to the curb, Omar's a loser, she said.

My stomach cramped and I wanted to blame the sangria, but I knew it was the *loser* that made me put my hand to my gut. Even though I half believed the things I told people at Rawlings about him, hearing Omar's name roll out of my sister's mouth as part of another lie to help me save face made me need to turn away from them talking and put the cup to my mouth. But I couldn't swallow another drop. I tilted my head back to mime drinking, the sangria lapping a cold band against my lip. Above us, an airplane was coming in to land—Zoila's house sat underneath the flight path of anything coming from the north and touching down at Miami International—and I wished the roar of it were worse: that it would cover up the new shouts in my head defending Omar, block the rush of him, how we'd known each other so long and so well. I wanted those feelings gone, smothered by sound, so that I could lie to myself and believe I would forget Omar, that he wouldn't matter to me months and years from that day. And I wanted the noise to block out the fact that though I hadn't called Omar since coming home, he hadn't bothered to call me either—that maybe *I* was the loser. But the plane overhead was a small one, the wail of it too high-pitched to flood the backyard completely and make everyone stop talking for the four or five seconds it usually took to fade away. People shouted over it; I could hear Leidy laughing and saying, Right Lizet? My stomach churned again. I watched the sky until the plane disappeared behind the canopy of leaves shading the street. I made myself nod.

—He was not a loser! Neyda said, and I swallowed to make sure those words hadn't come out of my own mouth. He had a car and stuff! And irregardless, he had a job, right?

I wiped my mouth with the back of my hand. It had taken exactly one big red oval around an *irregardless* in an early discussion paper in biology for me to leave that word behind, sequestering it for good to my Miami Vocabulary. I slid a step away from this cousin, impressed with myself for hearing now how stupid that word sounded in someone else's mouth.

—He has a job, I said. I just haven't talked to him lately. You know I'm away at college, right?

I looked at Leidy, hoping she'd stick up for me again, though I wasn't sure for what this time. She rolled her eyes, took a long gulp of sangria from her cup. When she pulled it away from her face, a red smear arched across her upper lip. She sucked it in to clean it off, but the stain remained. I drank from my glass—careful, now that I saw what the drink could do, to avoid it lapping over my lip again—the punch burning all the way down.

Over the course of the night, assorted relatives in various stages of drunkenness told me that I: looked skinnier, looked fatter, looked pale, looked sick, looked sad. One volunteered a cure for the faint bands of acne that had recently colonized my cheeks—egg whites mixed with vinegar. One asked if Omar and I were engaged yet (I'd slurred, Not yet!). One old uncle asked if I was jealous of Leidy for getting all the attention because of Dante—this after the baby made the rounds and charmed everyone just as Omar had the year before; another kept calling me Leidy but didn't call Leidy Lizet— Lizet just didn't exist. Neyda asked me if I was going to get back with Omar in a voice that made me think she would ask for his number if I said no. An hour or so before we sat down to eat, the new boyfriend of one of my older cousins showed up in his tricked-out Mustang, and after introducing himself as Joey to some, Joe to others, we all had to go out to the driveway and listen to the new tube speaker he'd installed in his trunk because my cousin had helped pay for it. The bass rattled the car so much that I swear the bumper vibrated, but when I pointed out the buzzing to a somewhat-drunk Leidy, she said I was seeing things and rightfully noted I was pretty buzzed myself, ha ha. She handed Dante to me and asked if I thought my cousin's new boyfriend was cute. I told her no just to be safe, and she stayed put, eventually taking Dante back into her arms.

The boyfriend had a seat assigned to him at the kids' table with us (the oldest person at the kids' table was twenty-six that year). I assumed he'd take Omar's spot—Zoila hounded our mothers about our breakups and new romances starting in November, gossip hiding behind the pretext of head counts and place settings— but when I passed the table later on my way back from the bathroom, the little card with his name on it (it read, for some reason, *Joey/Joe*) sat next to a card with another name: Omar. I picked it up with two fingers, balancing myself against the wall as I stared at it. It was the same card from the year before (the ink was blue, the same color as most of the family's cards, which Zoila kept and reused year after year) and it had an oil stain on the corner from where he'd dripped mojito on it while spooning oil-slicked onions from the plastic tub onto his own plate.

I scanned the back windows of the house for my mom outside. Hadn't she told Zoila that Omar wouldn't be here this year? Did she just assume that our morning breakfast (which hadn't actually happened, of course, but which she didn't bother to ask me about after getting back from Ariel's) hadn't ended in the breakup I'd said was inevitable, that I'd hinted at over a month earlier? I spotted her sitting on a cooler, waving away an uncle who was threatening to reach between her legs to grab a beer. She clamped on to the cooler's side handles and screamed so hard she almost fell off of it. I checked the area around my mom's seat for a place setting for my dad: there wasn't one. I checked each of the fifty or so spots. None of them were for him. So my mom and Zoila *had* talked at some point; my mom had told Zoila my father wouldn't be coming, but she hadn't said a word about Omar. Or maybe she had, and what she'd said was, *Leave it there.*

I crushed the card with Omar's name in my hand and rushed through the open glass door, almost tripping over the metal guide rail on the floor. My mom had moved off the cooler and was now sitting on Zoila's lap. Zoila was pretending my mom was a baby, bouncing Mami on her thighs and trying to force my mom's head down to her chest.

—You think I'm a joke? Mami yelled.

—Mom, can I talk to you? I said.

—Come, come let me feed you like you're Ariel, Zoila said.

My mom wrestled her head away from Zoila's hands and jumped off her lap.

—That is *not* what I'm doing, she yelled to Zoila. We're *right* to be worried. What I don't understand is how *you're* not.

The week before I came home for Christmas, the lawyers for Ariel's Miami family officially requested that Ariel be granted political asylum, and from what I could tell, most of Miami was pretty certain—or was pretending to be certain—that he'd get it. He was, after all, Cuban, and he had, after all, reached land. People like Zoila saw it that plainly; they didn't think about the complications— that he hadn't made it to land unassisted, that he was a minor with a father back in Cuba who was now asking the UN to step in and get his kid back for him. My mom, along with dozens of others who saw themselves as *close* to the Hernandez family, saw all those complications and allowed them to keep her up at night.

—Ay chica please, Zoila said, flicking her wrist and splaying her fingers in the air. Stop your preaching already.

My mom growled, Maybe you need to be paying more attention.

Zoila leaned back, her fingers now hinged around the metal arms of her lawn chair.

—He's not going anywhere, Zoila said. He'll get asylum with or without all those tears for the cameras. So cálmate, *please*, que you're making a fool of yourself, like those why-too-kay people on the TV.

—¿Qué tu qué? an uncle's voice howled.

The circle of cousins and tíos around Zoila and my mom crashed into mean laughter, the men slapping their knees, some of them laughing so hard it made them cough. Zoila turned to Tony in the commotion and said, The only reason she gives a shit about ese niño is because she's lonely and has nothing better to do.

My mom kept her eyes on her cousin and said, You know, Zoila, go fuck yourself.

Tony lunged to the edge of his seat but Zoila, without breaking my mom's stare, flung out her arm and blocked him from getting up. He held himself on the chair's edge.

—No, come on Zoila, Mom said. Let your grandson come over here.

—Mami, I shouted this time.

She snapped her chin toward me, her face and neck red under her streaky foundation, some cream a shade too light on her skin.

—What do you want *now*, she barked at me.

As if I'd been asking her questions all night rather than hanging close to Leidy and fending off stupid questions myself. As if she wasn't about to get smacked after spending the whole night trying to convince her drunk and largely uninterested relatives to join her on New Year's Day at a rally in support of Ariel's political asylum request, one she'd told us about (instead of asking about my fake Omar meeting where one of us may very well have dumped the other) while we got dressed. The corners of the card with Omar's name dug into my palm. My jaw tightened and I felt my words come out through my teeth.

I said, I need to talk to you. *Now.*

One uncle said, Oooooh shit! And another said, Lourdes is getting beat tonight by *somebody*! He flapped his hand like he'd burned his fingers on something.

As my mom stepped over to me, Zoila said an exaggerated *Thank you*. Then, to Tony and the other family, Let's see how la profesora handles her.

Zoila lowered the barricade of her arm from Tony's chest, but they both seemed to be waiting for me to say something back. I knew she meant the profesora thing as an insult to my mom more than to me, but I was thrilled to have some sort of acknowledgment of what I was doing. It meant they knew. They knew what me going away signified but hadn't said anything because they just didn't know what to say. Then I remembered the woman from the airport shuttle on Thanksgiving, my imaginary profesora, how much I'd ended up hating her for her accidental insult. And maybe Zoila was implying something like that instead, that I gave off the stink of thinking I was better than everybody. But that was fine right then. I needed it. I smiled at Zoila, but my mom grabbed the top of my arm—her nails digging into the extra-white skin of my arm's underside—and pulled me away. Omar's name card almost fell from my hand.

She dragged me back into the house, where no one outside could hear us.

—Who do you think you are, talking to me like that in front of people?

I pried her hand from my arm and said, Nobody.

She jammed four fingers, hard, into the muscle right above my left breast and said, That's *right*. She pushed me back—the side of my head bumped against the edge of a shelf bolted into the wall. She said, Maybe you forgot that up there. Maybe it's time you remember better.

I leaned my head away from the shelf and took the card from my palm, smoothing it out in the space between our faces.

—I just want to know, I said, why this was on the table.

She didn't even have to look at it. She knew what I meant.

—So Zoila forgot to take out Omar. So what?

She went to grab it and I snatched it up higher.

—She forgot? I said. Or you told her to leave it there?

—Maybe you needed a reminder, to remember what's really important.

—*Omar?* Are you serious?

—You think you don't need anybody. Four months away and all of a sudden you're too good for him?

—You don't even know what's going on with us! You haven't asked me one fucking question since I've been back. About Omar or college or *anything*.

She grabbed both my shoulders and slammed me against the wall for good, pinned me there. If I'd turned my head to the left, I would've caught the edge of the shelf in my eye.

—I have to ask *you* questions now? I don't need to ask you shit.

She let go of me but stayed in my face. Even though I should've kept quiet, I squinted and hissed, Don't you want to know what happened this morning? Who I was *really* with while you were out distracting yourself?

Her hand swept up—for sure she was about to slap me, and I would've deserved it—but instead she went for my fist and tore Omar's name away.

—*Distracting* myself? You don't get to talk to me like that! You don't know shit about sacrifice. You don't know shit about shit!

—Zoila's right, you only care about Ariel because what else do you have going on?

She shoved me again and the room spun, the sangria sloshing in me, and I lunged forward to keep her in one spot, reaching for her shoulders, but she took a wide step away from me—she was letting me fall. So I reached back instead and caught myself, slid my hands against the sandpaper of the wall, pressed my spine against it and sank to the ground, my butt hitting the floor too fast and too hard.

—You can go to *whatever* college for as long as you want, but about some things, you'll always be fucking stupid, she said.

She tossed the paper at me on the floor and said, You think you have problems? You, your sister, your idiot tía out there? You *made* your problems.

She turned her back to me and walked out of the room, screaming as she left, Nobody has *any* idea what Ariel and Caridaylis are going through right this second, but I do. I know what it means to lose so much. None of you know shit because you haven't sacrificed shit for anyone. Selfish pigs, that's what you and your sister are.

—Mami, I yelled after her, but she exploded from the house, slamming the front door behind her.

The room's walls swirled around me along with her words—how could we be the selfish ones when she was the one spending all her free time away from us, fooling herself into believing she belonged somewhere else? I was making my own problems—with Omar, with school, too, in her mind—but she *wasn't?* I worried maybe the sangria was coming back for me, that I would throw it up right there on Zoila's floor. I sat still until the spinning stopped, then looked over to a wispy pile of dust and hair in the corner. The crumpled name card floated on top of it. The years that my dad hadn't shown up to Noche Buena, someone—Zoila or her first husband or even Leidy assigned to do it by some other tía—was quick to get rid of his place setting, to make the paper plate and the plastic fork and knife and napkin disappear, the rest of the seats shifting to absorb and erase his space. From my spot on the floor, I looked at Omar's seat, the foldout chair squatting in the same spot he'd sat last year, next to me. He'd been a smash hit: spoke the best Spanish he could muster to every old person, drank a ton and didn't show it, called every man *papo* or *papito* and sold it as sincere. He'd only made me cringe once, when he'd told one of my cousins that the rum he was pouring for him from my aunt's bar was *one-hundred-percent proof.* My cousin had said, *Sweet,* and taken two shots with him, but I still logged it as something that would help me make the decision to leave for college if I got in anywhere far enough away. This year, Omar's seat was still there, even though my dad's place at the table was gone; in Miami, coverage of Ariel's first Noche Buena in the United States—footage of his first lechón, him dancing, him meeting a big Cuban Santa Claus—trumped all things Y2K; I sat on the floor of my aunt's house, there because my mom was mad for too many reasons, the sangria thick in my throat, and I thought of the excuse Leidy had used for Roly the year before, how I could recycle it—*Omar just couldn't get off of work*—and I promised myself I'd tell everyone at the table that Omar was really sorry he couldn't make it. *He's real sorry, but next year?* I'd say, *Next year will be different.* I didn't understand what my mom had accused me of, but I thought I knew how to undo it, how to back-slide into something more recognizable.

While we ate, Mami sat as far from us as she could. Omar couldn't get off work, I kept slurring, even after Leidy kicked and kicked my shin under the table each time I forced out the excuse. Dante crawled around on the floor next to her, moving from cousin to cousin, begging to be lifted. I kicked Leidy back and said it anyway—Next year, you'll see—to Neyda, to people who'd been whispering about my mom's outburst, her door-slamming and her curses to her cousins: Watch, next year, I promised them, my mouth and fingers shiny with the grease of familiar food.

21

I CALLED OMAR THAT NIGHT. I waited until my head was clear, until Leidy and my mom were asleep. I used the kitchen phone, my back against the wall and my butt on the floor again, this time in my mom's apartment. I was ready to hear it from him too now, for him to chew me out for being a baby and a bitch and a bad girlfriend.

—I was wondering if you were gonna pull another Thanksgiving on me, Omar said almost right away, after sighing at hearing me say, It's me, it's El.

Despite what I'd thought up to that moment, it felt good to hear his voice, to hear him say he missed me. He'd just gotten home from his own family's party and was sweet instead of angry because he'd been drinking. But only a little, he said. We were flirty, joking around in a way we hadn't since we'd first confessed to liking each other. He told me some of our friends had called him to go out, telling him to let me know too, since no one had the apartment's new number, but that he was waiting on me to call him first.

—You're the one visiting, he said.

He admitted he did and didn't understand what was up with

me, but that he knew I was freaked out about school and the hearing results. *I know how you get*, he said—the same phrase my dad had used at breakfast to warn me about my mom.

—I thought maybe they'd given you the electric chair or something, he said. You never called me back. How bad was it?

I kept quiet. Only a few days had passed since my last exam, but it all felt so far behind me that I couldn't go back to it, not with his voice so close in my ear, with how easy it was to talk to him about anything else.

—It wasn't bad, I said. It was a big misunderstanding. It's fixed now, it's over.

I closed my eyes, praying he wouldn't ask for more because there was nothing else about it I could bring myself to say to him.

—So you don't have to come home?

—No, I said. Are you sad?

I meant it sarcastically, but he said, Yes and no. He said he'd been thinking a lot about me, about how I pushed him away whenever I got stressed, but that he figured we were meant to be, so neither of us had to work too hard.

—What we are is bigger than talking every night on the phone, El, he said, and every little hair on my arms stood straight up. Maybe I *was* making my own problems. When he asked if he could come over the next day, on Christmas, I twirled the phone cord around my finger and said, Why? You got a present for me?

—I do, he said. Got it a while ago.

I let the cord unravel back into place. I hadn't gotten him anything and said so.

—I didn't expect you to, he said. Your roommate what's-her-name made it sound like you'd moved into the library. Still though, a Rawlings T-shirt would've been nice.

He waited and said, It's not like you don't know my size.

I pulled my knees to my chest. A tiny plastic Christmas tree on the dinette table was the only sign in the apartment of what tomorrow was; my mom made us leave Zoila's before any presents were given out or the leftover food divvied up, so there were none of the annual post-Noche Buena trappings: foil-covered containers on the kitchen counter; hunks of flan in the fridge; gift boxes of cheap booze—matching tumbler included, a shiny bow the only attempt at wrapping—left on the floor by the couch. There were no cards from anyone either—the only ones we ever got being from our optometrist's and dentist's offices, from the public library I'd volunteered at one summer, people reminding us of some obligation—and I wondered if my mom had forgotten to update her address with these places.

—I'm sorry, I said. You know people asked about you at Noche Buena?

—Really? he said.

—Yeah. It was kinda bad tonight actually. My mom?

I struggled to think of how to work the entirety of my mom's behavior into one sentence, the way she'd shoved me then let me just drop, the march around the block she took before deciding to come back and eat, the way she'd pushed Leidy away when she asked my mom to hold Dante while Leidy served herself some food, how she'd acted like nothing had happened when she talked to Zoila or Tony or anyone else who'd messed with her about Ariel, but then the minute after she'd helped clear the plates—when the party traditionally *really* got started—she'd yanked Dante off the floor and told us to say bye to everyone while she strapped him into his car seat—We're getting out of here, she'd said, and not added another word the whole ride home.

While waiting for me to say something, Omar let out what sounded like a little burp or a sigh, then said, You there? So I abandoned any hope of nuance or complexity and just said, My mom is super pissed at me, I think. She's not talking to me.

—Uh-oh, he said.

His voice sounded like he was ready to hear the rest of a joke, and I knew it could turn into that, so I said instead, You know they set a place for you at the table?

—Ha! Why'd you tell them I was coming?

—No, I didn't. It just *existed*. It started this bad fight with my mom.

He shushed me. He said, Everything's cool now, we're talking again, El. It's cool.

—Okay, I said. I was sort of thankful he didn't want to hear it, because it meant I didn't have to think hard about anything for a little while.

—Listen, I said, come whenever you want tomorrow. No, wait. Come as early as you can.

He laughed and said, So you want me to come early, huh?

—Omar, god! You know what I mean. Just – just come over to-morrow.

—All right, he laughed.

I inspected my knees, the spikes of hair on them I needed to shave.

—Hey, I said. I should warn you I've gotten really, really fat since you last saw me.

—For real? I heard him shift the phone to his other ear. I didn't expect him to play along with my joke, but he said, Like how big are we talking?

—I probably gained two, three hundred pounds I'm guessing.

He whistled into the phone. He said, You're still fucking weird, El, but that's okay I guess.

After a second he said, I can't blame you for beefing up for the winter.

I laughed, and he said, But is it okay if I'm still ripped as hell? Because I am fucking *fine*. I'm still lifting like crazy and I am so fucking cut up these days it might be hard for you to keep your fat hands off me. That's okay, right?

I'd blocked out so much of our last night together before leav-ing for New York—the humiliating tow truck, the birth control I didn't mention because he'd assume it meant I was planning to cheat on him. But the good parts of that night—him sucking on the

spot where my shoulder met my neck, the lick of cool air that rushed
over the tips of my breasts just as he'd snatched off my bra—flared
in the quiet of that moment like headlights through the windows. I
thought of his chest and arms stretching the fabric of the Rawlings
shirt I hadn't bought him, of the way Jillian had gawked at the
very first picture of him I'd ever shown her, her mouth an open O.

—I guess that's fine, I said.

I spent a good hour after hanging up sitting in the living room and
promising myself I would not have sex with Omar, no matter how
good he looked, no matter what else I ended up doing with him
out of sheer horniness. I will not suck his dick and I will not have
sex with him, I told myself as I thrashed around on the living room
couch, hoping to work out my frustration in advance of seeing him
while Leidy and Dante and my mom slept in their rooms. I told
myself Omar could suck on any part of me he wanted, stick anything he wanted into me, so long as it wasn't his dick. As long as
his dick didn't make its way into any orifice, I'd be free and clear
to let our relationship dissolve. We could be what Jillian called
friends with benefits, except the one benefit she'd talked about—
sex—would be the only thing we *wouldn't* do. Because sex with Omar
meant too much: Omar was my first, and I was his second (though
he'd only done it with the first girl three times—she was older than
him, an aspiring dancer for the Miami Heat that he'd met at a club
the summer before we got together). Sex meant, for both of us, that
we were a serious couple destined for something together, and until I had my grades—until I knew for sure what my future at Rawlings would be—I didn't want that pressure back again. I vowed
not to let it happen.

But over the rest of my break, we ended up fucking like crazy.
Not because I couldn't control myself, but because of what happened Christmas morning. Omar came over and lifted each of us

off the ground when he hugged us and he talked easily with my mother—the first carefree conversation between her and anyone else I'd witnessed since I'd been home. He played on the floor with Dante for over an hour while my mom served him café con leche after café con leche and asked him questions about his Noche Buena, and when Leidy sank into the couch and started crying because Roly hadn't even called, Omar slid across the carpet and told her Roly was a sorry bastard who didn't know how lucky he was to have a kid like Dante and a girl like Leidy. My mother rushed over and squeezed his shoulders, kissed him on the top of his close-shaved head, and then sat next to me, putting her hand on my knee and squeezing that too, as if our fight the day before were over. I stayed in one spot that morning, my legs folded tight under me, while he just belonged there in a way that made me want to choke him, and so later, once I'd broken my promise and slept with him, there was no point in not fucking him every chance I got until I was drained of everything. The only thing that got rid of the hole I felt in my chest at my failure to keep the don't-sleep-with-him vow I'd made less than twenty-four hours earlier—a hole that opened up seconds after I'd pull him out of me after finishing myself—was fucking him again, so I kept at it, tried to make myself wait longer and longer to come, to stave off the worst part of it.

So just before the first time that break that I had sex with Omar, after the morning in our apartment when I'd watched him maneuver through my problems like they weren't even real, we said bye to my mom and got in his car—my present still a mystery—and he drove to the beach because I told him I hadn't seen it since the summer. He grabbed my hand at the first red light and put it on the gear shift with his. The whole time I just wanted to seize his crotch in my fist and squeeze it until he screamed. But I kept my hand under his and he drove and parked and we walked around in the cold sand and he took me to the deserted lifeguard tower where we'd first made out back when we were both in high school, and he made us sit down on its steps. He put his hand in his pocket and I thought he was adjusting his dick in his pants, but then he pulled out this little white box.

He said, Don't freak out.

He said, I'm not asking you to marry me tomorrow. This isn't the ring you'll have forever, so maybe you can trade it back to me when I get you the real one.

He said, I want you to know that I think we should get married someday. I want you to wear this up at school so those nerds don't get any ideas about stealing you from me.

He tugged the ring—a silver band with three little diamonds on it—from the velvet-lined slit holding it and stuck it on my hand.

He said, There.

I felt so frustrated I couldn't stand it anymore. I pushed him against the steps and shoved my tongue into his mouth—our first kiss since August—then straddled him and felt his dick against my underwear (I'd changed into a skirt before leaving the apartment—we both knew what that meant, though I pretended otherwise, forgetting when I can that I facilitated my own failure that day), and it was all me that did it, right there with the bright sun showing us to the world, me that broke the promise to myself as I pulled my underwear to one side and I slid him in and rocked on him, mean almost, like I was angry, like I was getting back at him: I pictured the steps digging into his spine and hurting him, doing it this new way with almost no love, just want and gnashing teeth and grunts and fuck yeses and his fingers clutching my ass trying to slow me down but no, thank fucking god, finally, there it was—my turn. When I finished, I rocked on him a little longer so that he'd come and not ask any questions, and then I pulled him out with the ringed hand, lifted myself off him and tucked myself into his side, his dick glossy and still hard as he pulled his T-shirt over it.

—Damn, El, he said. Do I need to ask if that's a yes?

He laughed at his own joke.

I didn't look at him—I couldn't yet. I looked at the ring. My almost-engagement ring. A ring that said, You're a good investment. It felt heavy on my finger.

But to anyone looking, I was still dressed, still put together enough to get up and walk away. I turned the ring on my hand and felt the sun on my face, my skin waking up and darkening in that light.

22

THE MAIL CAME EARLIER IN Little Havana than it did in Hia-leah. We'd been a late stop on our old route and were an early one now, so most mornings over break, a rip of booms jarred me awake, the row of metal bins downstairs in the foyer all getting slapped shut. The registrar's office had notified us that our grades wouldn't show up before Christmas, so only after the holiday did I obey the leaping reflex at the slams and charge down the stairs—shoeless and usually wearing a long T-shirt like a dress—the mailbox key shaking in my hands. When my grades weren't there, it was over: I had the rest of the day to forget they were en route, and I'd head upstairs newly exhausted. Mami and Leidy were already at work, so I usually got Omar to come over almost as soon as I got my tooth-brush out of my mouth and his ring back on my finger (I kept it off and hidden at home to avoid Mami and Leidy asking any ques-tions), and between having sex on the couch and/or the floor and/or my sofa bed (that last spot only if Dante was at daycare—I consid-ered it really bad luck to do anything with a baby in the same room), we argued about New Year's Eve. He wanted to call up friends—other couples we used to hang out with—and go to a club, do something huge, and I didn't want to commit to anything out of fear that my grades, once they arrived, would after everything be too low. I couldn't imagine getting dressed up and smearing makeup on my face, seeing people from high school and pretending to be happy about the future. So I lied and said I just wanted the night to be about me and him, together at the end of the millennium. I was shameless in my attempts to avoid going out—I even suggested we split the cost of a few hours at a hotel by the airport. He argued that going to a club did not prevent us from going to a hotel afterward. This argument led to more sex, which by then I recognized as the best way to keep us both distracted.

That pattern lasted until my grades showed up on Friday, on December thirty-first. The envelope sat crammed in the very back of the bin, bent as if the mailman had punched it down the metal tunnel. I pried it from the box's back wall and ran upstairs, my bare feet slapping the steps, turning the envelope over and over in my hands and thinking of how it was Leidy, not me, who'd spotted the faint pencil marks on the gifts from my dad a week earlier. What if neither of us had noticed the scrawled names and she'd opened mine, seen what my dad had written about her and Dante? I'd hid that envelope inside a shoe and tucked the shoe into the front pocket of my suitcase, zipping it shut. I planned to shove this new secret in there along with that one.

Back inside, I scrambled onto the couch, folded my legs under me, and pulled my long T-shirt over them. The refrigerator rumbled against the kitchen wall, but otherwise the room was quiet— it hit me that the reason I could open my grades right away and with no one around was because Leidy and my mom's jobs had them working a half day on New Year's Eve. Their jobs meant I was always the only one home when the mail came. I should've felt bad, or guilty, but as I peeled back the seal in the same way I had with the envelope from my dad, I only felt grateful to be alone.

The sharply folded page stayed shut against itself as I pulled it out. I tugged at its corners and rested the paper on my lap. I'd expected, I realized, some kind of paragraph, some kind of explanation with words. I'd expected to have to scan sentences and search out the grades: for this information, like everything else at Rawlings, to feel hidden from me but also somehow in plain sight. So I was surprised to see, on the left-hand side, a list of the courses that had defined the last four months, and across from each, lined up on the right margin and connected to the course title by a series of underscores like a line of stitches, the grade. The only A listed was attached to my PE course, and I'd been expecting it (in fact, I think I would've been the most surprised by anything other than an A in swimming). What I wasn't expecting was the column of B-minuses leading to that A.

A column of B-minuses: I ran my finger down the line to make sure I was seeing each one of them correctly. I held the paper up to my face, inspecting the curves of each letter just to be positive the Bs weren't smudges. There was no need to sort through the conditions surrounding my scholarship money or what courses I would or wouldn't be forced to take; the string of B-minuses meant none of that mattered. The grades in bio and chem meant that I'd done so well on the finals that I'd counteracted my earlier failing midterm exam grades, but the B-minus in my writing seminar meant both that I'd done well on the final paper and that my professor had shown mercy. I latched on to that last aspect—mercy—and instead of basking in the idea that these grades were a huge accomplishment, I sobbed: they'd all let me off easy. I remembered the tone of my hearing and thought, *They want to keep their Cuban above water for another semester.* They know how bad it would look, with so few of us even being admitted, or maybe they wanted to see how things with Ariel Hernandez turned out, and here I was, an authentic source of information (they knew my address, didn't they?). But almost as quickly, another fact pushed that feeling away: the exams in the chem, bio, and calc courses were graded blindly—we were assigned ID numbers, and only those appeared on our answer sheets. So those scores were, in a way, pure. And somewhere inside of me, I knew this meant I was smart enough to be a Rawlings student, that whatever question I—or anyone—had about whether or not I deserved to be there should've stopped existing for me in that instant. But that's not what I felt, sitting on the couch in basically my underwear, the bottoms of my feet black with dust from the stairwell, my stale breath wafting back at me from the paper. As I ran my tongue over my caked-on teeth, all I really felt was relief. I didn't feel like celebrating because I'd proven I was capable of doing the work at a high level; I barely registered that that's what I'd done. No, I felt like celebrating because my worrying about those grades—the dread lurking under the last month of my life—was over.

I sank into the couch and closed my eyes, mumbled *Thank you* to the ceiling. I considered calling my dad to brag before remembering the money—that he'd think I was calling for the extra fifty dollars. And what was there to say really, when for sure he'd see my B-minuses as weak grades. *You haven't gotten a B since middle school*, he'd say. How could I explain it to him, or to my sister or to Omar—*These grades are different*—without sounding like an asshole? I decided not to call anyone, to instead give myself a few more minutes of just me and those grades and what they meant, to register the new subtext, even if I couldn't name it for what it was: I can do this. I am, already, doing this.

When Omar eventually showed up at the apartment that morning, Styrofoam cup of coffee in one hand, a greasy bag of buttered Cuban bread in the other, and with a visible boner I worked to ignore tenting his silvery basketball shorts, I told him that my grades had shown up—All As and one B, I said, a kind of translation of my real grades into how they felt rather than what they were—and he declared that news, as I knew he would, reason to *really fucking celebrate.*

We settled on Ozone. Omar got us on the list (which only meant

he'd given his name and phone number to random people with clip-
boards standing outside other venues in the weeks leading up to
that night) at three different clubs, but Ozone, because it was essentially a huge tricked-out warehouse in downtown Miami, was
the one he felt most certain we'd get into before midnight. Leidy
had always owned better club clothes than me, and now she willingly let me borrow something from her side of the closet—a big
change from our typical fights over, say, a mesh or fringe-trimmed
shirt that she'd claim I'd *stink up with my armpits*, her standard ob-
jection to letting me use her club clothes. She pulled out a ridiculous magenta halter top; I initially mistook it for a bandana and
said, No I need a *shirt*. She unwrapped its straps, like tentacles, from
around the hanger and held it up to her own chest. There was a
big cutout shaped like a teardrop down the middle of it, presumably to show off some major cleavage. It didn't seem like enough
material to rein in Leidy's chest—not after Dante. Her fingers
worked the various tangles in the straps, then she tugged the halter into place over her T-shirt, revealing its snakeskin pattern: jag-
ged zigzags shining in a darker magenta. I'd never seen this shirt
before. She managed to corral her breasts into it, and even though
she sucked in her stomach, a roll of new fat popped out under the
shirt's bottom edge. She put her hands on her hips.

—What do you think of this? she said.

I leaned back on my hands. That, I said, is one hot fucking top.

She laughed and undid the knots after glimpsing herself in the
mirror.

—I bought this like a month after Dante was born. It's my goal
shirt.

Her breasts spilled back out and she was able to breathe normally again. She held the shirt between two fingers like a rag and
dropped it on my lap. Go for it, she said.

I passed on her recommendation of her slit-up-the-side go-to club
skirt—I imagined some strain of skanky Ozone bacteria lurking

on Omar's hands finding an easy way into my body; people were already referring to that club as Hoe-zone—and opted instead for a tight pair of black capri pants that sat very low on my hips.

Later, as she and Dante watched me in the bathroom mirror while I smeared on eye shadow, she said, You look so hot Omar's gonna freak out when he sees you.

—What*ever*, I laughed.

My mom yelled my name from the couch, where she was watching the news and also on the telephone with a neighbor, talking through the next day's Ariel Hernandez rally. Neither Leidy nor my mom had asked about my grades, but neither even knew they were coming. I yelled back, What? And without getting up or lowering the TV, she yelled, Omar llamó ahora mismo que he's on his way.

I yelled to the mirror, Okay!

—You want me to take a picture of you guys before you leave? Leidy said. Mami's camera has film, though who knows if she'll let me use it on you in that shirt.

A brush loaded with more silver-gray shadow hovered above my eyelid.

—Do I look way too slutty? Tell me the truth.

She zeroed in on my reflection and said, Lizet, you look amazing.

I never showed my stomach that much, but the halter top only made it down to halfway between my breasts and my belly button, so there was a lot of exposed skin. The parallel vertical dents visible along my torso—almost full-fledged abs—surprised me, and I was mad at my body for taking a semester's worth of stress and looking better for it, for rewarding the punishment I'd put it through over the last month with results I hadn't been shooting for. Being that thin—thin enough that my ribs stuck out—was the best evidence for how miserable I'd been. But that was over; I could stock up on calories flowing back into me via alcohol. I was ready

218 JENNINE CAPÓ CRUCET

to be me again, and this slutty-looking version was getting me there. I piled on the eye shadow, went back to the little pot to load up on more.

We took one picture, and when I look at it now, I can't believe it's me, which is why I still own it; it's proof I was that girl once, that we'd all stopped to celebrate her. It's also proof I was happy that day, still basking in the glow of my B-minuses. I'm smiling so hard all my teeth are visible—more snarl than smile. Omar's arm is slung around my waist, and his face—goofy, his grin lopsided—still registers the shock of seeing me dressed like that. Leidy snapped it, though by then my mom had hung up to say bye to us before we left for the club. Mami followed me post-picture back into our room, when I went to grab my ID, Omar's ring, and the credit card I'd opened that fall, the one I'd used to buy my Thanksgiving flight.

—Tengan cuidado tonight, okay? Mami said. Don't let Omar drink too much. People get crazy on New Year's.

—Don't worry, I said. We'll be careful.

—And be quiet when you come back, she said.

She tugged my shirt down in a useless attempt to cover more of my stomach, pinching my skin by accident. She said, I have to be up early tomorrow.

—For the rally? I said.

She nodded. This year will be hard, she said. People are starting to listen to his father, as if *he* should get any say.

—I'll be quiet, I said.

She bent her head down and rested her forehead on my collarbone and mumbled, I'm so worried, Lizet. I feel so, so tired, worrying about all this.

In her voice lived the same exhaustion I'd felt right after finals, the voice I'd used with anyone I spoke to between that last exam and getting on the airplane home. I put my nose in the part of her hair and breathed in the salty smell of her sweat, of food grease. It was the closest I'd physically been to her since she'd shoved me against the wall at Zoila's house—and before that, since she'd hugged me at the airport. I kissed that part, that clear in-between space, the wiry hairs of both sides like threads across my lips. I said, Maybe I can come with you? Tomorrow, I said. To the thing.

She raised her head and shrugged. Bueno, you'll be home late tonight but it's a free country. Do you *want* to come?

—I don't know, I said. Maybe I should.

—Don't do it for me, she snapped. Come because you want to, not because of *me*.

—Well I'd do it for both, I said, my voice too quiet after hers. For both reasons.

She wagged a finger in my face, No no no no. Think about what you want to do, but don't come for *me*. I don't want that.

I kept my eyes on the sofa bed as she shuffled away, her house sandals scuffing against the hallway floor.

We slipped back north to the go-to Hialeah liquor store where Omar could reliably use his brother's ID to buy a bottle of lime-flavored Bacardi and two already-cold cans of Sprite: we'd have to pregame once we got close to Ozone, he said. He'd called Chino (who had a new girlfriend I'd never met) and some of the other couples we went clubbing with a few times before I left that summer, but people's plans were set—had been for weeks in some cases. If we wanted to drink—and we did—we'd have to mix our own shit in a parking lot, Hialeah-style.

I took a shot right from the bottle after Omar handed it to me when he got back in the car, the warm alcohol singeing as I took two long glugs. He seemed impressed but then pulled over and said, Well I better lock that in the trunk now. Cops, Lizet. The bottle rolled around behind us as he drove through our old neighborhood toward the expressway.

—I was thinking we'd pass by my place real quick so you could say hi to my mom, since she hasn't seen you yet. But not the way you're going, he said.

He poked me in the stomach, said, And not with you looking like *that*.

I opened my can of Sprite, sipped it to wash away the rum's burn.

—Thanks, I said.

I crossed my arms over my belly, spun the ring with my thumb. His fingers curled around the inside of my thigh.

—You know I'm just playing, he said. Though you do have to come see my mom at some point or she's gonna think something's wrong with you too.

The skyline zoomed outside my window, and I felt the alcohol seep into my fingertips and calf muscles, felt my chest expanding underneath my skin. It must've been that tingling coupled with the city, that double dose of booze and what felt like every light in Miami showing off like a rainbow, that made me not register the *you too* until later, after we'd parked, chugged, paid, and made it through the line, past the velvet rope—the cans refilled with Bacardi tucked into my purse—onto the middle of the packed dance floor. The bass shattered inside my body, every joint and bone humming, and when it moved up from my heart into my brain, when I felt it bounce back to me off the arms and hips of strangers pressed around me, those little words—*you too*—lodged themselves in my mouth and had to come out.

I lashed my arms around Omar's shoulders and screamed into his ear, You *too*! Wait! Who's *too*!

—What? he yelled in my face.

I read the word more than heard it, the music screeching around us. I stood on my tiptoes and put my mouth on his ear, his diamond stud scratching my bottom lip, Your mom! What you said in the car! Who's the *too*! Who does she think something's wrong with!

He shook his head no, winced while he did it. I fake-pouted and put one hand on each side of the V of his collar, bunched up the ·

material and yelled—little fist pounds on his chest partnering up
with each word—Tell me now! Tell me now!

He looked up at the club's ceiling soaring high overhead, mirror-
paneled in places to multiply the strobes and colored lights freaking out around us. I watched his throat—he swallowed—as lights
danced over his neck, bounced off his new silver chain and flashed
into my eyes. Omar leaned forward, his whole face pressed against
the side of mine.

—Your mom, he screamed down at me.

He leaned away, made the universal symbol for crazy—pointer
finger looping by his temple—and then came back close and said,
Ariel Hernandez.

The DJ's voice boomed around the room, and I jerked my head
around, searching the mirrors above us, thinking for an instant that
God was yelling.

—We got thirty minutes left before Y2K, people! Make it count
in case we all fucking die at MIIIIIIIIIDNIIIIIIGHT!

The crowd cheered over his drawn-out vowels, everyone throwing up their hands as a siren blared at the same pitch as the song.

—Are you serious, I screamed at Omar.

He came closer because he couldn't hear me, but I put my hands
on his chest and pushed him away, then plowed through the churning mob toward what I thought were the bathrooms. It turned out
not to be the bathrooms at all, but a freaky black-lit and people-
stuffed hallway leading to a semi-hazardous stairwell that came out
at another dance area of the club, this one on the roof and playing
remixed Spanish music. Smokers congregated by a railing far from
the speakers that looked out over the back side of downtown, and
I headed there, grateful for the bites of cooler air prickling my arms
and shoulders.

—El! Omar eventually yelled from behind me, his hand clamping onto my arm. You can't just take off like that, there's a million
people here.

I whipped away from his grip.

—Leave me alone, I said. Why does your mom think that?

—You asked, okay? You can't be pissed at *me*.

—How's she more crazy than anybody else!

I paced around in the small square I'd claimed by the railing. I didn't know why people like my dad and Omar were freaking out over my mom acting and responding like a typical Cuban mother to this kid. Wasn't she *supposed* to do that? Weren't we supposed to be loud and cry when someone put a camera in front of us? Weren't we supposed to fight, to see ourselves in Ariel's face and fate, to act our part? I put my hands over my eyes and dragged them down, likely smearing my makeup the way Jillian always did when she was too drunk. I wiped my palms on my capri pants with a smack and said, Isn't *your* mom watching this Ariel shit?

—Of course she is, he said.

He seized the railing with both hands and hung back from it, looked out at the city.

—But your mom started saying some weird shit, he said. And on *TV.* My mom doesn't like what your mom's doing, how she plays shit up for the cameras.

—My mom fucking cares, okay? Maybe she's a little overzealous about it, but who fucking isn't right now?

—Overzealous, he said, buzzed enough to repeat the word spelling-bee style, to come that close to admitting he didn't know what it meant. And I was drunk enough to skip right over disappointment or frustration or surprise and say, It means like obsessed with something, like *hard-core* obsessed.

He shrugged off the lesson by putting his hands up and saying, Whatever you want to call it, but that sounds like one way to put it.

—Isn't that what we're supposed to be? These angry exiles? I mean (—and here I borrowed Ethan's "community building" air quotes, though I wasn't quoting anything—), the world is watching us! My roommate in fucking *New Jersey* is watching us!

—El, *what the fuck* are you *talking* about?

Colored beams flicked over our limbs, parts of us bright, other parts in the dark. A red light flared above Omar's head, but instead of making him glow the way Ethan did the night he learned my name, Omar's head was just a black hole, his face all in shadow. I closed my eyes. I didn't want to see myself anymore—I recognized it as exactly that, even at the beginning of it, when I couldn't name it: Lizet playing a part. I'd thought a shirt from Leidy's clubbing stash would cover me by not covering me, would turn me back into El, but I was separate from her now, aware I was putting her on, and that colored everything. Omar was grabbing my wrists to stop me from running away again.

—I want to go, I screamed. I want to go, I want to go now!

He yanked me to his chest and said through his teeth, *Stop, stop it.* My body slammed against his and I turned my face to the side, smearing lipstick on his shirt as I did it. That's when I saw our audience: people were watching us argue. Women much taller and thinner and tanner than me—women who looked like the TV version of Miami that wasn't me but that my shirt was striving for—tapped their grinding boyfriends with a long fingernail and then pointed that nail right at me. *Look at her*, the thrust of one's chin said. Another's forehead tipping my way: *Check out that crazy bitch.*

—What you looking at, you fucking hoe? I screamed at one, but she ignored me.

Omar turned me away from the dance floor, pinning my arms behind me in a hug.

—Have you seriously lost your mind? he said in my ear. I dropped like a hundred bucks to get us in here. You want to get us kicked out?

I said into his armpit, I don't care.

I swayed for a few seconds and said again, I want to go. I want to go already.

He wrapped his whole hand under my chin; I thought of Rafael, how he'd done the same thing despite barely knowing me.

—El, it's not even midnight.

—I don't care, I said.

I wrestled my face from his grip to flick my eyes over the crowd, but I couldn't find the woman I'd just yelled at. She'd been reabsorbed into the dance floor's anonymous mass—or maybe she hadn't been there at all. I looked back at Omar to find him scanning my face. He might've been saying something. His mouth dimmed as he peered into one eye, then the other, then back again: maybe I was closing them? The sky behind Omar and his face— both were dark enough. That I was closing them made enough sense. I lifted myself up on my toes, my legs stretching, and smashed my mouth against his.

He didn't push me off, or stop me to say I needed to drink some water, or ask me to control myself. Omar was lucky; he was still just one Omar—not broken like me, an El and a Liz trapped in one head. Omar didn't have to analyze what Omar would do. He just kissed me back, biting my bottom lip in a way that would later cause it to swell and crack. He lifted me off the ground, my arms still trapped behind me, and hoisted my body against his. But I didn't open my legs. I let them hang, making him carry the whole deadweight of El until he eased me back to the ground.

—Okay, he said. That's what you want, then let's go.

I squeezed his hand as he dragged me through the mess we'd just navigated. I let him be the shield that pushed between dancing couples and around the swarm eight people deep at the bar. There was, incredibly, a line to *leave* the club—they were stamping hands for reentry because Ozone would be open until nine the next morning—and I hid behind Omar then, too, breathing slowly and deeply through my nose the whole time, assuring myself that thirty minutes couldn't have disappeared so quickly: I would not be here, standing among strangers, when Y2K brought with it whatever was coming. I would not have on this shirt, these pants. They would be on the floor of Omar's car, probably, but that was closer to starting over. That was something I knew how to do.

But in his car, after he'd moved it to the darkest corner of the emptiest floor of the parking garage and we'd made the customary climb—Omar first, then me on top—to the backseat, I moved in all the familiar ways, but it wasn't working. I shut my eyes tighter, made myself louder, but I couldn't stop thinking about home. I wrapped my hand behind Omar's head and shoved it down— ignoring his annoyed *Ow!* because I didn't want to see his face— but that only put me right back in my room, with Mami's head on my collarbone, my nose nestled between the two halves of her hair. The parts of me normally up for the work of sex started to feel raw, and I panicked I wouldn't come, that this time would be the first where I couldn't use Omar to escape anything. Omar must have felt my hips lose their roll, my movements become more mechanical, because he smacked my ass and huffed into my ear, in a voice pained with want, I'm close, I'm close, try to come with me, I want you to come, too.

And that was it, what I needed to do: I would drink my weight in water when I got home, I'd gulp it down in the shower I'd make myself take, and I'd wake up with the sun and go with my mom to that fucking rally, to see for myself what she was like, who she was that scared everybody so much. I screamed with relief, finally, at the simple knowledge of it, of having put myself back together with that choice. It felt almost easy—like floating, like letting a wave bring you back up after it's broken over you.

23

I LET THE WATER POUND ME on the back for another half a minute before turning the clear plastic knob and grabbing my towel. I had ten minutes to get ready before Mami left with or without me, she said, and I was more wrecked than I thought I should be. I'd felt pretty sober by the time Omar dropped me off and, once inside the apartment, my vision started spinning only after I plopped onto the living room couch to sleep, a spot from which I'd be sure to hear my mom once she was up.

Dante was standing in his crib when I went back into our room, my towel around me like a dress, and since the sun was all the way up, I lifted him out and draped him across Leidy's chest. I yelled, Happy New Year, as he said bah bah bah bah and pounded his fist against her chin.

—Shit, she said. She rubbed her eyes but sat up on her elbow when she realized I was on the edge of the bed, my hand still on Dante's back to keep him in place on her. How was it, she murmured. How was Ozone?

—It was okay.

She pulled her pillow out from under her head and threw it on the floor.

—Okay? *Oh-kay?* Do you *not* understand I was stuck here with *this* guy all night? You gotta do better than okay, she said.

Her breath smelled weirdly sweet beneath the normal badness of any morning.

—I don't know, he's pretty cute, I said. I pressed my hand down on his back and wiggled him on top of her. He put out his arms and stiffened his legs, some kind of reflex, his body curving up like someone in free fall from an airplane. You've done worse, I said.

—True. Last New Year's I couldn't even drink. Was Ozone crowded?

I stood, clutching my towel at my chest, and said, It was. It was crazy. I'm going with Mom now but I'll tell you everything later if you want.

She pulled Dante to her side and sat up all the way.

—Going with Mami *where?* she whispered.

She motioned for me to shut the door. I picked up her pillow and tossed it to her as I did what she asked.

—To this thing down the street for Ariel. The New Year's Day rally thing.

—Are you joking? You can't go to that.

—Why not?

I grabbed my plainest white underwear from my suitcase, figuring today would be a no-Omar day, and slid it on under my towel. I turned my back to Leidy, let the towel drop to the floor, and wrestled on a bra.

—Because it's gonna get out of hand, she said.

—We've been before. Remember at Thanksgiving? When we saw Mom on TV and ran down there?

—Then was different, she said.

Our mom had ended that day by talking to the media about her two little girls and how they were just like Ariel, and we didn't

contradict her there, in front of the cameras, didn't identify ourselves as those two little girls. But on the walk back to the apartment, after the camera crews left, Leidy hissed into Mami's red,
blotchy face, *Mom!* You can't exaggerate like that! What were you
thinking?

I stared into the closet and said, I forgot to tell you, your shirt
was a hit last night.

—I know what you're doing, she said.

I thought she meant changing the subject, but she whispered,
You want to see it for yourself. You're not going for Ariel. You're
going for her, right? So you can say you saw it.

I flipped the hangers on my side of the closet, trying to hide my
surprise at Leidy understanding my motives so precisely. I said,
Either way, so what?

—I did the same thing, she said. Back before you got home. But
I didn't tell her I was going, I just went with Dante like ten minutes after she left.

I kept my back to her, but I said, And?

—*And?* She cries a lot and finds a microphone and tells a bunch
of stories to make those people like her.

I turned around, T-shirt in my hands, and she moved to the edge
of her bed, closer to me, bending forward and whispering.

—She told that Caridaylis girl that she was a single mom. She
straight-up stole my life story with Roly but made it hers and put it
in Cuba twenty years ago! She tells people we all three came on a
raft together. She tells people I almost fell out of the raft on the
second day, and you were a baby she was breast-feeding until her
milk turned to dust.

The shirt I'd snagged off the hanger fell from my hands. I couldn't
move.

—She really *says* that, Lizet. She goes (—and here my sister threw
her voice so that it was an octave higher but even quieter—), Hasta
que mi leche se hizo como polvo. It's freaking gross. It's like she's
Miss Dusty Tits on the news.

—How can she say that? I said. I sat down on the still-made sofa bed, my head pounding from my hangover. How come nobody's called her on it?

—I don't know! Maybe because no one knows us here? Maybe because she's made all these friends that are saying the same shit? *I'm* not gonna be the one to say something.

I almost said, *Maybe she thinks it's true now*, thinking of the way I'd morphed my idea of Omar up at Rawlings. Instead I said, Dad must've seen – what you're saying –

—You think he's seen her interviewed?

—He did, maybe, I said. He didn't tell me anything, the stuff you're – but he seemed worried. Omar's mom I think, too. But I didn't know why.

—Well now you know. It's probably Dusty Tits.

I picked the shirt off the floor and yanked it down over my head, over my torso.

—You're still going, Leidy said. You don't believe me?

—I do, I said. I just – why didn't you tell me this sooner?

—I'm supposed to leave a message about Dusty Tits with your roommate?

—You should've told me, Leidy.

She said, Whatever, and clutched Dante against her stomach like a teddy bear. He held absolutely still in response. I did and didn't think Mami capable of co-opting Leidy's story and making it her own to get into the good graces of the family—but mostly of the girl, Caridaylis—taking care of Ariel. Her version of our life made me more Cuban than I technically was, degrees of Cuban-ness being something I'd never thought about until Rawlings, until the Where Was I *From* From question. Mami's invented version made me a more authentic Cuban, and part of me wanted to hear her tell it. I wanted to see how she pulled it off, if she had to convince herself before she could convince anyone else, or if just saying something and having people believe it could make it real. I stood up and rummaged through the drawer for my shorts.

—Lizet, please, she said. Stay here. I don't even want to know what's gonna happen.

—Then I won't tell you. So you can see how it feels.

—Fine, she said. Please, like there was anything you could even do from up there.

She stood from the bed and slipped over to me, her arm slung under Dante's diapered butt.

—Don't tell her I followed her before, she said.

—You don't think she saw you?

—I know she didn't. You'll see why.

I pulled my legs through the shorts and slipped into my flip-flops, but Leidy grabbed the top of my arm with her free hand. She said, You should wear real shoes. At least listen to me for *that*.

She let go of my arm and swung Dante to her hip, saying as she left the room, Remember I tried to stop you.

When I followed her out into the living room a couple minutes later, her eyes darted to my feet, where she saw I'd switched into socks and sneakers. She closed her eyes and mouthed the words, *Thank god*.

—You should wear this, my mother said.

She tossed me a flap of white material: a shirt with too many words in too many fonts. And down low—the shirt was an extra large, presumably the size needed to get all that information on it—was a big square iron-on of Ariel's face, grainy and faded, his eyes closed and his hands folded by the side of his face. The shirt had a version of almost every Cuban-affiliated slogan I'd heard so far—CUBA SÍ, CASTRO NO; TO HELL WITH FIDEL—plus a new one: WE'LL REMEMBER IN NOVEMBER!!

—It's too big for me, I said.

—Just take it with you, Mami said. Wrap it around your waist or something.

—Take it, Leidy said before drinking a long sip of coffee, Dante straddling her knees with his back to the dining table. He leaned forward, used her breasts as pillows, put his whole hand in his mouth.

—Where did you even *get* this, I laughed.

Mami turned and started rinsing off her coffee mug, then my already-washed glass of water from the previous night.

Leidy cleared her throat and said, She made it, while slicing at the air across her neck with a flat hand. She's made a bunch of them, she added while shaking her head no.

—Oh, I said.

I turned the shirt around to see the back: a black-and-white photo of a smiling Ariel and the words ARIEL NO SE VA!

—It's good! I said. It's informative.

Leidy put her coffee cup down and slapped her hand to her face. From outside came loud voices, women passing by.

—We better go, Mami said into the sink. She turned around, wiping her hands with a dishcloth she then folded and returned to the counter. You ready? You sure?

I nodded, avoiding Leidy's stare, even when she coughed and Dante smacked her on the chest with both his hands after she started, turning the cough real if it wasn't already.

Even from two blocks away, the rally hummed with voices and music. As we got closer, I felt a false chill: the humidity was low, even for December, and it made the morning feel cold enough that I was thrown off by the absence of the cloud of my breath—the face fog that had marked my every outdoor moment at Rawlings since October. It freaked me out to feel cold but see nothing.

Despite the growing number of people ahead, most of the houses and apartment buildings we passed were dark and quiet, and I pictured all the hungover people behind the windows, still in bed, sheets pulled over their heads, greeting the new year with headaches stronger than the one hiding behind my eyes. As we walked, the clumps of posters and displays increased in density: chain-link fences showcased slogans on banners and photos of Ariel, all attached to the metal with curls of ribbon—the kind used to wrap presents. Some posters had fake flowers—roses, daisies—glued to their corners: others were heavy on glitter or puff paint. On one poster, a crooked row of American flag stickers separated the handwriting of a grown-up from the unsure print of a child, revealing the poster to be a family project. Tied up right next to that one, the work of another family: the words *Welcome Home* in tall bubble letters around a black-and-white photo of Ariel—the same photo on the shirt my mom made, which hung against my leg, threaded through a belt loop on my shorts. Someone had filled in Ariel's brown eyes with an inexplicable blue, the artist having taken liberties with his appearance. The bubble letters were painted in with two kinds of green—the first green marker apparently running out halfway through the *m* in *Welcome*, a lighter green finishing the job. Stickers—this time, foil stars like the kind elementary school teachers put on A-plus work—framed the photo in a wobbly box. I imagined an adult's hand wrapped around a child's wrist, guiding their sticker-tipped finger despite a *Let me do it* whine, the frame closing in around Ariel's face with each press. The handmade signs went on and on, up and down the block on both sides of the street, each one a kind of story. I was about to see into the next one when a voice I'd never heard before yelled my mom's name.

Mami stopped to let the woman hug her. The stranger floated inside another handmade T-shirt sporting a smaller shot of Ariel looking forlorn and the phrase BACK TO NO FUTURE? on it. She wore her brass-colored hair parted down the middle and hugging her face like brackets—a more processed-looking version of my mom's style. They pulled apart and kissed each other on the cheek, exchanging hearty Feliz Año Nuevo greetings as they both turned to walk straight into the thickening crowd.

When the woman noticed me following, she reached for my

shoulder and said Feliz Año Nuevo to me but with a leftover smile. She leaned in to kiss me on the cheek, and I froze: even though I'd been doing it my whole life, to kiss a stranger in greeting now felt very weird. It was the inverse of what I'd first felt at Rawlings when I met Jaquelin. As this woman pulled away from me, she began talking as if I'd just interrupted some conversation.

—Bueno *yo* no salí anoche, she said.

—Me neither, my mom said. Too dangerous.

—¡Ay, sí! she said. So many crazy people out for New Year's. I'll stay in my house to drink. No drunk drivers there. You see how many people they arrested? Four hundred DUIs! And that's on the Palmetto nadamás.

—Four hundred! my mom said.

The woman nodded, but I had a harder time believing that large a number.

—Are you sure it was just the Palmetto and not *all* the expressways in Miami? I said, my voice sounding dry, not ready to be awake. Four hundred's just – that's a lot.

She sucked her teeth and said, I heard it this morning! On the news! They said it like eighteen times!

—Hmmm, I said, nodding.

—Y dicen que ese negro – ¿como se llama? – Puff Daddy? He was at South Beach and his security people made them shut down the club and take away everyone's cameras.

What club? Who is *them*? I wanted to ask her these questions but started with: Where'd you hear that?

She opened her mouth and looked at me, then my mom, then said to her, What is she, the CIA?

This is when it would've made sense for my mom to introduce us, to say, *This is my daughter Lizet* (or better yet: *My daughter, Lizet, the one I told you about, the one away at college in New York, remember?*). That Mami hadn't told me who this woman was made me think I maybe wasn't really there, but it also made me feel like a regular,

like the woman and I already knew each other—of course we did!—
from all the previous rallies. That couldn't be true, but maybe she
knew *about* me—well enough that my mom didn't feel compelled
to refresh her memory. Maybe she was my mother's more preoc-
cupied version of Rafael: *You must be the smart one.* I waited for some
hint of this, needing to believe that Leidy was wrong just to keep
walking. I tried to believe this woman already knew who I was as
my mom laughed and said, Myra, you're too much.

Then Mami smiled at me, too, so I tried to remember if I'd met
Myra at Thanksgiving, passed her on our way back to the apartment or seen her lingering outside the building next door. Myra
screamed out some other woman's name and waved her over—
another Ariel T-shirt, this one with a huge Cuban flag, the star replaced by Ariel's face. The new woman rubbed her arms and bent
toward my mom, then Myra, then me, planting a kiss in the air by
my cheek, the third in the line of automatic greetings.

Mami had warned me not to come for her but for Ariel, and by
then I saw why: she was not my mom here. She was Lourdes
who made T-shirts, Lourdes who had friends I'd never met. She
laughed at something the new woman said—a big laugh, one
that seemed careful to match the ones around her. She reached
forward and tugged the edge of this woman's T-shirt to stretch it
out and said, Oh, I really like this one—sounding years younger
to me, a girl-voice almost, trying and hoping to fit in. Leidy's freak-
out must've been about this. She must've seen Mami against this
new backdrop and wondered, *Who the hell are you trying to be?* But I
recognized the rise in pitch as something else: the effort—the
strain—of being a new version of yourself, a strain I knew. I held
my spot by Mami in the little circle of talking women, convinced
they knew by then that this friend of theirs, their Lourdes, was my
mom—it never felt more obvious to me.

And as more and more people arrived, I felt how easy it must've
been for Mami, finally surrounded by something that seemed like
love—or at the very least a shared sense of purpose—because I felt

it too, standing in the street, the whole crowd shifting to allow cars to pass, each of us waving at the drivers. No one was hysterical: people laughed, found friends in the crowd, perked each other up by offering each other café in tiny plastic cups. The Ariel T-shirts, the flags—all of it was just a uniform that said, *I belong here.* I yanked my Ariel shirt from the belt loop and slipped it over my head, smoothing the wrinkles I'd made in it as best I could. It hung to my knees, so—bad as I knew it would look—I tucked the shirt into my shorts: I didn't want the news portraying me as the weirdo Cuban protester refusing to wear pants.

A man near the front of the crowd yelled that the house's screen door was opening, but it was clearly still closed. No one came out, and I waited for my mom—who'd craned her neck between her friends' heads to see Ariel's house—to turn back around. I waited for her to see me in the shirt and to smile, to recognize me. The door stayed closed—no sign of anything. I waited for her to see how the shirt hung on me, to see that I understood what she was doing. I tugged at the shirt, made sure its message was clear. I waited and I waited.

Once I saw him, live and real to me for the first time, I forgave my mom for never turning around: Ariel, perched high on his uncle's shoulders and waving—both arms up and bent at the elbows, his hands a blur—wearing a Santa hat and squinting into the sun. Or maybe the pained smile and almost-closed eyes were his reflex against the sudden wall of noise that hit him, that must've filled his bird chest to bursting. That first glimpse of Ariel: chubbier in the face than the pictures on all those T-shirts showed him to be, he was an elf, his ears glowing from the sunlight behind him. There was no way I could've heard his laugh, but I remember his laughter, the high notes of it spiking out over us. His skin radiated the joy of tans from playing outside, of having a ready line of people to push him on the swing. His uncle's hands gripped his knees, and it seemed to me this was not to keep him from falling, but to keep him from floating away.

I say all this because I felt in that moment the power he held and wielded by accident. He was more than a cute little boy. I had the very strong desire to carry him myself, to fold him into a little ball that fit in the circle of my arms. Hidden behind the pebbles of his baby-toothed grin, you sensed a loss so profound it made anyone want to hold him, to cradle and rock him and say you were so sorry, over and over again. For so many people there, he was a mirror, some version or idea of yourself, some Baby You, fresh off a boat or a plane and alone but still hopeful that what's been set into motion around you is just fine. I wanted to lift him to my face, to ask him what it felt like to go outside and see yourself staring back at you from the chests of so many strangers. I say all this because if it wasn't for me wanting to see my mom's face more than I wanted to see his, I could've stayed in that trance—happy to be among a tribe, each one of us tapping into the love the person beside us radiated toward Ariel—for as long as anyone. I say all this because I recognized then how things could get out of hand.

Someone knocked into me, pushed me forward, then another push, and suddenly I was pressed up against Myra's back (she'd let my mom, shorter than her, slide in front). Myra wasn't as easy to jostle as I was, and soon enough my face smashed up against the back of her T-shirt. She held her ground by trying to step backward— right onto my foot. She planted it on the outside of my sneaker, managing to find the one blister I had from walking in heels the night before—I hadn't even known it was there until water first hit it during that morning's shower. Now it sent a charge of pain over my foot. It hurt, but I was grateful for Leidy's advice to wear real shoes. People yelled in Spanish and English, all hoping to say the question that would catch the uncle's attention: Did you stay up until midnight to greet the new year? What have you heard from the government? Then I heard my mom's voice, just a few feet in front of me: Where is Caridaylis? How is she?

The government question won out over the others.

—We'll know more Tuesday, the uncle said as if we were one person, a friendly neighbor talking to another friendly neighbor, nothing at all weird about the mass of us hanging out in front of his house.

—We're talking to the lawyer all the time, he said.

He shook the boy's sneaker-clad foot and said, Ariel, you wanted to say something?

—Happy New Year, Ariel said, suddenly shy with his voice.

Many in the crowd said it back. I didn't: I'd slinked around Myra, favoring my non-blistered foot, to get a clear view of my mom's face. Mami didn't say it back, either.

Her mouth threw me off the most—lips bent in a practiced, forced smile showing more bottom teeth than top. She looked like she was holding her face for a photo, stale lines fanning away from her eyes, which ticked back and forth, searching somewhere behind Ariel. I'd expected some glow, one reflecting what Ariel gave off, what I'd seen in him, but she looked used to this moment, content but close to bored. But then, as all around me rose new cheers of welcome, my mom's face broke open, her mouth cracking the mask-smile and coming back to life with one that reached her ears, tears rimming and glossing over her eyes. She stood on her toes, lifted her chin to see over the crowd. I sometimes forgot that she was still young, still two years away from forty, the flicker of gray that might've winked from her hair by then hidden under the dye job and the chunky blond highlights. Leidy was almost a year old by the time Mami was my age; she was weeks away from learning she was pregnant with me. Happy New Year, my mom yelled, and she raised her hand to wave, a strong smooth arm: she looked too young to have daughters as old as us.

Close to my ear, someone yelled *Cari!* and lifted a bangle-clad wrist in greeting. So I understood before I even saw her that my mom's new face was for Caridaylis, the uncle's daughter who'd been assigned, more or less by default, to fill the role of Ariel's mother.

I'd never seen her in person either, but when I took in her pretty round face, her tan shoulders under the straps of a white tank top, I had to look away—up at Ariel, then into the sky, at the dark shadows bellying from the clouds. Because I almost recognized her. Because she was, to me—and I hate that I still haven't thought of a better yet equally accurate way to put it—painfully generic, the quintessential girl from Miami, a girl who could've gone to my high school and blended in so seamlessly I would've flipped past her picture in the yearbook without really registering it: with her small hoop earrings, the gold chain from all the photos still around her neck, her thick, straightened hair and her long bangs skirting her face, her arms reaching up behind her uncle to take Ariel from his shoulders and carry him herself. Her *regularness* struck me as tragic, because to the people surrounding me she'd never be regular again. Ariel made her special; everyone around me saw it that way. But I must've been broken somehow, because as Ariel climbed onto her, wrapping his legs around her waist and his arms around her neck and tucking his head into her shoulder, he *lost* whatever specialness I'd seen on him. He was now some kid being held by some girl from Miami. I listened harder to the crowd as they yelled *We love you* and said they were praying and lighting candles, but I couldn't get it back, couldn't see Ariel the way I had seconds before, because I couldn't give that feeling to *her.*

Caridaylis sent a little wave—four fingers folding down to meet her palm in a curl, three or four times—right at me, and my face felt hot. She'd caught me somehow, sensed that I saw through to her secret that she was a regular person, but my mom's hand flicked ahead of me, waving back. Caridaylis was waving to my mom—she even mouthed, *Hi Lourdes,* which killed my hope that maybe I was wrong about the wave—bequeathing for a second her specialness to my mother by singling her out. She knew my mother's name. How could that be true? I wanted to launch over the fence and shake her, ask her why: Why on earth do you know my mother's name? She rested the hand she'd waved on Ariel's head.

Mami finally remembered me then, grabbed my hand and pulled me to her, making me step on the toes of people crowding the short distance between us. She clenched the meat of my upper arm and said, Did you see that? There's something so special in her. God bless her, she is trying so hard.

She looked back at Caridaylis, probably hoping for another wave, but my hands balled into fists. My mom knew I was the first student from Hialeah Lakes to go to Rawlings even though she never acknowledged it. In the grand scheme of human achievement, I recognize this is not a big deal, but still, when I eventually showed Mami the acceptance letter and pointed out the handwritten note near the bottom stating I was the first, she'd said, Maybe you're just the first one who ever applied? And I wrote it off as exhaustion because she was, at that point, the new grandmother of a sleepless two-month-old baby, a woman whose husband had just left her.

—Mom, I said. It's not the first time someone's taken care of a kid. I mean, I get it, but it's not like what she's doing is actually that *hard*. She's – she's a glorified babysitter.

She released my arm, almost threw it back at me. Her now-shut mouth, the way she rolled her shoulders to push out her chest, the ugly flash of a tendon in her neck: I knew then this was the wrong thing to say. I didn't even really believe it, but I needed to say it to her. *I* was trying hard. What *I* was doing was fucking hard. My mom stared at me so long that her eyes seemed to shake in her head.

—What? I said. It's the truth.

—I'm waiting for you, she said, to take that back.

What Caridaylis was doing was hard, too, of course it was, but I couldn't understand that. What woman who I knew from home *wasn't* taking care of a kid?

—Why does that girl even know who you are? I said.

—Because I've been here from the beginning, Mami said. She's my friend.

—No she's not, I said. She's *not* your friend.

She grabbed my face, hard, squeezing her nails into my cheeks.

—You know what? she said. I look at you now and I don't even recognize you.

She let go of my face, said, You're a bad person.

I took a step away, knocked into the side of Myra. Mami dropped her arms and turned her face up again, back to the house, to Caridaylis.

—No I'm not.

I shook my head and snorted out half a laugh to show how little I cared, but it stung to breathe. If there'd been a way out, I would've charged down it away from her, but people blocked me in on all sides. I'm not a bad person, I said again.

For a few seconds I thought she hadn't heard me. But then she faced me finally, her face tight like she was going to cry.

—Only a bad person could say that about her.

—I don't really think – I just –

But I couldn't speak. I wanted her to give me the kind of attention she gave so easily to Caridaylis, someone she barely knew, a girl she wanted so much to count as her *friend*. I wanted us home, not at that rally. I wanted Ariel gone.

The closest I could get to that was to say, I'm sorry. I just wish none of this were happening.

I let myself cry. She watched me. Mami, I said, I just –

—I know, she said. She let her tears crest and glide down her face. She wiped mine with her thumb and said, Ay, Lizet, none of this should be happening.

I hiccupped more tears, and she stepped closer and put her head on my shoulder, the way she had the night before, when I'd left with Omar for the club.

—We shouldn't have to be fighting for this, she said. It shouldn't be so hard. I don't know, I don't know.

I put my hand on her back but regretted it right away. I didn't know if I should move it or hold it there. Myra came over and encircled us with her arms, shushing and saying, It's okay, it's fine.

We don't know anything yet. Save it for Tuesday, huh? Everything's gonna be fine. Just look.

She tucked her hand under my mom's chin and pointed her face toward Ariel, now off the girl's back and scampering around the front yard, the Santa hat—abandoned on the grass by his uncle's feet—replaced by a teal Florida Marlins batting helmet. When he reached the porch steps, he crawled over the door of some four-wheeled contraption: a Christmas present, the uncle said, from a local congressional representative. It looked like a beach buggy, complete with a fake roll cage and fake lights and everything, but was powered by him—by his feet, which stuck out of the thing's plastic shell at the bottom. He steered it around the yard, growling out driving noises as he trampled every single blade of grass.

The camera crews and reporters hovering at the fringes of Leidy's and Omar's warnings eventually materialized when Ariel's uncle stood on the highest porch step and gave a formal statement concerning the motion for Ariel's asylum made before Christmas. He said they had every reason to be very optimistic, that they looked forward to Tuesday. The reporters asked a few questions. Cameras clicked with each calm, measured answer. Mami waved, yelled *Amen* when other people did, but I witnessed none of the craziness Omar and Leidy had described, though Mami did seem sensitive, and people did step on my feet. I read my mom's admiration of Caridaylis—or as I saw it, her admiration of the attention people paid Caridaylis because of Ariel—as displaced jealousy. She'd never put it that way, but that's what *I* felt—jealous—at how lovingly she looked at that girl. Mostly I was disappointed in Leidy and Omar for not recognizing what was really going on with Mami: she was becoming her own person finally, trying to learn who that even was via a newfound passion. So maybe she'd retrofitted the circumstances of her life to fit in to her new surroundings. So what? I of all people couldn't fault my mom for having the wherewithal to adapt her behavior, for being a creature thrust into a new environment and doing perhaps exactly what it took to survive there. I admit this was a flimsy conclusion given the small sample size, given my now-obvious observation bias. But it's easy to stand on the fringes and mistake your distance for authority.

24

OF COURSE THERE WAS ANOTHER RALLY on Tuesday in anticipation of the court's decision, and of course I went, convinced that
going was really just a form of supporting my mom. We were up
front, having gotten there early to meet Myra and the others near
Ariel's fence. A crowd hundreds wide and ringed with camera crews
formed around us, and at the promised time late that afternoon,
Ariel's uncle came out, Caridaylis at his side. Ariel was nowhere
to be seen—not in the shadow of the house's screen door, not in
any window. Caridaylis looked as if she'd been up all night, her eyes
puffy and strained underneath new makeup. The lines around the
uncle's mouth seemed more pronounced. He had his arm around
her shoulders, Caridaylis small enough to be a child herself, fitting
snug against his side like a purse.

From their posture and somewhat bloated faces, the people nearest them—us—intuited that the news was bad. A few feet away
along the fence, a woman let out a moan. There was a collective
holding of breath as the uncle made his way, while guiding Caridaylis, to the spot from which Ariel had wished us a happy new
year. People around me muttered preemptive *Ay dios míos*, and

even my mom—so calm on the two-block walk there, so eager to greet her friends after work and to again not feel the need to intro-duce me to any of them—held her breath longer than was, to me, safe.

The uncle's exact words are hazy to me, partly because I knew as he spoke them that his statement would end up outlasting that moment, recorded by dozens of camera crews, reported by dozens of writers. There'd be a transcript, and someday, if I ever needed to look it up, I'd be able to find it. So I could lift those words from a document now, put them here as what I heard him say, but even though that's the fact of it, that wouldn't be the honest way to tell it, because all I remember hearing—his voice isolated from all other noise like Ariel's laughter on the first day of the year—was this: Our worst fear is here. Everything he said after this is lost to me because as he spoke, I looked over at my mother, who appeared to be melting. Her chin went toward the sky as she sank. I remem-ber, more than anything, her scream. A long *No* with a softness to the vowel that told me she meant it in Spanish, though of course it means the same thing no matter which accent surrounds it. The wail ripped through her body, then the crowd surrounding her, then me: a scream fit for TV, and I felt them rush in—the cameras—their zooms finding and catching her.

She struggled against the arms of Myra and her other friends—it looked like they were trying to hug her. I reached out to grab her shirt and pull her to me, my hand squeezing between the shoul-ders of the women surrounding her, but she pushed herself forward, her upper body hanging over Ariel's fence.

—So his mother died in vain, she screamed. She died for noth-ing! Nothing!

Someone yelled, ¡Señora, por favor! But from elsewhere came a barked, No! Then more pushing, and Myra and the rest of my mom's group began yelling, a ridge of sound rushing at Ariel's house.

The uncle had stopped speaking and was also crying—or as close to crying as he would allow, his face suddenly red and blustery, hands rubbing against his eyes in wide passes. He walked to the fence, began grabbing the hands of the people there suffering with him, sputtering and nodding at us. This move made my mom worse. She fell to her knees, her hands still grasping the fence. When the uncle got to her, she pushed herself up again and squeezed his hand, said, No please, no.

The uncle nodded, wrapped his other hand around their joined fists, then released her to keep moving along the line of people. She reached after him, touching his back, her fingers trailing down it as he eased away.

—He can't! Mami screamed. He can't go back! Don't let them take him!

Nothing she was yelling made any sense to me; I turned to Myra.

—Go back? I said.

I hadn't had any more contact with her since meeting her three days earlier, but she slapped the side of my head the way my dad did whenever I talked back to him or said something he found especially funny or stupid.

—Are you deaf? she said. INS says his father has custody. They have two weeks until Ariel is deported.

This didn't seem at all connected to the news we'd come to hear: the family had filed for political asylum on Ariel's behalf—custody wasn't part of any conversation I'd heard or seen on TV, not yet.

—Wait *what*? I yelled at Myra.

—They don't have the right! she said.

I thought she meant INS, which if they'd weighed in meant they probably *did* have the right, but what I learned later was that Myra was trying—in the whirlpool of crying and the new chant of ¡No se va!—to explain a legal technicality to me: Ariel's *U.S. family* didn't have the right to apply for asylum on his behalf in the first place. Only his legal guardian could do that, and so only his father, in Cuba and apparently staying in the capital as a guest of Fidel Castro, had the right to file the motion that his son be granted asylum. The paperwork everyone had spent the last few weeks talking about, which Tía Zoila had called bulletproof at Noche Buena, was all a waste of time.

Caridaylis stood alone, frozen to the spot where the uncle had left her. She was not looking at anyone, not even at the reporters snapping photos and spearing her with questions. She stared at the ground a few feet ahead of her. One reporter—sunglasses atop a perfect helmet of hair—yelled, Cari, what will you do now? What are you going to do now? I pushed closer to him, the crowd having turned more liquid in everyone's rush to find a neighbor and spread the horrible news, and as soon as my arm could reach it, I raised my palm and covered the lens of his station's camera, blocking his shot of Caridaylis. The cameraman was used to this, though, and quickly pressed something that raised the machine out of my reach. I looked back at Caridaylis just as she covered her face with her hands. She must've watched the concrete path leading back to the house through the spaces between her fingers, because she ran the length of it with her hands still shielding her.

At Cari's sudden exit, my mom a few feet behind me yelled, No no no no! I turned around but couldn't see her. She yelled, This can't happen! We're her voice! You hear me? We are her voice!

A few seconds later, Myra was at the fence diving after someone who'd just collapsed, yelling, Lourdes! Lourdes!

I yelled, Mom, and lowered my shoulder, used it as a wedge to move sideways through the mass of people flooding against the fence to chase Caridaylis with their words of support, throwing them at the house like rocks. I ducked down, making myself as small as I could, and through the spaces between torsos, I caught flashes of my mother near the ground, limbs trampling limbs, her arms flopping around Myra and another woman's neck as they struggled to lift her.

Myra fanned my mother's face, yelled, Help! Somebody help!

The other woman said, Lourdes, stand up, please! These people are gonna crush you!

She was maybe seven or eight feet away. From my ducked-down

place, I pressed against stomachs, squeezed my shoulders past the butt pockets of people's pants. An elbow flew back and crashed into my ear, sending a blast of pain so bright and loud that, as spots tracked across my vision, I thought I'd been punched on purpose, thought I'd never hear again. I fell from the searing of it, almost all the way to the ground, lurching forward, my hands stopping my fall when they landed on and clutched someone's sneakers—my mom's shoes, her ankles turned and rubbery at the ends of her legs.

—Mom! I yelled, but her head lolled forward like she'd decided right then to take a nap. I climbed her, used her knee and then her hip to pull myself upright, and I scrambled to my feet, pressing a hand to the new pulse at my ear the whole time. The pain was so bad that when I looked at my fingers, I was shocked not to see blood.

I grabbed my mom's face the way she'd grabbed mine the last time we found ourselves in front of this house with these people. I shook her whole head and yelled, Mami! Mami! Wake up! Say something!

Myra grabbed my wrist and flung it away.

—Stop that! she hissed. Her name is Lourdes.

I blinked at her, the whole side of my head burning hot; blood had to be pooling *somewhere* in my ear. Myra didn't know who I was, had no idea, and so I couldn't ignore it anymore: my mother had never talked about a version of her daughter that could be me.

—You're making it worse, she said. You're not helping, just get out of the way.

Myra and the other woman began pulling my mom's body in the direction of the street, leaving the fence behind and yelling, Get away get away, as they charged against people whose faces glowed as red as some of their shirts. They pushed past people clasped in hugs, people still turned toward the house and vowing, in the form of various slogans, to fight this, to stop this from happening, to do whatever it took to keep their new family together.

—I'm her daughter, I said to my mother's back as the others

dragged her away. Protestors filled in their wake. ¡Soy su hija! I'm
her daughter!

But they didn't hear me. They didn't know who I was, and as I
tried and failed to push through to them, they never even turned
around.

25

IN THE HANDFUL OF DAYS BEFORE I flew north for the spring semester, Ariel's uncle, at the urging of a team of Cuban-American lawyers working pro bono in response to the INS mandate that Ariel return to Cuba within two weeks of the day my mother collapsed in front of his house, sued for temporary custody. So he was not Ariel's legal guardian—then he would pursue becoming just that, his daughter Caridaylis dutifully at his side. While I was on the plane back to school (somewhere over Georgia would be my guess), this custodial status was approved as an emergency measure by a Miami court as legalities got sorted out. I imagined poor Omar—who'd driven me to the airport because, when he came over that morning to say goodbye, I'd shown him the note my mom left saying that she couldn't take me; she'd gone to the courthouse before I'd woken up—stuck in the Ariel-related traffic that no doubt plagued his drive home.

That court's decision, according to some experts, nullified the order that Ariel be deported by mid-January. According to other experts, this decision meant nothing because a federal agency had already implicitly decided otherwise. I heard these news bites secondhand from the bank of TVs near the school store's cash registers while in line to buy my spring books, or from the sets I passed on my way in or out of the student union—and not from our apartment's window or my mom's mouth. Although at some point I'd likely be required to take a government or history course like the one Jaquelin took in the fall that would explain the origins of these legal complications, I was far from anything close to that kind of understanding, and the truth was I didn't want it; this was going to be some long, legal nightmare, and I planned to stay as ignorant about it as possible in order to avoid becoming the Representative Cuban at Rawlings College. But escaping that fate became almost as big a challenge as getting Ariel's status in the United States settled.

That first week back on campus, many of the people in my dorm asked me my opinion—while I brushed my teeth, in line at the dining hall—and they thought something was wrong with me when I'd shrug and answer, I don't know. They said, How can you not *know*? I wanted to hate them for asking—to prop the ever-gracious and ever-accommodating Jaquelin in front of them as the better Rawlings Latino Ambassador—but it was hard to do that because they were right: I *did* live two blocks from Ariel, even if they didn't know that. Two days after we returned, my RA knocked on our door, and right in front of Jillian, said she'd gotten an e-mail from a woman in the Dean of Students office asking her to check in with me, to remind me of all the people willing and able to support me. Support me through what, I said. And Jillian answered for her: Through everything going on back home. *Nothing's* going on! I laughed. He's not my freaking brother, sorry to disappoint you. This outpouring had nothing to do with my mom's participation in the rallies: I was careful to keep those facts from everyone but especially from Jillian, who thought she was hearing some nonexistent code in Leidy's messages. But I might as well have been Caridaylis herself, the way people kept asking me what I thought. I feigned disinterest because I didn't want their assumptions proven right. It was only a coincidence that I knew and cared about the protests, not a consequence of being Cuban, and so I denied caring at all. I just want to study, I told the RA, told Jillian again and again. I just wanted to lose myself in the spectacular classes on my schedule— spectacular to me mostly because they were courses I'd chosen rather than those I would've been forced to take had my fall grades been lower. I was enrolled in the next round of biology, the next round of calc, and the Spanish II class I'd placed into during orientation week but which I'd left off my fall schedule, thinking I knew enough Spanish and not realizing I'd need to prove proficiency in a foreign language in a Rawlings-certified way. I sat out chemistry just so I could tell my advisor, who now sent me a perfunctory e-mail every couple weeks, that I'd learned something about *balance* the semester before. In its place, I signed up for the Monday morning section of a weekly lab course called Investigative Biology Laboratory: Best Practices, a sort of boot camp for people hoping to do laboratory research someday. I figured it would help me, in some vague way, build the equally vague community clinic I'd written about in my admissions essay. I still worried that someone would hold me to the claims I'd made in that document, and I wanted to show I was already on my way to making good on those promises.

The classroom for the lab wasn't a classroom at all: it looked like a bona fide laboratory, though I later learned it was a teaching lab, a sort of Fisher Price version of the real thing. Six rectangular black benches—three on each side of a central, square bench—stood in the middle of a room lined with shelves of glassware and industrial-looking vents. We were each assigned the right or left side of a bench as we walked in the first day. There were twelve of us, and while we would share the benches for ease of use when it came to large pieces of equipment or distributing supplies, we'd be working alone, and I felt weirdly relieved by that—by having total control over my own space.

Our professor, Dr. Kaufmann, was a biophysicist, internationally recognized as a leader in population ecology. I'd looked up each professor running a section of the lab once I was able to register, and I signed up for hers because she was, technically, the only immigrant: she was born in Germany but came to the United States for her Ph.D. and stuck around after falling in love with our beaches (her faculty Web page said exactly that). I realize this was a stretch—thinking of Dr. Kaufmann as an immigrant the way my parents were—but I saw my very presence at Rawlings as a kind of stretch, and besides, I was basically *from* the beach, and maybe she'd sense that somehow and see it as a positive.

Dr. Kaufmann was very tall—six-two or six-three—easily the tallest woman I'd ever seen in real life and the only born-in-Germany person I'd ever met. As she assigned us to our benches, I couldn't guess her age. She was already a fixture at Rawlings, but if I'd seen her on the street I would've guessed she was twenty-seven or twenty-eight—impossible considering her rank in the department, which implied enough time there to put her closer to forty at the youngest. Her eyes were small, hidden as if always squinting from a smile, and she gave the same smile to each of us as she told us where we'd be standing all semester (the only chair in the room was behind her bench). She'd been featured on the Rawlings Web site for her groundbreaking study on plankton populations, and I'd read her write-up of the project twice, enthralled by her findings but also a little envious that she got to spend her time researching questions so simultaneously complex and simple: How did these get here? What does that mean?

Dr. Kaufmann spent the first half of day one orienting us to both the lab (This is the eyewash station; this is the emergency shower; pray you never need to use either.) and to the project we'd work on all semester: isolating genes from one organism and learning how to express those genes in another. She showed us a series of slides illustrating the steps the project entailed.

—The project itself is not exactly the point, of course, she said when she reached the last slide. But it will expose you to much of the lab's equipment, and *that* is our aim.

She pointed up to the slide, which featured a single-celled bacterium.

—For our final organism, we typically use bacteria such as these, but there's a chance this term we'll use *C. elegans*, a type of tiny roundworm.

The guy at the other end of my bench yawned behind his hand. I didn't know what *C. elegans* looked like and so hoped, for exactly that reason, that's what we'd get. As if reading my mind, she said, It will depend on what we have on hand when we reach that week, but let us hope for roundworms.

She raised the lights and went on to review how to properly keep a lab notebook, which she described as a research scientist's single most important tool. I'd bought mine already, and it was thicker than any notebook I'd ever owned because every page was backed by a carbon copy sheet. She explained why: we would tear those out and submit them to her each week without surrendering the whole notebook.

—You will always be working, so you can never be without your lab notebook, not even to submit it for review.

As she listed them off, I wrote down each of her lab notebook guidelines as if they were tomorrow's winning lottery numbers: always begin with the date; don't skip any pages or leave space to go back later and add things—you should represent your work in the order it was actually performed; keep track of every single step and everything you use—an outsider should be able to replicate whatever you do just from reading your notebook; never, ever use pencil.

—Can anyone guess why? she said.

Knees and ankles cracked as people shifted in place instead of answering; we'd been standing for almost two hours. She held up a lab notebook, raised it to face level, and let the pages flip past us. Several entire sheets were crossed out.

—This is mine, she said. As you can see, it is messy and has lots of scratching out, lots of mistakes.

She put it back down on the table and patted it like a pet.

—This is good, she said. We never, ever use pencil because we never erase anything. You must keep the mistakes there. Mistakes are vital to every scientist's process. Just put a line through whatever you did incorrectly and keep going.

I wrote down this sentence and stared at it. It made perfect sense. The forgiveness built into this basic research philosophy—so simple and obvious—instantly validated my first semester in a way I could finally accept: everything led to this moment in this lab, the beginning of a new challenge of my own choosing. Put a line through it and keep going—I looked around to the other benches to see if anyone else registered the power of what she'd just said, but I was the only one taking notes, the only one nodding as my pen hovered over the page.

She eventually explained that even though we had a standing weekly class meeting, she expected us to be in the lab much more than just three hours. There'd be organisms to grow and feed, enzyme reactions to initiate and time and halt, gels to run.

—Whatever the lab requires of you, you must fulfill, she said. There are no weekends in a laboratory. As I say each term, a lab is not a restaurant. This kitchen never closes.

I laughed with her at the comparison, but everyone else met this remark with dismay.

She spent the second part of class showing us how to prepare stock solutions and explaining—with almost religious devotion— the fundamentals of sterile technique. She demonstrated the correct (and incorrect) ways of handling the petri dishes, flasks, and pipettes, the various solutions and their vessels. She told us to wash our hands, snap on some latex gloves, and familiarize ourselves with the tools and methods we'd be using daily, to practice as she demonstrated, and I headed to the sink before she'd finished her sentence.

—The laminar flow hood is your best friend, she began as she paced around the room, observing our tinkering. Then she said, Not really, this is an exaggeration.

I tried to keep my gloved hands steady through my silent laughter. No one but me seemed to think she was funny; the guy on the other end of my bench checked his watch, inspected each instrument but didn't try them out. I considered asking him if I could borrow his squirt bottle of ethanol when I'd almost used mine up. After maybe fifteen minutes of watching us transfer liquids between centrifuge tubes using the various pipette sizes, Dr. Kaufmann handed out our goggles, showing us the sterilization cabinets that would house them whenever they weren't protecting our eyes. She then gave each of us a lab coat, and when she called my name and held one out to me, I almost died.

—Contaminants are everywhere! she said as I took it from her hands, a smile passing between us. Once we were all properly goggled and coated, she said with clear pleasure, I will use the final hour today to assess your sterile technique. This is your first exam.

Murmurs rose from the other benches. The guy I shared mine with raised his hand but didn't wait to be called on.

—Professor, some of us didn't practice very much before because we were focused on listening when you were explaining stuff? You didn't say we'd be tested right now.

I'd practiced plenty (she told us to!) and thought, *What are you, pre-law?*

—Well, working in a lab is full of surprises, she said.

I wanted to high-five her before remembering that contaminants were everywhere.

Because of my last name, I'd be going tenth, but my nervousness decreased with each person ahead of me, as everyone screwed up some major element. Everyone plunged their pipette way too far into the sample on their first try; no one seemed to be considering their immersion angle at all; one person scratched his face then touched the lid of a petri dish. Dr. Kaufmann chirped *Contamination!*

every time she witnessed a mistake, and after saying it four times—all on just the first person to go up—people stopped jumping when the word broke the silence. But her point was clear: it was hard to keep your work area and samples sterile, and we all had much to learn.

When it was my turn, I glanced down at my notes right as the professor called my name and decided to start at the true beginning. I walked away from my bench, tied my hair back at the sink, then washed my hands as she'd demonstrated. It probably wasn't necessary—we weren't dealing with live materials yet, and no one else had backtracked to the ultimate step one—but it felt important to start fresh, to practice exactly what I'd need to do every time I worked in that room from that day forward.

I approached the flow hood and was sure to work in the middle back so that I wouldn't accidentally pull my hands out from the sterile area. The hood acted like blinders on a horse, and as I focused on maneuvering the pipette into and out of the plastic tips that needed to be changed and discarded between samples, I forgot that there were eleven other students watching me, that Dr. Kaufmann was a handful of centimeters from my left elbow. The gentle whoosh of the ventilation system covered their breathing and filled my head with a kind of neutral music. I'd thought, while watching others go up, that I'd have to control my hands—figure out a way to keep them from shaking—but as I dipped the pipette's tip into the last centrifuge tube, avoiding any contact whatsoever with its edge, I wasn't thinking about anything but the work in front of me, how every small step led to a desired result. My hands took care of themselves.

I backed away from the hood and disposed of my gloves.

—That was great, she said. That was really great.

Hearing her voice suddenly made me realize she had not said *Contamination!* once.

—What did she do that no one else did, she asked everyone else.

Someone behind me said, She washed her hands. Another voice said, Oh yeah.

She said the next person's name, and as they trudged over to the sink, she leaned over and said, That was very impressive, Lizet.

I know it was only the first step of thousands and that I wasn't doing anything like actual research, but to have Dr. Kaufmann—whose own research had kept me at a library computer hours longer than I'd intended as my brain turned her into a new kind of celebrity—say this to me just after having lost myself in the work might've changed my life. When class ended and we'd cleaned our stations and stored our lab coats and goggles, after distributing the pre-lab worksheets for the next class meeting, she said to the group, Your student IDs should be set up to open the door by the end of the day. I imagine most of you will need to come back and continue practicing.

She picked up her lab notebook and held it against her chest.

—Some of you will just *want* to. She looked directly at me and said, That is encouraged as well.

Before leaving, she reminded us she'd be available during office hours and via e-mail should we have any questions or concerns. The syllabus noted her office hours were later that afternoon, and as I packed up and zipped myself into my coat—I had to go to the library to get my spring work schedule—I convinced myself that it wouldn't be sucking up to visit and ask about her research, to tell her that the project described on her faculty Web page had drawn me to her particular section, to mention that I also loved the beach.

As I left my supervisor's office and tugged on my mittens, a shock of red hair dodged behind a wall of shelves. Without meaning to, I said, Ethan? His face poked out from behind the corner a few seconds later, as if he'd debated answering.

—Lizet! he said. Hey, I've been looking for you.

—Well that's not creepy.

—Oh I'm totally being creepy, I freely admit that.

We walked up to each other, and I thought he would hug me,

but he kept one hand on the strap of that intensely buttoned back-pack.

—I thought you worked Monday afternoons, he said.

—I do, I did, last semester. This semester is different.

I flapped my new schedule in my mittened hand. A guy inside the closest reading room turned and shushed us, making more noise than either of us so far.

—It's the first day of class, nerd! Ethan shouted at him. I choked on a laugh and he pointed to the library's front doors, whispering as we headed toward them, Have you had lunch yet?

I had just over an hour to kill until Dr. Kaufmann's office hours started, and I knew if I went to my room, I'd let the cold keep me from coming back out. So I was, in fact, planning to go get food just then.

—Perfect, he said. Carter House? It's the only decent place within walking distance.

—I'm not twenty-one, remember?

—I remember. But it's only twenty-one-and-over after five. They have great sandwiches.

—Wait, why were you looking for me?

—It's not a big deal, he said. I wanted to invite you to this thing I run for my hall, but also just, you know, say hey, see how your break went.

He swung the door open for me and we stepped into the cold—no snow but the threat of snow—and after I tried saying *It was fine* into the freezing wind whipping at our ears, we both ducked into our coats and walked downhill in silence, a reflex for people like us—people from places where it never got that cold.

The bar was old and smelled damp, the walls covered in wood, that wood covered in names scrawled on and carved into it. It was dark and warm and felt in some ways like an extension of campus, but there were older people there and a couple families, all eating the sandwiches Ethan had mentioned, baskets of free peanuts keeping each party company. We ordered at the bar—Ethan got a beer with too many words in its name—then grabbed a booth by the window, our coats sprawled out on our respective benches.

—So how was Miami?

I tugged off my mittens, instantly worried at his word choice— *Miami* instead of *home*—thinking maybe he was circling around to asking about Ariel Hernandez, that that's what this was actually about. How could I have fallen for his invitation, considering how many people had asked me *how I was holding up* along with the fact that he was an RA? I imagined the e-mail he probably got from the Dean's Office: *We are aware you've befriended the Cuban.* I put the mittens on the table and said, What's that supposed to mean?

—*Jesus*, he laughed. It means just what I said! Here, I'll show you how it's done.

He cleared his throat dramatically, then said, Seattle was great! It rained every day I was home. I spent New Year's on the couch with my mom. But I went on some great hikes, wrote ten songs about Mt. Rainier, high-fived an orca. It was *swell*!

He leaned across the table, dropped his eyes to my level.

—See? he said. Now *you* try.

I felt like hiding under the bench, but as he lifted his beer, I decided to play it off like a joke. I said, Got it, okay. Miami was great! I went to the beach every day and had breakfast every morning with the Miami Dolphins and went to fifty-five raves. It was super swell.

—That's better, he said. He reached over and grabbed one of the mittens, smacked my left hand with it.

—What's that though? he said. He reached for my hand, then pulled all but one of his fingers back and poked at my ring. I'd started wearing it at Rawlings in the hopes it would distract people from talking to me about Ariel and instead make them ask me what a ring like that was doing on my left hand.

—Nice bling, but I think you're wearing it in the wrong place. Unless you and the Miami Dolphins got engaged.

—We did, I said. I did. Sort of.

—You *sort of* got engaged?

I nodded and he pulled his hand away.

—To your boyfriend?

—Yeah, I said.

—Not to the Miami Dolphins?

I smiled down at the table.

—Just making sure, he said. He knocked his knuckles against the table's top a couple times. Wow, he said. *Wow.* Congrats, yeah? Does this mean you're leaving Rawlings?

—Why would I leave Rawlings?

He wrapped both hands around his pint glass.

—I don't know, he said. I guess, when people get married – I don't know.

I realized what he might've meant—maybe I was pregnant— and I laughed to cover up the awkwardness. He laughed, too, but looked through the window at the cold as he did it. I tried to think of something I could say to correct his assumption.

—You think I'm too young to get married?

—No, no, that's none of my business, he said. My mom almost got married when she was eighteen.

I imagined his mother holding on to one of those high school boyfriends a little longer than the rest of her college friends.

—Before she met your dad?

—No, *to* my dad. Didn't happen though. He managed to escape before I came along.

I didn't say anything. He started shredding his napkin into strips.

—I know he lives in Portland now, he said. And, obviously, I know he's a ginger. Probably. Seeing as I'm the only person in my family who looks like this.

He flung a napkin shard at me, then pointed to his head. This was not the life I'd constructed for Ethan, and before our conversation got any more serious and confusing for me, I decided to protect us both and rework the truth.

—God, I feel bad now. I was kidding, I said. I'm kidding!

I turned the ring on my finger, tugged it off, and put it on my other hand.

I said, My mom gave me this. For Christmas.

He let out a burst of a sigh, his cheeks filling and then deflating, then shoved his hands in his hair and pulled it back from his forehead.

—Wow, OK, he laughed. That was a good one.

He took a long sip of his beer, then dropped his voice, made it deeper when he said, Sorry to get so personal there. I hope that wasn't weird. I was ready to be very happy for you. I said congrats, didn't I?

Aside from the existence of Omar, Ethan knew nothing about my life back home, and what he thought he knew thanks to Jillian's mittens was wrong. I pressed my thumbnail into the table's soft wood and tried to get his impression of who I was closer to accurate.

—When my mom gave me this, she told me the three stones stood for her, my sister, and my nephew. I'm an aunt, I said. My mom and dad aren't together either.

—Oh, he said. Cool – about the aunt thing.

He set his beer down slowly, exactly on the condensation ring it had already made.

—A diamond ring for Christmas? he said. You must mean a lot to your mom.

The mittens—Jillian's mittens—were still on the table, and I realized I'd made things worse in that respect: now I was a Rawlings girl who wore hundred-dollar mittens ice skating and got diamond rings for Christmas. I didn't know how I'd fix this, but it wouldn't happen then. I just said yeah.

When our sandwiches arrived (they were, in fact, pretty good), Ethan told me about the hall program he moderated called Happy Hours, a standing study group with a simple premise: every hour of work you put in around the aggressively silent book-strewn table equaled one beer you bought yourself later at Carter House. He wanted me to know I'd be welcome to hang out anytime; he'd been waiting around the library to tell me that.

—I'm legally obligated to say that the school's endorsement of this program officially ends with the studying, *before* the tallying up of beers, he said. And while I fully understand you can't join us for the bar portion, he said as he wiped his mouth, that doesn't mean you won't get work done. I mean it when I say we're aggressively silent.

He took another long sip of his beer. Plus, you know, it'll get you out of the library sometimes.

Thanks to the ring, we didn't return to the subject of my break. We talked about our schedules, and I eventually went through a play-by-play reenactment of my day in the lab, including what Professor Kaufmann told me about my sterile technique being impressive. We cracked open free peanuts for dessert while I talked about her research, what I'd read online about her work, how she'd determined the effects of plankton on seawater viscosity. He said she sounded *killer*.

—It would be weird if I went to her office hours on the first day, right? I said.

I thought he'd tease me for being a suck-up—I was looking for excuses not to go now that it was almost time—but he said, Absolutely not, you should absolutely go. I said, I don't know, maybe next week is better, and then he stood up and said, No, now. You're going *now*, no excuses. He jumped from the booth, grabbed my coat and held it out for me.

—And come by Happy Hours, too, he said on the way to the bar's door. We start next week. Thursday and Sunday nights.

I tucked my hands into Jillian's stupid mittens and said, Maybe I will.

The walk uphill toward campus went much slower, but I made it to Professor Kaufmann's office, which was neat and organized but sparse—like wherever she really worked was somewhere else. When I knocked on her already-open door, she said my name and declared me her very first visitor of the new year. Just as I'd planned, I told her I'd grown up near the ocean and that I'd read about her research on her Web site. She said, Oh, *super!* and launched into a description of some mutant microscopic organism off the coast of some island I probably should've heard of. I was able to follow along at first, and every time I contributed something to the conversation, she said, Yeah, super! (*Super* would prove to be her very favorite adjective; she'd write *Super!* across the top of all but the first of my lab write-ups, and I heard her voice each time I read it—not the Miami *soup-er* I'd always known, but her version of it—her *zoo-pah!*) But within a few minutes of that first visit, I was looking around the room for family photos—for anything personal—to turn the conversation back toward something I could handle. There was nothing to latch on to except her enthusiasm, but that, along with Ethan's encouragement to visit her office that afternoon in the first place, turned out to be enough.

26

THE FIRST WINTER OF THE new millennium would be the cold-est to settle over the Rawlings campus in sixty years, and the first few feet of snow that would harden into the icy bedrock encasing us through April fell pretty much continuously over the weekend between the first and second week of classes. So you can under-stand why I was confused when Jillian came home Saturday night flecked in snow, and as she peeled off her layers, asked, Liz, what are you doing this summer?

—This *summer*? It's negative a million degrees outside. Must you torture me?

She separated her fleece from its waterproof layer and spread each over the backs of our chairs. I watched her from my bed, where I lay on my stomach.

—Seriously, she said, what are you thinking of doing this summer?

—I don't know. Go to the beach? Hang out with Omar?

—No, I mean for *work*, for, you know, experience.

—Why are you asking about this right now? Where've you been?

She went back to our door and retrieved her boots, placed them inside. She pulled off her hat and finger-combed her hair to bring it back to life.

—Because what you do the summer between your freshman and sophomore years pretty much goes on to determine your entire career.

—That can't be true, I said, but I wondered: *Is that true?*

—I was at an arch sing, she said. And yes it's true. And I saw that guy there.

—What guy? What's an arch sing?

—That guy, Ian, she said. Hold on a second, you don't know what an *arch sing* is? They only happen pretty much every Saturday *somewhere* on campus.

—Oh *wait*, I said.

There'd been a few times when I'd walked around and/or through groups of men singing in a semicircle while people stood around and watched. I always looked for a hat full of change or something being passed around, but never saw one: for some reason, these people were doing this for free, possibly even for fun. Jillian told me yes, these were the aforementioned arch sings. The group for which she'd just risked hypothermia was one called the All-Nighters.

—In this weather? I said. People stood outside for *singing*? Did anyone get frostbite? Wait, before, did you mean Ethan?

—People huddle together, Liz. Life does go on when it drops below fifty degrees. And yeah, sorry, Ethan. You should go to one sometime, it's kind of a thing here.

—*Ethan* was there? I said, almost adding, *That is so lame* before remembering she'd gone to watch, too. What does an arch sing have to do with a summer job? I said.

—I was talking with Tracy about it on the walk back here. She lined up an internship over winter break and now I'm freaking out that I waited too long.

—For real? We're supposed to figure that out *now*?

—I started looking over break, but haven't nailed anything down yet.

—Oh, I said, trying not to freak out along with her. I haven't started, if that makes you feel better.

—It *doesn't*. But seriously, you better start looking. Seniors and juniors usually start looking in the spring, and they've been in school longer and have more connections and stuff. We're at a disadvantage as rising sophomores, so we're supposed to start early.

—So then how do you even get internships? What are *you* doing?

—I just went to work with my dad a couple of days and met the other partners there. Anything you find is going to be unpaid. It's more about asking people, asking to just be around and get some experience.

I thought of the lab, of how I'd gone in every day that week despite the weather to work through the pre-lab exercises and to practice my sterile technique. I'd already begun growing the cultures we'd need for Monday's work, had made a few extra as backups. Professor Kaufmann came in while I was working one night after dinner, and since I was the only person around, she showed me the part of the stockroom reserved for upperclassman researchers, walking me through her inventory check and letting me tag along as she looked in on some tests of her own in a nearby lab.

—Is there stuff for people who want to maybe do science research? I asked Jillian. Maybe a summer job here on campus where I can keep working in a lab?

—I don't know, probably.

—How do I find out?

—You just ask people who know. You talk to people in your network.

She sat down and began pulling off her socks.

—My network, I said. My network is you, I'm asking you.

—Like for me, she said, a sock dangling from her hand, what I *really* want is this internship in entertainment law in the city that *might* happen through a friend of my mom's.

So there was my summer: an internship babysitting Ariel Hernandez, or, if that didn't work out, one ironing slogans onto T-shirts. Fuck, I thought, if this is how things worked, I was done before I'd even started and there was no hope of doing anything in a lab that summer. Jillian draped her socks over the heater.

—Probably I'll just get a job down in Miami, I told her.

—That makes sense, she said. She brought her boots over to the heater, tucked them underneath it to dry out. Can I ask you something? she said.

She came over and tapped my right hand.

—So this can't be an engagement ring, because that would be crazy, but you did have this on your *left* hand when you got back.

—Why would it be crazy? I said. My mom was seventeen when she got married.

—Your mom's your mom. You're here, you're you, it's nineteen-ninety – no, two thousand. It would be crazy.

—Cubans are different, I said, regretting it instantly. I mean, not all Cubans, but it wouldn't be that weird, is what I'm saying.

—My point is, since the day you got lunch with that guy, it's been on *this* hand.

She tapped the ring the way Ethan had, said, So what does *that* mean?

—Jillian, please. One, I have a boyfriend. And two, Ethan – he's *really* not for me.

—Do you only date Hispanic guys? No offense, I'm just wondering.

—No, I – for now, yeah, I guess. But that's not what I mean.

—It's not a big deal if you only like Hispanic guys. I prefer Italian guys.

—Why are we talking about this? Do you want me to tell Ethan you're interested?

—He's really tall, she said. I think he's cute.

—I don't, I said. He's *too* tall, too skinny.

—He's not *that* skinny. Though he did look like he was freezing tonight.

I don't know why, but I said it again: So you want me to hook you guys up?

—No, she said. He's a senior. What's the point? Besides, I met someone cool at the arch sing. He's actually *in* the All-Nighters.

I really did believe what I'd said about not feeling Ethan was for me—the skin on his throat, which I'd watched as he swallowed his beer, looked to me like the raw skin of a dead chicken, and feeling bad about that association was not the same as not having it in the first place—but as Jillian described this new guy she'd flirted with, all I felt was relief that she wasn't talking about Ethan anymore.

By Thursday of the second week of classes, I had enough homework to justify going to Ethan's Happy Hours without it seeming weird of me; I didn't want him thinking I was going just to hang out with him. Though maybe I was: I'd missed his joking around, and since he didn't know my new work schedule, I hadn't seen him even once at the library. That night, after checking on my specimens in the lab and wishing them good night the way Professor Kaufmann had to her own cell cultures, I went to Donald Hall. I got as far as the ground floor's glass-walled study lounge before spotting the back of Ethan's head. He was all alone in the big room, sitting at a huge conference table—a modern version of the one from my hearing.

—Is this not happening? I said.

He jolted at my voice and I laughed, but he didn't. He looked at his watch.

—Great. I was hoping you *wouldn't* come tonight.

I stopped just outside the room, remembering Thanksgiving and Leidy's *What the fuck are* you *doing here*, her inflection revealing something the way his just had.

—Nice to see you too, I said.

—No, I mean, this started ten minutes ago. I don't think anyone's coming.

I took off my coat and hauled my books from my bag to the table. I slapped down bio, slapped down Spanish. Don't worry, I said, I brought enough work.

—I wasn't trying – I didn't know it would be just us, he said.

—So this is like the Terror Squad of study groups? His face looked as if I'd hit the pause button on his brain, so I added, Terror Squad's just two guys, two rappers.

He nodded vigorously. Oh, right on. Like how the Silver Jews aren't actually Jewish.

I didn't know them or their music, but I played it off and said, They're not?

—Maybe one of the guys is Jewish.

He grabbed his pen and scrawled something on the back of his hand, digging deep into his skin, which flared up red around the marks. He said, Facts to look up later, and he clicked his pen shut, showing me his hand. It read, *Silver Jews = Jews?*

—We're learning already! I said.

—I *invited* other people, he said. His back curled over the table as he bent across it to stare at me on its opposite side. He said, During study week last term there were fifteen of us. Really.

I tried to sound skeptical with my *Sure*, but I believed him—felt a little left out, actually, at having not been invited back then, after ice skating, like I'd failed some test that day. I thought of Jillian's mittens, the way he'd skated away after seeing them.

—No really, he said. Maybe since we're only two weeks into the spring . . .

He tapped his pen against his book so fast I almost asked him if he was a drummer.

—Stop freaking out, I said. Maybe everyone decided you're a shitty study partner.

—Ouch, he said. And for that?

In comic slow motion, he turned his face to his book, kept his eyes trapped to it. I thought he'd been kidding about the *aggressive silence* he'd described at Carter House, but he didn't speak at all over the next half hour, not even once—not when I said his name, or when I asked him what language his book was in (he told me later: Japanese), not when I said, If your balls itch right now, stay quiet. (He covered his mouth at that but didn't make a sound.) Thirty minutes later, I'd only read half a page, distracted by the effort of thinking up ways to make him crack. Then his watched beeped, and he clapped his book shut and yelled, Coffee break, before leaving the lounge.

He came back with two cups of the worst coffee I'd ever tasted. When I took mine from him, he said, Who's a shitty study partner *now?*

He took a thick gulp. I held the mug he'd given me—chipped and clearly swiped from the dining hall—in my hands, blew over the coffee's surface to cool it down.

—So listen, he said. I know we joke around a lot, and that's great – like actually great, not sarcastic great – but I want to say outright that I really wasn't trying to get you here alone when I invited you.

—What? I said. I didn't think that. Should I have been thinking that?

I gripped the mug like it was keeping me from running away. I sipped some coffee, winced at the bitterness.

—I wouldn't do anything *that* creepy, and I just want that clear between us. I don't want you to have the wrong idea about me.

My fingertips and palms started to burn where they met the mug. Dark oil swirled over the surface of the coffee.

—No offense, I said, but this coffee is *bad.*

He sat back down and blew air from his mouth, the sound like a wave crashing.

—The thing is, he said, I can't afford good coffee with four years of loans sitting on my neck, so since starting here I've trained myself to ingest this garbage. I buy whatever's cheapest, I'm talking the brands they use at gas stations, then I just brew the shit out of it.

I fought the urge to ask him how exactly brewing the shit out of something could be an antidote to anything. I sipped a little more, burning my top lip and barely getting a second taste, and he smacked his lap with his hands and said, So yeah, sorry you're a victim of what might be my ultimate Rawlings sacrifice.

—I wasn't – it's fine, I said. I took a good swig to prove it, like drinking dirt. I said, It's not much worse than Cuban coffee.

I made myself swallow more, knowing what this was a chance to do—not just study, but to let him know I was more like him than I'd accidentally made him think, that we were both making sacrifices, even if my mom didn't see that in me. I forgave my fingers and put my mug down.

—I have to tell you something, I said.

—We're breaking up already? Then he said, Kidding.

He sank down into his chair, hiding his height.

—I don't want you to have the wrong idea about me either, I said. Those mittens? Those ones I had when we went skating. Those mittens aren't mine.

He looked into his own mug, swished it in a circle. Color rose up his neck in blotches, connecting the dots.

He took too long to say, I don't know what you're talking about.

I felt sorry for him, the way his skin was such a traitor, but right then I wished for something that good at giving me away.

—Yeah you do, I said.

I leaned forward and wrapped both my hands around the mug again.

—My roommate gave them to me, I said. I guess she sees me as her charity case.

He still wouldn't look at me, but I needed him to understand I was an ally, a member of the same band. I decided to admit it: I said, So the thing about being an RA next year?

He slid up in his chair, tall again, his eyes hooded by his pale eyebrows but finally meeting mine. He said, I get it, you don't have to –

—I *do* need it. I gave a breezy snort and said, Where do I sign up?

He shook his head.

—It's too late. The deadline passed. But knowing you, you knew that already.

I nodded because he was right: I'd looked it up the day I got back to campus.

—Thank you for – for letting me know that about you, he said.

He spun his drained mug between us.

—So that ring, it's not really from your mom, is it?

—No.

—Did your roommate give you that, too?

—No.

—So . . . you *are* engaged to the Miami Dolphins?

That he was still joking made me not want to admit it exactly. I worried that if I did, Ethan wouldn't keep doing this, wouldn't continue acting like he enjoyed my company. Saying I was engaged to Omar would turn the way we kept trying to make each other laugh into a problem—at least to me. And unlike the first time I admitted it, I now knew his mom almost married young; I didn't want him putting me in the same category as her, as my own mom. And Omar did say it wasn't my real ring, that he only meant it to keep other guys away: certainly Ethan didn't count as *other guys*. With a thousand miles between us, couldn't I afford to be vague? It's not like me and Omar were a list of procedures in a lab write-up.

—It's OK if you are, he said. Even if it *is* to the Dolphins. You're really engaged?

—Only to their mascot. To an actual dolphin. That's okay, right?

His tense laugh shot across the table. He said, That's fine with me. Dolphins are smarter than us. Besides, I could never compete with a *dolphin*.

I pulled my bio textbook closer to me. He was too smart, too witty.

—Good thing you aren't trying to, I said. Because you're graduating.

—*Exactly*, he said, pointing at me. That is exactly right.

We'd saved it, whatever it was; we'd given each other permission to keep going.

—Now drink your shitty coffee and don't talk to me for another thirty minutes, he said. Time to get strict. I haven't earned a single beer.

—My roommate saw you at an arch sing last Saturday, I said.

—God I hate those things. Get to work.

—Did they cover any hard rock hits?

—The bonds of friendship coerced my attendance, OK? Now stop distracting me.

—You're friends with someone in an *a capella group*? What would Pearl Jam say?

—Seriously, he said. I'll kick you out of the group.

—One guy is a group?

—Lizet, really. Don't try me.

He stopped talking. I watched to see if he would smile down at his book, but he didn't. We both got back to work.

—The Mountain Goats, he whispered to a page ten minutes later. *That's* just one guy.

As winter got colder and the semester went on—and with Omar's ring on my right hand instead of my left—I stayed ahead of my work in the lab thanks to the extra hours I put in. I visited Professor Kaufmann's office a few more times, too, though usually about stuff I read for my bio lecture or even for calculus: it was helpful to get her take on things like parametric equations or the Krebs cycle. Ethan's Happy Hours became part of my week the way another class would. Other people did materialize, and in time I became one of what the group called the Regulars, even without the after-work beers. Leidy's calls dropped down to once a week when she got tired of leaving messages with Jillian, but even the weekly calls felt stilted and tired—she was annoyed that I'd asked to schedule our calls for a standing time instead of her calling whenever she wanted or needed. Scheduling shit like a white girl, she said, but I knew she was just mad, that she'd get over it. It didn't matter that things were off between us: I saved my real worries for Omar, who I could call as late as one or two in the morning when I'd get back from lab, and who I made check on my mom and sister at regular intervals so that I could shrug off my guilt long enough to get lost in my work.

She get trampled in front of his house lately? I'd ask, making it seem like a joke though I dreaded what he might say. He'd laugh and answer, *Nah, she ain't doing that anymore.*

Good, I'd say, thankful—but more than anything relieved—that my mom's adventures on the streets of Little Havana were dying down now that the legal battle over Ariel was so stalled and convoluted it was no longer fun being involved. *Don't worry about her*, Omar said week after week, and as my first set of exams came up, I was grateful for the permission to scratch her off the list, to put her out of my mind by believing she'd given up.

27

WHILE WAITING TO HEAR HOW I'd done on those exams, I got an e-mail from Dr. Kaufmann. We weren't getting our grades back from her that way—that exam had been a lab practical, so we already had some sense of how we'd done—but my history with e-mails from professors was not good, and even though we talked in lab and during her office hours, she'd never e-mailed me before. My hands shook as I swerved the cursor to open it.

She wanted to meet with me outside of class; she had something she'd like to discuss one-on-one. The e-mail was written with the same troubling vagueness as the one I'd received months earlier from my writing seminar professor, but this was much worse: this was Dr. Kaufmann. This was a class required for my major. And this—whatever I'd done—would be strike two, and no matter how understanding the one woman at my hearing had seemed, there was only so much Rawlings would tolerate.

I scanned my mind for what this could be about. Had I left a supply closet or fridge unlocked? Had I open centrifuged one of the specimens she'd asked me to look at when it was supposed to be closed centrifuged? Had she glanced over my shoulder at my class notes and seen the list of embarrassing questions only I seemed to have and which I'd scribbled under the heading *Things to Look Up Later*? I'd been so careful around her so far, hoping to make up for all the times I raised my hand and revealed how little I knew, all the times she caught me pretty much fondling the equipment—the elegant pipettes, the test tube racks that kept everything snug and in place, the magical autoclave incinerating all evidence of use and making everything perfect over and over again. It could've been any or all of these things: she was so smart that I was certain she'd put these observations together and conclude, long before I figured it out, that though I was eager and good at keeping contamination at bay, I wasn't cut out for the hard sciences. I wrote her back, composing my e-mail in a word processing program first to make sure the green squiggly line of grammar impropriety didn't show up under every clause, and confirmed I could meet with her Monday at noon, right after class. She wrote back a cryptic, *That will be more than fine.*

The three hours of that week's lab class felt like a goodbye. I stacked each petri dish as if it were the last time I'd be allowed to handle those delicate circles of glass. I swished saline solution for longer than was needed, looked at the agar coating the bottom of plates as if its nutrients were intended for me and were about to be withheld. When a question popped into my head, I kept my hand down and didn't even bother to write it in my notebook.

I watched Professor Kaufmann for clues all class but saw nothing, though she'd already proven herself good at masking frustration with kindness. You could drop an entire tray of beakers, and she would smile and in a too-high voice say, *That's OK!* I sometimes thought I was the only one in the class who saw through her, could tell how very upset she was at all that shattered glass on the floor: I knew it from the way she'd say *Hmmm* as she accosted the student culprit with a broom and stood over them, pointing out a missed shard here, a tiny speck there. She'd wait until they put the broom away before noticing another piece, then instruct them to go back to the closet and bring the broom again.

I approached her lab bench once everyone had left. She was scribbling something on some graph paper, and I glanced at what she wrote once I was closer. Whatever it was, it was in German— probably not a good sign—and it was underneath a series of equations that meant nothing to me and which were in no way related to our class.

—Liz! she said. Oh, super! Come here, please!

She stood and let me have her seat. I sat there for a good minute, watched her keep working as if she hadn't just asked me to sit down. Her pen dug into the paper and I wondered if she had two brains—wondered if there were a way I could split my own mind like that, be in one place but let my mind hang out wherever it wanted.

She slapped the pen down on her notebook, and without even apologizing for the awkward three or so minutes we'd been right next to each other but not speaking, she said, Thank you for staying after class. I see you're eager to know what this is about.

—Yes, I said. I tried to keep my back straight; I found trying to maintain good posture more painful than just slouching. Even seated on her high stool, I was still looking up at her. I said, Is everything okay?

—Yes, of course. Thank you for asking.

I figured then that I should stop talking lest I incriminate myself, but she smiled at me and nodded as if I'd kept speaking, as if I was saying something at that very moment.

—Yes, so, she said. You are enjoying the lab so far?

—I love it, I blurted out. It's my favorite class this semester.

—Super! she said. That's super.

She nodded some more. After a few additional seconds of painful silence and sustained eye contact she asked, Are you interested in becoming a research scientist?

I thought I wanted to be a doctor, but that didn't seem like the right answer.

—Yes, I said. I am.

—Good, super. Because there is something you should do then, a program.

She slipped a hand beneath her pad of graph paper and slid out a glossy folder. I closed my eyes, not wanting to look at it: here it was, the remedial program for students needing extra help, forced in front of me like that list of campus resources I'd printed out last semester as my only hope. The folder was white with a crimson stripe down the front of it, a gold logo embossed at its center.

—This is connected to my research group. It's a summer position at our field laboratory off the coast of Santa Barbara, in California. You would be perfect for it.

—A summer position? Like an internship?

—Yes, yes. You are perfect for it. I would like you to apply. I will nominate you.

She said this louder, as if the problem were not that I didn't believe her, but that I couldn't hear her.

—But it's your lab, you run it?

—Weeeeell, she said. She laughed in a sweet way. I do run it, yes, she said. So perhaps let's say you have a very strong chance of getting it since I'm nominating you and I also choose the students. You *do* have to apply, technically, but there is always a Rawlings student. Each year I bring the strongest freshman from among the various lab sections.

—Oh, I said.

I couldn't believe she meant me, that I'd been doing that well. My write-ups were getting good scores, but they were twice as long as anyone else's for all the missteps and questions they contained. I put my hand on the folder and pulled it toward me by the corner. I said, So is this for like minority students or something?

—No, it's for my lab in California, she said. I'm sorry if I'm not being clear. Your work in class is fantastic. I think you will be great. You should do it!

She put her hand at the top of the folder and pushed it all the way to me. She then clasped her hands together, dropped them into her lap, and said, Please open it!

I jumped at her voice, then did as she said. In the center prongs were creamy-feeling pages that explained the lab, the experience I would get, the projects I'd contribute to, and near the end, a page explaining the scholarship money for housing and the travel subsidies and something called a stipend. I figured out quickly, thanks to the numbers being stacked on top of each other like in my Rawlings bill, that a stipend meant I'd get paid to be there. I wanted to grab the folder and run to the dorm, show it to Jillian and ask if it was real. The experience alone was worth it: I would've gone for free—no, I would've taken out another loan to go all the way to California and work in a real lab, a for-real lab run by Professor Kaufmann. I was taking out bigger loans for less interesting experiences. I flipped back to the pages describing the projects, recognizing in some of them the language from Professor Kaufmann's faculty Web page. She'd singled me out to be part of her research, part of her network. I turned past those pages before looking too eager and embarrassing myself.

Tucked inside the folder's back pocket was the application. It asked for a short essay about why I was interested in the program and how I came to find out about it (though small, the program was open to applicants all over the country). It asked for a list of past research experiences and other extracurricular activities (freshmen were allowed to list activities from their senior year of high school, which made me feel much better) and a short explanation about how each extracurricular had *furthered or enhanced my interest in research*. It asked for a reference letter and the contact information for your reference—Professor Kaufmann had already signed this form and written, on a Post-it note pressed to the top right corner, *Lizet: Don't worry about this page*. It asked for a copy of a graded lab write-up. It asked for a transcript, for my grades.

Despite being proud of my B-minuses because I understood what lived behind them, I was fully aware they were not great grades by Rawlings standards. Professor Kaufmann had no idea that my GPA was below a 3.0. My work in her class—I was sure of this because it was my goal—reflected the grades I wanted, not the ones my past mistakes had shaped: put a line through it and keep going. I pulled out the checklist of the application's required parts from the folder. My hands shuddered as I held it, so I let it drop to the bench, only pointed, for a second, at the line that said *Official Transcript*.

—I think my grades –

I felt something sharp rise in my throat. I wanted so badly not to confess this to her, to preserve her idea of me being fantastic in lab. I swallowed, but it didn't go away.

—You get that from the registrar. Official only means it is sealed in an envelope.

—It's not that.

I pointed to the line again, then put my hands in my lap. I breathed in through my nose, willing my voice to come out at its natural pitch. Then I said something I'd never said before.

—My grades are not very good.

She blinked, the half smile never leaving her face.

—Oh, I'm sure they are more than fine.

The same phrase from her e-mail, the one that had made me worry. Her English was always perfect, but as I searched for reasons why she wouldn't understand me, for why she was making me admit my incompetence again, I let language be one of them. I closed the folder but left it where it was on the bench.

She asked, What's your GPA?

So I told her.

—Oh, she said. Then her smile came back, her spine straightened. But what is it in your *science and math* courses?

I could almost hear her rationale floating from her brain to mine: she'd defaulted to Occam's razor—all other things being equal, go with the simplest solution—so of course the problem was some wayward grade in an English or history course. *Those pesky humanities! That must be it!* Many a fantastic biologist had been foiled by a required literature course.

—The same, I said. It's the same.

She blew air from the side of her mouth. It billowed through her bangs.

—Well that doesn't make any sense, she said. Your grades should be higher.

I winced. They should, I said.

She turned to her pad, scribbled something down. When I sat up straighter to see it, it read *3.5 min a must?* She kept the pen in her hand and, as if it were a problem thrown to the class that she'd already solved but wanted us to puzzle out, asked, So why are they that low?

My hands sat curled in my lap. I thought of blaming Ariel Hernandez. I knew I could formulate a version of things where it really *was* his fault, and using him would make the grades seem more like a triumph than a mediocre showing. If other people could use him, why couldn't I? And maybe it was true: maybe I knew he was on his way over, could feel or hear, because of the salt water in my blood, his mother making plans from across the Florida Straits. The daughter of the president of Thailand was a student at Rawlings—surely she had big things on her mind, and surely those things got in her way of studying for an exam, and surely she got a pass here and there for it. For the past six weeks, I'd worked hard at being *less* Cuban, at trying to pass as anything *but* Cuban. I'd refused to be an ambassador, but to get this internship, maybe an ambassador was what I needed to be: I needed to play it up to explain away the grades. I could say I was the daughter of someone important and legitimately connected to the whole affair—a judge, a congressman. I could even play along with my mom, claim Caridaylis as a sister. I had to try; Jillian had just landed her dream summer in entertainment law through her mom's friend. It was my turn to hustle.

—There were some things. Going on back at home, I said.

She didn't budge, just sat there staring at me, holding her pen.

—There's this boy, I said.

I couldn't face her as I lied. I focused on the thumbnails I'd obliterated with my teeth, a habit I shared with Leidy and one I couldn't control, as it happened while I read and studied: I was in no way conscious of it. I'd drawn blood from the right thumb the day before, and that had stopped me—the sudden taste of iron.

I closed my eyes. I shook my head no—let her think what she wanted to think, but I couldn't say it. I couldn't pin the bad grades on Ariel any more than I could explain to her why I didn't think of them as bad grades.

—Oh, it's OK! she said, too loudly. You know, things happen, with boys.

I wiped my eyes with the heel of my hand before raising my face. She looked around the room, searching for an escape.

—But you must not be together anymore, correct?

She nodded, leaned forward as if to make me nod, too.

—This semester? she said. Because you're better now. Your work. No distractions, no boyfriend, so now everything's better.

I must've looked as stunned as I felt, because she said, Oh, I didn't mean – don't worry! There are more fish in the sea! Perhaps you don't even need a fish!

I laughed, not knowing what else to do, and she watched me laugh and joined in a second later, one moment past natural. I raised my shoulders, then let them fall.

—So you have no reason to say no, she said.

—But my grades –

—It's fine, she said. She crossed out the note she'd written. Just remain focused this semester. You're doing super so far. Everything will be better. There is no boy?

—There's no boy, I assured her.

She took the folder from the bench, held it out to me. I took it from her slowly to hide the true electric thrill running down my arms and legs at what her handing it to me really meant. I said thank you. I told her I'd let her know soon, after I talked with my parents, but that I couldn't imagine anything I'd want to do more.

Returning to my dorm room that afternoon—the folder in my bag, slapping against my back with every step—I whispered my half of a theoretical conversation into the evening air, the mist of my breath taking the place of any answers. I couldn't really afford a flight down for spring break, or maybe for Easter, to talk to my parents in person about the internship offer, but I also couldn't imagine asking over the phone: the phone would make it harder to explain that they could trust this kind of program, that it wasn't a scam or a trap or a disguise for a prostitution ring. This sort of mistrust, which had come up with my financial aid, only got worse with every document I'd signed and mailed back. They'd drawn the line at my social security card: my dad forbade me from mailing a copy of it and instead made me call to see if I could just bring one to the registrar's office during orientation (the registrar said that would be too late, and so I managed to get copies sent through a high school guidance counselor). But at least my parents had been in the same physical space when I'd had to argue for something—I didn't have to make all my points twice, because we all still lived in the same house. I shoved my ungloved hands deeper into my pockets and kept moving, wiggling my fingers to keep them warm.

It would make more sense if what happened a day later had happened right away instead, but the truth is I had all afternoon and the whole night to let it sink in, to fret and fantasize about my summer in the faraway fantasyland of California. I showed the folder to Jillian when I got to our room, and after saying *No fucking way!* to every page—the loudest one coming when she saw the stipend—she congratulated me before grabbing her toothbrush and putting it in her book bag; she wanted to have it with her, she said, in case she ended up *pulling another all-nighter with an All-Nighter*, a joke we'd said so many times it had lost all its humor then circled back and regained it. She left for her afternoon class, and I sat in my chair, debating which parent to call first.

I couldn't make myself pick up the phone though. I wanted to call Jillian's parents. Her parents—*her* parents—would know what to say if she called with news like this. *Oh my god, honey! That's fantastic! When does it start? Maybe we can come out at the end and make a vacation out of it. Oh, sweetheart, what an opportunity! We're thrilled for you, so thrilled.* . . . It was a good thing, a happy thing, something that meant their daughter was performing at a very high level. Jillian would never have to convince them of that. They recognized good news when they heard it.

I decided to hold the offer in me for one night, to let the invitation and what it meant be just mine. The moment I told either parent would be the moment the news started to erode, to be questioned and confused. I wanted to be selfish and keep it, let it run around unencumbered through one night's dreams. To put off for one day the fight toward not a Yes—I would never get a Yes—but toward the answer that got me to Rawlings: Fine, Lizet, do whatever the hell you want.

But I should've at least called my father that day. It turned out to be the only night when the internship offer stood even a chance of being received as good news, the last night before things got much, much harder.

28

THE WALK BACK TO MY ROOM from my Spanish section the
next morning brought with it a phenomenon for which very few
people or things—no ice-cream-infused orientation week assembly, no e-mail blast from the Office of Diversity Affairs, and certainly in my case no big sister or older cousin—could've prepared
me. Later, I'd see it: *Of course* my not calling home had a flip side.
Home, it turned out, was just as reluctant to talk to *me*. And much
later, I'd learn from other first-in-the-family-to-go-to-college
people—Jaquelin, other friends I made and sometimes lost—that
I wasn't alone, that at some point in our time away, we'd all had
our moment of familial reckoning: one friend's moment happening over a winter break, his first morning back home, when he woke
up in his apartment and found his mother still there, finding out
then that weeks and weeks earlier, she'd been laid off and was still
not working; another friend's moment coming in an airport, when
she saw, next to her mother, her father waiting for her and in a
wheelchair—a month earlier he'd fallen off a roof at work and would
maybe never walk again. *Why didn't you tell us?* we all asked, only to
be told, *You couldn't do anything from up there*, or, *We didn't want you to*

worry. Maybe they tried, *You're always so stressed, so busy.* And we each heard these excuses exactly the way we thought we were meant to hear them, with a confused rage pounding in our ears that translated their words into brand-new hurt: *Like you even care about who you left behind. Like you didn't decide to abandon us first.* We never admitted that we'd needed to believe them when they told us nothing was wrong.

I say this only as a long-overdue explanation to Caroline, Tracy, and the other two white girls—should they ever read this—who stood in the TV lounge as I passed it on my way back from class that morning. I was headed down the hall to my room, practicing in my head what I'd say to my parents to explain the internship, when I heard on the midmorning news show surging from the screen those girls watched a story about Ariel Hernandez. The last thing I expected to hear in the hallway was that voice, then to see, on that television screen, my mother's face.

I veered into the TV lounge and yelled toward the voice, What are you doing here!—not registering that Mami was still far away in Florida. All four girls jumped and turned around; I hurtled past them, my arms wrapped around my Spanish textbook. I dodged the couch and stopped just short of the TV, not caring that I blocked their view. My mom's name suddenly appeared on screen in a title beneath her head: Lourdes Ramirez, Madres Para Justicia (Mothers for Justice).

Nothing Leidy or Omar had said in our calls or their messages had indicated that my mother was still heavily involved with the Ariel protests—what was she doing on a national news show with some official-sounding words after her name? I couldn't make sense of her face, which was not wet or blotchy like the last time I'd seen her near Ariel. This face had foundation powder dusted over it, a little thick but evenly applied. This face had mascara slicked onto its eyelashes, brows gelled into submission, blush swooped on the right bones, lip liner with—I could barely believe it—coordinating lipstick. This face didn't shake or scream or let itself get messed with tears; this face had talking points. This face was professional. I was glad I'd heard her voice first, because I might've passed right by the face alone.

—Oh my gosh, can you move? one girl said behind me.

I answered her with *Shhh* and a slap at the air. My mother, answering a question I'd missed, said without blinking, We are here because his mother is *not*. That, sir, is our mission.

—Oh *wait*, another girl—Tracy—whispered behind me. That's Jillian's roommate, she's Cuban, from Miami.

—Jillian from your floor? another girl said.

Tracy must've nodded, because no one behind me asked me to confirm. *Lizet*, I almost said without turning around. My name is Lizet—you *know* that—and it's also *my* fucking floor. A man's voice off camera said, Can you tell us what else your group is doing to prevent this latest court order from being enforced?

So the phrase attached to my mom's name, Mothers for Justice, was this group, and my mother was, at least at the moment, its spokesperson. How could Leidy and Omar have kept the existence of this version of my mom from me all these weeks—and worse, how could I have tricked myself into believing them each time they said everything was fine? From right behind me, a chirp: Caroline's voice.

—Um, Liz? Hey, is everything OK?

—Why is she – what's going on?

There was a pause—maybe a silence during which the four girls searched each other's faces, ponytails shaking with their *No*s. I turned around and saw they'd all backed up, their thin legs pressed against the couch seat. It wasn't until I faced the TV again that one of them got brave enough to answer.

—Ariel Hernandez is going back home. His dad's coming to get him, Caroline said.

—What! His dad? Since when?

I pressed the volume button, kept clicking the plastic bar even when the set was as loud as it would go, like a lab rat desperate for more food from a dispenser. I looked for Leidy and her red tube top in the background—but nothing. Behind me, feet shuffled against the carpet, moving a step or two away.

—We've begun a twenty-four-hour prayer vigil, my mother said into a microphone, looking at the camera dead-on. She said, We started two nights ago and will continue through Easter. One or more of us will keep a constant prayer for Ariel, for his family here in Miami, and for the soul of his mother in heaven.

—Since when do *you* pray? I asked the TV.

My mom's face shrank down into a small box in the upper-right corner as some other footage played on the screen: a little boy sitting on someone's shoulders next to Ariel, who sat on his uncle's shoulders, the caption reading *Ariel and Friends*. Her face expanded to take up the screen again, and I wondered if the reporter would ask about the obvious cartoon series *Ariel and Friends* should spawn.

From behind me, as I tried to listen to the questions and my mom's answers and fill in the blanks set up by the people I'd trusted most, there was this quick, whispered conversation, the kind of semi-private banter I recognized from months earlier—the morning I first saw snow, when they'd watched me and play-by-played my reaction, me just their freezing spectacle: So wait, that woman is one of his relatives? They didn't say but I think so. Wait, she's his mom. No, I think she's just related to his mom. I thought his mom was dead. Then who was that before – the girl they showed? That's his cousin or something. But she's his legal guardian now? No, *this* woman is. No, she's just some lady. I think she's their social worker. Maybe she's their lawyer? She's *not* their lawyer.

I spun around, dropped my textbook on the ground, the pages splaying at my feet.

—Will you shut the hell up? I yelled. I'm trying to figure out how the fuck this happened.

I don't know why I cursed, sounding so much like Leidy all of a sudden—the one person supposedly still physically close enough to Mami to have stopped her from whatever Mothers for Justice was. When was she planning on telling me anything, when Mami got arrested? When Ariel and Caridaylis moved in with us? Caroline stepped up to me, her puffy lilac vest zipped tight over her flat chest, the same vest she'd worn the day of the first snowfall, when she'd made us all hot chocolate from scratch.

—There's no need to get like that, she said.

I put my hand in her face and said, Right, except that's not *your* fucking mom on TV right now, so just get the fuck out of here.

—Jesus *Christ*, she said, and the girl behind her said, You don't have to be nasty.

Tracy, standing farthest from me and wearing a wide mint-green headband, said, That's your *mother*? *Really*?

I felt the spark then—the flare that shoots up at being challenged—what Weasel must've felt and had thrown in my face before Christmas when I went looking for my dad, the rage with which my mom once fainted but that she now channeled into a microphone over a thousand miles away.

—Yes, that's my mom, I said to Tracy's headband, to her restrained hairline. You want to say something about it?

Tracy and Caroline and another girl drew together, their shoulders touching, instinctively clinging to the pack to avoid being picked off one by one. But the fourth girl, who had yet to say a word, crept backward, her eyes on the carpet the entire time, as if willing me to notice she wouldn't be able to identify me in a lineup later if it came to that. She slinked out of the room, her hands shoved in her pockets as she turned in the doorway and all but sprinted down the hall. No one but me noticed she'd left.

Caroline held her head at a practiced angle and said calmly, Don't get so upset, OK? Take a second to just calm down.

Why did she have to say that? Why did she try to step in and *help* me when the smartest thing those girls could've done was what their friend did and just walk away? I stepped closer to them, to her, and felt taller, stronger for the high-school-born pride and fear— the adrenaline churn of some hallway fight an accidental blow sucked you into. I scanned the room for a chair, for something light but significant I could eventually throw.

—*Calm down?* I shouted. Are you shitting me! Out of nowhere my mom is on national television, this whole fucking spectacle obviously *way* outta hand –

—No, exactly, Caroline said. That's why his dad's coming, to end all this –

—Come on, Tracy blurted. The man just wants his son back.

—That's not the fucking point! I yelled. Besides, the guy knew they were coming, he knew their whole plan, they had his blessing! His dad caring now is just some propaganda shit on the part of Castro and the Cuban government!

I'd heard all this while in Miami—was hearing it again behind me now, part of my mother's bullet points—but I didn't know, when I repeated it, if I believed it: it was easier to feel rage about Ariel than regret about not being home to have stopped Mami myself, so it's possible I wasn't really convinced of what I'd said until all three of those girls rolled their eyes like a reflex. There is nothing like the whites of someone's eyes to convince you how very true what you believe is, how very much you must act on it.

—Are you really too stupid to see that? I said.

I stepped over my book, the soaked toe of my sneaker hitting Caroline's boots.

—You want to tell me I'm wrong? You want to tell me I'm lying?

—OK, she said, putting her hands up. Wow, OK.

She stepped back and almost fell down into the seat of the couch, but she only wobbled, watching me the whole time like I was some animal she'd just failed at taming.

I shoved the beak of my fingers into the embroidered pattern of letters on her vest—*The North Face*, it said—and she let herself sway with the force.

None of them pushed me back. They were afraid of me, and I couldn't believe it. There were three of them, *three* of them, all taller than me. In high school, this was a no-brainer: *I* should've been the one avoiding physical contact, the one looking for the fastest way around them and out of the building. I should've been the one ready to duck. Instead, I let them keep this nonsense switch; I widened my stance and stepped right on Caroline's boot. I leaned all the way on it. She should've smacked me for it, or at least pushed me off—I even closed my eyes, ready for it in a deep-down way—and when she didn't do it, when my sneaker collapsed her boot's toe, I knew we were from very different places, and I could push her, push all three of them, as far as I wanted, as far as they expected me to go.

—No one's saying they don't believe you, Caroline said slowly. I slid my foot off her boot.

The third girl, now the farthest from me, said in too cute a voice, I just feel like he needs to go back, get back to his life, to his school and stuff.

—You *feel like*? Let me ask you, what kind of life do you think he's gonna have in Cuba? Tell me. You *really* think he can go back? He can go back to school and say to the kid next to him, Oh in Miami I had a puppy and I ate steak every day and we had soap and toilet paper and freedom of speech and the air inside buildings was freezing cold? You *really* think Castro's gonna allow a liability like that on his island? In a place where the news is censored? You're telling *me* that can really happen? After how good he's had it here?

They watched me with steady faces, with thin lips parted, as if dealing with someone holding a knife to their own wrist. I said, That kid's life in Cuba won't be worse because it's *Cuba*. It'll be worse because he knows what life is like *here*.

—He doesn't *belong* here, Tracy huffed. Just because he got a taste of the good life –

But Caroline raised a hand up to her and said, *No*, Tracy. She looked at the TV, and I wondered if she remembered how she and Tracy and Jillian had left me behind the night of the dance party before the last week of classes, if she saw this moment as karmic payback for leaving without me. She said slowly, her hand still holding off Tracy, If that's all true, then once he's back in Cuba, if something happens, can't his family just call the police?

I had no words. I smacked my own cheeks. I yelled, It's a communist country. The police? The *police*!

She tugged her vest down at the waist and looked crushed. Her attempt to manage my anger was over, and behind me I heard my mom say, Of course this is personal, of course we are taking it personally.

—But they showed his desk in Cuba, the quiet girl half whispered. His classmates are saving it for him. It had the saddest sign on it.

Tracy whispered to no one and all of us: Their news is *not* censored.

—How do you know that they can't call the police? Caroline said.

I said what I thought would convince them: I'm *from* there! Did you forget that's my mom on the fucking television? Besides, look it up! Look up *communism* and fucking learn something.

Tracy said, Wait, you're *from* Cuba?

—*Trace*, leave it *alone*, Caroline said as I pushed right up to Tracy's face.

—Yes, I blurted, because I was tired of saying no and then explaining that maybe it didn't matter. I said, I left when I was a baby. I still have family there and they all want out. And yeah, their news is fucking censored. You get arrested for speaking out against the government, or for being gay or trying to buy meat, so yeah, go smile at your fucking Che Guevara poster like you know some shit, you stupid bitch.

I spat all this out, my fury somehow making my mom's new version of herself a fact: I'd made myself the True Daughter of Dusty Tits. This invention was the only way to explain the woman behind me to the women in front of me. It was the only thing I could do from so far away. In the silence surrounding their shock—*of course* calling this white girl a bitch had been the thing to produce shock—I heard my mother say, How can we deny her wish for her son to have a better life? How can we deny him his inheritance?

Tracy tried to sidestep my body and said to the others, You guys, she's not really from Cuba. Jillian told me she's not.

—What people have to understand, said my mom's voice, swelling and cracking with grief now, is that this is our story, too. I came here with *my* girls the same way Ariel's mother came with him. Ariel's story is my story, the story of my daughters.

I took the help; I even wanted it. I got between Tracy's blank face and the screen and said, You're a fucking idiot.

She looked at my hands then, which I'd raised between us. I pulled them closer to my body and, because it came to this or hitting her, I said, Ariel's mother died to get him here. Do you realize that?

I couldn't believe I was saying it, but I kept talking.

—She *died*, I said. His mother drowned trying to get him here. That doesn't mean *anything* to you? That sacrifice?

Tracy nodded. Her hands checked the position of her headband. She jutted one foot out in front of her, twisted her lips in this ugly way, pointed with her whole hand at the TV. Through her smirk she said, So what did *your* mother sacrifice for you to get here? For *your* taste of the good life?

The quiet girl gasped, *Jesus, Tracy* as Caroline came up behind me before I could do anything, hooked her hands on my elbows in a way that was so assured, so soft but strong, that they trapped me. I pulled with everything against her, couldn't believe how much power her small frame held.

Tracy said, None of this would be happening if she'd stayed put.

—Trace, for god's sake *stop*, Caroline yelled.

I know Tracy meant Ariel's mother. But the proof that she meant me too was on the TV screen. And I don't know why, but Caroline was crying, and all I got to yell at Tracy as the other girl pushed

her down the hallway and away from us was, Who the fuck are
you? Say that to me again! I fucking *dare* you, come say it to me again!

I pulled and pulled then gave up. Once we were both breathing normally again and she saw I wouldn't chase them, Caroline
let me go.

She wiped her face and said, I'm sorry, I shouldn't have touched
you.

Her calm voice made me feel so much shame. What had my
yelling and my stepping on boots like in some fight at a Hialeah
dollar movie theater made her think of me, of any Cuban she'd ever
meet from here on out? Me and my mother on television, both of
us spectacles, the two of us and the rest of the crowd a big enough
sample size. My face began to burn, my eyes too, and as Caroline
turned to shut off the TV, now blaring with news of a shooting at a
Miami-area Chili's thought to be connected to the Ariel situation, I
swooped down for my book, then sprinted to the stairwell, ignoring her *Liz, wait!* and taking two steps at a time up to my floor,
barreling toward my room, where I grabbed the phone, panting
and dialing our house number with my thumb.

Of course it just rang and rang and rang, and I pictured Leidy
holding Dante in a crowd behind the cameraman, keeping the
knowledge of whatever the hell Madres Para Justicia was all to herself. My mom was lying to the whole country, was roping me into
these lies, and me being far away had let that happen. I was supposed to call about the internship, but I couldn't now: leaving home
had been a mistake—one I needed to undo as best I could. When
I slammed the phone back in the cradle as the answering machine
beeped on, I saw my hand was trembling but didn't feel it doing
that—the hand seemed not mine. I picked up the receiver again,
this time to call my dad. The day I'd seen him at Latin American
Grill, he couldn't even talk about my mom, couldn't even bring
himself to properly warn me. His phone would ring in that Hialeah apartment, and Rafael would reach for it, and my dad would
say, *Just leave it, don't answer, I don't want to hear it*—not guessing that

the person calling was me, trying to talk to him, trying to segue from what we'd seen on TV to my own news, the internship, which seemed silly and unimportant now. So a teacher, a weird one, thought I was a good student and wanted to work with me: Who the hell cared? It was garbage, a frivolous reason to miss summer at home, another selfish mistake.

I put the phone down and decided I wouldn't call Papi, that there was no reason to do so. And it was fine if I didn't do the internship, because I didn't deserve it anyway. My grades weren't high enough, and Professor Kaufmann knew that as soon as I admitted it but had wanted to spare my feelings. I sat at Jillian's desk, and while I could barely make out my face in the bright computer screen, I recognized what I was: Professor Kaufmann's pity case. Still applying for the internship meant that I didn't get whatever subtle clue she was either too weird or too smart to emit. I wasn't who she thought I was, and I'd tried to blame a boy and let her believe that lie—and I'd just done it again with my mom's help, had tricked a whole new group of people into thinking I deserved to be outraged about the wrong thing. I didn't deserve the spot. I knew it, and I couldn't face Professor Kaufmann in the lab, much less show up in California and work by her side. I knew, too, that I'd never take a morning shower in the main bathroom on our floor and risk seeing Caroline or Tracy in a towel again—I'd go back to showering at night, like I did when I lived in Miami. As I typed *MIA* into the destination field of the travel Web site whose link I'd clicked so hastily that I'd brought up five of the same window, I wanted more than anything to disappear, to fix everything by disappearing and reappearing somewhere else, to not be the person who'd lied and lied and caused a scene and who now only deserved to go back to where she came from.

I scrolled through the prices of the flights: spring break, being just a little over a week away, was out of the question, with every ticket available costing more than the meager limit on the credit card I rarely used. But the prices dotting the calendar later in the month said I could swing Easter, the final day that my mom would be—what? Sprawled on the floor in prayer? I had no idea. I'd never seen her pray in earnest, had never really been taught how to do it, but there was, on the screen, a flight listed that I could afford, that got me there to see that spectacle, to pull her off the ground my-self if I had to, this time before any cameras caught her and added importance to her name. I stood and rolled the chair away from Jillian's desk, just crouching in front of it with my credit card in one hand, my head down and bent over the keyboard, saying the numbers on the card out loud as I typed them, wondering if this was a kind of prayer.

29

MADRES PARA JUSTICIA BECAME A FAST favorite of the news
media thanks to one of their favorite pastimes: pressing their backs
against asphalt while acting as human speed bumps on the road in
front of Ariel's house. Equally camera-worthy was the way they
stood in a circle, hands linked and bound together by rosaries, praying in front of his house, always in head-to-toe black because they
were in mourning, they said, for Ariel's mother. When I saw a photo
on CNN's Web site of my mom on the ground with these other
women, I called home that night—it wasn't our regular day to talk,
so Leidy should've known I was upset about something. But when
I asked, So how's Mom, Leidy just said: Mom? She's fine. She's not
here or else she'd talk to you. But she's good. She's doing real good.

In the days leading up to spring break, Jillian wasn't ignoring
me exactly, but since hearing from Tracy about my outburst
(I guessed it was Tracy, though more likely it was all of them, probably sitting on my bed after shuffling into our room while I was at
work or in lab, somberly debriefing Jillian on what had happened
in the TV lounge, their voices measured and serious like in an
intervention), she'd practically moved in with her All-Nighter,

saying only *Hey* and *Sorry* and *Excuse me* when we happened to be in the room at the same time. Aside from her, no one but me and Professor Kaufmann knew about the internship, and though I'd been looking forward to bragging to Ethan about it at Happy Hours that week, I didn't want to tell him now that I felt I should turn it down.

In theory, Ethan was someone I could talk to about the problems back home. At the very least, his RA training would kick in— he'd listen and say *I hear you* in all the right places—but he'd be better than that: he'd actually understand the very real impact the cost of the Easter flight had on my budget; if anything even remotely urgent had called him home over the last four years, he could tell me what he'd done about it. But I didn't want to make Ethan work for me that way. I'd kept everything about my mom and Ariel from him because, unlike everyone else who knew I was Cuban and from Miami, he'd (purposefully, I thought) never asked. He was the only thing at Rawlings that home hadn't contaminated, and I'd wanted to keep him like that. No one but him consistently called me Lizet— not Liz, and never El—and though neither of us said this outright, I took it as some agreement between us to keep each other intact.

There were some Thursdays or Sundays, before or after the study silence began, where he'd seem more stressed than usual to me, and if I asked if he was okay, he'd say simply *My mom* or *Money stuff.* He'd say, *You know, the usual,* and having the same shorthand for our worries made me feel close to him despite the abstractions. I'd come to think of him as a version of a grown-up Dante, and I think it was this—that I'd found a way to metaphorically insert him into some hopeful version of my family—that made me realize I now wanted to confess everything to Ethan, to admit that I needed him.

So I got to Donald Hall early, to find him before Thursday's Happy Hours got started. My plan was to drop off my stuff in the lounge, then go up to his floor and look for his room (RAs universally announced themselves as such via the random shit they taped to their doors in an effort to seem approachable and cool, though it almost always backfired). I probably didn't need to talk to him in his room, but I justified wanting to by convincing myself that being alone—without the imminent arrival of the rest of the Regulars looming over us—was vital to us moving past our joking to whatever came next.

I set down my books and took off my coat, and as I draped it over the back of the chair I always sat in, I heard the crash of the building's front door—Ethan came bursting through it, caught me staring at him from the lounge. He yelled my name and ran toward me, through the open glass door of the study lounge, his bag on his back and a torn envelope in his hand. He charged at me full speed, then leapt and slid across the table on his stomach, his hand and the envelope reaching out to my face.

—Read it, he said.

But he started talking before I'd gotten the letter all the way out.

—I got into Berkeley. For grad school. My top fucking choice, fully funded.

He whipped off his bag and tossed it off the table, then rolled onto his back. He thrashed his arms and legs in the air like a dying bug and screamed, then he tilted his head so he was seeing me upside down, the acceptance letter stretched between my fists.

—You're the first person to know. Isn't that perfect? I am losing my fucking mind!

—Grad school? For what?

He flipped over to his belly and got up to his knees, legs spread wide on the tabletop.

—Dude, for history. For my doctorate.

He plucked the letter away.

—I didn't even know you were applying to places.

—I didn't want anyone to know. And most of the apps had to be in by January anyway. I only applied to four schools. That's all I could afford.

He marveled at the letter again, then said, Jesus H. Christ, I think I'm going to puke.

Without taking his eyes off the page, he scurried off the table and slammed himself into a chair.

—I haven't felt this kind of relief since getting in *here*, he laughed.

—Why didn't you tell me? I said.

He reared away, sliding the letter back into the envelope as if to shield it from me.

—Hey, I think what you meant to say was, Congratulations, Ethan, you are a pinnacle of human achievement, I hope to be half the man you are someday. Something along those lines.

—Sorry, I said. Congratulations, Ethan – assuming you would've told me had I not been just standing here waiting for you.

—Of course I would've told you! I couldn't wait to tell you.

—You didn't bother to tell me you were waiting to hear from places.

—Come on, don't be like that. I feel like celebrating. Don't make this into a thing.

He smacked the envelope against his palm. What *are* you doing here so early?

His face was as bright as a shark's belly. Something was gone from him: the stress of all those weeks of waiting, something I hadn't registered until it was missing. He'd kept his worries a secret, hadn't burdened me with them—a pattern we'd both kept so far and that I couldn't break now even though I wanted to, not in the glow of his good news, and not with his example of someone who'd kept it together shining in my face. I slid my books away from me, lined them up with the side of the table.

—No reason, I said. What do you mean, a *thing*?

—No, Lizet, come on, don't do that.

My eyes filled—I wondered if this was how my parents felt when I told them about Rawlings. Do what? I said.

—What you're doing. Finding a reason to get upset. I'm so fucking happy right now, please, *please* don't wreck it.

I still wanted to tell him about my mom, ask him what he'd do if he were me when it came to the internship, but now I knew he'd just tell me to go. Forget your family, your life is about you: that's what he'd say. That's what his keeping quiet until he found out for sure meant for him. That's why Ethan was going to Berkeley and I was going nowhere.

—I'm not. I'm happy for you. I just don't know why you didn't tell me sooner you were waiting to hear from grad schools. I don't why you'd keep that from me.

—Stop stop stop stop! He lunged at me and grabbed my wrists, squeezed them for a second before letting them go when the envelope crinkled.

—God, Lizet, I wasn't *keeping* anything from you, I – no, *no*, I'm not doing this. I'm not doing this!

—Doing what?

—I'm not playing into this.

He stood up, leaned over the table, his color rising.

—This isn't complicated. If you can't just be one hundred percent happy for me right now, that's *your* problem.

—I never said I wasn't happy for you.

—I see it in your face!

I put my hands on my cheeks to cover whatever was betraying me. He slapped his hands against his thighs.

—You're doing that infuriating girl thing where you make this about you, he said. My mom pulls this kind of thing and I hate it. I didn't think you were like that – you've *never* been like that. Don't start now.

—I'm not your mom.

I grabbed my jacket and pulled my arms through it.

—I know you're not my mom. But do you see how now *I'm* trying to make *you* feel better when all I want to do is get drunk and celebrate? When I want *you* to celebrate, too?

—You know what, whatever, Ethan. I said congratulations. What do you want?

—There's no reason for you to resent me for this! I didn't think you'd be this way.

I did resent him—that was exactly it—I resented him for having a future where he could put his mom in her place, and that that
place wasn't ahead of what he wanted for himself. I grabbed my
books and started shoving them in my bag.

—Well sorry to disappoint you. Sorry I didn't get on my knees
to suck your dick the second I saw that letter. Is that what you
wanted?

His hands went up into his hair, the envelope still in one of them
and so resting against his face. I waited for him to say *Fuck you* or
Maybe it is and grab his crotch—the way Omar would to keep the
fight rising. But Ethan folded over and hid his face. He heaved tired
laughs into his hands, but when he stood back up, the skin around
his eyes glowed red.

—*Christ*, I cannot believe you just said that.

—Ethan, I don't know what you want me to say!

—Not that! Jesus! Why are you acting like this?

I zipped up my jacket even though the room was too hot.

—Don't worry about it.

He held the envelope up in front of my face and said, I'm not
going to. *I* couldn't be happier. I thought you'd get that better than
anyone, but clearly I'm wrong.

He picked up his bag, slung it back over his shoulders.

—Ethan, I'm sorry. I'm just upset, okay?

He faced me again, his lips drawn into his mouth. It doesn't matter, he said.

He looked at the ground, and his hair flopped over his forehead.

—I was so happy when I saw it was you in here, he said. I'm an
idiot.

With the long edge of the envelope, he tapped the table twice,
then looked through the glass walls down the hallway. He said, Forget this, I'm getting another RA to fill in here, then calling my mom
to get that over with. Then I'm celebrating.

I tried to undo what I'd done by saying as he walked away, Your
mom's gonna freak, she's gonna be so proud of you.

He shrugged, tapped the glass door with the envelope like he had the table.

—She won't know what it means. But she'll be happy to hear I won't be moving back home for good this summer.

Someone came through the door—a resident who Ethan said hi to. His hello was just a nod, a stiff hand raised: serious and so Not Ethan in its perfunctory delivery that it proved how much I'd hurt him.

—I swear I'm happy for you, Ethan. I didn't mean what I said before to come out like that. I'm the idiot, okay?

—Have a good spring break, Lizet. Maybe I'll see you when you get back.

I wasn't going anywhere, not until Easter, but I couldn't explain why now, so there was no point in correcting him. The study lounge's glass door closed after him. He turned back with a little envelope-accentuated salute—the closest thing to a joke he could muster—before disappearing down the hall.

I was grateful that I had our room to myself over spring break, with no chance of Jillian walking in with only a *Hey* and stuffing a change of clothes in her bag before leaving again. Ethan was away—he'd gone to New York City with friends at the last minute as part of his celebrating—and since Jillian had put a password on her computer, I spent the days at the library, studying and writing then deleting e-mails to Ethan and also racking up work hours by picking up all the shifts abandoned by people who'd headed somewhere warm, money I needed to pay off the plane ticket. By the middle of the week I'd gotten lonely enough to e-mail Jaquelin—she *had* to be around—but she wrote back saying she was spending break on a service trip with some organization in Honduras, and I hated her so much for being this ideal Rawlings minority student that I deleted the e-mail without looking at the pictures she'd attached to it. *Sending sunshine your way*, she'd written; frustrated as I was, I believed she was really trying to do that.

During each library shift, I worried I'd run into Professor Kaufmann. Right before break, she asked if I was leaving town (she'd scheduled the lab work so that we wouldn't kill or damage anything because of a week's worth of inattention), and I lied and said I was headed home to Miami. She said she wanted to check in about the internship when I got back, about some forms I should be receiving in the mail. Any and every tall woman who came through the library's entrance that week was greeted by a half-hidden version of me cowering behind the library's security desk; I only emerged once I saw that it wasn't Professor Kaufmann pushing a coat's hood back from her face or stomping snow from her boots. And once classes started again, she didn't ask me to stay behind to talk, didn't e-mail me a reminder to linger after lab. The forms she'd mentioned never arrived in my campus mailbox, and I figured she must've realized I wasn't applying for the internship and was silently upset. In the days before my Easter flight, I kept waiting for her to make me admit I'd misled her, and the dread of that moment followed me around campus, sat with me during lab or at work, and was only eventually crowded out by fear—of flying, yes, but of so much more—the instant I heard the click of my seatbelt on the airplane.

30

THOUGH I NEVER TOLD OMAR I'd seen my mom on the news and that I knew about the weeks-long vigil, I did tell him a few days out from my arrival that I'd found some mythical last-minute deal on an Easter flight. When he asked me why Easter—his voice rising, sounding more than a little panicked—I said, I just feel like I should be home for the day Jesus resurrected himself. He didn't say anything except, Yeah I guess, and I worried I'd gotten it wrong and given myself away, that Easter celebrated something else: I hadn't been to church since my first communion, and even there I had no solid memories—only that I forgot to take off my lace gloves in the bathroom before I went to wipe. I asked Omar to pick me up from the airport, then gave him a chance to confess everything he'd been keeping from me. I asked him, Is there a reason *why* I shouldn't come home for Easter, Omar? No, he said. I even asked, Is something going on I don't know about? I really do think I gave him enough with that, that this test was almost too easy. Still, he failed it. No no, he said. He coughed for a few seconds then said, We'll go to the beach while you're here. So I knew he'd keep my trip a secret, since he was already keeping so many secrets from me.

Omar paid to park and met me at the gate instead of driving around until spotting me, which is what we'd agreed on over the phone. Under other circumstances I would've found the gesture sweet, but this was another Thursday night with me in Miami for a holiday my family didn't celebrate. This was me trying to—what? What the hell was I doing there? That's what I thought when I saw him waiting near a bank of chairs, because that's what his face said: *El, what are you doing here?*

The first thing he actually said after I pulled away from his stiff hug was, Where's your ring?

I told him I left it at school, that I didn't want to lose it on the plane, and I pretended to struggle with my bag to avoid looking at his face. I'd taken it off for good the night I booked the flight, had dropped it in the mug on my desk that held my pens and pencils right after clicking *Purchase*. He said, Really?—his voice so tight and uncomfortable that I knew he didn't believe me as much as he wanted to when he said, Right, that makes sense.

The ride home felt just as awkward, but he bought my *I'm tired*s as I leaned against the car door, the street rumbling too close under me. When I first sat in the Integra, my butt dropped into its bucket seat hard: I'd forgotten how low his car was, and as we zoomed through the concrete layer cake of the parking garage, I imagined my ass scraping against each speed bump that the car tipped its way over.

Once he'd navigated away from the airport to the expressway, he veered in what felt like the wrong direction, the sign for Hialeah three lanes away on the other side of the road, indicating a different on-ramp than the one we were hurtling toward. I said the first of many things neither of us expected over that trip.

—I'm not going to my mom's.

—What are you talking about? You can't stay at *my* place, my mom would –

—I know, I said. Drop me off at my dad's.

He huffed like I'd said something funny, asked if I even knew where my dad lived since selling the house, if I'd even talked to him since August. When I said yes, I did, and yes, I had—that I'd seen my dad over Christmas but hadn't bothered to tell him because it wasn't his business and please, could he just stop talking and take me to the Villas—he knew right then that I'd find a different way back to the airport come Monday.

I hadn't planned to see my dad, but the silence sitting between me and Omar the rest of the drive made me see how much I needed my dad's help, and that I could've never asked him in advance. The angry rumble of the streets beneath me, the cologne-saturated air wafting up from the car seats, the strict grids of the neighborhoods out the window: all these things confirmed that this was the only way to ask him—just show up, my bag behind me, and tell my dad what we had to do in the morning.

—I don't think anyone's here, Omar said as he slowed down.

I ducked to look past his head and worried he was right: my dad's town house was the only dark one of all those we'd passed on our way through the Villas. But his van was there. It was only ten forty-five—no way he'd be asleep already. All my life, even with my own late nights, he always stayed up past me as he shuffled bills and other papers at a living room cabinet that folded down, becoming, when he pulled a chair up to it, his desk.

—It's fine, he's here, I said. Open the trunk.

I was already out of the car and sliding along its side when Omar said from the driver's seat, I'm not leaving you in this place like this.

He wouldn't open the trunk. I asked him again. I knocked on the car, the metallic thuds sounding to me like the noise my fist would make against his head were I to knock on that. I knocked harder.

He still didn't open the trunk; he got out of the car instead.

—I said I'm not leaving you here. I can't. No one's even here, are you crazy?

I kept knocking all the way through that. He came around to

the back and laid his palms on the trunk, leaning forward over it after checking that his T-shirt covered his belt buckle, to avoid scratches.

—Get back in the car, he said.

I put my hand on the latch hidden below the boxed-in *A* ornament and flicked it over and over again, the sound of it worse than any damage I was really causing. Between these thunks, I said, Did you tell my mom I was coming?

—No, he said. Stop that already.

—You say anything to Leidy? Tell me the truth.

—No! Lizet, come on, quit it!

Inside the town house, at the window I remember being in the kitchen, a fluorescent light flickered and flickered and then finally stayed on.

I said in a singsong voice, I'm gonna *break* it.

Omar threw his hands up and ducked into the driver's side. The latch suddenly had more resistance, could go past the metal piece I'd been slamming it against, and the trunk glided open with a hiss. I grabbed my bag and began hauling it out, letting it scrape against the lining at the edge of the trunk.

—Watch it, Omar said, back next to me, but he didn't make a move to help. He knew better. And so did I: I slid my hand to the back of the suitcase to make sure the wheels cleared. I planted the thing on the ground next to me.

—Well thanks! I said. I shrugged my shoulders and smiled like a clown. Bye!

—El, are you serious?

—What? I said. Thank you for the ride here. What else do you want me to say?

—Who do you think you're talking to? he said. He closed his eyes, put his hand over his face, smeared it down—a reset. He stared at my bare hand until someone said my name like a threat—my dad's voice.

Omar stepped away and said with a forced laugh, Mr. Ramirez, hey, ¿como anda, como está? He put out an arm to shake my dad's hand, but my dad didn't take it.

—What are you doing here, my dad said to me. You're supposed to be at school.

He wore only a pair of jeans, paint splattered in the usual places, and a new gold chain I'd never seen circled his neck. He crossed his arms—the face of his watch flashing light at us—and opened his legs, leaned to the right to see me around Omar's big block of a body. I couldn't see my dad's face though: he was back-lit and still a little too far away, but from his voice I knew he was mad.

—I came home for Easter, I said.

—*Easter?* he said. Since when do you –

And then he stopped, looked up at the sky, said, Ay dios mío. He closed his legs and let his arms drop.

—Mr. Ramirez, Omar said. I just want to say I had no part in getting Lizet here like this, this was totally her idea, I didn't know she'd make me drive here to your place.

—Omar, he said, you should go now.

—Yessir.

He put his hands in his pockets as he backed up against the car. My dad jerked his head toward the apartment door, recrossed his arms.

—Lizet, come inside. *Now.*

—Dad, I said.

But he'd already turned around and was heading in.

Omar rushed at me with wide steps and raised his palm in the air between us. He looked angrier than I'd ever seen him.

—I don't know what you're pulling here, he said, but I've never been bad to you, you know that, so there's no reason for you to do me like this.

—There's *not?*

I grabbed the handle of my suitcase and jerked it past him. I waited for the sound of his car door to slam but it didn't come.

—Lizet, what the fuck did I even *do*!

—Like you don't know, I yelled. You should go now. You heard my dad.

He stomped to the car and dropped his body into it, slammed the door and lowered the window in one smooth motion. He said, more to the steering wheel than to me, I give up with this shit.

I slapped my own chest and yelled, Why don't you watch the news and figure it out yourself like I did?

—*That's* why you're mad at me? El, what the fuck were you gonna do from up there?

I pointed at him and said, Exactly, Omar. That right there, what you just said? That's *exactly* why I'm here. To fucking *do* something since you and Leidy obviously didn't.

—Oh! Okay yeah, he yelled. So now you know how to handle *everything*, huh? You got it all figured out, don't you. You think you're so fucking smart.

He threw the car in reverse, shook his head as he turned the wheel. I'd made it halfway up the concrete leading to my dad's door when Omar lowered the passenger-side window and yelled my name, made me stop.

—Whose fault is it that you weren't here, huh? Maybe you need to think about *that*.

I was ready for the tire screech of him driving off, a final flourish that would give me the space to yell *Fuck you* like the end of any normal fight, but the only sound was the mechanical whir of him putting the window up, the click of his locks keeping me out, the hum of the engine as he rolled away. And then unexpected, terrifying quiet.

My dad had left the front door open, so the cold air inside and the rattling of the window unit met me seconds before I crossed the threshold. All the lights were on now, and the door to his bedroom, visible from the apartment's entrance, was open. He sat on the edge of his bed, his hands rubbing his knees as he mumbled to the carpet. He'd grown back his goatee: he looked like my father again. The bed beneath him was neatly made, and the thought of him making his bed, scooting around it to pull the sheet corners tight, made so little sense to me that I almost sat down on the couch and held my breath to wait out the rocking feeling in my chest.

But I didn't have the chance. He waved me into his room, saying, Hurry up, come here. I left my suitcase by the couch but he said, No, that thing too, come on. I held my palm out toward it as if to ask why, and once I'd dragged it in, he murmured, Because Rafael, he's not home yet, I don't want him to think – why the hell do you make me explain everything to you! Why do you always ask so many fucking questions!

I blurted out, Oh *please*, don't even start. If that were true, I'd know why you sold the house like that.

The second surprise of the night for me—that I said that, that I let the *fuck you* trapped inside find its way out to the person who deserved it the most.

He sat up straight, stunned, and I backed away from the bed's edge. His chest stopped moving. His hands froze on his knees. He was in that instant making a choice: to slap me for what I'd just said and accuse me of the disrespect I'd shown, or to let it sit there in the room so as to find out if the reason I'd shown up out of nowhere was something more substantial, something even more worthy of punishment. His upper lip twitched, his mustache hairs curling into it like the spirals holding together a notebook.

—I sold the house because I couldn't think of a better way to hurt your mother.

He cleared his throat, and his next words came out a little louder.

—I thought you'd figure that out without me having to tell you. You're the smart one, remember?

His face puckered like he'd been hit with a rush of heartburn, his elbows locked and his hands still on his knees. He said, Why would *you* be hurt? You'd already decided to go.

He resumed rubbing his knees over his jeans, the sound scratchy.

—Shit, you'd already told that school you were coming. And

I thought your sister would move in with that asshole once he got over himself. So I figured, might as well make *Lourdes* miserable for once.

He shrugged but turned his face to the wall.

I focused on his room's disgusting ceiling, the same smear of lumps and stains as the rest of the town house, the rims of my eyes feeling less full with that shift. The water rings in that room had been painted over, though I didn't have to strain to find them lurking in the corners. I knew if I said, *Well you were wrong*, that everything would spill over in a bad way, into the kind of tear-laden brawl he was used to having with my mom. All I had to do was look at him and it would start, familiar and easy. So I pointed my chin higher.

—Lizet, come *on*. It's just a house, it's over. Please, okay?

He stood up but sat right back down when he felt how close that movement brought him to where I stood. The bed took up almost the whole room, only a U of a path around it on three sides, the head of it up against the far wall. He shifted over to the bed's edge farthest from me—his way of asking me to sit with him.

I left my bag—up to then an anchor, a podium—and sat down. Neither of us said anything. Then my stomach growled so loudly that it sounded fake, like I'd made the noise with my mouth. He jolted at the rumble but didn't make a joke about it or—as my mom would've done, as she'd done the very first time I came home to her, mere seconds after I surprised her at her door and without waiting for a growl to cue the question—offer me anything to eat. I felt dizzy again, the room swaying in the direction I'd moved to sit on the bed, so I focused on breathing in through my nose and out through my mouth to push the feeling away. The room smelled of damp carpet, of dirty socks and sweat, but the cloying cover of fabric softener and dryer sheets hovered over all of it. That wet air moved in and out of me, made me feel worse.

—I think I need to eat something, I said.

—They don't give you dinner on the plane?

He'd only been on one flight, ever: when he was fourteen, the forty-five minutes in the air between Cuba and Miami. I think he thought longer flights were more luxurious, maybe the way I imagined first class to be on the other side of the curtain blocking the aisle.

—Not really, I said. You get like a soda, some chips.

—Que mierda, he said. For all that money they should at least give you dinner.

I said, I know, right? And then I started rambling, fast, telling him a story Leidy told me about finding Dante's daycare, how she thought lunch was included—she hadn't even asked the white lady who took her on the tour about lunch, that's how pricey the weekly rate seemed to her—only to get a call at work halfway through his first day asking where she'd placed his food when she'd dropped him off. The story tumbled out in the hopes of keeping my dad from asking the next logical question, which would lead to why I was there, which would lead to me asking him for his help—something I was suddenly not ready to do.

—You got anything to eat? I said, tossing the question out with a voice like something shiny and distracting, a set of keys jingling in the air. I stared out the door, willing him to lead us to his kitchen.

—Did your mother pay for this flight? he asked. Because I *know* it's not in the budget.

—No, I said. I bought the ticket myself.

—You shouldn't be wasting money like that.

I reached for the suitcase and pulled it to me, blocking one path around the bed.

—She doesn't know I'm here, I said.

He laughed, a sad note, hung his head and said to the carpet, So that's why she didn't want to pick you up from the airport?

—No Dad, not here like your apartment. Miami here. I flew down because no one – because somebody has to get her away from those people, that protest vigil.

His jaw tensed. He did not look up from the floor.

—We get the news, you know, up there, I said, my voice ringing off the bedroom walls. I mean, do you have any idea how the rest of the country is seeing this? I'm tired of it. We look like a bunch of crazy people.

—What's with this *we* crap, he said. I'm not with her, you're not even here.

—We as in Cubans, I said.

He smiled with only one side of his mouth. He laughed again.

—You're not Cuban, he said.

This hurt me more than anything else he could've said—more than *Who cares what anyone up there thinks,* more than *Like there's anything you coming down here is gonna do*—and I think he saw it in my face, saw how impossible what he'd just said sounded to me.

—Don't look at me like that! he said. You're American. I'm wrong?

My stomach growled again, a deep, smothered roar.

—Yeah, I said. I'm – what do you mean I'm not Cuban? I was born here, yeah, but I'm Cuban. I'm Latina at least, I said.

—Latinos are Mexicans, Central Americans. You're not that either, he said.

—What? Dad, are you – other people think I'm Cuban.

He stood up from the bed and moved out through the door, leaving me alone as he said, Okay, sure you are. Whatever you say, Lizet.

This is my roommate, Liz. She's Cuban. Jillian said it just like that to every single person she introduced me to. I wanted to grab my dad as he left, shake him, tell him, Listen, if *Latino* means Central Americans, then why is that word on half the e-mails I get from my school's advising office, and why does it mean *me*? Shadows moved across his shoulders as he walked away; then I saw what they really were—new spurts of dark, grayish back hair.

From the bed, I said, You think I'm not Cuban but you also think our house was just a house.

He opened and shut the fridge, then a drawer; there was the sound of a metallic pull and snap. If he'd heard me, he was pretending he hadn't. He came back into the bedroom with a plastic spoon and an open can of fruit cocktail, the kind that's mostly peaches. He loved these little fruit-filled tins, made me or Leidy or my mom pour them, syrup and all, over two scoops of vanilla ice cream and bring them to him after dinner almost every night. It was a job we rotated, making and then delivering this dessert to him on the couch, and once, when he made me the maddest I'd ever been—a fight about Rawlings that led him to say he wouldn't buy me a plane ticket, that I wouldn't go to college *at all*, that he would never in his life allow it—I'd volunteered to prepare it. I was alone in the kitchen, and I blew my nose into my hand and then let the clear tear-induced snot drip out over the ice cream before covering it with the fruit, the syrup from the can matching the snot perfectly. I'd handed it to him, watched him eat and enjoy every bite.

—Here, he said, holding the can out to me. Eat this so you feel better.

I tried not to cry as I spooned the too-sweet fruit into my mouth. The cherry, only one per can as decided in some factory somewhere, was an artificial pink, more like a gumball than anything that had once been on a tree. I swallowed a peach slice without chewing it. There were maybe four in there total, along with something grainy and lighter that I took for a chunk of pear. I saved that for last.

—Do you need me to take you to your mother's?

—Well eventually, yeah.

—Lizet, he said. You cannot stay here.

I held the spoon in front of my face. He raised his arms up to indicate the walls around him and yelled, There's no room!

—I can sleep on your couch.

—That's not even my couch! It's Rafael's!

I drank the syrup from the can, tasting more metal than sweetness.

—No, I said. That's the couch from the family room. I remember it.

I finished off the syrup and said, You can take me on Saturday. Or maybe Sunday. It's gonna depend.

He should've asked *Depend on what,* and I could've used that to leap into what I needed from him: show up with me and tell my mom she wasn't going to any vigil.

—What! No! he said. No. I have to work tomorrow.

—You have to work on Good Friday?

—Yes, Lizet, I work every day. I'm not off reading books all the time on a four-year vacation. I'm *paying* for that vacation.

—One, I said, it's not vacation, but think whatever you want.

I got up from the bed and walked as steadily as I could manage to the kitchen, pretending to look for the trash. He followed me out there, pulling my suitcase with him.

—And two, you're not paying much compared to what you would if you'd stayed with Mom. So the least you can do is let me stay here until Saturday or Sunday morning.

To remain calm and distract myself from this mean truth, from how I'd said it as payback for him calling my time at Rawlings a vacation, I imagined myself descending on my mom's apartment, my dad at my side, the two of us barging through the door just as she was putting on her makeup and practicing, in the bathroom mirror, what she'd say to the cameras that day, all while Dante and Leidy slept in the room across the hall from her. Wash that shit off your face, I'd say, and my dad would say, *Now.*

—You think the money I have to give your mother every month doesn't go to your school bills? he yelled.

—I have to stay at least the night. At least.

—You're obviously not taking *math* up there!

I opened the lower cabinets one by one and in no rush, until I found—in the cabinet under the sink—the one with the plastic grocery bag hanging from inside its door, being used for garbage.

—I'm taking calculus. It's harder than math.

I held out the can and tilted it side to side, said too sweetly, Do you guys recycle?

—¡Ah carajo! he yelled.

I dropped the can into the bag, which was already full of used paper towels and the milky sleeves that once held stacks of saltines, and went to the couch, passing right in front of Papi with my shoulders as relaxed as I could make them. I sat down, ran my hands over the vinyl on either side of me, sweeping imaginary crumbs to the floor. I slipped off my shoes and pulled my feet up, my legs curled at my side. He put his hands on top of his head, laced his fingers. Flecks of deodorant clung to his armpit hair like snow.

—We need to call your mother, he said.

—Don't, I said, but I didn't move. I kept my hands on the couch cushions. I said, If you don't want me here, I'll go to Omar's. I don't want to do that, I'd rather stay here, but it's up to you. I cannot go to Mom's yet.

I made sure to keep my shoulders still and my voice calm, a posture that went against everything rocking inside of me, everything I'd ever seen or been raised to do when we were furious with each other, and then I said, In fact, when I *do* go to Mom's, I need you to go with me. I think it would work better if she saw us both.

I swallowed. I said, Because I don't think seeing me is going to be enough. I think everything that happened with you and her is part of why she's latched on to this kid. I'm not blaming you, I swear, I know it's my fault too, but I just – I cannot do this by myself.

I looked down at my hands, the skin on the backs of them still cracked from the cold that continued to reign over the Rawlings campus, refusing to let in the spring, a season I'd yet to meet. The one-year anniversary of the day's mail bringing news of my acceptance had passed a couple weeks earlier. What we were coming up on, then, was the anniversary of me telling my parents I'd applied and that I'd already sent in the paperwork saying I accepted the offer, that Rawlings had happily sent me a waiver for the deposit when I called to ask if I could have just a little more time to find the money. They said we qualified as a low-income family, I'd said to my father just before he'd torn through the house, making holes in the walls with his fists. Now, he put those fists in the pockets of his jeans. He almost smiled.

—You flew down here by yourself, he said. You found that school, you filled out all those papers, all by yourself. You got down here for Thanksgiving by yourself. You didn't need me then. You didn't even see me that first trip.

My hands went numb, my feet suddenly freezing at my side. If he'd screamed at me I'd have known what to do, but he seemed just as calm as I was pretending to be.

—The best I can do, he said, is you can stay here tonight. To-morrow I'll take you to your mother's. That's it, that's the best I can do.

—Okay, but –

—But nothing. I'm not getting down. I'm not going inside. I'm not helping with this. I see the news too. I'm not getting involved with whoever she thinks she is now.

—Okay, I said again, trying to find some calm inside me. Okay, but what about – forget her, what if you do it just to help me?

He reached over, and I thought he was going to touch my shoul-der or my cheek or something, and the thought of that kind of con-tact made my eyes water, made me worry I would undo this new way of behaving and throw my arms around his legs, my face pressed into his stomach as I cried, *You can't do this to me, you can't leave me on my own like this.* But he didn't reach for me: he grabbed the cordless phone on the coffee table. My suitcase waited in the middle of the living room, where he'd left it.

—You're still at that school, right? I'm helping you enough.

He dialed with his thumb and before I could ask who he was calling, he barked, ¡Rafael! ¡Oye! Quédate la noche allá con tu mujer, que tengo alguien – no, cochino, mi hija, que llegó aquí de sorpresa del colegio. Sí, sí. No, gracias. And he hung up.

When he saw me crying—only a little, and calmly, no move to wipe my face—he sighed and said, You can have Rafael's bed. He just changed the sheets.

—I'm fine here, I said.

I thought he'd try to convince me, maybe grab my suitcase and put it in Rafael's room, but he smacked the sides of his jeans and said, Do whatever you want, Lizet.

He walked to his room but stopped first at Rafael's door, turned the knob, and opened it all the way. When he got to his own doorway, he didn't turn around, but he yelled, I swear he just changed the sheets, I saw him do it this morning.

He didn't close his own door behind him. I gave up after a few minutes: more than anything, sleeping on a couch would set me up for everything to go worse from then on. The least I could do for myself was take the bed my dad had negotiated for me, get some real rest. I dragged my bag to Rafael's room, the wheels catching on the overly plush black rugs he'd used to pad the places around his bed. I lay in a straight line on top of the mattress and slept like that, all my clothes still on, without even washing my face or brushing my teeth, as much as I wanted to do those things. But I didn't want to open my suitcase, dig around for my toothbrush, ask my dad where he kept his toothpaste. Even after I heard his snores half an hour later, even after I peered in and saw that he was on top of his bed, facedown and hugging his pillow under his face, pants still on, also refusing the comfort of covers, even then I still kept that stale taste in my mouth, told myself I'd get rid of it come morning.

The sound of him on the phone again, but hearing it from Rafael's room: my dad told the office of the contractor he worked for that he'd be late that morning. He had a family emergency concerning one of his daughters and could he please make up the hours that afternoon or Saturday, and no, he wasn't fishing for overtime, he just needed to get his daughter to her mother and he just wanted that one hour of pay back. I don't know what the person on the other end decided; my dad didn't tell me and I didn't ask.

He drove me to my mom's apartment as promised. The only

thing he asked during the drive—the Miami sun blaring through his van's windshield, his tools and ladders rattling behind us, filling in the silence—was if I ever gave Leidy and Dante the money from Christmas. He'd asked me that before: when I called him in January from school to say I'd made it back safely and pretended I'd forgotten about the fifty he claimed to owe me.

I said, Yes I gave them the money. I said, You asked me that already.

He didn't respond, and I understood he wasn't really asking. He'd meant it to remind me he was a good person, a good father. Neither of us spoke the rest of the ride.

It was only eight thirty when he rolled away, leaving me and my suitcase on the sidewalk after saying through the van's open window, Be careful, but there were already people standing down the street outside of Ariel's house. Two blocks away, a long oval of women all in black pressed up against his fence. I went upstairs hoping to see my mom before she left for the day—unlike my dad, her job with the city meant she got Good Friday off—but it was Leidy who got the door, who looked surprised to find me behind it and then suddenly not at all surprised, who told me, a glob of wet cereal on her collarbone and Dante crying behind her, that Mami had left before the sun was even up—hours ago.

I pushed past her and hoped my suitcase would roll over her painted toenails, chipping the polish and screwing up one of the few perks she got from working at the salon. All I said as I wheeled toward her feet was, *You* must be happy to see me.

Leidy and I then fought the old way, the big way, the way that felt, after the night before with my dad, less like a fight and more like a script I was following. We knew what to do and where it would end: I called her a liar and accused her of pushing me out of our family. She called me a snob and said I didn't care about anyone but myself. I told her I'd stayed at Papi's the night before and she called me a traitor, and I said she'd been listening to Mami too much and told her if she really wanted to see a traitor she should look in the mirror. There was a lot of yelling and stomping around and picking up of a crying Dante and *Don't you dare pick up my kid!* threats. There was aggressive unzipping of suitcases and fierce proclamations of *You're not sleeping in my room* and rebuttals of *This is our room*, and *She's our mom* and *What gives you the right*, et cetera, et cetera. Until it wound down and flared up and wound down again, until the crap in Dante's diaper found our noses and made us gag through our stern mouths, the room eventually smelling so bad we had to step out into the living room, where the curtains were open and from where we watched the crowd down the block grow and grow, the line of people headed to join it passing like a parade.

Later I would see that I was wrong about Leidy, wrong to think I wouldn't need her and that being a mom herself hadn't changed her in a way that would help us deal with Mami. I was wrong to believe the stories we'd been told about ourselves: that I was the only one bright enough and aware enough to have some kind of plan. But in the quiet of the apartment—feeling loud in its own way for coming after the riot of our fight—Leidy said, I *am* happy to see you, you stupid hoe. *You're* the hoe, I said back, and there we were, two hoes staring out a window, one thinking the worst of the fighting was over, the other glad to have the opening act out of her way.

31

SHE ONLY CAME HOME TO SHOWER and to shit. She'll pee there, Leidy told me, but our mom drew the line at shitting in Ariel's house. It's disrespectful: that was Mami's answer when Leidy—in the gentle tone she'd learned to use with Mami over the last few weeks, as if coaxing a cat out from under a car—asked our mom *What've you been up to* and *Where've you been sleeping.* The day I'd seen our mother on national news was one of the last nights she'd slept in her own bed. She stayed up nights for the vigil, or slept at the houses of her fellow Madres or at the house across the street from Ariel's, which was made available to my mom and her crew after the home's owner watched them, from his front window, pray all evening through a rainstorm. His wife had joined the group after that, and now his house was host to a perpetual sleepover, with women snoring on his couch or underneath his dining room table at all times. He'd rented a tent, too, and it stood in his front yard, protecting protestors from the sun and rain and cameras in heli-copters.

Leidy told me all this when she got back from her half day at the salon, Dante in her arms, marker all over his hands and cheeks.

She'd already paid for the week of daycare—was paying a little less overall now that he'd turned one—so she turned down my offer to watch him after our fight. I was secretly grateful for the chance to shower and then sleep through the late morning, though falling asleep had been an accident. I'd only meant to lie down for a few minutes before figuring out what to do next, but my body demanded the rest. I hadn't slept well in Rafael's bed.

All afternoon, Leidy punctuated what she told me with *I just didn't want you worrying*, and the bags under her eyes and the grayish tint to her skin made me finally believe her. While wiping off Dante's face and then feeding him and then wiping him off again, she told me in one avalanche all the things I thought I'd have to pry from her. She just gave it all over, relieved to have someone to talk to, and I stoked the small fire of what remained of my anger with that thought: I could be anyone. She's so lonely, I could be anyone.

Leidy told me that in the days after what was my spring break, Mami's supervisor at the city left messages on the machine giving first and second warnings about missed shifts, and a few more days passed before Leidy caught our mom in the apartment and played these messages for her, asking—gentle again but blocking the front door—if everything was going fine at work. I told Leidy we should call Mom's supervisor, but Leidy sighed that she'd done that already, a week earlier. I got up from the couch and feigned wanting some water to mask how ugly it looked that I hadn't *asked* if she'd called but said we should do it, as if the idea couldn't possibly come to her on her own. From the sink I asked what he'd said, and she told me the only reason Mami still had the job at all was because her supervisor was Cuban, too, was in fact a Pedro Pan kid, sent alone by his family to the United States back when Castro first came to power. Of course he wasn't happy about her missing so much work, but he told Leidy that Mom was calling in, using the sick days and vacation days she'd stored up for years. I sipped my water, my heart stinging from the new fact that she hadn't used these days on me over winter break, but I tried to hide this from Leidy, who was spending almost half her paycheck on daycare and so had to deal with that kind of hurt every day. The supervisor told Leidy that he was relieved when Mami asked to switch to part-time—something Leidy didn't know until he'd told her, but she played along like she knew, to keep him talking—and that he so admired her work with Madres Para Justicia and what he'd seen her say on the news that he'd only hired a temp to replace her, had told Mami that when everything was resolved, she could have her old hours back. That's good news, I said, and Leidy said again: That's why I didn't say anything, no reason to worry you. It's all gonna be fine, she said. But we both knew that me showing up meant everything was more serious than she wanted to admit.

—I want to see Mom, I said.

—They did an Easter egg hunt today at the daycare, she said. I'm thinking I should try to get a part-time there.

The apartment looked the same as it always had, but when I'd poked into the fridge before showering, there was almost nothing in it. A carton of leftover white rice. Some jars of Publix-brand baby food—just the sweet ones, banana, peaches—and some Tupperwares filled with a couple different colors of mush. Half a two-liter bottle of RC Cola, which had gone flat. An almost-empty tin of Café Bustelo ground coffee.

—I have money from my job too, I said. Up at school. It pays okay, if we need it.

She nodded.

I said, Don't worry, okay?

—*You* don't worry.

She left Dante on the couch with me and went to the pile of papers on the table by the front door, junk mail and bills and notices I'd planned to look at after Leidy left, thinking I'd need them as clues. The fact that I'd thought about it in those terms made me feel ridiculous, though it had seemed like the right word considering how much I didn't know.

—Do you think we can go find Mom? I said. Down the street?

Leidy returned with a manila envelope the size of half a sheet of paper.

—This came here for you, she said, handing it to me.

Mostly what came to the apartment for me was credit card offers, but this letter was from California, from UC Santa Barbara. Postmarked three days before spring break had started, the envelope was sliced open at the top, very clearly opened. In it were all the forms I needed to complete for the internship—waivers, IRS papers, travel preference sheets, checklists I was supposed to consult and *retain for my records*. There was also a typed note from someone writing on behalf of Professor Kaufmann stating that they hoped getting the forms to me at my home address over break would help expedite their return. A postage-paid envelope, it said, was enclosed for my convenience.

—Are you switching schools or what? Leidy said.

It was like I was Roly and I'd cheated on her and she'd caught me: that's what her face made me feel. But now I understood why Professor Kaufmann had seemed baffled by me in lab since spring break—because I never returned these forms. I'd never even seen them, but in lying and telling her I'd been home for break, she thought I had.

—No, this was a job thing, I said. It's nothing.

—But then why's it from another college? You want to go even farther away?

—It was just for the summer, like a summer internship thing.

—So wait, you're not gonna *be here* this summer? You're not coming back?

I heard the panic, could sense beneath it all the times over the last few weeks she'd wanted to ask me this but hadn't, thinking *I* was keeping something from *her*.

—It's not happening anymore. Don't worry, I said. I promise.

She stood stunned for a second, then let herself deflate, flopping on the couch next to me and Dante.

—Oh god, I thought I was gonna die, she said.

She pulled Dante onto her lap and squeezed him. He tried to worm away, more interested in the remote control.

—You swear though? she said. You swear you're coming home?

I shoved the papers back in the envelope, some catching and creasing as they went in. I said it again, though I didn't mean it for the reasons Leidy assumed: I swear. I promise.

She kissed Dante, a big wet smack on his cheek.

—Who wants to go to summer school anyways, she said to him.

She stuck her finger down the back of his pants and pulled them away from his body, peered down into his diaper. The elastic band thwacked back into place, and she said, Okay, let's do what you want. Let's go find Mom.

Dante's stroller crunched ahead, his butt sinking into the cloth, the seatbelt harness too tight against his chest. He sat in a daze, eyes half closed in the sunlight. My eyes were partway shut, too—Leidy was smart enough to wear sunglasses—and through hazy slits, in the ring of black-clad bodies linked hand in hand in the street, I first saw my mom. Then, two women down in the circle, I spotted her again. The shape from behind of a third woman could've been her, too.

—I should warn you, Leidy said, she's gonna be weird.

—No shit, I said.

The mumble coming from the group as we approached suddenly snapped into something recognizable—a prayer, one they all knew. An Our Father or a Hail Mary maybe: I didn't know the difference, and they were praying in Spanish, which made it even harder for me to tell. The only place I'd heard those sounds before was whenever our parents dragged us to a church for some cousin's first communion or confirmation, or to see some newly born relative get baptized. Me and Leidy always seemed a step behind, everyone else knowing when to stand, when to sit, when to shout back at the priest up front. My parents were raised Catholic but never prayed outside of these instances, so it always disturbed me to hear those words pour from their mouths without a thought, like some language they knew but kept secret from us, some voice that wasn't theirs. And that's how it felt, once we were close enough to see which one was actually my mom—prayers falling from her lips, eyeliner wobbling across her closed, twitching eyelids, her hair pulled back into a tidy but shaking bun: that she couldn't really be my mom. That my mom wasn't there.

We stood behind her in the prayer circle, onlookers stepping out of our way thanks to the stroller and Dante and the sacred nature any little boy within twenty miles of that house had taken on. Strings of rosary beads snaked around their palms and dripped into the air below their joined fists. I wondered where my mom had bought hers, if one even buys a rosary or if they're given out at churches for free. We waited for the chant to end, and when it did (sort of— there was a natural pause and some of the women opened their eyes and looked around, but others didn't, and my mom was in this second group), I leaned close to my mom's bun and said, Mami?

She opened her eyes and turned, hands still holding other hands on each side.

—Lizet! she screamed.

And then the smash of beads against my back, whips coming from both sides. My face was in my mother's neck as she pressed her hands and the rosaries into me. The rest of the circle stood frozen and confused.

She pushed me away and held me at arm's length, then let me go.

—Es mi hija, she said to the women around her. Everyone! This is my daughter!

All the women in the circle gawked at me, like maybe I was a sign from God, or some evil visiting. Several of them whispered to their neighbors—only one or two words of shock—and I thought maybe I should twirl around or something, but all I did was pull my shirt down at my waist with both hands, which let me hunch my shoulders like a boxer readying for a blow. Mami tugged me closer to the circle's center.

—What are you doing here? she said.

—I came down for Easter. I came down to get you.

I worried someone somewhere was snapping a picture; Mami was grinning like this was a possibility. The circle collapsed in closer.

—Another gift this Easter, she said. I am so happy you are here for this.

My mom grabbed my hand and squeezed it too hard, like she'd either really missed me or was really mad: the kind of grip you'd throw on the shoulder of a misbehaving toddler as you dragged them around a corner to beat them. I had no idea what to make of her reaction and so searched for Leidy, to read her face and see if she was signaling anything to me: *Get out now* or *You're on your own* or *See, I told you* or *Oh my god you're bringing her back single-handedly!* I couldn't spot her through the ring of women, so I looked all around me and ventured, This is so great!

—Yes! Our faith is moving mountains. Do you want some water?

I tried shifting a little away from her, just to get her whole body into view, but the women around us made that hard to do. Their black clothes radiated heat, and some had cheeks so red and fore-heads so sweaty that I couldn't believe they hadn't passed out.

—No, I'm okay, but can we – let's go home, I said to Mami.

The women all got silent and I said, Just for a little while. It's so hot. It's Good Friday. And I want to see you.

—I can't, she said. We're here praying, we can't stop. The court said yesterday that his family has the right to refuse his return, and we are giving thanks and praying it doesn't get reversed. Because the others, they keep calling.

—The others, I said.

—Janet Reno, Bill Clinton's people. They think they are bigger than the courts, than history. We are praying for God to intervene. He will. He has. We are praying all weekend and then Monday we're marching to the courthouse to thank the mayor, God bless him.

—From *here*?

—He says Ariel will stay, and he told the news that the federal government can't overrule him.

—I don't think the mayor gets to say that, Mami.

A current twitched beneath her face, like when I was little and did something in front of people to embarrass her. It meant a secret viselike pinch to the back of my arm was on its way. But it never came, and the hard-line mouth slipped back behind the beatific face.

I took the reprieve and said, But I didn't know about all that, I was on the plane. I didn't hear, Mami. Of course you have to keep praying. Of course. Now more than ever.

The women began to spread back out. One close to me wore a large gold brooch in the shape of Cuba, and it pulled on her blouse and sagged at one end, the east end, so that it looked like a smear of metal dripping from her shoulder. It glinted in the sunlight like a just-brandished knife. My mother tugged my arm and pulled me to her, leaned in to my face, her breath another source of heat, and said, I'll come by later, after I eat with them. When we rotate I can visit you. You're at the apartment?

She squeezed my arm harder. It was a genuine question.

—Yeah, of course, I said.

She kissed my cheek and hugged me again, the rosary beads rolling over my back and clinking together a second time. The circle around us was almost intact once more except for her spot, the place through which I would leave it. And just outside of it was Dante in his stroller and Leidy, standing stone still until I stepped toward her.

As she charged away, the circle back to praying and safely behind us, Leidy said, What the fuck was that, Lizet?

—I don't know. You're right that she's weird.

Despite the heat, my arms and legs were freezing. And I couldn't walk fast enough. Neither could Leidy. For a step or two I was right next to her, and the sun shined off the tears on her face as they slipped from under her sunglasses, just before she swiped them away.

—Oh my god, are you crying? I said. Why the hell are you *crying*?

Instead of stopping to answer me, she wrapped her fists tighter around the handles of Dante's stroller and seemingly shifted into a higher gear. Her silver earrings rocked back and forth like angry kids on swings.

—You know how many times I came down here to ask her something and she acts like she can't hear me? Like I'm not even there?

I was walking so fast to keep up that it would've been easier to just jog. I managed to huff out, Leidy, she sees you all the time.

—Whatever, she said. It's not like you got her to come home. A lot of good you did, gracing us with your presence. All the way from *New York*.

—What the hell, I said to her back. I halted in the street. I said, You're jealous that she stopped for me and not you? Is that really so shocking?

My armpits were drenched, and my sweat-soaked shirt nudged itself cold against the insides of my arms. She kept walking, the stroller's wheels scuffing ahead of her. She got smaller and smaller until a car honked beside me; I was blocking a driveway.

By the time I locked the apartment door, she was in the shower with Dante—the stroller and her sunglasses and her clothes and his clothes and his wet diaper all in a trail from the front door to the bathroom. She came out over an hour later, all wrinkled and with her hair in a towel, had stayed locked in there long enough to make it weird for me to bring up what had happened. She spent the evening wandering around the apartment, playing with Dante and then feeding him and then hanging out in our room with him, leaving me with nothing to do but watch TV in the living room, though what I was really doing was willing the phone to ring, willing my dad to call and say he'd changed his mind and would help. Or willing Omar to call and just talk to me. I kept almost hearing it—the shrill bell about to make me jump—but I knew my dad wouldn't call, that Omar wouldn't call. Omar couldn't, not after the way he'd driven off, and I didn't even really want him to—what would I say to him? I just wanted the distraction, the chance to whisper with someone the way Leidy did to Dante, to feel less lonely for a few minutes. I turned up the TV's volume, pretending not to be listening for the phone or for Leidy's hushed voice spitting my name at her son.

Mami came home maybe an hour before the sun went down. Leidy had put Dante to bed, and she volunteered *The baby's sleeping* once it was clear Mami wasn't going to ask about him. Mami nodded at her and grabbed my wrist, tugging me up from the couch into the kitchen.

—I don't have a lot of time, she said. I don't feel right not being there if I can be there.

I let her keep her hand clasped around my wrist.

—But I'm visiting, I said. Can't you tell them I'm visiting? I'm never here.

—It's not them, it's *my* feeling.

She raised my hand with hers, made it look like we were both pointing at her chest.

—You don't know what it's been like, she said. This is so important.

A wrinkle formed between her eyes, like she was concentrating or trying to beam a thought into my head. She looked like me for a second, like the face in the mirror the night I'd practiced in front of it, almost a year earlier, after sending in my paperwork to

Rawlings, saying to what seemed like a serious, determined reflection, *There's something I need to tell you guys. It's about my future.* Though in the end, I hadn't said any of that, only: *I'm going to college in New York and it's too late to stop me,* starting the whole thing off even more wrong than it already was. Mami's tired face shined at the nose and forehead in the white light of the kitchen. She was trying to seem greater than herself, mustering up what little energy she had left to convince me of something.

—It's okay, I said. I understand.

She let out a breath I was scared to see she'd been holding. She said, So you'll come back with me?

—What?

—I just think, it must be a sign that you're here. Come back with me for the vigil.

Leidy, now steps closer and behind my mom's left shoulder, scowled at us like we were high school bitches in a hallway talking shit: *You hear she's pregnant? Yeah, you hear he's not gonna marry her?* She waved her hands in the air, a huge *No.*

—I just got here, I said to my mom.

—But you're here for *this,* she said, her grip tighter. Come tonight, keep me company. I have to be up the whole night for the prayer.

Her grip loosened and her hand slid down my wrist, her curled fingers hooking mine.

—I promise it's not scary, she said. It's really powerful. We all feel so strong together. You'll see it. Come, I'll wait for you to get your things.

I tried to hide my mouth from Leidy's view, but the apartment was so small, I knew she could hear me. I said, Okay.

Mami laced her fingers with mine and squeezed so hard my fingertips throbbed.

—I'm going to shower, she said. I *need* to shower. Get ready fast, okay?

Even from all those feet away, I saw over my mom's shoulder

Leidy's nostrils flaring, her head jutting forward as if ready to ram me.

—I'm happy you're here for this, Mami said, reaching for my hair and pulling it over my shoulder, fixing it a little with her fingers. I'm proud you'll be part of this with me.

—Of course, I said. Me too.

I caught only the tip of Leidy's ponytail snapping out of view as she ran away, the bedroom door slamming a second later.

Mami didn't even turn around. She only said, Your sister's got the baby.

She hugged me then, pulled me into her and rubbed my shoulders. She let one hand slide down to the small of my back, where she rubbed a wide, warm circle—a motion she'd always done when we were sad or sick and bent over a toilet, a small solace as our bodies convulsed with a stomach flu or shook with despair at the way we'd let some stupid boy hurt our feelings. I felt my back rest at the familiar touch, at the comfort her hand there still sent through me. She gave me a kiss on my forehead as she pressed one last circle and then let me go.

—The baby keeps her so busy but that's how it is, isn't it? she said as she walked to the bathroom.

Once the water in the shower was running, Leidy came out and went for my arm as I stepped around her and into our room to pack some things. I smacked her hand away.

—Don't play around with this shit, she said.

—I'm not, I said like a reflex. Dante was asleep in his crib, but I was the only one who lowered her voice. What was I supposed to tell her? I said.

She looked at the crib, then snorted through her nose.

—In case you're wondering, she said, this is why I don't tell you anything.

I dropped to her bed, which still held the chaos of my accidental nap, and stared up at the ceiling, the texture of it blinking back with hints of glitter to make it seem nicer than it really was. She walked to her dresser and grabbed her purse, slung it over her shoulder. Then she picked up Dante from his crib. He murmured but managed to stay asleep.

I pulled at the crown of my hair the way Ethan would—my forehead was shellacked in sweat left over from the conversation with my mom—and said, *Leidy*. Come *on*. Please don't be mad at me about this. Do I really have a choice?

But she was at the bedroom door already, Dante perched backward on her hip with his limbs dangling away from her, his eyes closed. I jumped up and followed her through the apartment, said, Where are you going, when she opened the front door, the exposed fluorescent tube lights in the apartment's hallway buzzing low under my voice.

—Don't worry about it, you've got enough going on, she said.

After the slam came Dante's crying, high and receding as Leidy bolted down the stairs. I ran to the window: Leidy strapped Dante into his car seat, then stomped to the driver's side. She rested her head on the steering wheel for a second and then turned the key in the ignition. She didn't look up at the window, not even once. Behind me, the shower shut off, and I scrambled to my room, to the things I was supposedly gathering.

I dumped everything in my book bag out onto Leidy's bed, then put certain things back inside: my toothbrush, my wallet, a pair of sweatpants and a T-shirt for sleeping in, underwear, a small towel of Dante's I grabbed from the dresser. Focusing on packing for the sleepover aspect of the vigil made what I'd be doing that night feel more normal. This was what I'd come for—to face this head-on and drag my mom away from it. The word *infiltrate* hovered in my mind, somehow feeling more cumbersome than the *betray betray betray* my dad had thrown around a year before. I tossed my deodorant back in the bag. I looked at my pillow and wondered if I could cram it in there.

Mami came into my room with her hair wet, but she wore the same black shirt and loose black pants she had on before. Did Leidy leave? she said. I told her yes, but Mami didn't seem at all worried. She looked at me—she'd redone her eyeliner—and said, Don't be so worried, your sister knows what she's doing. I let myself believe her, made myself remember everything Leidy had kept from me over these last weeks. Mami checked the buttons on her blouse and said, Ready? And I slung my bag over my shoulder and moved and we were out on the street, the moon low in the sky, Mami not even looking twice at the vacant parking spot, our steps falling into the same rhythm.

32

I WANTED TO ASK HER a million questions. How often do you sleep there? How much work are you really missing? But each one seemed too pointed, too worried, too quickly exposing why I'd ditched Leidy to come along with her. We passed the now-smaller circle of women praying outside of Ariel's house. She waved to them but we didn't head over to join it, and I asked her why not.

—Your clothes, she said.

My jeans were a little thin at the knees but clean, my T-shirt maybe a bit tight across my chest. She lifted the latch on the chain-link gate surrounding the house across from Ariel's, the one I'd seen in pictures on the news with the white tent covering the lawn.

—No, it's just you're not wearing black, she said. Come on, you can stay inside.

—Was I supposed to –

—It's fine. Just come inside.

—I can go back and change, I said, still standing outside the gate.

She climbed up the three concrete steps to the house's front door and pushed it open, waved for me to follow.

Once inside, it was hard to remember we were only a couple blocks from the apartment. The overhead lights of a small kitchen bled out into what looked like the dining room. Every window was covered with sheets and duct tape, but the sheets hung loose at the bottoms, allowing people to look out when they needed or wanted to. The house was packed and loud with talking. Right away I almost lost my mom in the crowd; she slipped between men and women she seemed to know, touching their shoulders as she passed. I tried to stay close, though my book bag made it tough to squeeze around people. When she stopped, I pushed up right behind her. We were stuck against a long table loaded with food: a platter piled high with grilled chicken drumsticks, pink and brown juices pooling beneath them; aluminum trays filled with yellow rice next to stacks of Styrofoam plates; hunks of Cuban bread cut from a long loaf and then sliced in half again. I was about to ask if I could grab a piece of the bread—I was starving—when my mom handed me a plate. She forked a couple slimy plátanos onto it.

—Eat something, she said.

I slid the bag off my shoulder and tucked it between my feet.

—Where'd all this come from? I said.

—Everywhere. People bring things, places donate things.

Someone pushed by me to stab a chunk of avocado from a bowl on my right—a younger guy with dark hair and a thin beard. He looked like someone I could've gone to high school with. My mom continued to load my plate for me—rice, chicken, tostones, black beans drenching all of it. The guy did the same thing, grabbing a handful of forks and stocking his plate mostly with sharing-friendly foods. My mom nudged the plate into my hand and said, Hi Victor, and the guy said, Wassup Lourdes. He leaned away from the table and bent behind me, kissed my mom on the cheek while chewing. I watched him leave, and he only looked back at me once—with green eyes so surprising they looked misplaced, transplanted into his head from some long-lost Cuban cousin of Ethan's—just before he looked down and hid them and pushed his way into the crowd, his plate of food held high over his head.

—You know him? I said to Mami.

She used a new, empty plate to gesture around the room.

—I know everybody.

I nudged my bag a foot or so along the floor and turned to lean against the table, my butt pushing over a stack of napkins. As I shoveled rice into my mouth, I saw the things I'd expected to see: banners with too many words on them, their messages confused and in two languages; Cuban flags propped in corners; women standing in pairs, bent in to each other, holding hands and praying. But it was creepy because it was not that creepy. People smiled, people laughed. People weren't posing; they had no clue how crazy the cameras blasting their images around the country made them look. My mom asked, You okay here for a second, and before I answered she left for the kitchen.

Near the house's rear entrance, in what was once a back porch now converted into a full-blown room, the guy named Victor and other younger guys—guys my age or a little older—stood on the brink of the cinder-block-walled backyard, the people outside smoking cigarettes, their caps backward or to the side, the smoke pouring from their nostrils as they talked at each other. I ran my tongue over my teeth, hoisted my bag to my shoulder, lifted my plate over my head, and moved toward them.

I stood just inside the house, eating and listening for a minute to the guys outside. People speared food off Victor's plate, but he didn't acknowledge it. He just stared at me with his borrowed eyes, with no shame in a way that made me nervous. He chewed and swallowed. Crickets cut in and out between the words of another guy's story about how he'd almost punched a reporter, and in the middle of all that, Victor blurted out, I know you.

The other guy looked at him but kept on with his story, turned a little to push Victor and me out of it.

Victor forced his way closer, came up a step to stand next to me inside the doorway. He pointed his fork in my direction.

—You went to Hialeah Lakes, he said.

He leaned against the doorframe and slipped another chunk of avocado in his mouth. I reached up and back with the hand holding the fork to tug my ponytail forward and drape it over my shoulder, but I accidentally poked myself in the cheek with the fork's tines.

—Yeah? Yeah, I did.

Having gone to the same high school didn't mean much when a few thousand people a year could say the same thing: he might as well have said, *I know you, you're from Miami.* But he still hadn't faltered in his eye contact. He didn't seem to need to blink. His chewing looked more like teeth grinding, the small silver hoops in his earlobes dancing a little with the motion of his jaw. Thanks to the help of the streetlights illuminating parts of the backyard, I made out the surprise of red hair glinting from his chin.

—Oh shit! he said. He repeatedly stabbed his fork into a greasy plantain and smiled. You used to go with Omar, right? You're that smart girl.

—I'm not that smart.

I'd said this too many times to guys from Miami, though the reflex had never kicked in up at Rawlings, didn't show up, for instance, when I talked about lab with Ethan.

—But yeah, I said, I go with Omar.

—Oh so you're *still* going with him?

I rolled my eyes, mostly to see if I spotted my mom anywhere. She hadn't turned up behind me, and I didn't hear her voice in the crowd. Victor stroked his chin in mock concentration. His fingernails were ringed with dirt, and I imagined his hands wrist-deep in a car engine. I let my bag slip off my shoulder, let it dangle in a way that I hoped looked casual and that tugged down my shirt a little from the side.

—No, I said. Sorry, I meant what you said. Used to. See how I'm not smart?

He laughed like fast hiccups—too rough—but still stared at me while he jerked his shoulders and bent forward. I decided to think of him as *intense*—as one of those *intense* guys looking always for the *one woman* who *gets* them—and made myself stare right back at him. He picked up the plantain he'd basically shivved and flung it in his mouth, all without looking at anything but me.

—So you know my mom? I said.

He shook his head no.

—I know *of* your mom. Like how I know *of* you.

I nodded and said, Okay. You know *of* my mom.

—Don't change the subject, he said. You're that girl that went to New York for some scholarship.

I smiled, said, Yeah.

He made ticking noises with his tongue. So did you cheat on Omar up there?

I squealed *What?* as my bag swung and hit the doorframe. Rice spilled from my plate.

—I see it all over your face, he said.

He laughed again, big stuttery bursts, shoulders jumping. Then he finally looked away and down at his plate, mumbled, I'm-kidding-I'm-kidding.

He smashed an avocado piece into mush under his fork tines. I decided to laugh, too, giggled a halfhearted *Whatever, bro* as I lowered my bag to the floor.

—Why have I never seen you here before? he said.

—I'm just down for the weekend. Just visiting.

His face snapped back up and I tried to match his new stare without smiling but couldn't hold it back. My teeth came out like a white flag.

—Oh so you're a *visitor*, he said. I got it. Hey guys, she's *visiting*. But no one outside even looked at him. He lowered his voice and said just to me, You might want to *visit* the beach too. While you're *visiting*. Fucking ghost.

—Funny, I said.

He used the edge of his fork to nudge a single grain of rice around his plate. He pushed the grain all the way to the plate's edge, then laughed at it for a few seconds.

—So! he said. He dropped his head down so that it was closer to my face, gave me an exaggerated scowl. You think Ariel should go back or stay here?

He reached out with his fork and stole a piece of avocado from me even though he had plenty on his own plate. I knew I should just say *Stay here*, but I still thought maybe we were flirting, the green eyes making me feel like we were someplace else.

—Why are you asking me that? I raised one side of my mouth. Why do you think I'm here? You know my mom is –

—I know *of* your mom. Get it right.

He pointed the fork at my face again and closed one eye, shifted his weight to his other foot.

—No wait, he said. Why *are* you here? That's actually a good question.

He chewed like the cows on the farms lining the one major road into Rawlings. I started to answer, but with his mouth full he blurted out, Because you left once, right? You're already a sellout, right? So what makes you think you can just come back like nothing? With no consequences?

My mouth went dry, and I could taste and smell my own sour breath despite the bits of food. I remembered I had on no makeup— no eyeliner, nothing on my lips. My hair was frizzy, freaked out by the sudden onslaught of Miami humidity, the ponytail on my shoulder fluffing up like a squirrel's tail. There was no way I looked pretty enough to flirt with. He reached for another avocado chunk from my plate. He pressed down harder—much harder—than he needed to snare it.

—I'm not a sellout, I said.

—So what, are you doing like a report for school on this?

He held his fork up and lassoed the air with it. A couple of the other guys turned and flicked their eyes over my body, waiting for me to say something.

Victor said, You like a little baby reporter? You reporting on us here, Smart Girl?

He bit his bottom lip—a chipped and turned-in front tooth flashed out like a warning—and lifted his chin. Stray grays sat shrouded among the reds I'd noticed before. He was older than I thought, maybe much older. The skin circling the base of his earrings, I saw now, was blue-black, the holes ragged and peeling. I fixed my bag on my shoulder, grabbed the strap with my free hand.

—I have to go look for my mom, I said.

—You do that. Say hi to Omar for me.

—I won't, I spit over my shoulder, trying to move away fast.

—Good, because I don't fucking know him or his stuck-up ex-bitch.

I pretended I didn't hear him or the snorts from the few guys who'd started paying attention to our conversation. I shoved my way into the crowd and moved in the direction of the kitchen, leaving my half-empty plate of food on a picture-lined table behind the couch. I pulled the rubber band from my hair and ran my fingers through it, arranged it on my shoulders, smoothed my thumb over each eyebrow. I lowered my head and pinched each of my cheeks as hard as I could stand it, trying to force some color into them. When I passed the bathroom, I ducked inside and slammed the door, the sound lost under the tumult of voices. I sat on the toilet and cried without wanting to, without letting myself look in the mirror at any point. I didn't want to know what a sellout looked like.

That guy Victor took off not long after I emerged from the bathroom. He waved at me before leaving like nothing had happened and said, Good talking to you, as he held two fingers and his thumb like a gun in my direction. He kissed my mom goodbye, hugged the owner of the house on his way out. I worked up the courage to ask my mom, How do you know that guy, and she said, His abuela spends the days down here. I think he went to your high school, but a while ago.

She watched me as I stared at the front door after he left. He's not for you, she said.

The crowd inside the house continued to thin as the night deepened, which was sort of a relief, but sort of not: with fewer people there, you could tell I wasn't talking to anyone, just standing around with my bag on the floor next to me or between my legs as I pretended to be part of conversations about the Easter march and how well negotiations were going, about the mayor's leadership and whether or not the attorney general was a lesbian, me just eating grains of rice one by one in an effort to look too occupied with food to chime in. My mom floated around the house talking to people, making them laugh, bringing them cups of water or soda or café, like she was part of another family's Noche Buena, a family she liked more and wanted to be in, one that understood her better.

Around midnight, she came up to me and said that anyone still there would be staying the night (most were women, most were dressed in black). I thought of them as the core; I recognized some of them from TV or from news stills, where they'd stood in Ariel's living room and prayed through phone calls, prayed before and after press conferences, put their hands on lawyers and blessed them.

—We're going to bed now to be up early, she said. But a few of us will stay awake to pray all the way through.

—What are *you* gonna do?

She shrugged. Pray, she said. Try to keep people focused. But *you* should sleep, that way you can take the couch. If you wait, someone'll take it. You don't want to be under there.

She pointed at the long wooden table with the food.

—They don't ever put the food away, she said.

After a lap of picking up abandoned plates and tossing them out, she set me up on the couch, pulling a flat throw pillow off another chair and setting it where my head would go. I tucked my bag beneath that spot, leaned it against the couch, and decided not to change into the sweatpants I'd brought since it didn't seem like anyone else was making themselves more comfortable. I pulled my legs up on the seat and out of nowhere my mom bent down and kissed me on the forehead. And so I ignored how the sheet she'd found for me smelled like cigarettes, how the couch was covered in material so coarse it paved a pattern on my skin. Her lips left a cold spot for minutes afterward, and I wanted to grab her, pull her to the couch, not let her go outside. I wanted to call Leidy and say, *I did it*, though I didn't do anything. All I can say is that her touch made me feel close to her in a way we'd never been, despite the fact that she would spend the night outside with strangers praying for a child that wasn't hers. She pushed my hair off my forehead and said, Tomorrow will be a beautiful day, and I closed my eyes and nodded.

I fell asleep that night trying to rewrite the conversation with Victor into something else, something where he was flirting with me and not trying to fuck with my head, not trying to tell me where I stood in the neighborhood now—an echo of Omar's last words to me. I remade his smile into a sweeter one, took the squint out of his eyes and reshaped them into something more open, something impressed with what he saw. And I put even more of Ethan's red in his beard, under his chin, which made him kinder, more familiar. I revised the memory so that his laughs were better timed, in sync with what I said the way Ethan's always were. I turned my face into the dank throw pillow I'd folded in half. When I still couldn't fall asleep, I told myself Victor's venom came from his knowing I was too good for him, out of his league. What did I want with him anyway? Why did I care what some loser thought? But a year earlier I would've given that loser my phone number. A year earlier I would've found a way to press my arm against his, would've laughed at his jokes in a voice higher than my real one. For years after that night, the real memory of that conversation made me wince—and it does, still, much too often, whenever I catch a decent-looking man watching me from a nearby table during the breakfast remarks at a research symposium, or at the beach bar my colleagues and I sometimes visit during happy hour on Thursdays to drink a beer and watch the sunset. I still perceive some intensity from someone and instead of recognizing it as attraction, I immediately assume it's disgust. I want to blame Victor for that reflex, but it was there already, had shown itself for the first time the day I saw my mother in the airport, waiting for me at winter break; all he did was verify for me that I would always use that double vision against myself. All he showed me was that I couldn't go back to not having it.

And then there's the bigger reason that Victor has stuck in my memory like a splinter. I didn't know it then, replaying and revising our conversation while falling asleep on that couch, but he was the last person to talk to me before this double vision became the *only* way through which I saw anything. My mind defaults to that small conversation with Victor because it's easier than thinking about what happened to Ariel hours later, about the different waves of betrayal that surged in and around me that night and since. I've focused first on someone I never saw again because he's an easier specimen to dissect, an easier result to write up—one where I'm only a small variable, one that my mother isn't part of at all.

33

I WISH I COULD SAY I woke up with the screams, with the sound of breaking glass, or even before all that—with the rumbling engines of the vans as they pulled up, with the boot stomps charging up and down the block and kicking in doors. But it was a stranger who woke me, a woman dressed in black who was not my mother. I had no idea what time it was, only that I'd been dreaming, I think, because I'd heard someone snoring and thought it was Omar, that I'd slept over at his house and I hadn't yet seen my dad or Leidy or my mom or anyone—that Omar was on the floor next to me and I wanted to pull him to the couch but couldn't move. Then a woman's hands were digging into my shoulders and she was shaking me and yelling in Spanish, They're coming! Get up! Get outside now!

Sleep evaporated from me—of course Omar wasn't on the floor, this wasn't Omar's house, I didn't know whose house it was. I sat up as the woman hurried away, the shapes of people following her out the door. There was no time to change, and then I looked down and remembered that I'd slept in my clothes. The bag I'd brought with me—I stumbled over it as I got up. I slipped on my sneakers and ran with the others into the morning dark.

Later I would learn that the raid lasted less than four minutes. Like the rest of the world, I'd see the picture of a screaming child with an assault rifle in his face, a soldier in riot gear carrying that rifle and demanding the person holding the boy let him go. By the time I made it to the gate of the house, that photo had already been taken by the one cameraman who, like my mom, had stayed across the street that night, and by the time the house's gate clapped shut behind me, the raid was in its final seconds. My mother was still inside Ariel's house, pepper spray searing her eyes as she groped the walls and tried to find her way back to Ariel's bedroom, careening against other screaming people left in the wake of rifle-lugging soldiers, the last few of whom I would see run from the house and into waiting vans. But the very first thing I saw—what I later thought I must've dreamed, because I remember the whole street going quiet when that couldn't be true, because I know he was crying, yelling for help, one small scream among dozens of others—was Ariel in the arms of a woman I'd never seen before, a blanket trailing useless from her side, his legs dangling and his feet hitting her knees as she ran into a van. He looked huge. His terrified wet face shined right in my direction as I stopped in the middle of the street, and I couldn't move, couldn't breathe, because I knew he was big enough, old enough to remember this, that when he would have the nightmares brought on by this moment, I would be in them.

The van door slammed—I thought I saw his skinny leg almost get chopped off by it, but that didn't happen—and I found my voice. Wait, I screamed. Not *No*. Not *Stop*. Not *Ariel*. I screamed *Wait* like there was something I needed to ask him, and I ran after the van like a bus I'd missed. My arms reached out toward it as if that would help, my fingers splayed and clawing. I thought I had a chance to catch up—there was a stop sign at the corner—but clearly they were going to blow through it. The men already in front of me came into focus: other people running, trying to catch the vans and—do what? One of the men veered to the curb and grabbed a metal garbage can, hauled it up over his head and hurled it through the air. It landed near the ignored stop sign, garbage spewing in an arc and more flying out as the can rolled into the intersection. Something smashed into my back as I slowed down, and when I turned around, a couple dozen people ran past me, all of them with anything they could find in their hands. They charged down the street, launching debris at the vans as they sped away, and I leapt sideways, toward the fence surrounding Ariel's house. People poured out from the front door, screaming and cursing, but none of them was my mother. I had no way of knowing she was in there, but I felt it somehow: no other place made sense anymore. A fire—seconds old—burned in another garbage can out front and someone ran up to it and kicked it over. I ducked beneath the carport, looking for another way in. I ran through the yard and around the house, darting between people with their hands digging at their eyes, all of them stumbling around like drunks. Sirens started up a few blocks away, and the yells from the front yard rose higher, sounded more organized. I stepped over a small bike with training wheels, the handlebars bent. A back door hung all the way open, the bottom hinge busted, and I rushed inside.

I'd never been in the house, but what I was seeing was not the way my mom knew it in the months leading up to that moment. Huge gashes at shoulder and waist height tore through the plaster in strips, exposing the wood partitions. The closet door in the room I'd entered stood propped up against another wall, ripped off, the closet's contents gushing onto the floor. A trail of mud and orange liquid—more pepper spray—splattered ahead of me. I followed it deeper into the house. I stepped over plastic toys, slipped on sheets and blankets strewn across the tile. People ran around me yelling, *He's gone! What happened! They kidnapped him! He's gone!* at each other in English and Spanish, moved from room to room with purpose I didn't understand.

—Stop, what the fuck's going on? I screamed to no one and everyone.

Nobody answered, but a bald man with a mustache put his arms around me and squeezed me so tight I couldn't breathe. He wept into my ponytail for a second or two, then ran outside. I pushed past people crying in the living room, all of them jockeying to find the front door, and I moved into a hallway toward what I figured might be Ariel's room.

—Mom, I screamed. Mami! Where are you!

The hallway walls were empty, but on the floor were picture frames: gold rectangles in all different sizes, the pictures in them curling at the corners and covered by fresh shards of glass. I put my hands on the walls to keep from slipping on the orange-slicked floor as I leapt over the piles. Something tore into the heel of my hand—a nail that minutes earlier had held up a frame. I wiped the blood on my jeans and kept moving. I stuck my head into what I saw was the bathroom, pink tiles gleaming, the shower curtain in a heap in the tub, a towel rack busted on one side, hanging straight down and useless.

—Mom, I yelled, the word cracking against the tile.

The next door down: the door itself was *in* the room, resting in a nest of stuffed animals against the room's back wall and blocking the window, the side with the hinges broken into splays of wood jutting from it like palm fronds. Inside, people cried to each other as they stood around what looked like a car—a racecar bed, red and low to the ground, though I could barely see it through everyone's legs. The crowd was two or three deep in some spots, and from its center—from the bed itself—came howls so raw I thought someone must've been shot, that the sirens—much closer now—were an ambulance coming to take this person to a hospital to be sewn up and saved. I stepped over a muddied Donald Duck—thought for a second that someone had ripped off his pants before remembering he didn't wear pants—and pushed into the crowd where the bed met the room's back wall.

My mother was on that racecar bed with her arms wrapped around Caridaylis—who now bolted her screams directly into my mom's shoulder. Caridaylis was pounding on my mother's chest and arms. She punched my mother in the sides, struggled to get free. My mother whispered *Shhhh* and *No no no* and dragged her hand up to Cari's head, her fingers wide apart and tangling in her hair and holding the girl's face in place.

—Ya, ya, she said into her ear. My mother kissed Caridaylis there, on the ear, then on her hair, then her temple, three or four more times at least, rocking her slowly until the girl's fists fell and she pulled them into herself.

—Go away, my mother begged us. Give us a minute. Please, give her *one* minute.

No one moved. No one even backed away. The chaos outside grew louder, pressing up against the window: glass shattering, every dog for miles barking and howling. Caridaylis hiccupped into my mother's shoulder, the soft sound unmuffled only when she turned her face to the side, to the back wall of the room, away from everyone. Only I could see it—her face—from where I stood on the circle's edge up against that wall. A face puffy with sleep and tears, a young face—no makeup at this hour of the morning, no lipstick to make her seem older—her eyes closed, the lids hiding them thin enough to rip. A face smashed up with grief I'd never known. It looked like my mother's face, which hovered close to Cari's in that moment, streaming its own tears over cheeks tinged the orange of pepper spray, over skin rushed old by the weeks of lost sleep. Both of them with their eyes closed like that, their mouths distorted and wet and swollen and open in breathy crying—they could've been related. Cari could've been her daughter.

My mom opened her eyes and I stepped back, feeling caught.

—Jesus I said leave her alone, she hissed.

She clutched Caridaylis to her chest, and her eyes passed over every one of us in that ring of people. They passed right over me. They kept moving until she shook her head no and then looked back down at the top of Cari's head and kissed it. She began rocking her again, cradling her tighter than before, and that squeeze pushed more of Cari's sobs out of her. She flung her arms around my mom's neck and wailed into my mom's collarbone, pulling herself up and leaving behind a patch of wet—saliva, tears, snot—on my mom's chest. My mom closed her eyes and ran her fingers through the length of Cari's hair. Her hand trailed down to the small of Cari's back, rubbed a wide, warm circle there, a comfort she'd given Leidy and me hundreds of times.

—Mami, I whispered.

—Ya, ya, she said to Caridaylis, as if she'd been the one to call for her.

I watched my mom's hand circle, press and circle, my own back cold against the wall.

Someone grabbed my elbow and tugged me toward the door. When my feet didn't budge, the pull came again, harder, then a clamp of fingers into the crook and these hot words from a stranger in my ear: Un poco respeto. No kiss followed it, no reassuring hand to guide me from pain, no sweetness or memory of sweetness. Just the lesson: Have some respect. Have some respect for the dead, grieving mothers.

Another pull, now at my hand, and a shot of pain seared up to my elbow. I brought my hand to my face. The chunk of skin the nail in the hallway wall had torn from the meat of my palm dangled in a strip, still attached to my hand's heel at the very edge of the tear. Blood smudged all the way down my wrist, and the cut was still bleeding. I put the gash in my mouth, thinking I could flip the strip back over it, press it into place with my tongue, set it up to heal that way. But at the taste of iron and salt, my teeth clenched down—an unknown reflex—and bit the sliver at the spot where it clung, the top teeth and the bottom teeth finally meeting as they severed it completely.

In the years since that night, I've reimagined what I did next every which way. In some daydreams, I ignore the people tugging my arm and tell them to get the fuck away from me, that that woman holding Caridaylis is *my* mother and I will not be leaving without her this time. In others I stand against the wall long enough that she sees me again, then she opens her arms and we all cry there, on that ridiculous racecar bed, her real daughter and her adopted one merging into one girl she could admire for a whole host of reasons. (In no version does Leidy show up, which reflects the real truth of that early morning.) My leaving had allowed for someone new to come in, and I'd been wrong all that time in thinking it was Ariel. The real replacement was right there in my mom's arms: someone she could be proud of, someone whose decisions she understood and would've made herself had it been her life, a daughter who'd taken on more than anyone thought possible but who'd done it through no fault of her own, who was blameless. My hand stopped bleeding, and there was nothing left for me to do except for what I did: I walked away, back to where I'd come from, grabbed my bag, then left that house and eventually that city, kept leaving, year after year, until where I was from became, each time, the last place I left, until home meant an address, until home meant only as much as my memory of that morning would betray.

Leidy never forgave me for leaving my mother there. She told me much later that she'd spent most of the night driving around, debating whether or not to take Dante to Roly's house for one of those surprise visits Roly hated before remembering that her last attempt (on Dante's first birthday, weeks earlier) had resulted in Roly's mother threatening to call the police. Eventually, the smell of shit worked its magic again, making its way to the front seat, and the thought of changing Dante's diaper in the backseat of the car rather than in the small comfort of the apartment made her turn around and head home. She'd slept through the raid, through almost all of its aftermath, only waking up when I got home hours later, after walking in the opposite direction everyone else headed until the sun was high enough that I wasn't afraid to turn back.

Mami didn't come home that day or that night, and Leidy almost murdered me when it occurred to her that our mom might've been arrested.

—You had the chance to save her! she yelled as she flipped through the phone book, looking for the numbers to the police stations in the area.

—No I didn't, I said, facedown on the sofa bed and shaking with exhaustion.

I was incredibly thirsty but also felt that drinking water would make me throw up. I was trying, above all else, to just hold very still, to calm my torn hand's pulse. I explained the following things to her and into my pillow: that I had a flight to catch the next morning, that I could not afford to get arrested myself, that they don't let people out of jail because they have to go back to school, that I was not about to wrestle Mom away from the group of people throwing things at the vans.

This last lie I told her because I couldn't hurt her with the truth. It was enough that one of us knew we'd been replaced. I couldn't tell Leidy what I'd seen—where I'd really found our mother— because *Leidy* should've been the focus of my mom's energy after I left, Leidy who should've gotten more from everyone who supposedly loved her. I kept the image of my mom with Caridaylis—a girl whose age split the fifteen months between me and Leidy—to myself, never told my sister about the kiss our mom pressed into the top of that girl's head, about the wailing and the rocking, about the hand making those circles on her back. When Mami came home, her face and hands still stained with pepper spray, I let Leidy think this came from the morning riot our mother wasn't part of. I've never told Leidy the truth, and when I think about all the ways I came to abandon her, I hold this one mercy close as redemption.

Leidy was mad enough that she refused to take me to the airport Monday when it was time for me to go. My mom didn't have the chance to refuse me this; she'd chained herself to Ariel's house the morning of my flight, and I couldn't bring myself to go over there and bend down and kiss her goodbye where she sat on the sidewalk. My father called to offer me a ride, having watched the news and figuring I might need it. Too embarrassed that he was right, I told him I was fine, that Mom was excited about taking me. He said, That's fine, and then hung up, and on the plane I realized that he'd probably seen not just the coverage but my mom herself on TV, her wrists bound to Ariel's fence, her legs dusty from the concrete beneath her.

So Omar—the first person I saw that trip to Miami—was the last person I saw, too. I met him several blocks from the apartment: I had to walk almost a mile to find the first street not blocked off by police. When I opened the Integra's door, his face was dry but it was clear he'd been crying.

—You too? I said. Did you *really* think the family could just keep refusing to hand him over? Jesus, does it really take leaving Miami to see that was impossible?

He stared straight ahead. He clenched and unclenched his hands around the steering wheel. I watched him swallow.

—So I guess we're over then, he said.

And I was so surprised at where his mind was and at how far my own thoughts now lived from his that I grabbed his arm and squeezed it. I said, God Omar, I'm sorry, but I can't do this. I can't.

He nodded slowly, nostrils flaring, and said, No I figured, then just drove, his lips pulled into his mouth the whole ride. He hugged me like I'd never come back when he dropped me off, but he didn't park like last time, the hug happening in the middle lane of the airport's departures area.

So there was no one to call when I got back to campus, no one who wanted to hear I'd made it back safely. Only Jillian, studying with earphones over her ears—she pulled them off as I walked through our door. And though she eventually asked about the raid and what she'd seen on the news, and though she wanted details

I'd never be willing to give her, she gaped at the bandage on my hand and began her interrogation with an almost sweet question, the first full sentence she'd spoken to me in weeks: Are you OK? Liz, please, tell me you're OK.

I sat down on my bed, dropped my bag at my feet, cradled and covered the hurt hand with the good one, and said, It's so good to see you.

34

DESPITE HAVING TRIED TO TRADE shifts with someone before leaving, I still had to work at the library that night, and I sat there dazed, lulled into a kind of desolate trance by the dozens of people passing in and out of the doors who didn't feel like they'd abandoned their families to be there, who didn't know how it felt to be ambushed by your country and your own mother in a one-two punch. For most of my shift, when someone set off the sensors, I didn't even call them back to my desk to check their bag—I just waved them off, because it felt wrong to be sitting there, a thousand miles from where I'd been that morning. What were a few lost books? I couldn't care less. I waved and waved while staring down at my other hand, a finger tracing the grain of the wooden desk.

But I raised my head after one very long set of beeps to find Ethan right in front of me, his arm reaching back, a book from one of the special collections in his hand that he'd used to intentionally anger the sensors, the word BERKELEY stretching across his chest on a sweatshirt.

—You're not supposed to let this leave the building, he said.

I hadn't gone back to Happy Hours since our fight—I'd missed the last two while in Miami—and since he hadn't e-mailed me to find out where I was, I figured he was waiting for me apologize. But I didn't know how to do that without bringing up problems his example told me to keep to myself.

—Thanks, is all I could make myself say.

He put the book between us on the desk. He'd gotten a haircut, lopped off all the length and buzzed the top almost as short as the sides. It made him look older, like someone on his way to being gone. It very much suited him—made his jaw look stronger, his eyes more brilliant without hair to obscure them. I stared at him until he waved his hand in front of my face in slow passes.

—*Hello?* Are you getting paid to be a zombie now? You look tired.

—Nice to see you too, I said. What's left of you.

The hand went to his hair, fingers spreading out to hide as much of it as he could. Maybe in the instant I was getting called a sellout in a Little Havana backyard, Ethan was chatting about his upcoming move to Berkeley with some stylist, some girl like my sister working the clippers around his ears and saying *So you're getting a doctorate, what kind of doctor are you gonna be?*—a mistake I might've made just a few months earlier, a mistake people like me made. I propped my elbows on the desk, leaned my face into my open hands, covered my eyes.

—So you don't like the haircut?

—You look like a different person.

—Is that a good or bad thing? he said. He pretended to laugh.

I kept my eyes covered and tried to keep all feeling out of my voice. I said, I haven't seen you in a while.

—You stopped coming to Happy Hours.

—You've been avoiding me too, right? It's not like you don't know where to find me. You found me now.

—Yeah, well, I figured you were still mad at me for getting into Berkeley.

—I was never mad about that.

—Whatever it was, it wasn't OK. Can you maybe put your hands down and talk to me?

I pressed my fingers harder into my eyelids until I made false light glow from them, just to the point of pain. I wanted to be back home, not having what now felt like a frivolous conversation. His sweatshirt, the glass doors, the rare book on the table—all of it felt so pointless, so small. I kept my hands up.

—Ethan, I just got back from Miami like hours ago, and I'm sorry but I just can't talk to you about this right now.

—Why were you in Miami? he said.

I couldn't handle Ethan the RA trying to console me about something he didn't have to think about unless he wanted to—another reason to resent him. I blinked into my fingertips. Please go away, I muttered.

—You're not wearing your ring, he said. Did something happen?

I pulled my hands from my face.

—I wasn't home for that. Seriously, what part of *Go away* do you not understand?

—You know, Lizet, I don't know why I'm standing here either. If anything *you* should be apologizing to *me*.

He was talking too loud for the library's foyer, but I didn't care. There were worse things in the world than talking too loudly in the library. There were much worse things than hearing the basest version of what you might want from someone thrown at you right when you're the happiest you've been in weeks.

—Okay, fine. Sorry I told you the truth. Are we done here?

He surprised me by saying, No, we're not.

He leaned over my desk and said, I don't know what's going on with you. I know you're – or were, I don't know – serious about someone, and I've tried to be respectful of that. But I still thought we – look, it's not what you said. It's how you said it. You insulted the fact that I like being around you. You made me feel like an asshole when I've tried really hard not to be an asshole with you.

I slid the book to my side and dropped it with a slap into the return bin even though special collections books were supposed to get reshelved immediately. The sound was meaner than I wanted, but I needed him to leave me alone—there was no room left in my imagination for a version of my life that included someone like Ethan. I pushed my fingernail into a knot in the desk's wood, tried to scrape away some of its shine.

—Did Berkeley send you that sweatshirt? I said.

It was the closest I could come to the way we'd always played around, so easy and so quick and subtle, like before. I hoped he'd heard the compliment beneath it—*That just looks right on you*—but he shook his head.

—OK, I think I'm done here, he said.

—Come on, Ethan. Do we really need to do this now?

His Adam's apple churned at his throat, like an animal fighting its way out. If he'd found me at work before I'd gone home, I would've asked him to come back after my shift—maybe even feigned sickness to leave early—and I would've confessed everything: *Do you watch the news? Have you heard about this kid?* I could've told him about the internship happening on his coast, how I wanted to do it but felt like I shouldn't. If he'd found me before I'd promised Leidy I'd come home, I could've asked him how far Berkeley was from Santa Barbara. *Maybe you could visit me this summer.* Except now none of that mattered: I needed to be home and Ethan didn't need to be anywhere he didn't want to be. I sat up in my chair, tired of how he made me feel, jealous of how lucky he was to have survived long enough at Rawlings for his priorities to change for good. There was no way to explain to him and his sweatshirt why I no longer cared how many books were kidnapped from the library.

—No, Lizet, we don't need to do this now. Don't worry, we won't do it at all.

He backed away from the desk.

—I'm just saying I'm sure we both have real things to worry about.

—I'm sure we do, he said.

He reached out his arm and drummed on the desk with his fingers, and I remembered the day he introduced himself to me at that exact spot, and I think he was thinking the same thing, how it would make perfect sense if this ended here, too. We both knew I wouldn't go back to Happy Hours; I'd gotten through finals once without them, and I would do it again. The day his bag triggered the sensors, I'd been mean—I didn't even give him my name— because I was busy puzzling through my probation letter. He'd been charmed by it then. All these months later, his future was so much closer to what I'd wanted for myself, before accepting my real fate.

—I'm going to go, he said. I better go.

He knocked on the table once. I said, Yeah you better, to keep myself from grabbing his hand, to make myself help him go.

—Have a nice life, I said to the swinging door, and I imagined the quip Ethan could've tossed back at me, the meanest, most true reply: *I will. Unlike you, I can plan on it.*

When I showed up for lab the next week, Professor Kaufmann glided by my bench and said, We missed you last Monday. I thought she was about to ask me the same questions Jillian had inevitably ventured—where was I during the raid, did anyone I know get hurt or arrested—but instead she asked me to speak with her after class. This resulted in me mismeasuring and mishandling anything that required measurement and handling during the lab. At the end of class, as I waited for the room to empty, Professor Kaufmann sorted papers on her lab bench, and I thought about

how lucky she was to have nothing but her work, her research—
how lucky she was to be able to lose herself in project after project.
Maybe she'd seen the news, had recognized me in the face of a
woman chained to a fence in Miami, knew that that woman being
there meant I was chained to something, too. I thought she'd make
it easy for me this time by saying not to worry about the internship, that she'd nominated someone else.

—So do you have your forms? she said after the door shut
behind the last student.

—Huh? I said. Then I remembered the envelope from California at the apartment, the papers Leidy had kept from me until I
showed up there, papers I left in the top drawer of my dresser in
Miami after promising to come back for the summer.

—I thought you'd bring the forms, she said. You never mailed
them in.

She looked at my bench as if they'd be there, as if I were just as
awkward as her when it came to talking to another human.

She said, Your name wasn't on the list of flights, and when I
checked with Santa Barbara they said they never received your paperwork. So you must have it now, yes?

—No, I don't have it. Are you – have you been watching
the news? About what happened, what's happening down in
Miami?

—No, she said, but she smiled and nodded. Oh, she said. You
mean the little boy. It's very sad. It's very complicated!

—Right, yes. Well I didn't know until now but it's not going to
work out, I think. I can't participate this summer. At the internship with you. I need to be in Miami then.

—Oh no! she said, genuinely surprised, but she didn't ask for
details.

After a pause filled solely with her nodding, I said, Because
of that boy. My family – well, my mom is sort of involved in the
protests, and it's been tough on my sister and her baby. I have to
be there this summer to sort of help deal with that.

She nodded slowly through my whole explanation and stopped just after I stopped. She said, Why?

—Well because. Because it's my *mom*, so I should be there.

She blinked. I don't understand, she said. What will you be doing down there?

—Like, supporting them. Her and my sister.

—Oh! You've found something with better funding?

—No, no, I mean like other kinds of support, I guess.

—I see, she said.

She picked up her pen and wrote something; I recognized it as some sort of integral. She scratched it out, wrote something else.

—It's hard to explain, I said.

And I regret what I said next: It's like a cultural thing, I said.

—Ooooh, she said. Oh, well, then I'm sorry it won't work out.

She rested the pen on the pad and smiled again, said, It's a shame that your family won't let you participate.

—No, it's not like that, I said. I just feel obligated to be there for them.

—So ask them! Perhaps they will let you come!

—It's not them letting me or not letting me, I didn't even talk to them about it.

—I don't understand. I had the forms sent weeks ago to your home address.

—It's just very bad timing, I said. I'm really sorry.

—Bad timing?

She picked up her pen, clicked it closed, returned it to the exact same spot.

—This is fine, she said. Thank you for being clear. Perhaps just keep thinking about it? About the offer? Perhaps that's all for now, she said.

I thanked her for understanding even though she obviously didn't, but her confusion about how I'd be helping my mom and sister opened up a place for all the disloyal parts, all the parts that were jealous of Caridaylis. Still, in declining the internship, I was keeping my promise to my sister and making up for other failures. Of course Professor Kaufmann didn't understand. She was destined for a bigger life than I was—was already living it. I'd been stupid to see myself following in her footsteps and having a life like hers, and the severity and intensity of the protests and counterprotests in Miami over my last weeks at school proved me right. And so did Ethan, with his silence; I didn't see or hear from him again until the onset of study week, when he sent me an e-mail. The subject line read only *Hi*, and all he wrote was, *You OK, OK?* As if our first joke were a magic spell that could conjure the swagger I'd wielded at that party months earlier, back when something as silly as *wielding swagger* could even count as a priority. So I didn't write back. And anyway, there was no point: we were leaving campus in a matter of days, him for good, and I didn't deserve whatever goodbye he imagined. I was proud of myself for giving him that, for releasing him from the obligation I might've let myself become. I felt in those weeks that school was a job: finish my courses with the highest grades possible and get back home. It brought me a sense of calm, to recognize my place, to admit I could only rise so far above where I'd come from and only for so long. It was even a relief—to have removed the pressure of long-term success by accepting that it was just beyond me—one that led me to have the second-best semester I'd ever have at Rawlings.

35

ARIEL HERNANDEZ LEFT THE UNITED STATES for good on a Wednesday in June of that year. I'd been living under the cold war of our apartment for just over three weeks on that day, back in time to witness the worst of a different set of protests, the ones aimed at letting Cubans know that Other Miami had suffered enough of our antics.

Leidy was behaving in what I now think of as a civil manner. She'd started dating this guy named David, a cop she met while trying to track down our mom the day I flew back to school. They were the ones to pick me up from the airport—in David's patrol car, Dante's car seat in the back with me—when I came home for the summer. I was the first one to be nasty: You don't mind that my sister has a kid? I said through the air holes in the Plexiglas separating him and Leidy from where Dante and I sat. I was cranky, dismayed at how much summer loomed ahead of me, embarrassed to be in the back of a cop car like a suspect.

—No way, he said. He had a buzzed head and wide, clean fingernails, the tips of his fingers the only thing steering the wheel, and he did that with such ease that I was jealous of him, of Leidy for having him.

—Dante being around is how I knew right away that your sister puts out, he said.

Leidy smacked his arm but laughed with her whole body. I liked him from that moment on.

We were careful with and around each other: it was the only way to deal with our mom, who vacillated between distraught and enraged. She'd been fired from her job, and though Leidy had corralled her into applying for unemployment, the money wouldn't last long, and it wasn't enough anyway. They'd scaled back on Dante's daycare since Mami was around to watch him more, but twice Leidy had come home from the salon to find a note on the fridge from Mami saying she'd stepped out to go lie down in the street in a protest on Calle Ocho, or to speak on camera with a news crew she'd seen pass by on their way to Ariel's old house. Both times, Dante was still in his crib, playing alone, or, the second time, sleeping in a wet diaper, but this was *Definitely not okay*, as Leidy had put it, and I agreed with her.

—I'm here now, I said the night I got home, when she filled me in on all this as her way of apologizing for how we'd left things the last trip. I told her I didn't need to get a job right away; I'd earned good work-study money from all the extra spring break hours, had almost seven hundred dollars saved up even after buying that April flight home, plus I had my credit card. We'll be okay, I told her. We'll be good. I wished I had footage of that conversation—evidence for Professor Kaufmann. I could've shown her that tape, could've paused it and said, *Now* do you understand?

It became my summer job, then, to watch Dante, and to watch Mom. To pack up Dante's diaper bag if Mom wanted to head out to a march, where I'd stand on the sidelines like a chaperone. To make her sit down and read the classifieds and look for another customer service job that didn't ask for references. To take her and Dante with me to the library every day when I checked my e-mail while my mom read a book to Dante in the kids' section. On that June morning, I got an e-mail from Jillian, who was two weeks into her internship in New York City. I could barely read the whole thing: she was subletting an apartment in the city itself, splitting the place with the girl she'd be rooming with off campus next year. The internship sounded boring despite the ways she tried to fancy it up (*A file crossed my desk that had Marisa Tomei's name on the label!*), but I couldn't help being jealous. The last weeks in our room were a lot like the first in the way we were careful around each other, but she almost always slept over at her All-Nighter's apartment now that they were serious. There was one night when she was around, on the eve of some campus-wide debauchery, a year's-end tradition called the Hill Spill that involved not much more than drinking outside all day on campus property. A friend of Jillian's stopped by to pick her up for a midnight party that was a noctur- nal pregame for the Hill Spill, and the friend—a girl I didn't know and who didn't live in our building and so wasn't aware of my his- tory there—said to me, You want to come? I surprised us all by saying, Yeah sure, changing out of my pajamas in just a couple minutes. Several hours and too many cups of sticky vodka-laced punch later, Jillian and I had our arms around each other's necks, singing along to the same rap songs at the party. We were the only two who knew all the words to anything the laptop—set to random and plugged into high-quality speakers—could throw our way. Hours after that, Jillian was vomiting into our recycling bin, my hands holding her hair back from her face, and she marveled at my ability to *keep it together*, and we confessed how we each thought the other was *so gorgeous*, each of us taking compliments where we could've just as easily found insults: she said I was *exotic* before clamping her hands on the sides of the bin and retching more vomit over our aluminum cans, while I stroked her unbelievably slick ponytail and slurred, I'd *kill you* for this white-girl hair. I spent the next morning—the day of Hill Spill itself—recovering from the punch I'd kept down as she'd puked hers up, while she stumbled back out to keep the celebration going. She considered us friends again thanks to that night, had promised to e-mail me over the summer, and in the absence of anything from Ethan—my *I'm okay, OK?* response lingering unsent in my head—I'd been looking forward to hearing from her until the e-mail actually appeared and hinted at everything I was missing by being home.

There was also, that day, an e-mail sent on behalf of Professor Kaufmann to all the students participating in the internship, which started soon and which would run through most of August, ending right before classes began again. The e-mail detailed how to check in once we arrived at the facility, where to pick up our keys and meal cards, driving directions for those coming to Santa Barbara by car, important phone numbers to call if we had any difficulties or changes in our travel plans. I'd clearly been added to the recipient list by accident (there was a reference to separate, prior e-mails I hadn't received), but it killed me to see it. I read it over and over again, inspected the list of names—only nine other people, from schools all over the country, some I'd never heard of: Reed, Pomona, Grinnell—and I opened another browser window and looked up all these places, these schools like Rawlings that didn't exist before that moment. I sat there reading and rereading that e-mail and the Web pages about the colleges until my mom snuck up behind me with Dante on her hip. She dipped him over my head and put his hand in my hair, and he took the bait and pulled.

I'd promised my mom we'd leave the library in time to drive to what she assured me was a tame protest, a silent march Madres Para Justicia had organized in response to the fact that the U.S. Supreme Court was, at that very moment, deciding whether to hear the case that argued Ariel *himself* had legal standing to file for asylum despite being a minor. Even though she guaranteed its subdued nature—*We have a permit, there'll be police escorting us and everything*—I would not be marching with her. Dante and I would wait down the street at the Cuban restaurant that was sponsoring the march, meaning, I thought, that it would be empty and quiet once the protest got under way. I checked out a book about the world's oceans for the pictures—something to keep Dante entertained—and we drove down there, me dropping off my mom a few blocks from where we would wait for her.

At the restaurant, we had to sit outside: the inside was home to a meeting run by another, separate group of organizers glued to a radio and also watching a live broadcast of the courthouse in Miami, despite the fact that the deliberations were happening in Washington (and isn't that perfect, the way so much of Miami thought itself the center of everything, even that late in the fight?). I ordered a café con leche for myself and a plate of French fries for Dante, to function more as toys than food. He grabbed fries by the fistful and dropped them on the patio while saying *bye-bye*. I pushed the plate away when he wouldn't stop doing this, then I busted out the ocean book and read to him about calcium carbonate shells and anemones and a whole host of organisms and structures. The pictures—glossy and full-color—promised us that places even farther away than California really existed, promised that the world was so much bigger than our block and the disappointment of that summer, that there was something much more vast than the despair sitting there with Dante brought me. The pictures did their job, occupying his attention for a few seconds at a time. I wiped off his hands with a paper napkin and let him flip through the pages himself, watching to make sure he didn't rip any of them.

After about twenty minutes, something came toward us from down the street, louder than the traffic already passing, than the voices suddenly rising inside the restaurant, though this new sound was way too loud to be my mom and her group's silent protest. It rang like a celebration, cars honking and people cheering, like the party in the streets after the Marlins had won their first-ever World Series. Within a few seconds I saw them coming: a brigade of pickup trucks and SUVs, some with oversized wheels, big banners flying behind them, American flags, Confederate flags. Car horns blaring, white men hanging out of the windows, banging hard on the roofs of their own trucks like they didn't care about dents. As they approached, some people on the street just stopped and stared. Some dropped the grocery bags they held. But others waved back, pumped fists in the air. When the first of the trucks passed me, I read the banner twice before understanding everything it meant. The letters and numbers on it, spray-painted in wide, black script on what I now saw was a king-sized white sheet, read: 1 DOWN, 800,000 TO GO!!!

Something in me said to pull Dante out of his high chair and, though of course he couldn't read, turn his face away and in to my chest. Within seconds that high chair was on the ground, knocked over by one of the screaming men who'd jostled to be the first out the door of the restaurant to throw whatever he could at the passing trucks. Other men followed, and the only thing that kept it from being a full-blown riot was the fact that the trucks sped up when they saw the rush of red-faced Cubans sprinting toward them. They kept going but turned off Calle Ocho a few blocks later, when it became clear that each man would chase them for as long as his body could handle.

As that high chair crashed to the ground, as Dante turned and turned his face where I held it because he couldn't really breathe, here's what I thought: It's over, he's gone. I thought: I'm one of those 800,000. I thought: Fuck you, we fucking *made* this city. I thought: Who fucking wants to be here anyway. Dante finally pushed my hand with his head hard enough for me to let go: Why couldn't I be the one? I couldn't admit this to anyone, but *I* wanted to be the one to go. Get me out of here, I thought. Get me the fuck out of here.

Dante started to cry and scream, and the group of people who'd left the restaurant regrouped in a parking lot a block down. Their running left them in front of a car wash, where they met other angry spectators, and they bent over and leaned on their own knees, heaving air while cursing and crying. Then one of them stood up and put his hand to his forehead in a salute, looking down the road in the direction the trucks had come from. He pointed there with his other hand, and the people around him watched as a group of

370 JENNINE CAPÓ CRUCET

women—all of them in black, each of them silent—moved toward us with arms linked.

And as the women came—just a couple thin lines of black stretching across the four lanes of the street, cops on motorcycles zigzagging ahead of and behind them, lights flashing silently—my mother, somewhere near the end closest to me, did not turn to us at the sound of Dante's shrieking, which I tried and failed to control. She kept her head tilted down, as if her steps were the most important thing in the world, the only thing she had any power over. She watched herself walk and either couldn't hear Dante or refused to look up if she recognized the crying as his. She kept moving forward. Nothing would distract her. Dante gulped in a huge swallow of air and came back twice as loud, shrill as a siren, and my mother's eyes slammed shut, stayed shut, her legs still moving her forward.

I bent over and grabbed the wooden high chair, righted it as best I could with Dante on my hip. Then I put him in it, buckled the flimsy plastic seatbelt around his hips. He reached his arms up to the sky, his face a red fist of insistence, and when I backed away, he tore himself open with wet roars. But I moved a little more, just to the other side of the table, to see what it felt like. I turned from him and watched my mom focus, watched her keep moving in silence.

—You'll be fine, I whispered, the words lost under Dante's agony.

I ignored the glares from the people around us, angry at the broken silence, at me for not being able to do anything about anything.

—You'll be fine, I said again and took one more step away.

You'll be fine, you'll be more than fine.

Before the next morning's news could pick up where it left off and replay every image ever of Ariel during his time in the United States, I snuck out while everyone slept to run to the library and be there when it opened. I called the emergency number in the e-mail from a pay phone in the library's lobby. The program coordinator, sounding somehow not at all groggy despite the time difference, explained that no, I hadn't been *replaced* exactly: Professor Kaufmann had understood too late that I'd declined my spot, and she'd opted not to invite another Rawlings student, as the grant could be spent in other ways. This woman took down the pay phone's number and eventually had me call Professor Kaufmann myself, who just seemed happy I'd be on board—*That's super!*—and didn't ask for any of the explanations I was more than prepared to give her should I be forced to beg. All she asked about, again, were the forms and if I could just bring them with me then. Yes, I still had them. Yes, I'll bring my social security card. Yes, I'm happy this worked out, too. She hung up with me to call the program coordinator, who called me back at the pay phone within minutes and who seemed too happy to tell me that the cost of the flight, initially covered, would now fall on me—the funding for that had already been reallocated. I'll figure it out, I told her. I gave her my social over the phone; she gave me the airport to fly into and the name of the car service that would pick me up there: I was to e-mail her my itinerary the second I purchased the flight so she could book my shuttle.

The cheapest ticket that got me to Santa Barbara by the day they wanted us there cost just over six hundred dollars. My hands shook as I typed in my name, the numbers on my credit card. The confirmation screen came up with that large number behind the dollar sign—an amount so close to the one in my bank account, one just shy of the figure scrawled on our rent check each month— and I choked down the word *No.* I tried to find a way to forward my itinerary without that shameful price showing, to cover it up or delete it somehow, but there was none. I retyped my arrival information—the flight number, the airline, the time—at the top of the e-mail and hoped the woman wouldn't scroll down.

I told Leidy first, but I hadn't planned that. She was coming out of the shower, her hair wrapped in one towel and her body in another, when I got back.

372 JENNINE CAPÓ CRUCET

She startled when she saw me, the towel around her chest slipping a bit, and said, Shit! Where were you at so early? I thought you ran away or something.

I did not laugh or answer—I only winced from the thought of the money I'd just spent and doubled over like she'd already hit me.

She said, Oh god *what?*

Mami woke up along with Dante when Leidy screamed *You fucking traitor* at me. Mami's hair was plastered down on one side, her arms still weak in that sleepy way when she wrapped them around Leidy from behind, pulling one daughter off the other. Once Leidy's arms were pinned, I let my hand fly to smack her in retaliation, but Mami spun her around in time so that all I caught was air.

—You're no better than Dad, Leidy spit at me.

—Leidy! my mom yelled.

Evoking my father was still the ultimate insult, the power of it tripled by all the hatred focused on Ariel's father in the weeks between the raid and their final departure a day earlier from Washington, where he'd been waiting for his son. But Leidy shrugged off our mom and got back in my face, squared up to me like I was someone she'd never met but was ready to rip apart. She shoved her hand in my face.

—No, you know what? You're *worse* than Dad. At least he has the balls to go away and *stay* away.

The long nail on her pointer finger glanced my nose, her elbow jutting up high in the air, her chest pressing into mine, her next strike so imminent, so close, that I almost looked for the balding bouncer from the talk show she must've been channeling, willed him to jump out from the kitchen and stop her.

—You're *worse*, she said. You came back and talked all this shit, you fucking promised me, and now you're fucking bailing on us *again*.

—What is she talking about! my mom cried at me.

—She didn't tell you either? Leidy said, raising her arms in the air. Of course she didn't! She took a fucking job in California, Mami.

—California? my mom said. *California?* Lizet, how can that be?

—It's not a job, it's an internship!

But why was I trying to explain it? What did that distinction mean to anyone but me? Still, I tried to get it across; I wanted Mami to understand that I wasn't leaving just for a job, that this chance was much more than that. And I wanted to confess that I didn't even understand how much it might mean, that I was acting on a promise that wasn't clear to me yet, but only acting on it would make it clear. That making this choice was terrifying.

I pushed Leidy out of my face and said, Mami, listen, it's this amazing chance to work in a real lab with one of my professors who thinks I'm really good and I said no at first, but I can't, I can't say no to it.

—A lab? she said.

And I said, Yeah, like a real laboratory, like a scientist's laboratory. The professor only asked one person in the whole school and it was me.

—Why you? How do you know this man?

—It's a woman.

—A *woman?*

—Yeah right, Leidy said from behind me now. She's obviously lying.

—No she's not! She really has her own lab.

—No, you fucking idiot, *you. You* are lying.

—Why would I lie about this?

—Because you obviously think you're too good to watch a kid all summer!

I'd fed Dante and put him to bed the night before, the only one of us who could walk away from the footage of Miami's varied responses to Ariel landing back in Cuba late that afternoon. Caridaylis had refused to comment: she hadn't been allowed to see him since the raid.

I said, So what if I do? What if one of us is?

—Lizet, my mom said. That is *enough*.

—So you're too good to deal with this shit but I'm not? Leidy yelled. Must be nice to not give a shit about anybody but yourself!

I thought Mami yelled, Leidy, let it go. But Mami was staring at me.

—Let her go, Mami said again.

—*What?* Leidy said.

—You got your problems and she's got hers. She wants to go spend her summer with some woman professor she doesn't even know, let her go.

—That's not what –

—Mami, are you *serious*? Leidy said.

—Yes I'm serious! She thinks that's what she's gotta do, fine. You think *I'm* gonna get in her way?

—Yeah, that's your fucking job, Mom. It's your *job* to get in her way.

—Not anymore it's not.

—You guys, I yelled.

Mami turned to me and said, You know where the door is. You know where we live.

—This has nothing to do with either of you, I said.

—Bullshit it doesn't, Leidy said.

—No, she's right, Leidy. This is all about *her*. Her whole life is gonna be all about her from now on, right, Lizet? I say go for it.

Mami watched my face, her mouth twitching, and I didn't know what to do.

—But we're not going anywhere, she said. *You* go.

Her eyes flicked back and forth, not even the threat of tears in them. I waited for Leidy to jump in and say something, to make it easy for me to spit more rage at either of them, but her head turned from me to Mami, trying to decide who she hated more.

Then Mami shrugged. She said, When do you leave?

—In two days, I whispered.

—Mom! Are you for real just gonna let her –

Mami raised a hand and silenced Leidy, and in the calmest voice I'd heard out of her in months, she said, You know what? I say you go *now*.

She turned and walked down the hallway.

Leidy said, Get back here, we're not done talking about this!

Our mom passed through the doorway into her bedroom, and Leidy screamed at her closing door, Mom! This is for real! This is not Ariel!

We heard the lock click shut. Leidy stood in front of me, breathing through her teeth. She yelled, You *know* I can't leave Dante with her. You *know* you're supposed to help her find a job. You *know* we're next to broke.

She grabbed my shoulders and shook me, saying, You can't do this. You can't leave me here with her again. Please don't leave me here like this.

If I let her shake me for a second longer it would work, so I stopped trying to fight her grip and decided instead to go *through* her—I could tell she thought for an instant I was collapsing into a hug—and into our room. I ripped my clothes from the hangers on my side of the closet, wiped tears and snot from my face with a T-shirt before tossing it in my suitcase, which was still propped open on the floor even three weeks into being back. It was already half filled with the dirty clothes I'd planned on dragging down to the laundry room—like the suitcase knew before I did that I'd be out of there so soon.

And my dad knew before I did, too, but only because from her room, from behind that door, my mother called him. Even Leidy stopped screaming when she heard it.

—Come get your daughter, we heard Mami say.

All that time, our mom knew his number and never let on that she did. All that time, she'd maybe even known it by heart.

—I don't care, she said. I want her gone. I want her gone *now*.

The first time they'd spoken to each other in months.

I waited for Papi downstairs. Before he even hoisted my suitcase into his van, he said, What the hell did you do to your mother?

—I got a job in California, I said.

—You're quitting school?

—No, it's just for the summer. It's an internship.

—Then why didn't you *say* internship? he said.

He tapped the side of his own head and held his hand out afterward, like offering me something. He looked up at the building, searching the windows for anyone he recognized.

That night, over some yellow rice and chicken that Rafael had bought for us at a food-by-the-pound place near the Villas, I told my dad and his roommate everything about the internship, about my lab class, about Professor Kaufmann and how weird she was, about how much better my spring term at school had gone than my fall.

—Even with all this shit going on back here? Papi said, his mouth crammed with rice.

I'd never told him about how close I came to being asked to leave. I don't think he even knew my roommate's name. I filled my own mouth with food.

—Even with all that, yeah, I said. My work helped me not think about it.

—Thank god for work, Rafael said to his plate.

The three of us nodded, chewed and chewed.

Papi took me to the airport two days after that night, the lines through security extra long because this time around, Ariel had already been through and upped the chaos; unlike our arrivals, our departures wouldn't have the date in common. My dad parked at the airport without me asking him to, and he made the security line with me, and I was careful to act like this was normal for him, to not show him how happy it made me that he'd be seeing me off at the gate, something he'd never had the chance to do. This would be the last time, too: September 2001 was fourteen months away, and in that time, before the rules changed, he wouldn't need to take me to the airport again.

We sat at my gate in a part of the airport I'd never seen, one of the renovated terminals that catered to the airlines dominating the sky in that direction—Southwest, Northwest, Frontier—airlines someone like Ethan flew to get to Rawlings. My dad asked me questions about the technicalities of air travel: Do your ears keep popping the whole time or just at the beginning and end? Will they feed you on this flight since it's longer? When you land over there, what time will it be at the airport?

—You don't remember your flight? I said.

He shook his head, snickered and said, That was so many years ago, the whole thing was over before I knew what was going on.

I tried to imagine my dad on his one and only plane trip, at fourteen—more than twice Ariel's age—crossing the Florida Straits. I wished he was the kind of man I could ask about that day, but that would make him more like my mom.

—When the plane takes off, he said, is it really rough, or does that turbulence stuff only happen once you're in the air?

I could still count on my fingers the number of flights I'd ever been on, and none of them had ever taken me out of the only time zone I'd ever known, but now I was the closest thing my dad had to an expert. I answered everything as best I could, let my nervousness about flying show so he could see I wasn't used to traveling this way, not yet.

When they called the section to board that included my row, he stood up faster than I did and said, Go, go, before they shut the door.

—They won't shut the door. Getting everyone on the plane takes forever.

I hooked my thumbs under the shoulder straps of my book bag, my real suitcase—the big one, stuffed with the clothes my dad and I had washed at a Hialeah Laundromat I'd passed hundreds of times but never entered—already somewhere inside the plane's belly. My dad looked up from his work boots.

—Listen, he said. Call your mother when you land over there.

—Are you *serious*?

His eyes went up to my forehead. Don't make that face, he said. Just do what I tell you, okay?

—She won't talk to me if I call. Neither will Leidy.

He looked at the jetway, at the line of people trickling down it.

—Just do it, trust me, he said. Call me too.

He swallowed, still looking down the tunnel that would take me to the plane. I watched the skin of his throat move up and down. I said, I will.

—It's good you're going, he said.

The agent at the counter scanned in ticket after ticket. She took one from someone's hand and had to turn it around before holding it up to the scanner. My dad elbowed me and said, Here, then slipped a folded bill under the strap of my book bag up by my thumb, into the curled grip of my other fingers.

—It's what I owe you, he said.

I put my other hand over my eyes so he couldn't see that I was about to cry.

—Stop, he said. It's gonna be fine.

I felt his hand grab my shoulder, too rough at first, but then the fingers relaxed some. The money felt wet in my fist. I kept my eyes covered. I squeezed the bill tighter.

—Come on, Lizet. I don't know what you want me to tell you. You could've stayed here for school. Are you doing the *harder* thing? Yeah. Maybe you can think that's better even if we don't.

I pulled my hand away from my face. He shrugged and said, You're learning something, we'll see what it is. We'll see where it takes you, right? It'll take you somewhere. Look, you're going somewhere already, right?

He turned his face from the jetway to the ceiling. He shoved his hands in his pockets, jangled the keys and coins in them, his face examining something above him. Then his arm shot up, and I jumped away, but he pointed to the ceiling, his hand bouncing as if he wanted to be called on in class.

—There's a leak up there, see? Right where that fixture is.

He scooted in closer to me, aimed his finger at a ceiling tile, at a light ringed by metal. I looked hard, turning my face at different angles, but I didn't see the leak; I don't think one was there. I'd bet money on it.

—Yeah maybe, I said. Right there?

I lifted my arm parallel to his, our shoulders touching.

—Right there, yeah. He whistled through his teeth. He said, And they just remodeled this whole fucking place.

His arm dropped, the hand back in his pocket but his shoulder still pressed against mine. He said, I can't fucking believe that.

We stared up at that spot until I made myself say it: I better go, Dad.

—Okay, he said.

He hugged my book bag more than he hugged me, his hands touching somewhere near the bag's zipper. He put his lips on the top of my head and held them there. He breathed into my hair. Then he pushed off from me and clapped me twice on the shoulder.

—Don't lose the money, he said. Be good. Be safe. Keep warm.

—Dad, it's hot in California, just like here.

—Some parts are cold, he said. Where you'll be it's cold at night. Look it up.

I stood on my toes and kissed him on the cheek, the rough starts of his beard poking my lips like barbs. He wiped the back of his hand over it and said, Go already, go.

He flapped his hand at me, shooed me toward the gate, looked up at the ceiling tile again, squinting at it now.

I took my place in the line, and just before I made the turn onto the jetway—a move that would take us out of each other's sight until at least Christmas—I spun around to wave at him one last time. He stood there, arms crossed over his white V-neck shirt, his feet shoulder-width apart, his jeans tucked into laced-up work boots, the soles of them so thick he looked rooted to that cheap carpeting, his face still turned to the fixture, his neck, with its shadow-beard, the color of a tree trunk. I kept craning my own neck around the line that trailed me, waiting for him to look away from the ceiling, for his gaze to meet mine, until the person behind me said, Miss, you can go now, and made me keep moving.

I found him again after I sat down, my bag tucked under the seat in front of me, the safety card—something I never, ever look at anymore—unfolded on my lap. My dad still stood there, his face turning between that imaginary leak in the ceiling and the dotted line of windows on the plane as he scanned them for me. I waved and waved, willing him to see me, to wave back, and we both kept at what we were doing, our attempts at saying something never understood, until the distance between us made it impossible to know when the other gave up.

36

SKIRTING THE EDGES OF THE ISLAND on which my parents were born—the island both even now still think of as home—are some of the most pristine and healthy coral reef systems in existence today. The industrialization of farming that's likely contributing to the death of reefs elsewhere in the world (with its runoff of pesticides and fertilizers, the things that make canals everywhere such nasty places) just never happened in Cuba, and so that country, inadvertently and thanks to unrelated measures outside of its control, has managed to preserve the very thing I've spent my adult life studying and working to understand.

My PI is careful around me when he brings up these facts—or I should say, he is careful to stick to facts, which I very much appreciate. Over the last few months, it's become clear that a research trip to Cuba will be necessary: we both know that the data we'd collect from Cuba's reefs would be invaluable to our current research project. If those reefs were anywhere else in the world—if they didn't surround the island at the root of my family's biggest heartaches—I would've jumped in their waters years ago. I've seen the abstracts float across my PI's desk with the phrase *Pending State Department approval* leading them off. Our group has submitted the grant pro-posals; I've seen my name on them; I know what will happen should they be funded, should America choose to send me back to a place I've only visited via stories, photos, and dreams.

Don't be worried that I'll do something ridiculous like go look-ing for Ariel. For the most part, the world knows where he is, what he's doing. The Cuban government is good at giving us updates, at releasing photos, year after year, of Ariel in crisp school uniforms, of Ariel speaking before groups of students, of Ariel in his army uniform. And I stopped most of my searching a couple years ago anyway, after a trip back to Miami as the ten-year anniversary of the raid approached, when I went to that house-turned-museum in Little Havana and saw so many of the photos and artifacts I'd already seen from three thousand miles away on my computer screen; I saw many of them again last year, when my mom moved into the other half of Leidy and David's duplex. I'd come back to help pack up her old place, cleaning out the drawers and closets stuffed with all those useless relics.

—Who's *this* kid? asked my niece Angelica, named after David's mom, who died the year before he married Leidy.

—Oh *god*, I said. She *kept* all this?

I took the stack of pictures and flyers from her hands, flipped through the mess of them. Mold framed the edges of most of the papers, and my scientist brain wondered, since Angelica was then only seven, if I should find her a mask to wear while we cleaned up.

—These are from before you were born, I told her.

—Oh. She frowned down at them. Who cares then?

She took the stack back, her hands dirty and her fingertips gray from the long day of sorting through my mother's memories, and shoved it all in the latest trash bag.

—Keep moving, Tía, she'd said. No time to get reminiscing!

She's a smart girl; out of all of them, she's the one who uses the computer to call me out in California, and she does it often enough that I feel like I know her. Leidy brags during our phone call each week about how well Angelica and Dante are doing in school. She knows me enough to give me that kind of update, to keep me from worrying about them too much. Leidy says she's not worried either, even though Dante and Angelica (and their other two boys, once they master potty training and fine motor skills) will eventually go to Hialeah Lakes, which is supposedly *better* now (Leidy's word) than it was when we went there. She and David moved to Hialeah—right back to within a few blocks of the old house, a handful of streets away from Omar and his wife (a girl we both knew from middle school whom he re-met at some evangelical church)—after they got married. A six-year-old Dante was the ring bearer at his mother's wedding, Angelica their barely walking (and therefore largely ineffective) flower girl, who I ended up holding for most of the ceremony.

I would've been Leidy's maid of honor had she asked me, but she didn't. She claimed I was too busy with grad school—*your extra college*—for the role. She only asked that I read some poem during the ceremony, and then I went back to my seat in the crowd, to one of the hundred or so metal folding chairs lined up in rows on the banquet hall's dance floor—chairs that, once the dancing started, would disappear.

The maid of honor was my mom. My dad didn't come—I'm not sure if Leidy even invited him, and I knew better than to ask her or Mami—but he sent, through me, the ludicrous set of copper pots they'd listed on their registry (the registry itself a sign that Leidy was more American than she wanted to admit—at least as American as I was). Those copper pots were the most expensive item on that list: I know this because I'd also wanted to prove something to my sister, but my dad beat me to it and bought the pots for her himself.

The wedding took place the summer before my third year at Berkeley; I'd inadvertently followed Ethan to grad school, but he was gone by the time I made it there. When I found out I'd been admitted, I wrote to him with that news, hoping only that he'd remember me and not think I was crazy for looking up his Berkeley-issued e-mail address. But that e-mail bounced back, and once I moved out there and looked him up, I learned he'd left before finishing to take a position as a regional union organizer in the Midwest. The hint of a receding hairline blinked at me from his photo on the union's Web page; he was still young, and so I thought it seemed unfair—that backward-creeping edge—and it shocked me almost as much as the fact that I was one of only a handful of minority students in my department's entering class.

That Ethan was no longer at Berkeley—not hiding on campus somewhere finishing his dissertation, maybe in a carrel near what would be my lab—really was for the best: the person I'd started (and still am) seeing, another Rawlings senior who swore along with me that whatever happened between us couldn't turn serious, decided on UCLA for law school partly so we could be within driving distance of each other. We ended up living even closer once I quit my program; I might've beaten the odds at Rawlings, but I figured out quickly that I'd never be the imaginary profesora I met on that airport shuttle years ago. I have a better idea now as to how much she might've been suffering the day she corrected my grammar on our way home. And while I hope she survived her postdoc, I'm glad I learned early on that I was only happy in the field or at a lab bench, far away from anything having to do with *The Department*, from the advisor who told me my dissertation proposal (about the effects of toxins from coal-to-gas plants—found almost always in poor communities of color—on aquifers) would never find more *general interest*, that sticking with such a project could *limit my options* when it came to funding sources. Lizet, there's not a lot of money in . . . *those* kinds of . . . questions, he said when I pressed him for what he meant. Sorry, that came out wrong, he said, but . . . you know what I mean—I'm interested in developing you as a scientist, not as an activist.

I pictured Ethan hitting this same kind of roadblock—What am

I even *doing* here? Who decides what counts as *general interest?* Why does no one else's research make *them* an activist?—and realizing the same thing about what he needed to do. A few months after Leidy's wedding, I found and applied for the lab manager position here at the Institute, knowing I was perfect for it, though maybe a little young for such a role. But I knew (or knew of) many of the researchers affiliated with the lab—including Professor Kaufmann, who served as one of my references—and after driving hours and hours (and missing many meetings with my advisor) for the various rounds of interviews down in San Diego, I successfully convinced them of what I'd known all along. The day after I signed the contract, I quit the grad program, channeling some imaginary combination of Ethan and Leidy as I picked up the one box all my things fit into and left, my middle finger the only part of me waving goodbye to my advisor's empty lab.

My parents each approved of the move for the wrong reasons (See? You didn't need more school to find a good job!), but that could change if my work took me to a certain Caribbean island. I already know what each would say should I ever have to tell them about an upcoming research trip to Cuba: my dad would talk about being *a little disappointed* in me, about the unfairness of me being able to travel to a country he can't enter, but he'd mostly not say anything, only leave me guessing at his meaning from the way he'd wait a day or two longer than usual to call me, the way he'd not leave messages on my voice mail for a while, choosing instead to just hang up; my mother would bring out familiar words—*betrayal, loyalty, traitor*—words that have come to define our relationship no matter how much time passes but whose sting has faded and turned into something I can manage, something Leidy is just as tired of hearing. My mom would, she'd say if I went, not be surprised.

To tell them would also mean inviting them along in a way. We still have family there. Go see this cousin, that aunt, I can hear either one of them demanding. Or more likely now: Go see this grave. And when I tell them there'll be no time for that, that this is a *work* trip, that I'll mostly be on the water, in or under a boat, that what they want me to do takes me clear across an island I don't know: Oh, I *see*. You don't have time to take a piece of paper and a crayon to your *grandmother's headstone*? You don't have time to do that for me who will never see it? Oh, that's right, *of course* you don't. I should've remembered how busy you always are. I shouldn't have even asked.

Truth be told, I don't know if I would tell them, since keeping quiet would be the easiest thing, the familiar thing, the way I've dealt with so many of my choices ever since that first year away. I'd say only that I was traveling again, to one of the dozens of islands I've already been to over the course of my career, so there'd be no expectation of presents. But it would make me sad to keep Cuba from them, because I'd want them to know I brought a part of them back to where they started, that some part of them had finally returned home. Even if—thanks to the summer I left them behind—they wouldn't see it that way.

After that first summer, I left straight from Santa Barbara to Rawlings with enough time to move my stuff from the college-owned storage place to my new room—a single, more expensive than a double, but what was another grand each term on top of my other loans? It was peace of mind, a year I could be alone and not worry about how people saw me. I used the days before classes began not to track down Jillian in her new apartment or enjoy the sun-soaked campus the way Ethan would've, but to write letters to my mom and sister—something I'd never, ever done. Earlier that summer, I had a test run at writing as a way of apology: I'd written to Ethan a couple weeks after getting to Santa Barbara, after learning that the work I'd do that summer would lead to my name appearing on an actual publication. He was the only person to whom I could imagine telling that news who'd understand its significance, so I finally replied to his *OK, OK* e-mail, trying to open things up again with just one line of my own: *I'm in Santa Barbara and therefore on your coast*, I said. But he sent only this single line back: *You're still a long way from where I'm from.*

So in writing to Leidy and my mom, I tried harder. I tried to say what I felt, thoughts that seemed big and important back then but that I can't even remember now. I imagine I was trying to explain myself as a way of asking for forgiveness. I imagine I was trying to figure out why I could never be like Caridaylis but how at the same time I was already like her—I wanted my mom to see that. A week after the letters would've arrived, my sister called the new phone number I'd written in each.

—You are so weird, she'd said. A letter? Who *does* that?

I asked how things were in Miami. Ariel was being used yet again, this time for the presidential election happening in a couple months. My mom had thrown in with George Bush Jr.—her newest cause, the first of many until David and Leidy moved her back to Hialeah. I was not surprised.

—The news down here is saying that Al Gore was the one who basically made the actual phone call to raid Ariel's house, she said.

—That's not true, I said.

—How do *you* know?

I said, It's probably not true.

—Mom says she forgives you, Leidy told me just before we hung up, after we'd stopped trying to prove each other's certainties wrong.

But my mother didn't come to the phone. She never said it herself.

Months from that moment, on Thanksgiving Day of my sophomore year, I'd be sitting in my dorm room, my back to the window and the snow falling outside, blinking at the screen of a laptop I'd bought with part of my summer stipend. I'd see a banner hanging from a pedestrian bridge over the expressway, near the exit that got you closest to Mami's building. THANK YOU ARIEL, the banner would say. WE REMEMBERED IN NOVEMBER.

That was the first election in which I was old enough to vote.

When my voter registration card showed up listing my polling place as my old elementary school, I followed the directions in the mailing and sent away for an absentee ballot. When that arrived, it took up my whole mailbox and, when I opened it up in my dorm room later, seemed excessively complicated. There were multiple envelopes, multiple places where my signature needed to be *affixed*—a word I'd never heard used that way before. I was to vote in private, it ordered. There were to be, it stated ominously, no witnesses.

I almost threw the whole thing out. *This is too hard*, I thought, and I tossed the flapping pieces of the ballot and its instructions on the radiator, hoping they would sizzle and burn away. How easy it would've been to drive to my old elementary school, to park in its familiar lot, to walk into the cafeteria I sometimes smelled under the brighter, cleaner scent of the campus's dining hall, and slip into a voting booth. How easy—how much less of a burden—than what I had to do, what I would end up doing.

But we all know the history, and I'm sure my vote was never counted. I'm sure it sits—even now, probably in that state's capital—in some vault, the envelopes unopened, the paper moldy and dank like the Ariel artifacts my mother kept, at the bottom of some bag filled with ballots like mine. I wish I'd known as I sat there hovering over that radiator-warmed punch card—having waited until the postmark deadline to commit a decision to it; the little pin that I'd detached from the instructions, which mandated I use only that tool to puncture the spot that proved where my loyalties lay, slipping in my sweaty hand—how pointless it would be. I wish I'd known that no one would ever see it or count it. I wish I'd known, as I pushed through one choice over the other, how little it mattered which side I ended up betraying, how much it would hurt either way.

Read on for an Author Interview
and Discussion Questions for

Make Your Home

Among Strangers

An Interview with Jennine Capó Crucet

What is your novel about?

The simplest answer is probably: It's about Lizet Ramirez as she becomes the first in her family to go to college, which coincides with the arrival of a kid named Ariel Hernandez, who comes to the U.S. from Cuba on a raft. It tells the story of the year where their lives intertwine in significant and devastating ways. It's about people landing in places and having no clue who they are as a result.

I wrote this book in the hopes that it would eventually serve as a kind of roadmap for the first-generation college student's experience, but it was also my way of thinking through my own questions and worries about immigration and how broken and crazy our current barely-a-system is.

Ultimately, it's about big things and small things: family and identity; class and access and privilege; Miami heat (the weather, not the basketball team) and New England cold; academic integrity; finding yourself surprisingly attracted to gingers and lab equipment; the successes and failures of college diversity initiatives; the successes and failures of the American Dream.

You used to be a sketch comedienne. How does your comedy background inform your writing?

I sometimes joke that I'm a writer because I'm a failed comedienne, but that's not actually funny so I stopped saying it. But yes, I started off writing sketch comedy and would sometimes turn those sketches into short stories when they didn't make it into a show or when I felt like the sketch form wasn't doing my characters justice.

From writing sketches, I learned a ton about dialogue and the sense of timing that good dialogue must have. I also learned a lot about pacing. I have a whole craft lecture on how humor can enrich very serious literary writing, the gist of which is how I apply a lot of the "rules" of sketch writing to literary fiction—the rule of threes, for instance. Writing humor taught me how effective it can be as a setup to something much more serious—think David Sedaris, how he usually has something really funny before something deathly sad comes up. It's like taking someone up a cliff before pushing them off: the effect is much more substantial than if I were to just shove them over.

You worked for a time as a counselor/mentor at a non-profit for first-generation college students. In what ways did you draw on this experience when writing *Make Your Home Among Strangers*?

During the years I lived in Los Angeles, I worked for a college access organization called One Voice, and it was the most rewarding job I've ever had. I had no business doing it, as I had no real counseling experience, but I thought the fact that I was also a first-gen college student who'd gone to a pretty fancy school (like the ones my mentees would be going to) would help me get by. I was right and wrong; it was also the hardest job I ever had.

I think what I drew on the most for this book was that there's this idea in the (largely white) cultural imagination that everyone who is the first in their family to go to college has the full support of their family behind them, and that's not always true. I worked with families who were dead set against their kids going to college—particularly the parents of girls, who saw college as unneeded or just a waste of time for their daughters. While my family was not against me going to college in general, they did outright question why I needed to go so far away, to a more expensive school, when we had Miami-Dade Community College and Florida International University right down the expressway. And they initially took my leaving very personally—like a rejection of them and the way they'd raised me.

Many of the students I worked with at One Voice had this same issue, or worse: they had families that were outright opposed to them going to college for a whole host of reasons (they'd been anticipating the income their child would bring in once they graduated high school, or they'd planned on relying on their son or daughter for child care, or because they didn't trust their child to have that kind of freedom, or some other reason). My point is, the narrative of the mother and/or father working hard and sacrificing so that their child can someday go to the best college they can get into—while absolutely admirable and wonderful and sometimes accurate—isn't in any way across-the-board true for low-income families. Some families sense—either consciously or unconsciously—the riff that such an opportunity will inevitably cause, and so they act in ways that prevent it from happening. And sometimes that comes out of love and fear: the families have experienced tremendous disappointments in this country, so they want their kid to have reasonable dreams—dreams that also happen to keep them close to home. We don't get these stories often despite how common they are, so I wanted to write a book that told that story, one that expanded the cultural imagination.

Lizet, the protagonist of your novel, leaves Miami, a large city strongly shaped by its significant Latino

community, to attend college in a small northeastern town. You made a similar transition for college. How are some of your experiences reflected in the book?

Nate Silver would probably say that Lizet is about 32+/–2.5 percent me. But she's not really me: she is taller, and she made the wise decision of going into the sciences.

I'd say the experiences she has are versions of what every first-generation college student goes through, so of course she and I have some overlap (though my undergrad institution was much better at recruiting and retaining students of color; Lizet's Rawlings is based more on smaller liberal arts colleges with much smaller minority populations). More broadly, though, they are what *anyone* who finds themselves having to build a life in any new, foreign place goes through. Some people fair better than others.

I think, in Lizet, I tried to create someone who I'd like to hope would've been a good friend had we found each other in college, but sadly and more likely, we probably would've felt ourselves to be in competition for the role of Everyone's *Sassy* Latina Friend. That's ugly to admit, but it's also accurate.

Actually, one of my own factually true experiences that shows up in the book is something I gave to the character of Ethan (a white dude!): he's an RA, and so was I. His attitude about the job is pretty much mine, though I was much better at making bulletin boards than he is.

There's a fictionalized immigration debate in your novel that draws upon the Elián González case. Why did you choose to look at this subject?

Because I felt totally torn and confused by my own reactions to the Elián situation, and my head and heart couldn't make peace with each other over it as it was happening—and really never did, until I wrote this book. More than fifteen years after Elián was deported, we still have the same broken immigration system, and

I wanted to show how that system impacts real families and real people, how that broken system is still hurting Americans every day. The events of that year and their aftermath haunted me and didn't stop haunting me until the day I wrote the last sentence of the book.

Discussion Questions

1. Lizet is on a very different path than that of her older sister Leidy, a single mom living at home. Describe their relationship as sisters. Where do they have common ground?

2. Do you remember the Elián González story from 2000? If so, did you recognize the fictionalized references in this novel? How did they contribute to building the picture of Lizet's hometown and Cuban-American culture in Miami?

3. Describe Lizet's relationship with her mom. Do you feel compassion for Lourdes as she tries to navigate the parallels between Ariel Hernandez's journey and Lizet's own?

4. Why does Lizet feel like a fish out of water both at Rawlings and at home in Miami?

5. Which scene was most powerful for you as a reader? Why?

6. How are Lizet's goals for her future aligned with her mother's, and how are they different?

7. How does Lizet cope with the challenges of being a minority student at Rawlings? What could the school administration do differently to support her?

8. Have you ever experienced culture shock like Lizet does at Rawlings? How did you cope?

9. Who was your favorite character? Who was your least favorite?

10. What could Lizet do, if anything, to bridge the cultural and generational gaps with Lourdes?